TERROR TALES
OF THE SOUTHWEST

BY
FRANK THAYER

A Sun Cross Publication
P.O. Box 3136
Las Cruces, NM 88003 USA

TERROR TALES OF THE SOUTHWEST
By
Frank Thayer

ISBN 978-0-692-96867-3

ACKNOWLEDGEMENTS

•Cover art and color interior illustrations by Graham Kennedy gkilius@aol.com
•Black and white text illustrations for "Horror of the Yellow Flowers" provided by Graham Kennedy
•Photo for illustration of Hillsboro, N.M., main street by Pamela Porter
•Sign of the demon Marbas from The Lesser Key of Solomon
•Photo for illustration of Mount Geronimo by Frank Thayer
•Photo of Hurley lightning by Frank Thayer
•Photo for illustration of Silver City, N.M., cemetery by Frank Thayer
•Venus illustration courtesy NASA/NSSDC, enhanced by Graham Kennedy

Book design by Pamela Porter

This book is a Sun Cross Publication
Contact: Frank Thayer, Box 3136
Las Cruces, NM 88003 USA
gticruiser@aim.com

TERROR TALES
OF THE SOUTHWEST

& Bonus stories
Two Missions to Venus

By
Frank Thayer

With artistic contributions by Graham Kennedy and Pamela Porter

Dedicated to the tradition of true supernatural horror and the authors whose stories have enriched the imaginations of readers across the centuries. This volume is also dedicated to the original spirit of the Canadian online forum "Writer's Cramp" wherein some of these stories found their beginning. Finally, I dedicate this book to the spirit of Mirella. She will always be in my thoughts, and there may yet be one more story left to tell.

Terror Tales of the Southwest
Table of Contents

TERROR TALES OF THE SOUTHWEST:
AN INTRODUCTION

It is a land of brilliant sun and long shadows, where the west winds blow curtains of dust, and the plains rise up to cruel, rocky hillsides—a land where explorers, ranchers, and miners became part of the mountains and the deserts but never tamed them. In common with all other peoples in all other lands, people here have their whispered stories of magic, witchcraft, unexplainable events, and of horrors beyond description. The Southwest guards its hidden traditions as known to the people of the Pueblos, the Spanish Conquistadors, the Hispanic culture, and the latecomers named Anglos.

The perennial interest in the supernatural presents a paradox. If there were no supernatural or paranormal, there would be no need to invent it, because human beings are capable of unspeakable acts beyond reason, most of it related to the abuse of drugs. Yet the folklore persists, and the horror story, be it simple campfire tale, or elaborately constructed literature leaves the indelible stamp of reality in those whose minds are open to invisible realms.

The 20th Century brought a shift to the literature of the supernatural horror tale, abandoning the classic ghostly encounters and the confrontation with unspeakable monstrous manifestations from beyond, choosing instead to become fixated, particularly in movies, upon the grisly and endless destruction caused by unlikely semi-human killers with superhuman strength who are almost impossible to kill, whether a Michael Myers in the "Halloween" movies, a Jason from multi-part "Friday the Thirteenth," or an army of walking dead under the direction of George Romero. This modern manifestation of horror relies upon repeated visual shocks and an ever-increasing body count. The result is a brutalized audience but lacking the sense of cosmic fear that classic tales have the power to evoke.

The effectiveness of the classic supernatural horror tale lies in the fact that its premise is, indeed, possible, and it leaves the reader with a sense that he or she is in the presence of a mystery that remains as a subconscious reality long after the tale is finished. Masters of the supernatural horror tale penetrate the veil separating the mundane world from a frightening dimension of the inexplicable and the demonic whose forms are beyond the description of special effects. There too are the explorations of humans who are faced with supernatural forces beyond anything they have before imagined and which changes them, shakes their consciousness to its foundations, or destroys them in inexplicable ways.

HORROR OF THE YELLOW FLOWERS

Such are the words— Shade, Spirit, Spectre, Ghost— but they are inadequate to describe the reality. Even today I have a recurring dream, the nightmare, of a darkened room, of stale, choking air, and a horrifying presence enclosing me in an embrace, so frightening that my heart threatens to burst my chest. I am powerless to resist until I throw myself awake in terror with the cryptic word "lamia" echoing in my solitary bedroom. Such are the memories.

The wellspring of those memories festers in a shunned ranch house more than 60 miles away from my hometown of Silver City, near the rustic foothills town of Hillsboro, New Mexico, on the eastern side of the Black Range Mountains. Sequestered behind a hill south of Hillsboro, it sits vacant as though waiting. At the north side of that two-storey house is a small patch of land overrun with yellow wildflowers and perhaps concealing a grave not recorded in the county registry. Of those flowers? I learned of them from the ranch owner's foreman, never thinking that common blossoms could be so costly to a lifelong friend. Those too are the memories.

* * *

Mary Ann came up behind me, pressing against my back, her cheek hard against the back of my left shoulder, arms tight around my mid-section. I could feel her smile spread through me, but when I recoiled and turned to face her, the sudden shock of my withdrawal stung her eyes to wetness.

Clumsily, I embraced her, but the light-headedness I felt was not the usual exhilaration of being close to her; it was something else—something born of revulsion. She started to pull away, reacting as I searched for words.

"It's not you, Mary Ann. Never think that." We kissed, and I felt the cold in me dissolve through the heat of her lips. She was still holding the buttery yellow flower in her hand. Her eyes followed mine, questioning. Revulsion at a perfect blossom? I could tell that she sensed an incongruity in me she had not seen before.

Unknown to her as yet, the only reason we were here in this New Mexico field together was because of that flower; otherwise, Mary Ann would be in Dallas. In the two days she had spent here, I had delayed telling her the story I knew I had to tell, trying to milk as much joy from our moments as I could. The time had come, though, even as my hands stroked her long brown hair. Here in the bright summer sunshine, I had to sketch the darkness for her.

Mary Ann looked at the flower again and laid it gently down, taking my hand and leading me back to the blanket where we had lunched. She wanted to know the truth and I could not deny it to her.

* * *

Herb Holbrook and I had always been friends, which was surprising since we thought much in common and should have exhausted each other's resources early in life. We had first met in the small New Mexico town of Silver City at age 9 or 10, and decades later we were still friends despite taking divergent career paths and in spite of discovering the opposite sex.

We had both fancied ourselves writers and had both failed miserably at it. Herb finally ended up working for the county as a surveyor, and I had spent nearly a decade working for small newspapers in the Midwest.

Two years ago, the cold shower of divorce had driven me back to home ground in southern New Mexico, and now I was employed with the local college, preserving as much free time as possible to become re-acquainted with the New Mexico outdoors.

Herb was not quite fortunate enough to be divorced, but he lived under its threat. It was his wry comment that community property was the most perfect leg hold trap ever devised. He welcomed the chance for us to roam the New Mexico hills again as we had in our miscreant youth.

Southern New Mexico has much to attract the person who is uncomfortable with urban culture. There are vast stretches of arid plains, wind-haunted rocky hillsides, and even thick wilderness forest. In the West, towns are either booming, comatose, or decaying, with little grace in any of the three conditions. Several of these frontier survivals formed the backdrop for our sojourns.

Herb's cousin Mary Ann was five years younger than me and not much more than a blurred memory when I had last seen her during my college years. In the interim she had married well, acquiring sophistication and charm as an interior decorator and wife of an oil company executive.

I could not have anticipated what would happen between us when circumstances threw us together one afternoon at Herb's house. Mary Ann had come to visit her cousin, and her re-introduction to me led to sudden and inevitable consequences. Though our attraction had not passed beyond a kiss, the penetration of her lips had been enough to open my imagination. Suddenly I felt truly alive as only one can when the inner mind is not fettered by its self-imposed limitations. Though I didn't see Mary Ann again that visit, the brief electric contact plummeted me into a new phase of creativity which was reward in itself. The lady with long hair and hazel eyes surprised me by calling me a week later, and that was the beginning of a correspondence warm and stimulating, untainted by real world limitations. I sensed somehow that the laws of this other world were very different, but as inexorable as gravity.

At first I said nothing to Herb of this fiery desire for his cousin and, naively, I hoped a discussion would never be necessary. While women take compulsive delight in discussing with each other the intimacies of their lives, men traditionally keep such things private unless circumstance gives them no choice. Even the bitter feud that passed for marriage in Herb's life was something I knew little of and would never ask about.

Soon after my discovery of Mary Ann, Herb had his own collision with enticing fate. The clarity of that rich Saturday in March 1981 has remained with me. Herb and I had

climbed aboard his 4-wheel drive Chevrolet pickup nicknamed "Old Blue" for a full day's journey over the Black Range mountains east of Silver City and down into the valley of the Rio Grande. After reaching the 10,000-foot level at Emory Pass, Herb guided the truck through the many switchback curves leading down through the eastern slopes of the range on N.M. Highway 152.

Just outside of the town of Hillsboro the right rear tire went flat. Changing the tire was a quick ten-minute job but, lacking a further spare, and having at least another hundred miles on the itinerary, we stopped at the Texaco service station in Hillsboro to get the tire repaired.

Hillsboro is one of those 19th century mining towns that almost died in the mid-20th Century before finding a new lease on subsistence through tourism. Substantial stone and stucco buildings shaded by towering cottonwood trees attest to the town's vintage. A few moldering structures stare vacantly, but antique merchants have kept other buildings from suffering a similar fate. Most people have forgotten that Hillsboro was the county seat of Sierra County from the mid-19th Century until 1939, when the seat transferred to Hot Springs, later Truth or Consequences, named after a popular television game show of the 1950s.

Some prominent buildings present the scalloped multiple arch facades of mock-Spanish architecture while others show flat store fronts with large, quartered, rectangular windows common to the southwestern storekeepers of the 1930s. It was inevitable that the atmosphere of such a place would bring the counter culture people of the 1960s—at least when the weather was warm. Hillsboro did not boast more than 176 permanent residents in those years, so denizens and visitors alike were all highly visible.

Herb and I left his truck with one of those attendants who promised to get the job done in "five minutes or less" but whose wandering, indefinite gaze assured at least an hour's wait.

We sauntered across the street in the manner that only westerners wearing jeans can walk. We were looking for homemade apple pie at one of two local cafes; it was a good bet because apple orchards had long been a part of the Hillsboro economy, culminating each Labor Day in an Apple Festival that multiplied the population by a factor of ten for the long weekend. As we walked, the welcome heat of the sun was punctuated by a breeze that raised light eddies of dust at the edge of the paving. Several young people were lounging outside one cafe. They wore slouch hats, patched jeans or coveralls; the men's hair was unkempt and their beards were scraggly, while their female companions wore their hair long and untended. One male entering the cafe was wearing motorcycle leathers, the jacket made with Marlon Brando zippers.

These young people have been described as hobos of the modern age, but most of them fancied themselves artists, frontiersmen, or settlers hearkening back to the 19th century. They sold handcrafted jewelry, pottery, painting and weaving—most of it undistinguished. Herb and I suspected that the majority, regardless of the protestations of independence, were supported by the nation's taxpayers, sustained by the middle class they had abandoned and rejected. They probably stayed at the camp outside of town that also hosted recreational vehicles in the summer.

One girl here was an obvious exception. Her jeans were clean and new-looking; her print blouse fresh and stylish. She sat on a folding camp stool with a large sketch pad on her lap, making rapid shading strokes with a pencil. Her hair was tied back but lustrous from brushing; its brown color was so light as to be almost blond.

She looked up as we approached the cafe, her blue eyes narrowed against the sun, her pencil hand shading her brow. She smiled, more at Herb than at me; as long as I had known him, such preference seemed inevitable. Herb was impossible to upstage, and his rugged looks got him the female attention I had always wanted but seldom got enough of. I sensed that subtle spark of interest in both of them even though Herb never broke stride as we entered the cafe.

Terror Tales of the Southwest

The other thing I knew about my friend was that he had a knack for inadvertently finding trouble. While he and the young lady were looking at each other, I was scanning the street. Nobody else seemed to remotely aware of us or the sketch artist.

The chintzy frame aluminum screen door into the cafe creaked, and we went in to take a table by the wall.

The first thing I noticed about the man in the leather jacket was his eyes. They were dark and glowering, fixed in our direction He was seated alone by the window and I immediately sensed the connection my subconscious had been uncomfortable about. If there could be a stereotype motorcycle club member, this man would be him. He slouched arrogantly in the chair, head slightly tilted, his eyes boring into us. For a shirt, he had only a denim vest with an embroidered Harley-Davidson badge, a line of metal studs and one or two other insignia, one of which was a strange flash that had the meaningless embroidered initials "IT-COB." His sun-darkened skin covered arms formed of muscle and sinew whose contours were mottled with tattoos. He wore tight, grease-spotted jeans, the cuffs fitting tightly over the shanks of scuffed motorcycle boots; his hair was wind-whipped and oily, the brow line showing the hint that it was receding up the center. The only other sign of his vanity was a carefully waxed handlebar mustache that might have looked pleasant or even comical on a gentler face.

As he stared, more at Herb than myself, the biker used a fingernail to pick at his strong but stained teeth; one canine booth was broken off close to the gum line, and it called my attention to an obviously recent scar on his left cheek.

For his part, Herb seemed oblivious to the presence of the man. The presidency of Scorpio in him could make of his face an impassive mask, but he seldom missed anything.

Hillsboro, N.M.

We ordered pie and coffee, dawdling over it, with no particular schedule to keep. Herb never looked toward the man by the window so I assumed I was the only one with a queasiness in my stomach; malignancy seemed to pour in our direction like a wave of black oil. I avoided looking toward the window until the biker stood up. He easily reached 6'1," and he faced our table momentarily, deliberately, then walked to the door, looking back once before leaving. If ever there was a carrier of misery, we had just seen him.

"You were aware of the prototype Hell's Angel who just scraped the top of the doorway?" Herb just nodded, sipped at his coffee, and looked around the room for the first time.

Out on the sidewalk, the man with the mustache towered over the long-haired artist. His mouth contorted with suppressed rage, and his fists clenched and unclenched, bringing out rope-like tendons in his arms.

She looked up and then back to her sketch pad, apparently not frightened or surprised. I felt apprehension for her, but the window glass that filtered the sounds was a motion picture screen into an uncomfortable world.

As I stared, the man stooped over as if on the verge of striking the girl, but she did not look up this time. He pivoted and walked across the street to where a swayback, high handlebar Harley Davidson motorcycle leaned. Within seconds, man and machine were shooting off to the east along the state highway, the grumble of the motorcycle exhaust loud and lingering in the air.

When we left the cafe, she was still there, sketching in the sunlight as though no cloud had passed. Herb walked up to her with the familiarity of someone who has been a friend for years, "I get the feeling we caused you some grief without really meaning to."

Then she really smiled, wrinkling her eyes in an engaging half-wink. "It's not really a problem...I mean it happens all the time. I guess Turk is a classic case, but he stays around anyway. He'll go off to T or C, get drunk or stoned and come back tomorrow." Her voice was lilting, but the seed of meaning in the words said something else. As the two of them talked, I learned that, true to character, her boyfriend Turk had found her two months before in Albuquerque and had spent most of his waking time since then trying to control her. Her given name was Feather Symonds, suggesting that her parents must not have been conventional people either.

At one point we broke off the conversation in the expectation of continuing our trip but, predictably, the service station attendant had gotten only so far as to dismount the tire. He promised to be done in ten minutes. We understood what that meant.

We spent the lunch hour with Feather Symonds. As well as being attractive, she turned out to be an engaging conversationalist. She was one of those people who looked intensely at the person she was speaking to and, as well, when that person was speaking. Although Herb did not show it, I knew by the way he had shelved whatever schedule we had that he was more than mildly attracted to this girl.

In the cafe she leaned her sketch pad against the wall and I noticed that the sketch she had been drafting was a neat and detailed view of the Hillsboro street, built up on paper in minute and perfect detail. Sometime during the period we had been talking she had inadvertently smeared it, marring its static, unchanging perspective.

Later, when the tire was finally repaired, she accepted Herb's invitation and the three of us drove south from Hillsboro toward ranch land and the ghost town of Lake Valley. A little more than a mile out of town, Feather suddenly directed Herb to turn onto a dirt road angling to the right and disappearing around a hillside.

A weathered white metal "Private Property" sign warned off trespassers and hunters, and a sturdy metal gate reminding me of the British flag hung open, reddish w/oxidation. Around the hill and nestled in the elbow crook of two ridges was a white stucco two-storey ranch house. Herb applied the brakes. "That's it. We'll turn around here. I thought you knew where we were going."

Feather waved her hand at the windshield, "Go on. It's abandoned. Really." She looked at Herb, then me.

The truck crawled forward and, as we approached the house, empty window frames and flaking white stucco came into focus, replacing the illusion of occupancy. A windmill in the back yard cycled in metallic creaks as it brought water up into a metal stock tank. As often was the case in New Mexico, the water was more valuable than the house, and there were signs that a local rancher was still using the tank to water stock, while the house seemed to be neglected.

Tumbleweeds had found their way among the sheltering trees and had piled up against the east wall of the former home and its front yard. The sight impressed me, "It really looked inhabited from the entry road."

Feather was genuinely excited. "Isn't it a great place? I mean, all the privacy you could ever want. I love it! Look, see how the overflow from that tank feeds all the wildflowers." I could see swatches of color against the drab, cattle-trampled earth of the back yard. We got out of the truck and walked around the house, following Feather who ran ahead to look at flowers. At the rear we found a screen door off its hinges and the inner door wide open. Herb and I went into the gloomy interior. It might have been a pleasant home once, but now plaster lay in chunks on the rubble-strewn floors. One or two names of nothing people, now-forgotten, probably never worth remembering, were spray-painted on what plaster remained on the walls. We tested the cluttered stairway and found it firm enough to try.

The second storey was less wasted than the ground floor. One large bedroom was almost clean, the windowpanes intact. The honey varnish of the pine floors could still be seen under the coating of dust. There was no furniture, and the air was warm and close.

I heard a noise behind us and turned around with a sharp intake of breath, somehow thinking of Feather's boyfriend Turk.

Feather stood in the doorway to the bedroom. She had untied her hair, and it flowed down past her shoulders; in her hand was a perfect yellow blossom. She ceremoniously gave it to Herb.

"Hmmm, Hibiscus coulteri unless I miss my guess." As Herb spoke I thought he was letting his degree in biology get in the way of practice in the field, but his smile was more expressive than his words. From the look in her hazel eyes I knew she probably would have kissed him had I not been there. The fragrance of the butter-yellow flower was strong perfume in a room whose neutral staleness had lain unaltered for years.

Inexplicably, I was overcome with a sense of melancholy, and I walked across the hollow-sounding floor to the window, looking down behind the house where Herb's truck was parked. In the midst of my thoughts of Mary Ann, I could feel a warm tide of desire mixing with the other feelings, so filled with images that the here and now seemed to dissolve.

It was only when Herb called my name that I snapped out of the reverie to become aware of him and Feather again; yet, the exquisite bittersweet of my feelings remained with me through the rest of that day and long into the night, a night of fevered longing.

The passage of the rest of the day was touched by those few moments in the upstairs room of that abandoned house; Herb and the girl hurtled down a dimensional tunnel, while I traveled in my own reality, parallel to them, but separate. Our spoken words seemed to jump great distances—clear but straining as with short wave radio messages.

The sun was fading in the west behind the looming peaks of the Black Range when we got back to Hillsboro. The sky was bright, but the shadows were deepening as the late afternoon air cooled rapidly. I left them in the truck, talking, because I wanted to be alone for a few minutes to tend the flower of my own imagination.

For almost 20 minutes I walked to the top of a hill, smelling the spring air, listening to the miles-away barking of a dog, seeing in my mind the details of the house and barn as it must have gradually faded below me in the growing twilight. As I thought of Mary Ann, I felt as though I was not alone at all, and it seemed to be more than the strength of my imagination, magnified by the thoughts in that abandoned bedroom.

I got back to the truck in full dusk; Herb and Feather were two close silhouettes by the front fender. It was time to go, proving that the most magical of days must also pass away.

"Well, I hope I'll be seeing you again soon." Feather addressed the comment to me, and the sincerity with which she said it told me more than the words. Herb and Feather said their good-byes and we were again in the truck roaring in the darkness back over the mountains toward home.

Herb was silent for a long time before he put it into words. "Nossir, love and marriage and not necessarily the same animal."

"Something about that house?" The two-sentence exchange was the extent of full male disclosure and discussion of feelings.

"I'm not used to things happening that suddenly." I could tell from his words that things had gone out of his control in his feelings for the lady with the sketch pad.

I stared out of Old Blue's cracked passenger side window at the trees rushing by in the darkness. "Maybe it's for the best that it happens all at once, because that biker Turk is the kind of psycho who'll massage your skull with his brass knuckles before you have the chance to enjoy yourself."

Herb squinted through the windshield, "Just another loser. I think she's had more misery in the last two months with him bothering her than most people get in a lifetime. Old Turk is one of those people who think they decide what other people want. I think we call them sociopaths—no inner voice. Feather said she feels like she's a prisoner, and she didn't want to tell me about some of the things that happened to her in the past eight weeks." Maybe Herb felt they shared a similar desperation, knowing that if they jumped overboard, a weight tied around their ankles could take them right to the bottom.

He didn't have to explain the strange manner in which his own marriage had devolved into one in which his wife now sought and extracted the punishment from him for wrongs real and imagined, meting out revenge for the gaps in his character that she had expected to fill in 11 years of domestic training. The lawyer she had retained for discussion of separation and divorce was, unfortunately, one of Herb's high school enemies. From what Herb had told me, though, his wife's greatest pleasure was in staying married so that every day could provide the opportunity for an inquisition. I felt I knew all that from experience.

His grin was sardonic. "Give me Chinese water torture, dripping water on the forehead and all that. Besides, today was just a nice daydream." His voice lacked conviction, but it was something he had to say nonetheless. After we reached the top of the Emory Pass and started down the serpentine roads of the other side, we remained silent, lost in our private thoughts.

The following week I received a letter from Mary Ann, a letter I had not expected—certainly not one with the feelings she now put into words. It brought back all the emotional force of the weekend, and I knew I had to see her again, even against my better judgment.

The following Saturday was a day of mistakes. Overwhelmed by my own imagination, I made a telephone call to Dallas and, heedless of the popular warning, I did not hang up when a man answered. I knew that Mary Ann could face repercussions for that call. Fresh from that uncomfortable experience, I called Herb. His wife explained that he had gone on an excursion—with me. Hastily, I claimed that I was calling to see when he would pick me up; she then informed me that Herb had left several hours before, and I suspected that any further protestations I offered would just make things worse, if that was possible.

Wherever Herb was, and I was certain where that would be, he would come back to a well-laid ambush. Oh well, he was tough, and he must have considered the risk worth the punishment—the only way to live.

Herb's wife and her lawyer picked the following Monday for what Herb would refer to as "the raid." Knowing that Herb would not put up much of a fight, she packed off most of the household goods while Herb was at work, emptied the checking and savings accounts, slapped a lien on Herb's truck, and left him with their house which was carrying only a few thousand dollars worth of equity and monthly payments of $900.

I had to hand it to him, though; when he came over to tell me the news, his face was frosted with impassivity. If it bothered him, he did not show it directly. His major gripe was that the sheriff's department had come to take his truck; it was unfortunate that his wife had put up the down payment from her account three years before. Herb said he would get it back as soon as he paid her the lump sum.

Herb threw up his hands, "My God, she even took the food from the refrigerator and cupboards. All that's left is a half quart of milk, some longhorn cheese and a can of sardines." A short silence. "I hate fish." He sat there with an expression of mock perplexity on his face, and then we began to laugh.

The serious possibilities in the moment were gone, and I half-regretted it because I almost wanted to mention my feelings for his cousin and the haunting passion without respite. Maybe he would advise me as to whether there was a chance for Mary Ann and me…but men didn't discuss things like that.

"I assume you went to Hillsboro Saturday?" It was more statement than question, and it was answered by the slight raising of an eyebrow.

"I'm not sure what I'm going to do about the Harley dude—his insecurity probably started when somebody stole his training wheels. He pushed her around some since last week. She can do without him. Maybe he should go back to California, where most maladjusted garbage comes from these days." His words were light but he meant all of it.

"That's okay; now that your truck has been snatched, you're not going anywhere, anyhow." It wasn't unusual for Herb to find himself in some kind of trouble but, as his friend, my subtle suggestion that he give up his infatuation probably would not be heeded.

"That's just what I wanted to talk to you about."

I prepared myself, "And here comes the hook, right?"

"Right. I'm sure you feel like taking a drive this weekend, and since we used my vehicle last time, it seems only fair…"

"Of course, he said, against all notions of common sense." It was hard to pretend that I wasn't concerned about his safety. If we both went, I was concerned about our safety. Yet I knew I wouldn't refuse him, because there was something in his situation that was my own. Because of our New Mexico heritage, at least we always were armed in our travels.

When I picked up Herb the next Saturday around 1 p.m., I could see the strain of his domestic problems in the set of his mouth and the bleariness of his eyes; underlying this was an eagerness I could understand. Without it, he would have no support for his ego. Whatever the risks, it was worth it to him, and that was enough for me. He brought with him a portable plastic cooler with sandwiches and soft drinks—the normalcy of a picnic in the making—the contents of the cooler were not for me.

Once more we went over the mountains and down toward Hillsboro. Herb told me of Feather's frequent but hurried collect calls and how they arranged their meetings. In Hillsboro we turned south on that same road I remembered from weeks before, and we looked for her.

Just before the turnoff to the abandoned house, I saw Feather walking alongside the road; her hair was almost golden in the sunlight, and it fell evenly down onto her shoulders. Her figure was smooth and supple as she walked, the ever-present sketch pad under one arm.

I stopped beside her, and she came over to the car in a bouncing run, smiling broadly, her eyes bright. As she got into the car, she handed Herb another of the butter yellow flowers she had picked somewhere along the road, and then we went the rest of the distance to the house; as we had planned, I left them there, promising to pick Herb up just after dark. The sight of the house infected me with the incomprehensible swell of desire I had felt the first time in that vacant upstairs bedroom. I wondered, if I ever saw Mary Ann again, if I would bring her here. Just the idea of being with her, anywhere, was a fiery hunger lurking beneath the seat of consciousness, rising undiminished at almost any hour of day or night. From Mary Ann's letter I trusted that she knew the same inexplicable emotion.

With an entire afternoon to spend, I decided to wander Hillsboro's main street. I looked into a souvenir shop, walked past the café where Herb and I first stumbled onto the biker and the counter culture remnants. The iconic bulk of the old courthouse and jail reminded me of Hillsboro's famous trial in 1901, when Oliver Lee and two gun hands were tried and acquitted of murdering Judge Albert Fountain out in the White Sands desert in 1897.

The afternoon sun was clear and intense as I walked, and it was just at a whim that I went through the rustic pine door of the Bar None where a horseshoe painted with red enamel was nailed at eye level. It was there I met Ebenezer Hickson for the first time. When my eyes adjusted to the dim light, I could see he was the only other person in the place as he sat nursing a beer. I ordered a draft with some chips and salsa, and he greeted me in a way common only to people in very small towns. Together we wistfully wondered about the prospects of rain and then avoided conversation for an obligatory five minutes before I mistakenly asked him if he knew anything about available property in Hillsboro. He said, "Yup," and that was the beginning of a story that made my other activities that day seem commonplace.

It was only when I casually mentioned the elegant but forbidding white house nestled between hills south of town that Hickson gave me his name. He began telling me of Big Jim Carmody and his lover Mirella who had lived in that very house.

He stretched his lanky frame in the straight-backed wooden chair, grimacing slightly and squeezing his thigh as though feeling a twinge of pain,. "Y'know, I told Carmody that Colt .45 Peacemaker would get him in trouble someday." He was telling me about his decades of working as a ranch hand, years as Carmody's foreman, and as an aspiring Old West story writer. His angular face was topped by a trimmed mop of coarse grey hair, narrowed blue eyes creased like bellows at the corners, and the planes of his face rough and sunbaked. An old, sweat-stained tan Stetson w/rolled side brims sat on the table between us. Ebenezer Hickson said he preferred to be called Barney, after his middle name. He could pass as a Louis L'Amour character.

It is a time-honored protocol never to go straight to the topic of greatest concern when two guys are sitting in a bar, so I asked him about his writing, revealing that I too was one of the many with unrewarded aspirations.

"Well, after Big Jim went to visit Louisiana …" Hickson pronounced it "Looziyana," and I got comfortable in my chair. "…I found myself with time on the weekends for writing. I kept thinking about a movie I saw in 1954 called "Dawn at Socorro," with Rory Calhoun and Piper Laurie. It starts out showing a plaque down there in Lordsburg—supposed to commemorate 'the Shooting at Keane's Stockyards' June 12, 1871. Point is, I never heard of such a gun battle and neither did anybody I wrote to or talked with in three counties. I wondered if the movie got the idea from the OK Corral story."

Hickson recalled how he drove over the Black Range one long weekend, and down all the way through Silver City and to Lordsburg that sits on the playas alongside Interstate 10 and the Southern Pacific railway tracks in Hidalgo County. He stopped at Silver Office Supplies on Bullard Street in Silver City to buy a ream of easy erase Corrasable Bond typing paper made by Eaton's and not easy to find in T or C. "The short version is that Lordsburg is not the cattle boom town it was 100 years ago, and the people I talked with said they never heard of such a shooting. They didn't even remember the Rory Calhoun movie. I came away with a sense that there were stories to write about Lordsburg, but probably the story I should have been writing happened right here in Hillsboro."

I gauged the way his shoulders relaxed and sensed an opening for what I really wanted to ask. "So, that rancher Carmody owned the big house south of town?" I didn't say I had a personal interest in that strange, abandoned house. "Why isn't it occupied now?"

Glasses clinked as the bartender arranged a shelf behind the bar. The room was cool, and there were no other customers at the tables or the four booths at the front and side of the rustic establishment. Hickson moved the toothpick in his mouth from one corner to the other. His head moved but little, and the negative nod spoke volumes. "Nobody wants to live there, and the stock tanks are the only thing the place is good for—somethin' bad about that house."

I shifted in my chair, suddenly anxious about the house the three of us thought we had discovered south of Hillsboro, and it turned out that Hickson was a regular at the Bar None in Hillsboro. I did not know that first afternoon that I would be sitting with him more than once as he told me a long story in true serial form about the woman named Mirella and an abiding mystery of the Black Range. In the weeks that followed, neither of us learned whether there was a shooting at Keane's Stockyards in 1871 Lordsburg.

***

James Rourke Carmody had that inexplicable ability to prosper even in a bad economy, building a two-section ranch south of Hillsboro at a time when cattle could still be shunted south past the almost-abandoned town of Lake Valley to the cattle pens on Southern Pacific rail line at Nutt, that same line that went west through Deming, Lordsburg, and on to the West Coast. He was 5'8", and he walked with almost bow-legged swagger; the locals usually called him "Big Jim."

As Hickson described him, Carmody's round, clean-shaven face, reddened by the New Mexico sun, was usually topped with a black Stetson that shaded his confident boyish grin. He carried his right shoulder slightly lower than the left, his right hand hovering beside the ivory grips of a nickel-plated .45 Colt Peacemaker that he inherited from his father and holstered at a silver-studded belt. He was seldom without it. He often rode his appaloosa into Hillsboro, but that was before Mirella came.

It was a common scandal when Carmody suddenly divorced his wife of ten years, sending her and the two children to live in Silver City. His friends pointed out that Big Jim gave her a generous settlement and long-term support for the children before he went for an extended visit to Louisiana, where his relatives had lived for generations in Houma. Hickson was delegated to manage the ranch in his absence.

When Carmody returned, he brought Mirella with him, and when Hickson described Mirella, his pale blue eyes narrowed as though he were looking into infinite distance instead of the 60" ancient water damaged bar mirror of the restaurant and saloon.

To the chagrin of Chapo, who was tending bar, I made one beer last all afternoon; however, Hickson was happy for me to buy him several rounds that afternoon.

As Hickson talked about Mirella, I could not help but think of Edgar Allen Poe's "Ligeia" in which the author quoted Bacon: "There is no exquisite beauty without some strangeness in the proportion." After a few minutes' conversation, there was also no doubt in my mind that Hickson probably was in love with Carmody's consort, whom he described so minutely that I could picture her clearly.

Carmody had brought her from Louisiana, variously saying that she had family in Lake Charles, Baton Rouge, and Houma, but it seemed from the start she would be ill-suited to the life of rural New Mexico. Mirella stood easily two inches taller than Carmody in her high heels. She wore her glossy black hair in a wave that flowed down over her right shoulder almost to her breast, her luminous brown eyes framed by groomed brows and naturally long lashes. Her red lips were full and striking against a naturally tanned skin, smooth and unblemished but for a small mole on her cheek. For some reason, Hickson dwelt upon her sculpted hands, whose unusually long, slim fingers were highlighted by immaculately manicured, pointed nails, painted a lucent red.

She moved languidly, preferring always to wear figure-enhancing dresses rather than ranch wear. In contrast to Carmody's boyish grins, Mirella smiled but little—yet she had an inexplicable charm that sprang from her ability to focus her deep eyes on those with whom she spoke. Her high cheekbones accentuated the planes of her face and her distinctively Italian nose. When asked, Mirella said that she was of Italian and French descent, with a grandfather from Calabria and a grandmother from the Provencal. According to Carmody, the family came to New Orleans at the turn of the century, though he never explained exactly how he had met Mirella. Hickson was sure it was a collision of the heart that upended Carmody's life. All of this was very understandable to me.

Perhaps it was Mirella's indeterminate age that puzzled Hickson most. He said that, at once she seemed a decade junior to Carmody's 41 and when glimpsed a moment later seemed to be almost his age. Through any prism, she was the definition of desire, and an aura of strangeness seemed to surround her, even in the midst of the ordinary activities of New Mexico life. As Hickson described her, I developed a clear mental photo of Carmody's woman.

As Hickson put it, Mirella had an undeniable sexuality in the way she moved and pursed her lips or the liquid manner in which she crossed her legs when she sat. Carmody doted on Mirella, remodeling the house south of Hillsboro into one of the few two-storey homes in the area. As a couple they appeared ill-matched, but Mirella seemed adoring and attentive to Carmody when they were seen in public. She always drew stares of men and disapprobation of the men's wives. "What had he got himself into, I wondered." Hickson chuckled and rubbed the back of his neck.

Though she and Carmody were affectionate in public, Hickson mentioned that Mirella was often sullen and had a vile temper that could explode into shouting fits without warning. Combined with Carmody's own, rare hair-trigger rages; it was in essence a fulminating mixture. "Y'know, sometimes I got the idea he was afraid of her, particularly when she was in a hot temper. More than once I went to the house and heard her shouting and the crash of dishes breaking against the walls of the kitchen that opened into the back yard. On days like that, Big Jim's grin wasn't so big, and he had this curious tic in his left eye that wouldn't stop. Funny ain't it, how a man not afraid of anything can be afraid of a woman." Neither of us laughed.

One evening when Hickson joined the pair for dinner in Hillsboro, Carmody and Mirella were disagreeing about some new living room furniture they were ordering, and she smiled at him, then said something like, "Then we won't order anything. We can sit on the floor." Carmody cajoled, asking her to be reasonable, and she looked at him affectionately, and replied, "Mon Cher, if you want sexy, you get bitchy along with it." Carmody rolled his eyes toward the ceiling and then kissed her.

Hickson said that his boss was never candid about the divorce or the mysterious visit to Louisiana. "He said that, despite family acquaintance with the Carmody relatives of Cajun country, Mirella's family made him swear to certain 'things' he would not repeat, except to say that it was more binding than marriage—whatever that means."

Two hours went by as Hickson talked about the ranch, about Carmody, the house, and of course Mirella. What did this exotic woman see in a rough-edged western rancher? Of course she demonstrated a taste for finer things, and Carmody could afford to be generous. Mirella seemed to enjoy being well dressed far beyond the practicalities of New Mexico ranch life, and within a year after her arrival at the ranch, Carmody bought her a brand new Cadillac Eldorado with that iridescent San Mateo red paint scheme of the era and with a cream-colored leather interior, fully equipped. With all that, there was no doubt that there was an intense physical attraction between the two that was obvious to anyone who saw them together.

Hickson called for another long neck and twisted in the hard chair, grimacing. "Every Friday evening, they would take that Caddy into town or drive all the way down to Tor C. Actually, Chapo over there and his wife have made this place a weekend attraction. They grill their steaks on mesquite coals out back, and you can smell the aroma all the way up and down the highway outside."

He returned to the story, recalling how Mirella and Carmody would sit next to each other in the booth by the window, and she always ordered tea. "It was…I don't know…peculiar, but she said that nobody out here knew how to make tea. She purchased an expensive electric tea kettle and a supply of imported tea— presented it to Chapo, taught him how to brew the tea in a floral china teapot and then bring it to the table, along with her personal painted rose teacup. Even the way she sipped tea was sensual."

Hickson said that Big Jim often invited friends to join them on Friday evenings, sometimes buying his foreman a juicy rib eye as they planned the work of the next days. "Jim loved to talk, but Mirella mostly just sat silently as Jim held court. Mirella always looked at other men, but you couldn't say she was flirting. She just looked—her eyes could lock onto you like no other woman I ever met. Of course that all ended one night right outside this front door. I'll tell you about that when you come back." He saw me looking at my watch and sensed that I had somewhere to go. I didn't tell him I was due to pick up two lovers. I forgot to ask him about the biker and his accidental associates hanging out at the café across the street by the intersection. I really wanted to know what happened to Carmody on that night Hickson remembered, but it was growing dark, and I had to make my apologies. I told Hickson I would be seeing him, and I was correct about that.

* * *

By dusk I was back at the metal gateposts, motor silent, waiting for Herb and Feather, but it was fully dark when I heard their voices preceding them down the dirt track leading to the Carmody house. The happiness of Feather's laugh in the growing night made me smile

Terror Tales of the Southwest

as I sat, and I realized that I had been uneasy about them being discovered. My nervousness had been groundless, and I knew Herb would never worry about such inconsequential things.

I got the idea that this rendezvous was something very carefully worked out, to be repeated as often as Feather could manage it. In an oblique discussion of the dangers involved, Feather smiled and passed it off, "If I ever fail to show up, then you'll know something has happened. Otherwise, don't worry. He could never do anything that would keep me away." They had obviously discussed the situation.

Herb looked at me with mock smugness, "See, I told you she had spirit."

Somehow that was the right word, and I didn't say anything further.

We left Feather at the edge of Hillsboro as she requested, and we were once more off into the mountains of the night. It was late when we arrived back in Silver City, and we decided to stretch the evening over an order of Mexican food in a small local restaurant that stayed open past midnight on weekends.

Against a jukebox background of mixed country and Tejano music, we attacked plates of enchiladas smothered in blood red chile sauce so hot that it brought perspiration to the brow and made the eyes and nose run regardless of the quantities of soft drinks we imbibed with it. Herb said only, "I'd rather have a beer."

There was something in the ambiance of the night that made us both less-guarded; perhaps it was in doing things that had only been possible long ago before the responsibilities of life and work had revoked our freedom license.

The sound of plates being stacked and the aroma of salsa and frying corn tortillas kept our senses alive, and I once again let fall the hint of what was going on long distance between Herb's cousin and me. No details needed to be filled in, just as he had little need to tell me of his own involvements. Yet, in those few words, we shared the confidences, stripped of normal posturing.

Outside, the midnight air was brisk, a natural factor of 6,250 feet of altitude that made even summer nights a relief. Hillsboro nights would also feel this cool. A passing parade of adolescents in their vehicles crawled down Bullard Street, the main drag, just as they had since the 1950s. "Things don't seem to change much here." I was trying to be incisive, but failed miserably.

Herb reflected a moment, "Nothing dies unless we let it. It's simple."

That didn't sound like a profound statement but, later that night I tossed in bed with desirous images of Mary Ann and Herb's comment grew larger, applying to levels far deeper than the physical. Perhaps it was the axis upon whose pivot the great levers of all ideas survived. But then, in the darkest part of the night, ideas have far more substance than the objects surrounding us in the daylight. Many times I wished I could dwell in the world of those ideas and feelings exclusively.

While Herb and his wife's lawyer battled head-to-head over the beloved blue pickup truck, it fell my lot to drive Herb to his assignations; it was a good excuse for me to get out of town. Herb and his artist love became a fixture in my activities for the next few weeks, their reflected happiness bringing joy to my own secret life.

This particular afternoon I was hopeful that I could find Ebenezer Hickson again and learn more about the house that had become the focus of Herb's life and my fantasies.

It was almost with Herb's emotions that my breath quickened when we caught sight of Feather walking alongside that dirt access road south of Hillsboro, or when she was just sitting, waiting for him to appear. The empathy I felt for their situation was unique for me.

Feather always seemed exuberant and her beauty radiant, something she could not help infecting others with. She never failed to bring Herb her gift of the yellow flower, the fragrance of that single bloom always filling the car. While Herb made light of the gift, it was plain that he expected such small things as a part of the one good thing happening in his life.

In contrast to other members of her generation, Feather impressed me as a person who kept appointments and promises. Over the mountains from Hillsboro was wrath, enmity, and prolonged legal agony; on this side of the peaks were sweet smells, trusting embraces, and a peacefulness that could make one forget the foolishly imagined dangers of a jealous boyfriend.

Never did I see Turk's motorcycle when we passed through Hillsboro, nor did Feather mention his name.

She almost always brought her sketch pad to show us, but the tenor of her drawing was changing; now, most of them dynamic in their motion, with sculpted clouds, blowing grasses forming the background for racing horses or human faces alive in detail and expression. She seemed prolific at all she did.

I became more and more familiar with the abandoned house too, until my eyes had restored the flaking stucco, had erased the piled up tumbleweeds, and I wondered how far the mind could go in altering the reality of environment as well as speculating how Herb and Feather had peopled that empty upstairs bedroom with the furnishing of their imaginations. In those idyllic hours we all found happiness in a very real sense that made the mere physical world but an excrescence to be cosmetically hidden.

Without a backward glance at the house, I returned to Hillsboro. The welcoming orange neon Coors sign was lit in the window of the Bar None, and the board floor interior was cool—the smell of cooking mixed with the yellow fragrance of draft beer. Much as I was committed to helping my friend make his assignations with Feather Symond, I had to admit that I was almost relieved to walk into the Bar None and find Barney Hickson. This afternoon I was in luck, not knowing that I could probably be just as fortunate most weekend afternoons after Hickson had finished his work on the ranch. I had to again ask him about Carmody, the house, and of course Mirella.

Hickson's cowboy hat was even more soiled and sweat stained than when I saw it the first time, and he kicked at the chair across from him in invitation when he saw me walking in the door. He had half-finished a cheeseburger along with a mound of fries smothered in catsup. I was suddenly hungry and ready to order my own.

"Mr. Hickson..."

"Barney," he muttered with his mouth full. A faint odor of cow manure wafted up from his boots.

"You remember that there was a particular night you were going to tell me about..."

"In due time. Everybody 'round here already knows the story. You young guys are always too much in a hurry. Gets you nowhere." With that he raised his hand toward Chapo and picked up where we had left the story at our first meeting as the bartender brought two cold long necks. The record playing on the Rock-Ola jukebox in the back corner was the George Jones recent country hit, "He Stopped Loving Her Today," and I felt a peculiar chill.

Hickson said, "Before I tell you about that night, you need to understand Mirella and her influence on Carmody, me, and most people hereabout." His story continued as the afternoon seemed suspended.

As he described her, it could not ever be said that Mirella was jealous, but Hickson noticed that when another man's wife or even an older female friend was in Carmody's presence, Mirella's arm was around his waist, her hip pressed against his as though to denote complete possession.

Hickson took a long swallow of his fresh beer and reflected, "Not sure how to put this, but that woman seemed more intense about living than anybody I ever met. One Friday evening we were all three sitting in the booth talking about religion and philosophy, and she looked at Big Jim, then at me, then said without smiling, 'it is my will that makes me immortal, yes, Jim?' and she kissed him on the mouth right there in that booth by the window." Hickson pointed toward the window booth, and I noticed that his fingers were still grimy from work.

"At the same time…" He paused and shook his head, "I read that quote, 'Woman, thy name is vanity,' and vanity thy name was Mirella. One evening they were sitting there, and she was dabbing at her makeup, a compact mirror close to her face. Carmody said, 'You're pretty enough, Baby,' and she snapped back, 'You don't want me to look like a gorilla, do you?' and then she sulked until the food arrived. Big Jim was constantly walking in a minefield around her."

I learned from Barney Hickson about the intensity of Mirella and her possessive spirit. She sometimes took the Eldorado and went by herself to Albuquerque or El Paso. One July, she went back to Louisiana for a month or so, but apparently Carmody kept his own counsel, not even telling his foreman where she went. Hickson said he could tell how much Carmody longed for her return, because he drank more than usual and refused to talk about it.

Hickson said they were out repairing a fence line one hot August afternoon, Carmody, Hickson and a temporary laborer. The day had been long, and their shirts were dark with sweat. Just as they finished they were confronted by the neighboring rancher who objected to the fence and who had a long-running feud with Carmody.

The other cowboy, named Parrish, was leaning out of his pickup with mud up to the headlights and a gun rack in its back window. Their shouting match didn't bother the work crew, and they figured the pistol hanging at Carmody's right hip was not thought of by either disputant.

When Parrish finally sped off, spewing dirt, Carmody turned to Hickson as though to explain the mild insinuations Parrish had thrown out concerning Mirella's fidelity, uncertainty in his expression. He had controlled his anger with Parrish but not his blood pressure. He roughly shoved the webs of his gloved hands together and spat into the dirt. "Barney, I worry about Mirella. I have to tell you she's been sick for a long time, but nobody can tell. It's that thing they call multiple sclerosis—it doesn't show, but the doctors say they can't predict what it will do. It's mild with some and awful with others." He shuddered, "I never told anybody about that, but she has a will stronger than anybody I ever met. She will not let it control her." Hickson recalled Carmody's pained expression as his breathing came back to normal.

When they climbed into the pickup, Carmody was speaking into the steering wheel, "Her mama was a conjure woman." That was all Carmody said, but he was not grinning when he said it.

The jukebox had gone silent, and both our plates were clean. "Uno mas, Chapo," Hickson said as he leaned back and looked for the bartender, who had momentarily disappeared back to the kitchen, talking to his wife.

"I've been thinking since you was last here. I think before we get to the night that made Hillsboro history, you have to understand Mirella and what she did to Big Jim."

Hickson told the story about how Carmody indulged Mirella's wants, aside from the Cadillac and his money. "Naw, she wasn't a gold digger—she really wanted him, always making him uncomfortable, if you know what I mean." It was not more than a year after she arrived that Mirella had a strange demand.

"She wanted to grow weeds—really. It's those damned yellow wildflowers, and she wanted to grow them." Carmody and Hickson spent two days running a system of pipes to a half-acre field north of the ranch house. The supply pipe ran from the windmill reservoir down under the parking area behind the house and into the field. When wind was strong, the reservoir filled, and the water flowed into the field. Particularly in late spring, the windmill was productive, and the water streamed all the way out along the access road. "In the spring and summer, she made that field and the access roadside like a yellow carpet with hundreds of wildflower plants.

"Many an afternoon she would take her tea and lie on a luxurious chaise lounge outside at the north wall of the house, protected from the sun, and she was usually wearing her bathing suit and her high heels." Hickson scratched the back of his neck as though it itched. "On days like that, the boss would quit early and leave the rest of the work to me as he went back to the house. Well, wouldn't you?"

I could only smile.

* * *

A week later, we made the trip again, and I was enjoying the adrenaline rush of taking the switchbacks fast enough to squeal the tires in the turns, the steep mountain slope on one side of the road and precipitous drop-offs just off the shoulder on the other. As planned, I dropped Herb off at the access road and looked forward to meeting the cowboy writer at the Bar None. Saturdays always seemed to be his day for storytelling, and I was his audience.

"That night was history, I'm here to tell you." I was momentarily scared that Hickson was going to meander back to Lordsburg and the Old West story of Keane's Stockyards, but I realized that, finally, Hickson was about to tell the rest of the Carmody story, or so I thought. "Another one of those Friday nights, and I was here when it happened."

At Carmody's request, Hickson was already at the Bar None that evening when the iridescent red Eldorado slid into a spot at the side of the road, and it was followed by a white Chevrolet truck owned by Ted Parrish, that rancher whose property abutted the Carmody land. Their dispute over a stand of grass on public land and supposedly under the control of the Bureau of Land Management. Since their last confrontation, they had traded letters from each of their lawyers. At the suggestion of the attorneys, they had agreed to sit down together, and it looked like this was the time.

Big Jim opened the door and ushered Mirella into the room. Hickson recalled vividly that she wore a low cut sleeveless black dress hemmed just above the knee, and her matching high heeled sandals clicked noisily on the hardwood floor as Carmody escorted her to the booth. Her long hair was wound into coils and piled atop her head, cinched with a chain of narrow elliptical gold links. She slid in on the leatherette bench seat with Carmody sitting beside her. Mirella's smooth throat was adorned by a ruby pendant surrounded by diamonds, and a wildflower was pinned to the top of the dress, an inch below the swell of her breasts.

The door opened again to admit Ted Parrish, the 6-foot barrel-chested man with a ruddy face and beard stubble. He wore a fresh white western cut shirt with snaps, his beige slacks sporting a knife-edge crease and held up by a wide belt and a worn silver and turquoise buckle he had won as a bull rider a decade before. He looked as though he had just showered and quickly run a comb through his thinning hair before coming into town.

Chapo came out from the bar and greeted all three, assuring Mirella that the tea was brewing, while Carmody ordered beers for the two men as they traded guarded surface pleasantries, trying to ignore a document with a blue cover sheet that Parrish put onto the table between them.

"There were several people I knew there that night—everybody laughing, eating the best steaks in the county. I was by myself and far enough away from Carmody that I couldn't hear exactly what they were saying." Hickson described Mirella, her bare elbows on the table, long fingers of both hands caressing the floral cup, her lips kissing the gold rim. Her eyes seemed fixed on the florid face of Parrish, and the big man had begun to perspire as the two ranchers argued about fences between vigorous bites of medium rare steak and baked potato topped with sour cream.

"My boss had a talent for thinking ahead, and he asked if I would be in the room when he and Parrish sat down together. I'm tellin' you, a bad feeling was growing in me, and I nursed my beer with one eye on that table over there by the window." Hickson told me that on more than one occasion, Parrish had goaded Big Jim, making veiled and suggestive comments about Mirella, but Carmody always ignored them, though once I saw his eyes narrow before he thought better of it. The meal passed with agonizing slowness for Hickson, the document being pushed back and forth as the men argued. Flatware clinked at the occupied tables as conversation rattled meaninglessly; the tight argument of the two ranchers rose and fell, but it was not quite audible at Hickson's table. There were six brown bottles in the center of the table when Chapo came to clear the plates.

"After the table was cleared, Parrish made a chopping motion with his hand and said something like 'my lawyer is gonna…' and he was staring at Mirella. Know what she did? She leaned back against cushioned backrest, putting her hand on Big Jim's shoulder while her eyes were on Parrish. As she threw her shoulders back, it seemed like her breasts under that tight dress were the biggest things in the room." Hickson was shaking his head, remembering every detail.

"My boss shrugged, cocked his head and grinned as if to say 'OK,' and pulled a couple of 20's from the folded bundle he kept in his shirt pocket; then they got up to leave." As he talked, Hickson was looking toward the window booth, remembering.

Hickson made a knife edge with his hand and pointed it at the door. "Big Jim and Parrish stood up, glaring at each other. Parrish picked up the document as Carmody held out his hand to Mirella to ease her way out of the booth. She led the way to the door, with the two men following, and that's when it happened. I saw it. Parrish, at least three beers to the wind, reached out and put his hand full on Mirella's rear end. She turned halfway around and moved to her right as Carmody jostled Parrish. Parrish pushed past Mirella and pulled the door open. Carmody was right behind Parrish as I pushed my chair back and started after them."

Hickson described what happened next as though it were a sharply focused movie scene. Carmody barreled through the door right behind Parrish, putting his cowboy boot in front of Parrish's trailing foot and then shoving viciously. The sidewalk is right outside the front door, with two concrete steps going down to the dirt at the side of the blacktop highway. Parrish tumbled down the steps, landing on his face in the dirt. The legal document came unclipped and four pages blew into the street.

Parrish thundered, "You sumbitch, I'm gonna kill you," as he scrambled to gain his feet.

"You'll have to," Carmody grated as he sprinted for the Cadillac. Parrish threw open the driver's side door of his truck, reaching for the carbine in his rifle rack while Carmody jammed his torso through the open Cadillac window, also grabbing for what Hickson knew was within reach on the carpeted floor. Carmody's black Stetson went flying and landed crown up on the sidewalk.

Parrish came around the front of his truck, a Winchester Model 94 in his right hand, as Carmody pulled himself out of the car and turned—too late. Parrish thumbed back the hammer and pulled the trigger. It was only a fraction of a second, but it seemed eternity. The hammer clacked—onto an empty chamber—and Parrish's mouth went wide as he grabbed the forestock with his left hand and with his right hand threw down the lever to jack a round into the chamber.

The twilight was split with a BOOM, as Carmody's .45 single action revolver bucked in his hand, and a 225-grain flat nosed lead slug slammed into the center of Parrish's chest. Parrish did fire the .30-30 Winchester, the bullet making a tiny volcano in the dirt as he staggered back against the hood of his truck, already dying as he slumped, one arm on the truck bumper and the rifle still gripped in a dead right hand.

Terror Tales of the Southwest

Even as he told me the story, Hickson seemed fixed on Parrish's sightless eyes staring into the growing darkness around him and in him, but his memory was more shaken by something else before he ran to his boss and took control of the revolver still pointed in Parrish's direction.

Hickson's description was like a photograph in my mind. "Mirella was standing against the dark wood planking of the outer wall of the Bar None, her black dress almost indistinguishable from the wood, but her smooth shoulders and legs pale by contrast. Her face was expressionless in its cold beauty, lowered eyelids masking her expression.

I remember that her lips were slightly open and her perfect hands, one covering the other, were on her lower stomach. Her hair was piled like midnight on top of her head as she stood against the wall, and she had eyes only for her man. I swear that her lips were forming a smile, but I didn't dare say anything. That woman was so damned beautiful as she leaned against the wall. Like nothin' had happened. She scared me down deep, more than Parrish lying there dead in the dirt."

Hickson said the rest of the evening was blurred. It took almost an hour before the black patrol car of the New Mexico State Police came screaming up the highway from Truth or Consequences, and the Sierra County Sheriff's Office was even slower.

The flashing red lights splashed a pulsating ruddy tint to the faces of Hillsboro residents who had assembled on the roadside and the sidewalk. Sheriff's deputies photographed the scene before an ambulance arrived to load Parrish's body. "The cops interviewed Carmody, Mirella, and me, but they didn't even take Carmody's Colt. Finally, when the cops finished, Mirella embraced Carmody, and I heard her say, 'You will always be mine,' and they got into the Eldorado without another word. I don't even remember going home that night, but I do remember that Parrish's truck sat in front of the bar for days after that, gathering a coating of dust."

I had almost forgotten about Herb and his lover as I listened to the way Barney Hickson wove his story, but as I stood up to take my leave, Hickson looked at the empty bottles on the table and shook his head, "That's been ten years gone—seems like last month."

"Some story, Barney, and sure worth writing."

Hickson shook his head. "You write stories, and you shouldn't give up before you've heard the mysterious part." His smile stretched across his face. "You'll be here next week or the week after. You need to hear what happened to Mirella. Also, I want you to read the first part of my latest effort." The manila envelope was weighty, perhaps 25-40 pages of typewriting, and I promised to read it.

As I headed for the door, manuscript in hand, Hickson added one more thought. "That night when I looked at Mirella's hungry eyes, I realized why I never got married. She wasn't looking at me, but I felt a hand gripping my chest. A cold memory came from my childhood when my own mother told me, 'Don't forget, Ebenezer—girls grow up to become their mothers'."

I walked outside into the cool evening air, looking at the concrete sidewalk and the two steps that led downward to Ted Parrish's sudden death. A lone car came from the mountains, its headlights briefly illuminating the quiet town after passing the almost-ghost town of Kingston, and now through Hillsboro to Interstate 25 and Truth or Consequences or down to Las Cruces and El Paso, Texas.

My passengers were waiting at the access road and in that exuberant mood that only lovers know. Once again, Feather got out at the outskirts of Hillsboro to walk back to the where she was staying with friends. I was never sure where that was. The now-familiar drive took us back over the mountains and down to the Mimbres Valley, then on to Silver City. It was necessary to concentrate on the treacherous two-lane paved forest road, but I did tell Herb about the rancher and his confrontation in front of the Bar None. It was more difficult to talk about Mirella, and I realized I was confusing my secret feelings of love for Mary Ann with the image of a woman I had never seen.

For his part, Herb was obviously fixed on Feather Symond and her counter culture associates as well as his obvious protective feelings, and I sensed that he was not certain he could extricate her from the life that had brought her to Hillsboro.

By the time we got back to Silver City, we were both tired and decided to call it a weekend. I did not regret the long drive, and I went home to think late into the night about Barney Hickson's story and with a promise to myself that I would read his manuscript.

* * *

As circumstances would have it, Herb pressed me the following week to make the journey yet again, and I was curiously eager to go back. We left a little earlier, and with the drill so well established, I could go back to find Barney Hickson and learn what happened to Carmody and his lover Mirella. Meanwhile, Herb and Feather would find their own destiny at the house abandoned by the rancher and his consort.

I was hungry to hear from Hickson every detail of Mirella's life, and I found myself longing for her almost in the same way I longed for the heat of Mary Ann's embrace—so vividly did Barney Hickson describe Carmody's woman.

I returned Hickson's typescript, and we talked about his developing Old West story. I was pleased to admit his skill in recreating the atmosphere of 1870s New Mexico. The beginning of his novel *Destiny in Silver and Lead* described the brutal McComas massacre when Apaches slaughtered a ranch family between Silver City and Lordsburg; the story then following three fictional men who hunted the Apache and rode toward a rough destiny in the cow town of Lordsburg.

Hickson created again the harsh and thankless life of cowboys and drifters in the real West of the 1870s. His story described the heat and the dirt at branding time and how the smell of burning steer flesh stayed in the nostrils for days. Hickson had obviously experienced his own gritty life on the range. In the 1870s, Lordsburg was a burgeoning cattle town just waiting for the railroad to come through southern New Mexico. At the same time, 100 miles to the east, the mining town of Hillsboro had its own growing pains. Critiquing Hickson's story was the tariff I was happy to pay in order to hear the final revelations about Mirella and Carmody.

* * *

Hickson was a natural story teller like most cowboys, and he set the scene. The call came in the middle of the night in that hour before dawn. "I don't remember the day, but it was early March, and I'll never forget that it was a moonless night. The air was freezing when I ran out to jump in my pickup. I'd never heard Big Jim's voice breaking in hysteria. He said her name two or three times, and I thought maybe he'd shot her. God knows she drove him to the brink of violence more than once."

Hickson raced from his house outside of Hillsboro, screaming along the empty highway through the sleeping town, and south at the intersection. He hit the access road and bounced along the potholes of the gravel track. "Every light was blazing in that house, and I hit my brakes when I rolled in behind the house, jumping out, my heart in my damned throat."

Carmody met him inside the door. "She's dead, Barney. She's dead." He was wearing his plaid shirt hanging open, but he had forgotten to put on his pants, his black socks almost comical as he led Hickson up the stairs mumbling that he had called the ambulance but it would be almost an hour.

The elaborate 12-bulb bedroom chandelier with its multitude of hanging prisms sent shimmering colors around the room. Mirella had selected it when Carmody remodeled the house. "She lay there, the maroon comforter pulled back to reveal the top of her red satin nightgown." Hickson said he swore he saw her breasts moving as though she were breathing.

"She won't wake up. She's gone…She's gone." Carmody dropped into the cushioned bedroom chair where his jeans had been thrown the night before. He covered his face with his hands as Hickson reached out to touch Mirella's throat. Hickson jerked his hand back as he felt the cool skin under his touch. Yet her lips were full and red, her breasts swelling, her beauty intact as she permanently slept.

The next hour was chaos, getting Carmody into his clothes and coffee into Carmody, trying to keep the rancher from dissolving from a shock that he had obviously never known before. Hickson said it was almost dawn when the flashing red lights announced the arrival of the EMT ambulance from Truth or Consequences. "I didn't know somebody could die like that. We followed the ambulance down to I-25 and up to Sierra Vista Hospital on 9th Street. I remember the fluorescent lights in that ER examination room." It wasn't more than 20 minutes before the doctor on duty came out, her face impassive but with the expression showing she had told this story too many times. She said that Mirella had died from bleeding of the brain— an aneurysm.

The doctor assured the inconsolable Carmody that she had not suffered…there was nothing they could do…could he contact next of kin…would he like the number of someone who could help. Her voice was even, measured, as though she had done this probably a hundred times.

Hickson's eyes were damp as he remembered that night and said it was one of the most horrible nights of his life. He said that for Carmody it was soul destroying. He leaned forward, elbows on the table, the sleeves of his Wrangler denim work shirt rolled up onto his forearms, and I started from my concentration, my mouth dry despite a half full glass of draft beer in front of me. "I can still see her lying there in the bedroom." Hickson was not talking to me, but I was certain that I could see her too.

"Chapo, get us another round and bring me a menu." Glass clattered and Chapo assured Hickson that he didn't need the menu—the burger was on the plate. Chapo almost shouted across the room in a friendly manner, getting the attention of two older men sitting together at the bar. The bar owner's arrival at the table eased the tension.

"Young fella, I'm saying as bad as that night was, it was the last normal night me and Carmody ever spent." Hickson could see the consternation on my face.

"Let's start with the collect call he made from the waiting room of the hospital. I figured he must be callin' Mirella's people back in the bayou country. He was making hand gestures and promising to pay their way to come out here. Then he started yelling at the staff when they said an autopsy had to be performed, and they told me to get him out of the hospital until the body was released." Hickson said he grabbed his boss by the arm and took him to the parking lot.

The drive back up to Hillsboro in the cold mid-morning sunlight was funereal. "That tough guy who usually carried a pistol on his hip was all hollowed out. He was trying not to cry, but he couldn't hold it back."

Hickson stayed much of the day with Carmody in the living room of the house with its expansive white leather U-shaped sofa, the glass top coffee table, the antique dining room table, and a hand-carved sideboard taller than Wilt Chamberlain, its marble shelf supporting a set with three crystal decanters, engraved silver lozenges hanging as necklaces around the shoulders of each. The elegance was incongruous with Carmody's personal style. Mirella was everywhere here.

The sense of emptiness was made even more oppressive by the 8-foot wide picture window framed by heavy velour draperies and looking outward to the S-curve of the access road. "Drinking makes everything worse, but I couldn't get that damn bottle of Chivas out of his hands. He opened the record cabinet and began playing songs from Mirella's record collection. Finally he threw me out—said he had to be alone." Hickson said Carmody's phone started ringing when he left.

"It was before dawn the next morning when he called me again." Hickson spoke between mouthfuls of cheeseburger, and I dipped tortilla chips into the salsa, eager to hear him continue. "His voice was slurred, but he was my boss after all. He told me to get a couple workers and meet him behind the house. Even though it was our slow season, I could always drive over to Hatch and pick up *mojados* who wanted a day's work, so I climbed into my work clothes and headed down the road. By 8 a.m. I was pulling in behind the house."

Hickson said that Carmody looked haggard and was unshaven. His shirt was only half-tucked, and his eyes were bloodshot. "Me and the two illegals brought picks and shovels, like Big Jim instructed, and we walked to the north side of the house where that field of wildflowers grew untended. I didn't get too close to him because he smelled of alcohol, but he grabbed my arm and led me out about 20 feet."

At that point, Carmody pointed to the ground and described the rectangle, telling him to "dig it here," and Hickson knew it was to be the grave for Mirella. The field was a mass of brown plants awaiting a new season, but the earth itself was saturated that morning with the overflow from the pipe system of the windmill. Hickson described how they started digging in the wet ground while Carmody went back into the house.

"We were digging, spelling each other, and all the while, Carmody was playing records in the living room of the house—George Jones, Hank Williams, Ray Price, one after another. Then he put one on I didn't know, and he started playing it over and over. Some guy singing in Cajun French. We was now down about four feet when Big Jim came out of the house, and I asked him what the hell that song was. There was somethin' mournful, sad about it."

Carmody told Hickson it was song by a Cajun who called himself Cleveland Crochet, and the song was "Drunkard's Dream." Hickson may not have known the song, but I realized that I have the record, even though I never knew what the French lyrics were. I could hear the song in my head, the pained Cajun voice, the whine of the concertina, the plaintive steel guitar, the hopelessness. It was a perfect threnody, a song of lamentation.

Hickson asked his boss what the song was about, because Carmody knew a few Cajun phrases. Carmody looked at him through bleary eyes and gave him phrases from the song: "arrive hier a La maison…j'ai crié,j'ai pas de réponse, and finishing, C'est si dur, c'est d'connaitre mais t'es pas lá. That's all I remember except for his pain. He said it translated it to something like, 'I came home… I cry but I got no answer… It is so hard to know you're not there."

Personally, I had never understood any of the words in the years I owned the record on Gold Band, but I had always intuitively known the message. I had the same experience listening to "Jolé Blon." I reminded myself that Mirella was not blond, and I was listening again to Ebenezer Hickson, now the gravedigger.

"We got the hole dug by mid-afternoon, with dirt heaped on either side, and Big Jim paid the *mojados*, dismissing us so that I could drive them back to wherever they were camping in Hatch. Carmody told me to come back in the morning and that he had to go pick up the family at the El Paso airport. Perhaps halfway sober, he got into Mirella's Eldorado and headed out.

Hickson said that he usually rolled into the ranch headquarters to get the day's marching orders as the sun was coming up, and this day he was a little later but wanting to coordinate activities as the ranch moved into calving season. "I parked behind the Cadillac and when I switched off the engine, I heard the arguing. Anyhow, I piled out of the truck just as all four of 'em came out the back door of the house. Carmody raised his arms to chest level, 'She stays here,' as he walked in my direction. I was thinking about the hole dug on the north side of the house."

Suddenly aware of his ranch foreman, Carmody introduced "Mirella's folks." Hickson said, "They were strange…yeah, that's the only word. I don't even remember the names, but the first guy was on the heavy side, wearing a grey fedora with the brim turned down. He was wearing chinos and a silk shirt. He looked like he was in his 60s—long, drawn face, mustache, puffy eyes, with oily grey hair sticking out from under the brim of the hat. I figured he was bald on top. The second man was tall and slim, maybe 25, maybe 30, with dark hair combed into a shiny Elvis-like pompadour. He was good-looking and dressed in suit pants black shirt, shiny shoes, but I thought he had cruel lips. They stood on either side of the mysterious woman—Mirella's mama. She was almost as tall as the young man, slender, and wearing a black mourning dress. I didn't really see her face because of her black veil. I could see her eyes, and I got the feeling they were accusing me. You know what it's like to feel nervous around someone? Well, it was more than nervous, but I can't explain it."

Hickson expressed his sympathy and asked her how she was. Carmody spoke to her in Cajun French "Comment les affaires?" She turned to him and then back to Hickson, "Ça va pas du tout," and Carmody translated for Hickson. "Not good." The conversation foundered. The younger man shook Hickson's hand, speaking to him in accented English, and the three went to the Cadillac to retrieve some belongings. They spoke in guarded Cajun French the way New Mexico Spanish speakers sequestered their language when they did not want to be understood by Anglos.

Hickson described how the younger man looked up at the creaking windmill, then at the vista of open sky to the south, and he said something to his mother that sounded like a question, "At-elle sortir?"

The woman nodded from behind her veil, "Oui—Je le pense." Carmody asked the young man what he meant by "got away," but got no answer, and thus let it drop.

Carmody called Hickson into the house, and he found the kitchen in chaos. As his boss sloshed whiskey into an iced tea glass, Hickson got the list of instructions for the next few days. The counter was littered with coffee cups, empty glasses, trays and cartons from half-eaten TV dinners, empty bottles. "There was a small pile of stuff at the end of the counter, and I'll never forget seeing Mirella's Louisiana driver's license just lying there on the tile counter top. I didn't pick it up, but I saw the DOB." Hickson shook his head.

When asked about the visitors, Carmody said they were Mirella's parents and her grown son. Hickson looked at me. "That's when I knew my eyes weren't playing tricks. Mirella was 59 years old. Maybe it couldn't be true, but it was a fact."

"He also told me they had come to take Mirella back to Louisiana—had something to do with what he had agreed to when he brought her out here. As he said the words, his fists were clenched, his mouth showing the grit I hadn't seen since the day she died. He told me to take care of the ranch and not to come back to the house until the visitors had departed. This was indeed the Cajun Carmody had labeled a 'conjure woman,' and as sure as I was standing there, I felt afraid of that woman and the eyes behind that veil."

"When I shook Big Jim's hand to wish him strength, his grip was softer than I had ever known it. His grief was deeper than the grave we dug." Hickson said he went away that day wondering if the Louisiana clan would claim Mirella, and then it was back to the plains and the herd that occupied him most of the next two days.

Hickson was very clear that on the afternoon of the second day he had by chance seen a hearse followed by a second funeral service car from T or C heading east out of Hillsboro, glossy black paint jobs lightly coated with the usual pale grey dust. Had they released the body to Carmody? Were they transporting Mirella to El Paso for passage back to Louisiana? "Not my business, y' know."

According to Hickson, it was three days before Carmody called him back the ranch headquarters. "I rolled in behind the house and first thing I notice was that the Caddy was gone, and the next thing I couldn't avoid seeing was that the hole we dug was completely filled in and tamped down. Seemed to me it was level with the ground. I was burning up with curiosity, but I promised myself not to say anything." He snorted, grimacing, "Not my business. Besides that, I was still feeling heavy with sadness for both Big Jim and Mirella."

All that Carmody would tell him was that he had signed over the pink slip to the car and given it to Mirella's son. They took the Cadillac and headed back to their home the next day. Whatever else they took, and whatever oaths they extracted from the rancher was none of Hickson's affair, thank you very much.

My conversation partner seemed agitated now, and my own curiosity had made me lose track of time there in the dim interior of the Bar None. "Yeah, we went back to work, but Big Jim couldn't shake the grief. He was still drinking, and he that tic in his left eye was getting worse. His shirt hung loose on his shoulders, and the ready smile was gone. One day we were putting out salt blocks close to the earth tanks at the south end of the range, and we were leaning against the door of my truck when he looked off into the distance and started talking."

Carmody blurted out, "My God, Barney, I can't help dreaming about her. Last night I looked at her and asked her if she wanted to…uh…" He hesitated and substituted the words "…uh, make love, for another 40 years, and she answered 'Will that be enough?' I heard myself say, 'It would be a good start.' You don't know how beautiful she was as I reached for her and woke up. I felt as though I was having a heart attack." Hickson responded that the dreams were normal but time would ease the pain. He said he hated to lie to Carmody's face.

For another week, Carmody seemed to decline, his sorrow and visible depression lengthening like the shadows that grew from the Black Range in the very late afternoon. He was still drinking heavily, but he seemed physically strong and capable as he worked the ranch alongside his foreman. Hickson took a deep breath as he remembered. "His sorrow was thrown over him like the black veil on that weird conjure woman from Louisiana. He was fighting it, but he sure wasn't winning. He went on like that for days, and I wondered if he would ever come out of it. Didn't really blame him."

Hickson's plate was clean, and the glass in front of me was still half full and warm by now. I was already behind schedule for picking up Herb and his lady love, but I couldn't seem to get up from the table. Several Hillsboro residents had come in to take their places and begin the undercurrent of chatter, but I was only listening to one voice.

"It was late on a Wednesday afternoon that I thought he might have hit bottom. It was close to sunset, and he told me he was going back to the house—he never considered my invitation to put him up at my place—said he was just sick at heart. That was his word, not mine. I watched his truck headed up to ranch headquarters and then I worried half the night."

Hickson recalled the next morning, bright and clear, when he saw Carmody coming down the access road riding the appaloosa he hadn't saddled for at least a month. "My jaw dropped when I saw his trademark grin, pistol belt in place. He looked tired, but that veil of sorrow seemed to be lifted, and I didn't ask any questions as we made plans to count calves."

Hickson said he was relieved "big time" at the sudden change in Carmody's demeanor, and for the next week or two the man was cheerful, enthusiastic, though not willing to talk about what he had been through. He threw himself into the ranch duties, and though he seemed to tire easily, there was no doubt that his grief had weakened him, and it would take time to recover his full health. "He stopped drinking entirely," Hickson said simply as if it were something close to a miracle.

One Friday evening Carmody invited Hickson to steaks and conversation at the Bar None. All was reminiscent of the days before Mirella's death, although Hickson said his boss seemed to be avoiding direct eye contact. "Hell, why not? The love of his life was dead, and he had killed a man right outside the door of the bar. Still, we talked cattle, politics, and he even encouraged me to get started writing a novel. I appreciated that. I was looking forward to the future, and he was talking about new electric branding irons and other possible changes to make our work easier."

As he sat talking to me, Hickson seemed to be struggling to describe the paradox of Big Jim Carmody who radiated the light of enthusiasm in his eyes and voice, but with a sense of frailty about his formerly robust physiognomy. "He was almost happy and eager to go back to the house at the end of the day." Suddenly Hickson stopped and stared at me almost accusingly before shaking his head vigorously and wiping a dab of catsup from his lips with a crumpled paper napkin.

"Two weeks later he was dead."

I felt a catch in my throat as I forgot to breathe. Hickson's eyes bored into mine, and I felt almost hypnotized. I couldn't move.

"Got your attention, didn't I?" Hickson described how he had phoned Carmody at sunrise on a Monday morning after not hearing from him on the weekend. No answer. When he pulled in behind the house, he walked toward the back door to see Big Jim Carmody lying face down at the threshold, half out the door, and wearing nothing but boxer shorts.

"I couldn't believe it. He looked so small, his body stiff and almost emaciated. Of course I went inside and placed a call to the sheriff and the ambulance service. As I stood in the kitchen, I felt scared, like there was something in the house. I wondered if the conjure woman had put a curse on Carmody or that some illegal had killed him. He was stone cold, and I was scared. I couldn't get out into the back yard fast enough."

Waiting for the authorities, Hickson went to the barn to feed the appaloosa, not daring to look into the windows of the house. "Something was in that house. I could smell it, feel it. No, it wasn't a bad smell, just something…something watching. That's it, something watching."

My dry mouth betrayed me when I tried to speak, and I was thinking about a Cajun conjure woman's spells, and I was thinking about Herb and Feather out there. It was dark out, and I couldn't make myself stand up. The Saturday night crowd had taken the booths and several tables, the chatter from the locals bringing the armor of normalcy to the dim interior. But what about my friends out there in the dark. Suddenly I was really afraid of that house. Why was there so little vandalism in a place vacant so long—and only a couple of broken windows? Why didn't somebody take it over?

"OK, long story short, Big Jim died of 'natural causes,' and no trauma except what the doctors said was dehydration. He was buried in T or C, and his ex-wife and kids were at the funeral. Seems he had left the ranch in trust to her and the kids, so she kept the property and kept me on to run it any way I pleased. Carmody's teenage daughter had the appaloosa taken back to Silver City. The family hired some people from T or C to clean out the house, right down to the light fixtures, most of Carmody's possessions, and especially the bed. They burned a pile of stuff in the back yard, and I'll bet the bed was on that pyre." Hickson snorted. "They said I could fix up the house and move in if I wanted to. I didn't. Oh yeah, and they presented me with Big Jim's pistol belt and Colt .45. That means a lot to me. Gotta tell you that I still feel jittery even when I'm anywhere on the property—Jittery and something else I don't like feeling." He didn't elaborate.

We stood up at the same moment. I looked Hickson in the eyes and shook his hand. I thanked him and said I hoped to see him again in the next week or two. I was wrong about that.

* * *

Then came that ninth day in May, a Saturday. Just the night before, I had talked on the telephone with Mary Ann, and both Herb and I were in a particularly ebullient mood. He had come up with the ransom his estranged wife was demanding, and he would have his truck released to him the following Monday. Things were going right. Even the long drive over the mountains seemed brief in the current of the brilliant day whose dry heat was tempered by a gusting breeze. This was the strong sun that brought New Mexico natives back from wherever we had wandered in our lives, to feel the pleasant harshness of the air, the powerful flavors in the food, and the lack of pretense in the people.

It was still early afternoon when we rolled into Hillsboro, and the wind had increased. The highway running through the quiet town was scoured by sworls of dust. Nobody was in sight, and there were no motorcycles outside the café on the south side of the intersection. We turned south as always, expecting every moment to see Feather's trim figure by the roadside. We drove to the iron gate and back to town three times in the face of wind and blowing dust.

"Did you confirm this appointment?" My comment was probably unnecessary considering the agitation that showed in Herb's tight-set mouth.

"She called me last night. Enough said." His eyes remained fixed on the road.

Finally we drove in behind the abandoned house; while Herb went inside, I stayed out front listening to the wind rustle through the tree limbs. After all these weeks I had suppressed all sense of foreboding concerning Herb and Feather, but now it came back with a familiar queasiness seething in my stomach. Herb emerged from the house as though it were his own. He got into the car and sat there for a moment, staring straight ahead.

My unease became a wave of panic as I thought of a dead girl lying in the old Carmody house, a victim cloaked in my worst imaginings.

Herb slapped the dashboard suddenly. "She's not there. Time to go to town."

The next hour was spent walking the street in Hillsboro—the bar, the Texaco station, the cafes, antique stores, grocery store, the RV campground: Nothing. It struck me that neither of us knew where Feather had actually been staying. After walking up and down the long street, Herb saw a younger man emerging from the café. Herb buttonholed him, and he said he had been awakened the night before by the roar of a motorcycle echoing through town before dawn. He had gone to the window, but it was too dark to see anything save a dark mass shooting through the town, blue flame coming from the header stacks of the machine's exhaust.

We stopped in at the Bar None, but Ebenezer Hickson's favorite chair was empty, and Herb was in no mood to sit down over food and beer. I waved to Chapo as we walked out.

My thought was pure sarcasm. Maybe Turk had left for good so everybody could live happily ever after.

By the time darkness came it seemed that we had talked to almost a dozen of the town's denizens—anyone out on the streets or clerking in a store—to no avail. The heat of the day was dissipating quickly and with it came a fatigue that could only be generated by disappointment. My mouth tasted of dust, and I didn't argue when Herb suggested we go back to Silver City.

Herb's personality was always an object of study to me; he was able to act quickly in emergency situations or when physical force was required, but his face could remain a stone mask, and he was imperturbable in most social situations. As we wound along the so-familiar mountain road, I felt, for the first time since I had known him, that he was crumbling at the edges like an ancient granite obelisk.

When I called him the following evening, Herb had still not heard from Feather, and the level quality of his speech could not conceal his depression. He did say that he was due to get his truck back the next day and that he was going to be taking a few days off from work. I didn't have to ask what he was going to do with the time, and I knew he wanted to be by himself.

For myself, the following days' demands took my mind off the whereabouts of Feather Symond. The deceit of appearances was an old nemesis, and I knew how possible it was that she had turned her life around and decided to make the best of it with her other boyfriend.

Mary Ann and I talked long distance four times that week. I knew that I loved her despite the limited time we had spent together. The softness of her voice and its promises were like nothing I had experienced; the way she could make me feel, too, was a blazing jewel in the everyday pewter setting of my life. We seldom discussed the future or social arrangements because we understood how difficult it was that to ever reach that stage. When I thought of marriage and social permanence I could not help but think of my own and Herb's experiences; the disappointments natural to life made me a foe of reality, but there was something in this ethereal contact that colored the thoughts of my days, the dreams of my nights, with the white stain of indelibility.

Several times I picked up the telephone and punched in Herb's number, but he was never home. It was two weeks later that I saw him at a local gas station. I pulled in behind him and got out to talk with him. Was it my imagination? His face seemed strained—his normally intense eyes red-rimmed and almost glazed with fatigue. Never before I had I seen such an accentuation of the lines in his face, which normally carried only the squint lines common to those who worked outdoors under intense sun.

"Where you been, Guy? I called about nine times in the last week."

Herb shrugged characteristically, "Told you—I was taking some time off. Guess I haven't been at the house much."

I pressed him, "Come on, what's the news? I've been wondering."

Herb re-hung the gasoline filler nozzle on the big, chrome-trimmed self-serve pump. "I was a little concerned, but it'll be all right. Just a mix-up the last time we went over." He rubbed his hands together and his eyes seemed fixed on a distant point down the street behind my shoulder. I noticed that his hands were dry and cracked, the fingernails untended. In the two weeks since I had last seen him, Herb had also begun to grow a beard, as yet it was uneven and disreputable looking.

"She's fine…okay. Nothing's changed." I hadn't asked about Feather.

With the mystery cleared up, I felt awkward now, and our conversation dwindled into a receding spiral of banality. Herb still had other things on his mind.

A day later he called me, asking if I would drive him to Hillsboro yet one more time. The alternator in his truck had unexpectedly quit. This time it was later afternoon when he wanted to be picked up and dark when we reached our destination. Herb indeed seemed changed; he was taciturn, but his eyes were eager, his face strained with exhaustion. Most of my questions were answered in bluff monosyllables. Perhaps it was his impatience or the tension in the air, but the whole trip seemed only half real.

Finding the road to the empty house required much more concentration this night, and Herb instructed me to stop at the turnoff, right by the metal gate posts and cattle guard. He got out of the car and walked through the pale shafts of the headlights into the moonless dark. In the glow from the headlights I could just perceive Feather almost floating at the limits of the headlight beams. Barely visible, her dark clothing sketched the flimsiest of outlines to her figure and her hair appeared darker in the night.

Hillsboro was shut down for the night, and I naturally parked in front of Bar None simply because it was open. Three locals were keeping Chapo occupied, but he greeted me and gestured to an empty chair.

"Not here, is he?" I was hoping to see Hickson.

"Haven't seen him all week. You here with your friend?" Chapo leaned on the bar, and he flashed a trademark smile of welcome. Hickson had obviously told him about our peculiar sojourns over past weeks. I ordered chips, salsa and a soft drink while I asked him what he knew about the rancher and his lover.

Chapo shook his head and glanced toward the kitchen area, but his wife had probably gone home. "There was never anybody like Mirella in this town. Never will be, Ese."

"So I heard from Barney."

"Ol' Barney was loyal to Big Jim, and he still is, but I think Mirella's eyes still haunt him. She had that power." Chapo talked again about the night of the shooting, and I was wondering if Hickson was sitting in his house typing his own story about the shootings of another era on the frontier streets of Lordsburg.

As Herb had requested, I came back two hours later and waited in the darkness, listening to a distant AM radio station while I waited for him to return. I think it was KWKH in Shreveport, Louisiana. I prided myself on my punctuality, but Herb just said I was punctilious. For his part, Herb was seldom anywhere on time. This night, however, Herb came walking down the access road only about 20 minutes late. For some reason, Feather didn't ride back to Hillsboro with us, and she didn't even come down to the car before we left. Her perfume lingered in the vehicle with us, and Herb had a yellow flower protruding from his shirt pocket.

In the days following I called him several times but he only picked up once, and that at a time when he should have been at work. He said he'd been sick and was slow getting back on his feet; his voice sounded febrile, his breathing forced. Once again our conversation was superficial, leaving me feeling as though I were an intruder.

* * *

May became midsummer too soon, the June heat wave broken by occasional afternoon clouds that would become the annual monsoon flow. The phone call was from Herb's wife of late; she was looking for him, and I had to admit that it had been two weeks since I had even talked with him. I queried her, but she had already called the Grant County offices and found that Herb had never returned to work after his vacation, a vacation that had ended two weeks before.

The uncomfortably recurrent stomach shifting was back again. I drove to Herb's place, but his truck wasn't there. There was an aura of disuse about the house—scraps of paper, an unlatched gate, certainly little things that Herb was meticulous about. Yellowing rolled-up newspapers were scattered on the front walk.

I made my own round of phone calls, but nobody had seen Herb more recently than I had. My next impulse was to call the sheriff, but Hillsboro was in Sierra County, next over from Grant.

Next morning as I headed out of town, I thought of the seven times I had made this journey so far this year, and I wondered how many times Herb had gone over the mountains to see Feather in the weeks after he got his truck back. The 60-mile trip was interminable this time and, when I coasted to a stop in Hillsboro, it was just past noon.

The day was hot and bright, but a wall of stately white cumulus clouds with darkened hearts were building up to the east, moving west as they often did this time of year. I went into the cafe where I remembered it all starting. The pie was as good as I remembered, and I asked the waitress if she recalled recently seeing anyone answering to Herb's or

Feather's description.

As I described Feather, the waitress chewed her gum in reflection and shook her head with a dissembling smile, but a slim man with hair tied back in a ponytail turned around in his chair across the room. "You know her, Man?"

I nodded. "Just looking for a friend of mine…thought she could help."

"You haven't heard?"

"Heard what?" The pie tilted in my stomach, and the waitress found something to do in the kitchen.

"Bad scene…really bad scene." He was shaking his head as he ambled over to my table. "Fine lady, artist and all."

He pulled out the chair opposite me and sat down, unbidden; the vaguely unpleasant odor of a man too long without bathing made me lose interest in finishing my food.

"We just heard about it a week ago. She had this motorcycle guy she couldn't get rid of. He was weird, really weird. They got him in the can up in Albuquerque."

"What about her?" What happened to Turk was not the first line item in my ledger of human concern.

"He wasted her, Man—beat her to death with a tire tool or something and dumped her body in an arroyo between here and Socorro, just off I-25."

The blood was racing through me; my head was giddy with pressure, and I sat there silently, images of Feather and Mary Ann juxtaposing as a rapid montage in my mind. Feather couldn't be dead. I remembered the last time I had seen her, walking toward the car on that dirt access road in the May night to meet Herb, just barely visible in the peripheral glow from my headlights. It was little more than a month ago, just before the end of May.

The young man across the table seemed oblivious to my rising anger. "I talked to one of the people who found her; they said her body was almost unrecognizable for the blood and the dirt and…"

I shoved my chair back, nauseated, and headed for the door, leaving two dollars on the glass top counter by the register. Then I had an afterthought, turning back toward the table I had just vacated. "You say it happened last week?"

He spoke through a mouthful of the pie I had left, "No, Man, I said they arrested that biker dude Turk last week. He killed her before, way before that."

My insides were gripped as if by a relentless iron chain. "When was she killed?"

"Musta been, let's see…two, three weeks, Saturday before that, well, it was May. Oh yeah, I remember, because it was my second day here in town and everybody was talking about it. It was May ninth exactly. I remember because…"

He was still talking as I bulled through the doorway, my vision swimming. The images came faster now. I hadn't realized how closely I had compared Feather and Mary Ann, almost as though they were the same. Because of my time spent with Hickson, I realized that Mirella was also resident in my melancholic images. I could not help but hear the thunk of a metal bar smashing into Feather's skull, and the end of a life as exquisite as the flowers she bestowed upon her lover.

The date…the unwashed fellow in the cafe had to be wrong because I knew I had seen her after that, and I was certain Herb had been to see her regularly. The man had to be wrong, but he seemed so definite. I sat behind the wheel of my car alongside the highway, seeing the street as a silent canyon of malevolence. What if Turk had found Herb too? No, the biker would have had a much harder time dealing with someone closer to his own size.

Then I thought of the house, the one place I hadn't considered—the only place the three of us had shared. I started the engine and drove south, aware that the heavy afternoon clouds were now touching the sun. By the time I reached the seldom-used turnoff, the sky was gray.

I stopped in front of the house, taking in its outline. It seemed more dilapidated than when I first saw it. Window caverns gaped, front door panels were splintered, rubble choked the front porch, and tumbleweeds rose up like lapping waves against its walls. On impulse I shoved my .45 automatic into my jeans pocket and walked toward the barn with its sagging rear wall on the west side of the house. I saw a swatch of blue through gaps in the planking.

Herb's pickup had been backed inside, and the red-painted door rolled shut to hide it. When I pushed the door open on its rusting track, I found the truck was lightly covered in a film of dust and its doors were locked; the strong smell of hay filled the interior. I looked from the truck toward the house, now ominous in the grey afternoon, with cumulus clouds building over the mountains. My feelings cycled from sorrow at what I had just learned into unreasoning fear of my own isolation.

The windmill creaked as it rotated in the breeze, and at the north of the house, a riot of yellow flowers lay like a carpet. It was quiet enough that I could hear the hum of bees tending to the blooms.

Looking at the intimidating bulk of the vacant house, I drew the pistol and jacked a round into the chamber as I approached the rear entrance, with that irrational fear eclipsing anything else I felt. With no sun outside, the inside of the house was dark, empty, and forbidding. I made myself go in by virtue of the momentum I had built up all day. Nothing had changed since the first time I had been inside. Scattered debris in the kitchen area assumed Rorschach shapes in the dimness.

I looked up the stairway and hesitated before putting my foot on the first step. Leaning against the foot of the stairs was a sketch pad, sprawled wantonly on the floor and leaning against the first step. I didn't have to guess whose it was, and I went back to the outside door with it so I could see better. A sprinkling rain had begun outside, and I could hear a drip coming through the roof of the house to drum slowly on some part of the floor upstairs— the only sound in this silent world.

The sketches in this pad were different, chilling to me as though they portrayed some alien landscape. The shading was dark, the detail gone; in the place of form was a web of shapelessness that spoke not to the conscious mind. It was Feather's work, but different from anything else of hers that I had seen. Somehow the drawings evoked in me the feelings I had first known in this house, but everything was overlaid with fear. I identified Feather with this house and with my best friend.

I put the sketch pad down by the door and began to ascend the 12 steps, the only sound other than the protesting of the creaking stairs was the plunking sound where the water was finding its way into the house.

My footsteps were loud and clumsy as I reached the second storey. I took hollow-sounding paces to the doorway and reached for the knob of the bedroom door. I remembered so clearly, the fear becoming a physical force inside of me, trying to operate my muscles against my will. I gripped the metal knob, twisted and pushed; at first it would not yield. That was strange because that room had been empty. I took a deep breath, pushing my

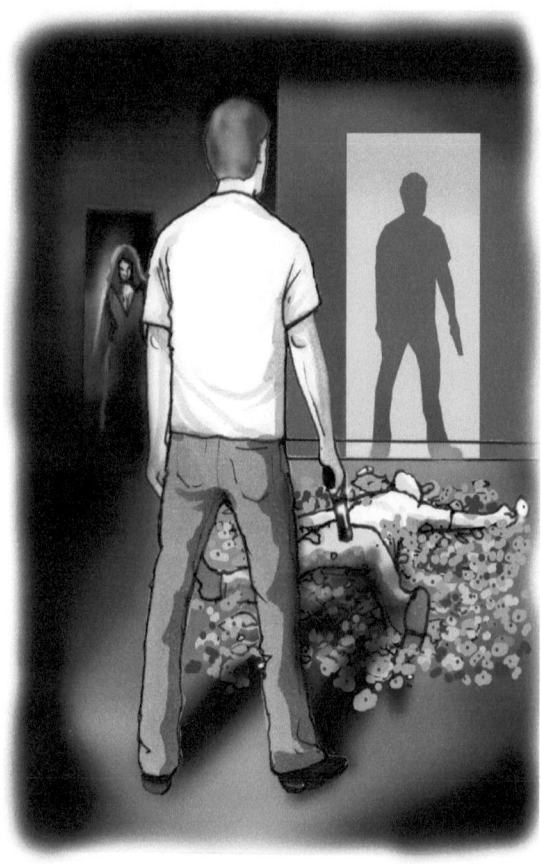

shoulder against the panel. The door came loose from the jamb and swung inward with a dry, rustling sound. Almost carried by the sudden freeing of the door, I blundered into the room then. Just as suddenly I stumbled out. Leaning against the corridor wall, I lost control of my stomach, retching helplessly in the gloom.

I told myself it was the abominable stench of death that gripped me, but it was far more than that. I knew without examining Herb that he had not died at the hands of Turk. He had been dead at least a week and now his body was lying on the floor of that vacant room, eyes sunken, his lips shrinking to reveal the rictus of that most final of grins. The blue and yellow plastic cooler lay open, the contents, uneaten save by insects, the cans of soda unopened.

Leaning against that upstairs wall, being supported by that wall with a gun in my hand, I knew there was little I could tell anyone. The body of my friend, now desiccating in the foul, dry air, was not the person I knew; but, there was something I knew that I could never tell another person save Mary Ann—an awful reality that required no explanation.

That empty room in the house, undisturbed by the outside elements, that room which I had first seen with a bare floor, was ankle deep in dry, dead flowers, each as though they had been picked and dropped there as at a shrine. And, in the right hand of the corpse, resting on that nest of dead, shriveled flowers, was a blossom of most perfect yellow; its stem was still green, its petals just now losing their fullness. It was a few moments before I realized that the ghastly perfect yellow flower in Herb's dead hand could not have been more than 24 hours old.

There was someone, something else in that room! I knew it, and I felt my self-control eroding, a tide of emotions swelling inside me. The horror that emptied my stomach was overlaid by the terror of an almost uncontrollable desire. No, my physical arousal was not for Mary Ann, but it was for…for whatever was in that room. Something was waiting there for me. Blindly I turned like an automaton and approached the threshold again, still gagging from the noisome stench. My mind seemed shout to me that I had to run, but I stepped inside again, my foot crunching on the bed of dead flowers.

Rain was splashing on the bedroom window, the semi-darkness palpable as the breath caught in my throat. An amorphous shape was moving in the room, and I was almost on fire with lust. Shadowy hands were reaching out, and my eyes were closing in anticipation of the impending touch. I would give myself…

The explosion in the room was deafening. My hand must have convulsed, because the .45 fired into the floor, my arm feeling the recoil shock. Off balance, I threw myself in headlong panic through the hall and down the stairs, gasping. The sketchbook still leaned against the outer door of the house and, as I catapulted myself into the yard, I know I heard a mournful beckoning sigh from within the house. As I fled to my vehicle, pelted by the rain, I turned. Behind rivulets streaming down the window pane, I saw a shadowy face of haunting eyes, red lips, and a Stygian river of flowing hair. As I fled in terror, I saw fearsome beauty beckoning through the glass.

* * *

In the days after finding my friend dead, I knew I would never again go near that ranch property, or even find cause to drive over the mountains to Hillsboro ever again. I did hope that Barney Hickson would allow the shunned ranch house to collapse in upon itself, though at times I can still hear in my mind the creaking of the windmill pulling water out of the ground, its overflow nourishing that hellish patch of wildflowers next to the north wall where Mirella had basked in the sun.

And of that horrifying presence that was as much desire as terror? Could I ever make sense of what happened? What presence lurks in that house—the spirit of a beautiful artist who loved a man to his death? Or was it the ghost of the beautiful and willful Mirella, daughter of a conjure woman?

I turned to reading the old books, from Sinistrari's *Demoniality* whose purpose was to expose the evils of the incubus and succubus, to the *Malleus Maleficarum* that infamous handbook used for the discovery of witches during the Inquisition. None of this explained my sense of dread. Joseph Glanvil did not add to my understanding, nor did Old Cotton Mather's accounts of the New England witch trials. By accident I stumbled upon the enigmatic words of the 19th Century French occultist Eliphas Levi who wrote of the astral light that underpins the physical universe, and I thought about his peculiar phrasing: "It is possible to die through the love of certain people." A chill gripped my solar plexus. Then I read the mystical writings of Arthur Machen and his tale of a human mind swept into chaos by "The Great God Pan."

It was that book and others describing the ancient philosophy of the Qabalah that I found in my sleepless hours a philosophy of the girders of consciousness and what the sages termed the machinery of the universe. Of ten spheres and 32 paths, I read and remembered, coming away with a warning in the Tree of Life diagram that threatened to carry me away in a torrent of inner tumult.

For those who seek understanding, I refer to the learned Qabalistic author Gareth Knight who essayed the paths and spoke of the most dangerous linking the sphere of Netzach and of Yesod—the 28th Path, in his words, "for by it the pure forces of the creative imagination flow into the subconscious mind."

He was writing of the girders of the human personality, and the sphere that represents the wellspring of the urges of nature flowing into the sphere that is the treasure house of infinite images. Herein the mind can feel the surge of ravening nature projecting into forms of beauty and compulsion. As I read this, I felt I was propelled along that path, but sometime before dawn, I sensed a clear analogy to a phenomenon that went beyond mere witchcraft or conjure magic.

In my teenage years of the late 1950s, a family vacation took us to the Grand Canyon and a side trip to the Hoover Dam. We were able to take a special tour that took us down, down into the cavernous core inside the bottom of the dam. I walked into a cool, massive corridor where more than a dozen giant generators were turning. I could feel the rush of water slamming against impellers that turned the shafts, creating a magnetic field in a hallway as clean as a hospital corridor. The guide spoke above the deep hum of the generators, telling us that each one was wound with approximately 20 tons of copper wire.

I remember the torrent of water gushing outward in plumes from the towering wall of the dam, while the belly of the dam, each generator was pumping 130 megawatts of electricity racing irresistibly through massive insulated cables, its powerful current illuminating most of the western states.

Though I could not shake the terror I had felt in the Carmody bedroom, what I had sensed in the Carmody bedroom was not an evil, but a confluence of invisible, living force, the swelling juggernaut of nature's primal procreative force brought into focus in a spiritual form so powerful that it manifests a vortex of desire, and the human brain reaches into the astral plane to bring forth the form of a beloved so real that it destroys the will and offers a union more powerful than that of any narcotic and more pure than the radiance of the sun. So powerful is it, that the merely human organism cannot survive its embrace. It was the Lamia of the ancient Greeks, the succubus of Sinistrari's *Demoniality*, the Great God Pan of Arthur Machen, yet more than either of those. Had it not been for the power of my love for Mary Ann, I knew that I would have been lost within her unnameable embraces inside the bedroom of the yellow flowers.

* * *

The memorial service for Herb was subdued but not somber. Friends and family offered remembrances of his virtues and even his ex-wife was kind in her elegy, confirming that we don't speak ill of the departed.

Because Mary Ann came to New Mexico for Herb's memorial service, we were once more together. We drove up into the pine forest above Silver City and we found a private location where we could spread a blanket on a carpet of light brown pine needles at the base of a 70-foot tall ponderosa pine tree that was surrounded by a platoon of smaller trees. Near where we parked my car, a ring of stones circumscribed the black and grey remnants of someone's dead campfire. We took each other hungrily as the afternoon shade grew darker. Nothing existed for me but that blanket and the power of a woman.

Then, it was time to tell Mary Ann, and all the feelings returned to me in a flash flood— the longing for her, Herb's Quixotic romance with Feather Symond, the fear of that house and its field of flowers, the horror of the ghastly upstairs bedroom. And there was that stench that came back to me sometimes at night, followed by a fist clutching my solar plexus when a wraith drifted toward me.

Of course I described Carmody's cowboy foreman and his sweat-stained Stetson as he sat in the Bar None telling me the story of Big Jim Carmody in an even voice with only a hint of twang. I tried to use Hickson's words to describe the vision of the exotic Mirella, daughter of a conjure woman, and how she could almost hypnotize those who met her.

I likened Ebenezer Hickson's obsession with the apocryphal story of a shooting at Lordsburg's Keane Stockyard to my own compulsion to know what lived in the empty and mouldering house south of Hillsboro. When Mary Ann asked if we could go to Hillsboro someday, I put my finger to her lips and just shook my head, perhaps too violently.

Mary Ann remained silent as she listened to the story of Feather Symond and the shunned house. She lay quietly beside me on a blanket, her skirt rearranged, and her white silk blouse still partially unbuttoned. Her lustrous long brown hair spread on the blanket, framing her face.

My mouth was dry from talking, and the afternoon light of the forest was failing as I gestured toward her with both hands as though to ask for her absolution. I tried to describe what I thought lived in that house, but the words were clumsy, and I watched a single tear making its mascara track on Mary Ann's cheek, as a genuflection to Herb's memory.

Now she shifted her body and turned onto her side. "He was nobody's fool, and he must have known what he was doing. It was more important to be with her than to be without her. She looked down for a moment and then back directly into my eyes. "Remember that he believed that nothing dies unless we let it." There was a silence except for the afternoon breeze.

I looked into the bright hazel of her eyes, sensing a meaning deeper than words, and it did not matter whether we would be able to be together in everyday life. The ghost of Mirella and Feather Symond were here with us, sighing with the breeze wending through the pine branches. "I don't understand any of this."

"We are not supposed to understand. We just serve love.' Her smile was distant and enigmatic, her eyes half-closed against the brightness of the sky. Her fingers were at the buttons of her blouse as the false twilight crept toward us, and she whispered, soft as the air, "Come to me."

I was in her arms, feeling the heat of her body against mine, the perfume of her long brown hair an aura about me, her lips feeding an aching hunger. As we absorbed each other's passion, I could see no end to what we had begun. The fresh-picked but now discarded yellow flower, lying vivid on the brown pine needles.

THE GRAND ORDER OF MARBAS

"What makes us good or evil is a decision of the soul,
not an accident of circumstance."

Amelia's hand shook slightly as she handed me the classified ad page ripped from the morning edition of the El Paso Times. She seemed to sense my frustration as I took the page, and she edged toward the office door, just as she had done the first time she had made veiled references to her family problems.

Circled boldly by her yellow felt-tip highlighter was a classified ad nestled in the personals section, between 900-number solicitations for phone sex and people seeking lost relatives. The classified ad itself was puzzling and vaguely sinister:

> Esoteric Order of Marbas—Magnes potestas
> venient. Oct. 31. Instructions 1890 E. Ochoa.
> Muchos son los llamados. Many hear the call.

"So, what has this got to do with you saying the other day you might have to leave school?" In those years of the early 1990s, before I found a teaching position at the university, Amelia and I shared a communal office with three other master's degree students. She and I had become friends through shared classes, financial crises, and late-night study sessions during the past year.

"I told you before that education doesn't solve every problem like you think it can." Her gaze was veiled under long-lashed eyes, her full mouth firm under a long, aquiline nose. She reached up and toyed with the waves of her luxuriant dark hair.

Maybe she was right. The muted sound of my small digital clock/desk radio carried monotone news of another woman's body found in a field south of Juárez, Mexico, just across the border from El Paso. As of Oct. 24, 1991, the woman was number 314 in that chronicle of victims killed and dumped over a nine-year period, according to the newscaster. The story was familiar, and I dug out my copy of the Times from last week's stack. With a rustle of pages, I found the Borderland Section and spread the newspaper page in front of me, displaying the two-column story beneath the photo of a garbage dump being searched by uniformed Federales.

Three more slain women found in a Juárez field Sunday afternoon

by Jorgé Sifuente

JUAREZ—Three young women were found murdered in a field south of this border city Sunday afternoon, bringing the total to 311 since the early 1980s.

Federal Police said that investigation was ongoing, but that no evidence had surfaced to link the deaths to the drug cartels or to possible serial killers.

One police source said that the killings were the work of a "misteserial rioso psicópata."

The idea of a crazed serial killer has spread fear throughout the city and leaking across and into the Borderland.

Authorities are quick to quash some rumors of satanic cults, and say that no evidence found at the body site show any signs of ritual abuse.

The same officials decline to describe how the victims died or in what condition the bodies were found.

(see "Women" 3-B)

The story, though chilling, had become familiar to residents of southern New Mexico and West Texas. As a New Mexico native, I had grown up Anglo in a strongly Hispanic environment and was well aware of their unique and inflexible family systems. I knew her family would prefer that Amelia be married and raising a large family rather than pursuing higher education.

As I folded the newspaper again, I considered the classified ad and tried to reconcile it with the story of the murders across the border. "I still think it's just a story like shape shifting and skinwalking in the Indian tradition. Nobody ever proved that either." It was not the first time Amelia had mentioned the superstitions of South El Paso.

Amelia smiled dismissively. "My grandfather is 119 years old, and I think he knows what's happening to those women down there. How do you explain that?" I tried not to chuckle in disbelief at that number and rubbed my forehead instead. "We've known each

Terror Tales of the Southwest

other for about a year, and you never said anything like this before. Why now?"

"Maybe I could really use your help."

"Oh, sure. Isn't that what your boyfriend is for?" I threw out the words with a twist of lemon. Amelia knew that I found her attractive but, as with most Hispanic women, she had a long-standing relationship with a boyfriend who had not finished high school and whose list of DWI charges and scrapes with the law were as long as a ristra of red chiles.

Amelia stood at the bank of tall, steel-framed windows, looking out toward the bright southern New Mexico sunshine blanketing the campus. "You know I told you I can't really talk to him. You're the only one I've ever met who could possibly understand. You've read so much— not just academic stuff, and you know strange things can happen."

I shrugged and got up from old swivel chair with its ripped leather seat, walking over to her but without touching. Silently, we both looked out at the campus basking in the warm October day. Students ambled in t-shirts; girls were uniformly dressed in shorts and flip-flop sandals. I was thinking, however, about a terrifying night experience in the desert that haunted me. While I had an urge to reveal it to Amelia, I held back and stood, thinking.

It was the midsummer of 1989, and I was taking one of the long, late-night desert drives I loved so much. As an amateur naturalist, I spent as much time as possible in solitary after-dark searches to study those desert creatures that hid during the blistering heat of day.

It was after 10 p.m. as my light blue 1984 Volkswagen Rabbit rolled slowly down one of the hundreds of miles of dirt roads crisscrossing the arid plains. Away from the light pollution of Las Cruces, the sky was deep and black, the stars diamond bright. With the windows down, I peered fixedly at the pool of light thrown by my headlights, hoping to see a western diamondback rattlesnake or perhaps a tarantula crossing in front of me. My camera was on the passenger seat beside me. I had just passed a metal sign post painted with a fading "D23" labeling one of the county's maintained dirt roads. The sign was recent enough that there was only one bullet hole damaging it.

So intent was my concentration on the road that I didn't see the glow from the fire until I topped a small rise. Just off to the side of the road I saw the flames of a bonfire flaring and shimmering reddish-orange in the dark. It seemed strange to see such a large fire when the temperature was still over 80 degrees at 9:30 mountain daylight time. I had no fear of whom I might encounter because I always carried my .45 automatic when I was out in the desert.

I was passing what appeared to be an impromptu campsite. Roaring flames illuminated the stark landscape of ghostly mesquite and creosote bushes. Five men were standing around the fire, moving slowly in a circle, arms lifting, oblivious to my passage. They were unshaven and shirtless, their hair shaggy and tousled. The ground around the fire was littered with beer cans, and even from 30 feet away I could smell cloying marijuana smoke. I thought perhaps they were singing in low voices, but then I was beyond them, back into the darkness. I had not seen a vehicle, but 20 miles from town, there must have been one hidden in the brush, unless perhaps they were illegal aliens who had walked the 45 miles of desert from the porous southern border.

A half-hour later, I found the county road too rutted for me to pass. Summer rains had cut through the track, leaving an unrepaired gash that was not passible except to a 4-wheel drive vehicle. I turned around and began my return. Suddenly a coyote sprinted across the road just in front of the headlights, a gray-brown flash with glowing eyes. It was gone, but the unexpected encounter sent a wave of alertness through me.

Ahead I could again see the glow of the fire I had encountered while I was outward bound. I slowed as I approached. The blaze had diminished, now more reddish than orange. The litter of beer containers was scattered on the trampled sand, and the men I had seen were no longer visible. I slowed to a cautious crawl, aware of the wavering shadows cast by the desert brush and cacti.

I flicked my eyes back to the road and slammed on the brakes. In the glare of the headlights was an animal almost as high as the car hood—it couldn't have been a Mexican gray wolf this far north—in the center of the road, its lupine head turned toward me, jaws open in a snarl, eyes luminous, shoulders hunched and bristling, confronting me rather than running for the dark. At the campsite to the left of the car, I was sure I glimpsed two or three other large creatures loping through the mesquite beyond the fire. The engine stalled! I looked down as I twisted the ignition key, and the reliable VW 4-cylinder motor caught immediately.

When I looked through the windshield again, the wolfish animal that had stood in my path was gone, and there were only the pale headlights lancing into the dark, the dying fire, and the sharp fragrance of burning mesquite coming through my open windows in wisps of dirty smoke.

Why then did I panic? To this day I don't know, but I rolled up the windows as I shifted into low and stabbed the accelerator pedal, filled with a nameless dread whose spectre looms whenever memories of that night are recalled. Those shadowy animal shapes in the darkness, that abandoned campfire, the vanished human figures, were still with me now as I stood beside Amelia at the window.

She interrupted my unintended reverie, "Will you at least go to El Paso with me to find more about this? I have this feeling something terrible is going to happen." Amelia knew I wouldn't deny her.

"You know I'll help, but what will tattoo guy think about this?" My reference to her boyfriend and his jailhouse skin art didn't seem to faze her.

She pursed her lips, trying not to smile, and slapped me on the shoulder. "Oh, stop it! Seriously, did you ever think that maybe he's part of it? His family and my family are connected all the way back to Ciudad Chihuahua in the old days, and my grandfather has a lot of power with both families."

Of course I agreed to drive the 45 miles down to El Paso with her the next day to follow up the classified ad that she was sure connected her family to the vaguely sinister Marbas.

Amelia leaned against me briefly, "You know when you were talking about possibilities of the occult world and the hidden cults that could be all around us? Well, right then I should have told you more about my life. We can talk more tomorrow." We then went back to our work as teaching assistants, work that occupied us from Mondays through Thursdays. Fridays offered relief, aside from the usual graduate assistants meeting that had thankfully been canceled this week.

The next day, we rendezvoused on campus and got into my car for a drive down Interstate 10 toward the border city. Amelia began to tell me for the first time what she knew of this order of Marbas and why she was so anxiety filled. The landscape of desert with boundaries of jutting hills lay around us, with the Rio Grande valley to the right and the memorable craggy peaks of the Organ Mountains to the left. The warmth of a New Mexico October day was pleasant and sun-soaked. An overpowering manure smell closed in on the car as we

Terror Tales of the Southwest

passed the dairy farms to the west, next to the highway, and I wished my 1984 car had been equipped with air conditioning.

As she talked, Amelia tore chunks from a piece of tissue and rolled each chunk into a tiny ball that she threw out the window, one by one. "You read books, but I learned awful things from my grandfather. When I was only 12, we sat in our tiny kitchen in south El Paso and my grandfather read out loud from an old book. Some of the words were strange, not Spanish, English or Latin, but I remember that he read from right to left. He described horrible things, but his face lit up, and he grinned as though each word was a delicacy to roll around on his tongue."

I reached out and stilled her hands for a moment. "You don't like him much."

Amelia bit her lip and mumbled an assent. "But, I had—I have—no choice. My parents fear him and the Order that has been part of our family history." She was quiet for a moment, moving her hips softly in the bucket seat of the car as she tried unsuccessfully to get comfortable, her thoughts causing her to squint.

She rolled another tissue ball, and she twisted in the seat. "You don't like it, but you know that reality isn't just physical…"

I laughed as I interrupted her, "Yeah, I think I read all the Carlos Casteneda books back in the '70s. I think it was the mushrooms that made him so wordy. Ah, the *brujas*…"

Amelia socked me on the bicep, smiling for the first time on the trip. "My grandmother could tell you something about brujas! She never told second-hand stories, but more than once she told me about being young in Vera Cruz and going with a friend to the plaza there on certain nights when the witches gathered to dance and cast spells. The people there feared them, and she says they are still there."

"Were they good looking?"

"You're impossible." She shook her head trying not to laugh. "Something else my grandmother told me about shape shifters—this is too strange to be a lie. She had a friend when she was about 12, and one day they were arguing whether people could change into animals. My grandmother told her friend it was impossible. The friend stared at her and said, 'turn around, querida,' which mi abuela did. In a few seconds she heard the sound of a turkey gobbling—don't laugh—and she turned around to see a large bird standing before her, its feathers fanning out. As she told me, her eyes were wide and frightened, even decades later. She ran away and never spoke to her friend again."

I listened, staring straight ahead at the traffic flowing sporadically around me. Amelia was speaking from her heart, I knew. The soft hum of the engine seemed louder.

After a few seconds, I broke the silence. "Is Marbas some kind of street gang like the South Side Locos?"

Her laugh was stifled, almost helpless, and I could sense tears being held back. "My grandfather was at the apartment last night, talking about the time being 'close'—cerca— and I could hear my mother crying in the bedroom. Then…then he came into the kitchen with a bottle in his hand; his beard was sticky with tequila and lime juice that had dripped from his mouth. The corners of his mouth were all crusted with salt. He started touching me…"

She stopped, visibly ashamed that I should know an ugliness in her life that she camouflaged with perfect nails, elegant makeup and fashionable dress. She turned her head to look out the window, avoiding my glances.

Fascination and revulsion wove a net of curiosity about me. "Maybe I should talk with your grandfather, and..."

"No!" Amelia's voice sudden and almost terror-stricken. "My grandfather is a powerful man. Even though nobody hardly sees him out of doors, he controls many people in south El Paso. I've always known something was wrong with him, some kind of evil sickness. His face, his legs and arms..." She shuddered and suddenly gripped my hand.

We had reached the outskirts of the city once known as Paso del Norte, and as we drove past the smokestack of the abandoned Asarco copper smelter I saw that division of worlds that never failed to make me thankful for where I was born. To the left of the Interstate, wrapped around the Franklin Mountains, was El Paso, with its modern infrastructure, broad ribbon of Interstate highway and prosperous homes and businesses. To the right was the channel of the Rio Grande and the sprawl of Juárez in a haze of smoke and dust beyond the riverbed. Mostly rude adobe homes were crowded along dirt streets and slopes, only some of which had electricity lines. Most of the city had no sewage treatment, but its two million inhabitants pressed ever closer to that riverbank separating them from the bounty of America. Here, the Third World was just a short walk across the bridge on Santa Fe Street in south El Paso.

"My grandfather said it comes time to make me part of the Order, and I only know there's something very bad connected with it, something the Church would forbid."

"Well, why doesn't macho vato protect you?" She was used to my sour grapes sarcasm.

"Because Tony has done many things for my grandfather, and I'm given to Tony. That offends your sense of righteousness doesn't it?" Her eyes looked almost oriental in the afternoon light, her gaze intense. She told me that her grandfather's current wife was 38 years old, while Amelia herself had just turned 24 on Oct. 12.

I just nodded. It is not a good idea to park a car on the street in south El Paso, so we picked a commercial lot near the Santa Fe Street bridge to Juárez and walked three blocks to the address on E. Ochoa. Amelia never told me where her family lived, though I knew she had an apartment of her own somewhere in the northwest section of the city.

We walked together on sidewalks where English was seldom spoken, effectively re-annexed by Mexican immigrants, legal and illegal, many years before. Amelia's heels clicked on the concrete, and the late afternoon sun painted the buildings sepia and added tint to the naturally tan faces of the natives. The older buildings in this oldest part of El Paso were constructed of red brick, and the address on Ochoa was a classic storefront from the 1930s with a large front plate glass and a full length glass in the door whose white painted wood frame was flaking. Sometime since the 1960s, protective black iron grillwork had gone up over the glass in these store windows to protect against vandals and burglars. Discolored brass numerals were nailed above the door frame and read "1890." The place appeared to be abandoned, but it was the number in the newspaper ad, so I tried the knob and the door opened noisily.

The store was indeed empty, the floor covered with dust save a track leading to another closed door at the rear. My vivid imagination conjured any number of horrible surprises waiting, but I knocked just the same and received a guttural "Venga" command to enter. When we went through the door, we found this back room to be just as unkempt as the front. Only an old oak desk and straight back chair sat in the center of the room under aging and flickering fluorescent ceiling lights. Behind the desk sat a lone Hispanic with long black hair that should have been tied in a ponytail. His feral eyes were too large for his head, and his mouth was puckered, revealing unusually sharp-looking teeth. Sitting before him was a bowl of stewed beef and green chile, a rolled flour tortilla in his hand. A bottle of Carta Blanca Cerveza stood open beside the bowl, its colorful label the only life in the room. The pleasant aroma of the food masked the stale smell of the vacant building.

With a brief glance at me, Amelia showed the man the ad and asked in English, "The Order…will it…will we meet here?"

As he answered her, he grinned with all his protuberant teeth and scribbled on a photocopied flyer. He looked at me directly, "I never see you before, Ese." It was then I noticed the length of the man's fingers and nails so long that they had started to curl. He seemed to be scrutinizing my arms and face.

Amelia tossed her head toward me and charmed him with her Libra smile, "He's a friend of my father's."

The feral man handed her a sheet of paper while I wondered just how secret an order like this could really be. It would seem commonplace if it weren't for Amelia's discomfort. The date and time of the "meeting" were the most prominent words on the page. Obviously all of El Paso could find out about this secret meeting. This could hardly be more dangerous or secret than an underground rave party for adolescent drinking and drug use. I couldn't understand Amelia's fear. And yet I wanted to get out of that arid and dirty enclosure as quickly as possible.

We left the empty storefront and paused next door where a neighborhood store attended to several customers. Behind the grimy windows were stacks of canned jalapeños and other imported Mexican products. From the ceiling, traditional Mexican piñatas were hanging. We didn't plan to enter the store, but I saw something peculiar, and I urged Amelia to take me inside.

In a rack near the cash register was a series of cheap paperback books, but not only the Spanish language novels I would have expected. Next to the current editions of *El Fronterizo* and *El Diario* newspapers were the books. Most of these were nothing but a collection of grimoires, mostly in Spanish, but some with covers in a mixture of Hebrew, Latin, and even one in English. I recognized The Sixth and Seventh Books of Moses, and the famous *Albertus Magnus*, and a poorly printed paperback of the Goetia.

All of the books I recognized as containing medieval spells and nostrums for everything from gaining health and money, to curses and transformations of all kinds. In one corner of the rack were several 8 1/2 x 11 stapled booklets, slightly yellowed, and which appeared to be old mimeographs. Hand-lettered on the cover sheet were the words Livro Marbas and a seal consisting of two concentric circles with the letters M.A.R.B.A.S. encircling a stylized tripod with tiny circles appended to the top and serving as feet for the three legs while with two stylized Maltese crosses angled at 11 o'clock and 2 o'clock connected to the outer legs of the tripods.

I took one of the booklets to the cash register and paid close to $15.00 for a booklet that could not have comprised more than 16 pages. Given the date of the ceremony and its relationship to All Soul's Day and Dia de los Muertos, I was beginning to think that Amelia was perhaps creating something frightening out of a large Halloween party of some kind. No, I was just hoping that was the sum of it. I planned to read the text or have Amelia translate parts of it for me.

On our drive back to Las Cruces, where she planned to spend the late afternoon and evening in the university library working on her thesis, Amelia told me more about her grandfather. He claimed to have come from Chihuahua 80 years ago, walked across the Rio Grande into El Paso and subsequently had become rich bootlegging in the prohibition era and smuggling aliens and drugs in more recent times. The legend of his wealth was whispered by Mexican-Americans everywhere on the border. It was peculiar that he claimed such great age and that he seldom came out of doors, particularly in daylight.

As she talked about her grandfather, with obvious disgust, she described him as almost goatish in appetite while he had abnormal amounts of body hair, particularly on his arms and legs. On the rare occasions that he walked the littered streets of South El Paso, he wore baggy pants whose cuffs dragged the sidewalks, and the sleeves of his shirts extended over his hands. He always wore a broad-brimmed black felt cowboy hat pulled down over his brow, and he was attended by at least three men whom Amelia said looked the same as the feral clerk in the abandoned store we had just left. It was an uncomfortable mental image she sketched for me. All the while, the crude mimeographed booklet with its discolored fly-specked pale blue cover lay between the front seats, separating us, with the pages sometimes ruffling in the breeze that coursed through the open car window.

We spoke little on the return trip, and back at the campus I matched steps with her as we were walking toward the library, when I spotted a large dog walking parallel to us on the other side of a hedge bordering the parking lot. When Amelia saw it, she gripped my arm and started, her dark eyes widening with panic. The skulking dog, screened by the foliage, suddenly broke into a run, disappearing. I did not understand why Amelia was distraught.

Shortly after I left Amelia at the library, I was walking back toward the parking lot when I heard my name being called, and I turned to see Bruce Dearing bearing down on me with his usual energy, a Nikon F4 hanging around his neck.

I greeted him, "So, how is it with the tenured elite?" Because I also was a decent photographer with my own darkroom, I admired the accomplishments of Dearing's documentary work and photojournalistic successes. His restless hands and dancing eyes translated to credits in media across the state, and even occasionally in *The New York Times*. Some of his friends affectionately named him "the Great Brucini."

Always up for a gripe session, Dearing raised his head as if to look down at me from under the rim of his glasses, "You sure you want to go into the servitude of the professor? I'm telling you that most of the people on that bus are bozos—probably including me." His hair was slightly greying, but his energy was contagious as was his laugh.

"Yeah, I guess I'm a masochist at heart, or at least I can't get the kind of assignments you seem to get." As I talked, we walked toward the parking lot, as he was no doubt ready for his own daily trip back to his downtown El Paso residence.

"Teaching is a blast, you know, but the rest of it usually sucks. I'm tired of driving 45 miles to get here and then driving back during rush hour on I-10."

"Then why don't you buy a house here in Las Cruces? Makes sense, doesn't it?"

He shook his head and sneered amusingly, like the Chicago street kid he still was at heart. "I've been in that 2nd floor El Paso loft for almost 20 years. I hate to move, but…"

I stopped and looked at him, squinting in the powerful late afternoon sun. "But what?" Suddenly there was something I wanted to ask him.

Dearing scratched the back of his neck and wrinkled his brow, "Ah, I don't know. The place has changed. There's something…" Then he shook his head as though he had bitten into something distasteful.

"I was down there in your neck of the woods today—except there's no woods in El Paso. There is something down there, and it's bothering my friend Amelia…"

Dearing grinned and threw his head back, "Oh, that hot babe! How are you doing with her?"

"The score is zero, just like the last time you asked me, but she's got some sort of superstition about South El Paso. Her family's there."

As we reached the parking area, Dearing looked at the sky, debating in his head, then back at me, and said, "Let me buy you a beer, and you can tell me the story. I know a few things."

He drove west, up University Avenue to the bar of the Holiday Inn, where we ordered chips and salsa along with Tecate, a beer served with a slice of lime. The squeeze of lime juice was followed by a dash of salt that added foam to amber liquid in the tall glass. I told Dearing about the strange tale surrounding the Marbas notice and the feral store clerk, along with describing Amelia's very real fear.

Dearing made a sweeping gesture with his hands and rolled his eyes. "That's a new one on me. Jesus, you have no idea what goes on in that part of town. We've got the Santos worshippers, Penitentes, Brujas, Curanderas, even some practitioners of Santeria with their goats and chickens. Hell, I even met some crypto-Jewish Mexicans hiding out this side of the border. What you're telling me is a new one, though."

I took a deep breath, not wanting him to think I was one taco short of a combination plate, but told him what I had seen in the desert two years before.

He squinted his right eye and leaned back theatrically with one of those "You're a loon" looks, then smiled and shook his head. "You're behind the curve, Guy. You don't know this, but when I first came out here from Chicago, I landed a job as photog at the *Gallup Independent*—you know, up there plop in the middle of Navajo territory."

My nod was sufficient. I had barely touched my glass.

"They're real, you know."

It was my turn to screw up my face in disbelief, knowing what he was alluding to.

"You can believe me or not, but I've been out on the rez, and I'm telling you that they made me believe in skinwalkers. The people there are terrified when there is a walker out in the night, killing their sheep or taking one of their children. They say there's no way during the day that they know who has the skinwalker power, but if you cross the wrong person, he or she just might shift into the body of a wolf, an owl, or something worse. They catch you after dark." Dearing did his one-eye squint, daring me to rebut him.

I must have been smiling indulgently, because he leaned toward me. "Next week I'll bring you a photo. The *Independent* didn't use it with the story, but I was there when the reporter interviewed old Joe Begay inside his double wide out there. The skinwalker attacked him one night—hey, it really gets dark outside of Gallup, let me tell you—and he was lucky to survive. It happened two days before we did the story."

"That's pretty creepy. What else did the guy tell the reporter?" It seemed unthinkable, but Dearing had high credibility in the field, especially his photos in *The New York Times*.

"It could have been bullshit, but I looked into Joe Begay's eyes while the reporter scribbled notes and knew he believed what he was saying. Not only does the skinwalker change into an animal at night, but he has the power to project his consciousness into animals at will to spy on his enemies or his victims." Dearing cocked his head and stared at me to judge my reaction, but my mind was suddenly on stray dogs.

Of course I respected Dearing as a photographer, but he could have been taken in by a wild tale. We let it drop, but I wanted to see the photo anyway. Right now the weekend beckoned, and he did not seem to know anything specific about the strange group that was so disturbing to Amelia.

After a weekend of studying and writing, I was eager on Monday, more to see Amelia than to attend our experimental research methods class. The class ran from 5 p.m. until 7:30, and the discussion on statistical analysis of experimental data was prefaced by the professor's favorite subject of how experimental science had effectively eliminated superstition, and his particular anathema to magic, something all academic scientists seem to irrationally hate as the enemy of empiricism.

As I looked at Amelia in the chair next to me, I was not thinking about statistics, but wondering if what I had been told years before had to be true, that romance can never be stronger than culture. Are we always prisoners of our upbringing, or is it a choice we make from day to day? I watched as she crossed her legs, though I was sure she was not aware of my sidelong glance.

After class I was walking Amelia to her car in the mild evening darkness. She said, "He's wrong, you know."

"Well, you have to admit that science has been pretty good for civilization."

She fumbled in her purse for the massive set of keys she always carried with her, the one with the whistle and university logo key tag. "Isn't it obvious to you? There's nothing more powerful than belief. People believe in science and they seek chemical and surgical cures for disease when most doctors admit that they don't understand what actually causes healing."

"I'll give you that, but…"

Amelia cut me off, "No, look at the hundred million fanatic Muslims who are willing to blow themselves up for their religion. Is there anything more powerful than that belief? People believe in alcohol, in money, and those things become their salvation. Where people believe in magic, it works."

I didn't argue with her as I had read books from Rudyard Kipling's era that had convinced me of the power of the fakir and how belief had an almost physical effect upon an individual and his appearance, susceptibility to pain and so forth.

We were so busy talking that I didn't hear Bruce Dearing gaining on us from behind. We both started when he said, "Hi there!" in his enthusiastic tone. I returned the greeting and formally introduced him to Amelia.

Dearing held up a 7x9 manila envelope. "Maybe she'll be interested in this photo too. Remember, I promised you. Let me know what you think." With that, he strode off purposefully, headed for his own vehicle.

I could tell that Amelia was curious, and when we reached her Nissan 280 ZX, she opened the driver's door and we leaned over together in range of the dome light. I pulled out a semi-gloss 5x7 color print. Amelia gasped, and I could sense her shudder.

The photo showed the back of an older man whose black and grey hair was woven into a braid that pointed below his dark tan shoulder blades. The arms were raised, but the focus of the image was on three cruel parallel gashes, still blood red, that raked his back from his pigtail to his lumbar region. There were two inches between the furrows.

Amelia put her knuckles to her lips. "The skinwalker."

"How did you know?"

She just smiled. "It goes with our conversation. Put that thing away."

I backpedaled mentally. "OK, so what does this have to do with South El Paso?"

"Perhaps more than you know. Anyhow, thank you for being being there. I know it won't be easy, but you're the one person I can depend on. Meet me at the address we got from that guy on Ochoa?"

"It's a date," I said, nodding, perhaps trying to put more meaning to the word than she would. Perhaps it was the photo, but despite our light conversation, I felt a faint sense of foreboding, remembering the strange man in the vacant store.

Amelia moved get into her driver's seat, then stood again, turned quickly and her lips were gently on mine, tasting of warm, rich fruit. When she drove off, I was still standing there in the night, feeling better than I'd felt for a very long time. The foreboding was gone.

While I was supposed to be studying from Borg & Gall's text on educational research methods, I had another book I had found in the university library, wondering how it got there. Of course the library did have Blavatsky's *The Secret Doctrine*, so why not? I read somewhere that Albert Einstein found Blavatsky's work one of his favorites.

This little book in my hand was edited by the early 20th Century occultist Aleister Crowley, and it was *Goetia, The Lesser Key of Solomon*, or book of evil spirits—a grimoire without redeeming academic virtues. Perhaps that was why it had been checked out at least 21 times as shown by the sectioned card in the standard envelope pasted inside the book's front cover.

In the Lesser Key, I read of all manner of things I didn't really understand: how to use the magical rod, the sword, the incense, the magic circle, the conjurations. While the intricate instructions seemed impractical, I sensed a connection with what I had seen on Ochoa Street.

Thus I turned to the mimeographed booklet *Livro Marbas*. Just the look of it was unpleasant, and the 60-pound rough cover stock of pale blue was faded and indeed dotted with what could only be insect droppings. I recalled that mimeograph disappeared with the rise of Xerox, but it was common in schools and offices when I was younger. The process included typing, writing, or drawing, on a stencil that was then wrapped around an inked drum that turned as pages were fed through the machine.

I peeled back the cover to reveal the 16 musty-smelling pages of yellowing cheap, pulpy paper, streaked with discoloration, the stenciled words still clear. The first page was typed with overstrikes and irregular spacing. I used my computer to transcribe the first section of words that I could read only haltingly:

```
La Llamada---
Los aulladores en la oscuridad, los bebedores de sangre.
Tomamos la comunión de los espíritus.
Buscamos la casa de cadáveres sentir el poder de ese espíri-
tu del mal. Promete que nunca podemos morir. En los cañones
de Sonora somos bautizados. Hemos pisado los escalones de
la pirámide y juró obediencia eterna en el cráneo de Quet-
```

zalcóatl en los lugares secretos del azteca. Nos convertimos en el jaguar y el lobo. Vamos a violar esta noche, vamos a matar esta noche. Caminamos con la sombra y desgarrar la carne de los vivos.

Traemos terror en la noche. Las ovejas del mundo se arrastrará por ante el poder de nuestra magia.

Tales son las palabras:

BEBER LA POCION---
ESPIRAR EL ESPIRITU DE LA LLAMA---
CON LA ESPADA, QUE PERFORAN LA OSCURIDAD Y LLAMO A SU TERRIBLE MAJESTAD
(see appendix)

The hour had turned late, and the pages blurred before my eyes, but I knew enough now to pronounce the book as hellish, not merely unpleasant. It was typed and scrawled by one either insane or truly evil.

The pages were dry, and one of them tore slightly as my fingers leafed through the book. The next pages were inscribed by stylus onto the stencil and almost impossible to decipher. The script was shaky and fragmented. I could make out the first three words, "Los ancestros hablan—The ancestors speak," but the rest was frightening.

From my reading, I knew of what is termed "the barbarous names of evocation," that are meaningless, multisyllabic words and gibberish: shouted, growled, screamed, sung, muttered, in rhythmic sequence. They were sometimes accompanied by drums and flute music. The goal is to alter consciousness and usher in the magical phenomenon desired. Of course in black magic, drugs and hallucinogenic incense speed the effect, as the soul spirals downward, plunging into the depths below Tartarus.

I could make out some of the tangled letters, and I know they were not Spanish. I transcribed a few of those rambling and disturbing conjurations:

ACAMAPICHTL!…RGAHCULHUACAN…NGLORGAHAHUITZTL… AMIQUI…

NGAYTILYL…ACXOYATL…NNNNNNGGGGGAHHHHHHH… ACXOYATL…

These disjointed, stylus-scrawled words went, line after line for two pages but, in my fatigue, I saw no point in transcribing more of what appeared to be repetitive nonsense. Still, I felt a revulsion as my eyes followed the string of letters, words—if words they were— and spaces between them. In my mind I found myuself sounding out the syllables. I did not dare voice them aloud.

Then followed pages of crude sketches, including the sigil of the evil spirit Marbas. Respecting the grotesque and arcane design of that sign, those who can locate the 1916 DeLaurence edition of *The Lemegeton*, sometimes titled *Goetia: The Book of Evil Spirits* may find in that octavo edition a dissertation by Aleister Crowley, though signed only by his order name from The Golden Dawn society, explaining the diagrams of the many evil spirits. He wrote that each diagram of an evil spirit is designed to affect a different part of the human brain so that, when the eye contemplates the symbol, the ritual environment overwhelms the subject. Now, all these years since those frightening events, I searched again for this book in the university library and was told it has disappeared, even though it was transferred to the rare books collection not long after I checked it out.

Two or three of the drawings in *Livro Marbas* were captioned in Spanish. There was a rough outline of a tall house with pillars at the front with the caption *"Entra en la casa,"* as well as another drawing—this one assisted by a straight edge— showing a stage or platform with the magic symbol in the center and a pulpit with an "x" drawn in the center and with devices in the corners that appeared to have tiny lines emerging to represent smoke. The diagram was labeled "La Plaza" or The Square.

Another page presented a mass of curved lines and spirals, with jagged lightning-like strokes coming from each of the four corners of the page toward the mass of lines that appeared to represent clouds or smoke. At the center of these random lines were two narrowed ovals that formed eyes with vertical pupils, made black by deep strokes of the author's stylus on the stencil as though they were emerging bodiless from the clouds.

At the end of the booklet appeared the scrawled name of the author, none other than Fernando Valles, Amelia's grandfather. He was the damnable sorcerer, the wizard who was somehow intimidating the superstitious residents of South El Paso.

The next day in the office Amelia was different, and I noticed a slight bruise on her cheek that makeup was unable to hide. I wondered if her low-grade boyfriend Tony Hinzo had suspected something between us.

"I have to tell you that maybe I over-reacted to all this. Maybe you shouldn't go down there Thursday night after all." Amelia had a maddening way of not quite looking at me when she was lying.

"Look, I'm in this for whatever happens. Maybe it's something like a gang initiation. It'll be all over by Friday morning, and you'll be safe."

Suddenly she exploded, eyes flashing, "I thought you were smarter than that. Three hundred years ago, people believed in witchcraft—even in the United States—and some things happened to people that cannot be explained. It's even documented in court records. You saw all those books in that store." Her hand was flailing, and a perfectly manicured finger pointed south through the office windows. "What if there are thousands of people in El Paso and south of the border who still believe in things modern science doesn't accept? They don't live in the world you know, but I grew up in their world. Terrible things happen down there."

"Hey, I believe enough to think you could be in danger, even if I'm skeptical of the spells in most of the nonsense in those old grimoires." My defense was only half-hearted. I wanted Amelia to look at me as she had the night before.

She pursed her lips and spoke with her eyes closed. "Mexico festers with the recipes in those old books, printed and reprinted in Spanish, Latin, English. Maybe you do not know, but children are still sacrificed at rituals in the hills south of the border. Oh, and you think it is just random crime when hundreds of young women are being killed just across the border from El Paso and nobody can do anything about it?" Her hair-trigger temper was suddenly exposed.

"You said your grandfather knows something about those murders." I tried to mollify her.

"You have to know that many of those killings are not simple murders. After our walk

Friday, you saw that south El Paso is like a sponge, soaking up the poison of Mexico and Central America into its belly where it grows—never acknowledged, never reported. There's something else I haven't told you too."

I grimaced. "If you're pregnant, I don't really want to know."

"What if it's worse than that?" She wasn't smiling.

"Well, that would be pretty bad from my point of view."

"Believe me, querido, there are worse things. You know I told you about my grandfather being 119 years old, and his wife being 38. I didn't tell you the whole truth. The woman is my mother—she was 15 when she had me. And he is not my grandfather. My mother says that Fernando Valles is not my grandfather—he is my father. He says that it was Marbas who keeps him from dying."

I was silent for a moment, doing the math. I wished her to be deluded, but she was a very smart woman. Suddenly I knew she was telling the truth, even if she exaggerated the old man's age. "So you're really saying that the Order of Marbas is…a…one of those…"

"You don't have to use the words. It is only in the last 50 years that the words have become ridiculed in this country. The bruja has not lost power south of the border any more than has the curandera."

"But, Amelia, why you? It doesn't make any sense."

"It's just a matter of payment. In Mexico it is much easier to have your wishes taken care of by an expert than go through courtship. You see, Tony has performed some service for the man I call my grandfather, and the Grand Order of Marbas seeks to repay him. I am the payment, only after la noche del ritual. Most gringos are still ignorant of the culture, especially you—especialmente tu!" She said the last with a soft grin as she slapped me gently on the shoulder.

I realized that I did not understand the Order of Marbas, but I was somehow inextricably caught up, feeling enmeshed in the strands of a silky web that was leading to a possible horror beyond my experience. "So the day is important to their purpose?"

Amelia talked to me as though I were a child. "All the foolish occasions and stories we play with today were once very serious things. This is the time when the ceremonies must be held. I think we would be terribly afraid if we knew how many still worship old gods and even worse things on that night."

"And what is Marbas?"

"He is one of the evil spirits, that's all I was ever told, one of those who should be called from inside a magic circle, but my grandfather's followers have no circle, so they don't rule Marbas—Marbas rules them, and he—it… changes them."

It sounded to me like the old story of intimidation where the ignorant were exploited by unscrupulous men possessed of more cunning and showmanship than they.

Amelia shuddered, anger now gone, a pained expression on her face as though she were remembering something; she plainly thought I was in over my head. Yet I knew the power of violence and threat, and though I wouldn't tell her, I planned to bring the business to the attention of the El Paso Police Department so they could deal with the situation as they saw fit—if only they saw fit.

She stood and went to the window, looking out at the campus. Suddenly I heard her gasp. I bolted upright and went to the window just in time to see the dog I recognized from the previous week loping around the side of the building out of sight. I was no expert on canines, but it appeared to be a mixture between a husky and a wolf that should not be wandering loose. Animal control was like the police—never there when you needed them.

I didn't understand Amelia's fear of dogs, but I was more and more sure that her grandfather was hip deep in some criminal enterprise. Was it murder, smuggling, white slavery? It was my turn to shudder inwardly as I realized the commitment I had made. All the infamies running through my mind were commonplace in Mexico. Someone once said that Mexico is not just another country—it is another planet.

Amelia had told me earlier that, on Thursday, I could follow her to El Paso, but I still spent a night of anticipation in unsettled desire combined with a greater uncertainty than I could ever remember.

October 31, 1991, was sunny in the Southwest, but by 4:30 I realized that Amelia wasn't going to show up on campus. I was worried, and I didn't relish venturing into that part of El Paso without her. Anybody who lived in the region as long as I had knew that you had to be very careful in south El Paso after dark. Roving youth gangs protected their precisely divided turf with mindless violence Yet, I had made a promise, and I was naive enough to redeem it. It was fortunate for me that Prof. Dearing still made his home in that neighborhood.

I made a call to Dearing, and he invited me to drop by his place if I insisted upon following through with a risky venture. He said he knew I was involved only because of the "babe," and that I should be careful what I was wishing for. I pretended that I didn't know what he was talking about as I wrote down directions to his loft apartment, using the Sacred Heart Catholic Church as the landmark. Somehow the confirmation that traditional religion still had a firm base in El Paso was calming.

Driving down, I thought about stopping at the EPPD, but I knew the police would just tell me they knew all about those strange meetings and that there was nothing illegal about them. They would then warn me not to wander about South El Paso alone at night.

The disc of the late afternoon sun burned copper orange through dusty haze as it sank toward the edge of the sky. This time I turned left from Santa Fe Street to find the Oregon Street intersection. I parked the car near the front of the Sacred Heart Church as though its facade would offer protection from auto burglary. Also, I could find Dearing's residence easily from there. It was not yet cold, but I was wearing a sweatshirt with a hood that I could use to hide my anglo face if need be. I then set out for Dearing's apartment and darkroom.

It was a walk of two blocks, and I found the entrance to his stairwell next to a Carnaceria that was closed but whose interior fluorescent lights dimly glowed, illuminating meat counters emptied for the night.

I opened the clattery window door next to the shop, walking up the hollow-sounding dark wooden stairs and touching the wobbly bannister whose rail varnish had worn down to the pale tan of cheap pine. The stairs were lined with ribbed black rubber treads under a dim ceiling bulb, and on the second floor landing I found only one door. Dearing responded to my knock, and I was ushered inside.

I was not surprised to find a spacious interior with a high ceiling that covered the area over the business downstairs. The walls were adorned with framed photos documenting Dearing's photojournalistic career, and at the back of the apartment, next to the kitchen area, a door stood open, revealing the darkroom where strips of negatives were hanging to dry like limp eels on a line. The faint smell of fixer mixed with the fragrance of bratwurst being grilled on his stove.

"How about sausage and potatoes for dinner?" He grinned, but I declined, being too concerned with my goal.

"No thanks. I just need some guidance to find the place I'm looking for." I showed him the sheet of paper where I had written the directions.

Dearing sliced a chunk of sausage with a steak knife, speared it and blew on it before popping it into his mouth. "What about your *chica*? Thought you were here to see her." He flexed his eyebrows Groucho Marx style while he savored the chunk of meat.

"She's not my…never mind…you know, but I don't where she lives—only the address of the meeting place she was afraid of." I hid my anxiety, wondering what had changed Amelia's mind. She was so determined that I help her. Why hadn't I heard from her?

Dearing swallowed and grabbed the piece of paper. "Ah, no problem finding the place, but you don't want to go there, and I don't either."

"I know that, but I promised her."

With a sweep of his hand, he pushed his cameras and flash units to one end of the kitchen counter; they were hooked up to chargers whose colored indicator lights winked; then, he invited me to sit on one of the bar stools. He pointed at me, squinting. "There are good people down here. I've lived here for a long time, and we've got problems that grow every day. It's not just the drug dealers. My friends may be poor, but they're honest and most have a respect for the religion they were brought up in. Then, there are 'others'." Dearing's emphasis had an ominous sound. We both knew the potential of underground cults and criminal organizations on the border.

I just nodded, thinking about Amelia's fears and her resignation to that secretive family and its unspoken directives.

His sudden laughter was almost braying. "Remember, I'm from Chicago, so I know about real evil. Once you've seen the Daley political machine in action, you're not scared of anything after that. In that toddlin' town, unless you are a registered Democrat, a 9-1-1 call won't even get you to a pizza delivery service."

Dearing jumped up and grabbed a stack of 8x10 prints from a shelf in the living room area and shoved them at me. I looked at a survey of El Paso images, his documentary style juxtaposing settings with the faces indigenous to the old part of the city and recognizable locales across the bridge in Juárez.

There were pretty young girls, business people, viejos, illegals, all weaving the fabric of a culture. When I uncovered the seventh print, he stabbed his finger onto the high contrast black and white late afternoon scene. "That's the place."

I was looking at a residential block not far away, with unassuming houses on the south side of the street, a small park on the north side, and two stooped figures striding along the pavement, walking away from the camera, their black shadows jack knifing away from them at a 30-degree angle on the cracked, grey pavement. As I stared at the photo, I wished it were still late afternoon.

As Dearing offered simple walking directions, I stared at the photo. He said, "I don't think you should go there, but if you have to do this, I'll just say if you don't show up here in an hour, I'll drop a dime and send the cops after you."

"Hey, I grew up in New Mexico, and I can handle it." Of course I wasn't as sure as I sounded.

"Then you know you don't walk around South El Paso at night unless you live here. You just have a thing for that hot babe."

I started to protest, but realized I would appear even more foolish trying to deny it. We shook hands, and I headed almost reluctantly for the door. He was looking at the photo when I closed the door behind me.

Back on the sidewalk, I breathed the mixed cocktail of city smells, and immediately my imagination began to badger me. I walked east to the next street, then south for a block. Padding along at my pace, across the street, I saw a large, ugly dog so similar to the one that had frightened Amelia on campus days before. Its half-open jaws were drooling and it snarled at me. My remembered fear from the desert night came suddenly back to me.

Two Hispanic youths in baggy pants were walking on the other side of the street. They saw the animal at the same time as I did. They crossed themselves and hastened across in my direction. Suddenly the dog slunk into an alley as I walked on.

With twilight thick and darkening, a cool breeze set up, blowing the smell of Mexico across the riverbed, over the Border Highway into El Paso. There was a foulness in the smell that was redolent of raw sewage, wood smoke, and indescribable industrial emissions from the maquiladoras. The breeze turned chill, and I pulled the hood up over my head, stuffing my hands into the slits in the front of the sweatshirt. Clouds had come up on the horizon, and the long shadows swiftly faded with the dimness of twilight.

I had expected the evening streets to be empty, but there were people everywhere. Children in brightly colored costumes and masks ran past me or into the streets as they looked for homes and apartments whose residents might be home.

Amelia had said that south El Paso was a sponge, and I could sense the surge of human flotsam that came across the Rio Grande wherever the fence could be climbed, ripped open, or tunneled underneath. These shadowy figures filtered into the part of El Paso that Juárez embraced like a wanton prostitute.

As I passed a narrow recess separating two buildings, I saw a toothless old woman in a shapeless black dress trying to entice a giant orange alley cat to come to her; from the darkness, she proffered a shiny wet piece of raw meat, and I could swear that her words were Latin, not Spanish. I quickened my pace.

The words from the Goetia echoed in my head, "Thou shalt know and observe the Moon's Age for thy working." The book was specific in that magical ceremonies should be done when the moon was 2, 4, 6, 8, 10, 12, or 14 days, and at no other time. I had no idea how old the moon was, but the moon had been full more than a week earlier and it had not yet risen tonight.

The light crowd moved aimlessly, interspersed with masked trick-or-treaters, and a heavily bearded man passed me with a coat drawn tightly about him, hat down over his face, shadowing all but his eerily bright eyes; perhaps it was the distorted camera of my imagination, but I felt that his entire face bristled with hair. He was making sounds deep in his throat.

Dirty yellow lights began to appear in windows, and I was certain that some of them were from kerosene lamps rather than electric bulbs. Two other men going in my direction jostled me as they shuffled past, grunting. I did not speak. Now I admitted to myself that, were it not for Amelia, I would still be safe in Las Cruces.

The gathering dusk silhouetted the building I was seeking. It was a two-storey house with a one-acre park on the north side, across the street—the location in the photo. The park was in name only, because only a few brown patches of bermuda grass remained, the dirt beaten down in it, and the several trees at its perimeter were obviously gnarled and dying. Milling in the open park were seven members of a youth gang in baggy clothing, smoking marijuana and throwing empty Bud Light® beer cans as they postured to each other with their shaved heads, their hands flashing gang signs. These spiritual descendants of the old pachuco had brought them as far as they would go, and they were as doomed as the trees surrounding them.

The crowd milled around the almost-Victorian style house of red brick with a high porch and broad concrete steps leading to ostentatious wooden doric mansion columns supporting a roof overhang, and whose white paint mostly flaked off. They still stood like sentries in the dusk. No lights could be seen except for a dim bulb behind an orange, stained glass panel in the fanlight above the front door.

At least a dozen men were lounging on the steps of the house, smoking and drinking. A group of four was hunched around a guitar player on the sidewalk, and they were singing ballads whose lyrics I recognized as the popular Mexican narco-corrida—songs romanticizing Mexico's drug dealers.

The restive attitude of the people on the street was disturbing, and I watched the front of the house to see if anyone entered or left. Even as darkness inexorably grew, the dirty glow from Juárez only a few hundred yards away outlined the tall, ugly border fence along the riverbed that was only a temporary barrier to the polyglot invaders who were trying to enter the United States by any means possible.

I walked on down the street past the house, feigning nonchalance, waiting for full dark to return and make my entrance. It was no surprise to me that the police would only pass through this area in patrol cars with windows closed and doors locked. Parked automobiles scattered along the street were dead animals squatting at the curbs. I saw one or two coated figures enter the house, and now I had to have the courage to walk past the loiterers to fulfill my promise. Fear made the blood thunder in my ears, but I could see Amelia's oval face before me, imploring, frightened.

The impromptu mariachi group paid no attention when I came back and walked toward the steps of the house. The yard and sidewalk was peopled with a handful of Halloween revelers, some wearing deathshead masks, drunkenly howling their approval to the music. For all practical purposes this was Mexico.

Again, nobody paid attention to me, and I was ignored as I walked among them, the hood shielding my face. Once I reached the concrete porch in the dim orange glow of the fanlight, I could see that the front windows of the house were cracked, and one pane was newly shattered. The doorframe had once been painted white but was now gray with age as though a thousand filthy hands had left residue caked on it. On the lintel above the door was a fading black legend, partially effaced, in block letters painted long ago. I tried to read it as I shivered from the stiffening breeze:

ARS   OETIA ET THEUR IS MARB S.

The front door itself had once been hand-carved oak with scrolled artistic inlays. Neglect and weathering had done their work, stripping the original finish and leaving the wood to warp and crack, the fine grain lined and gray like an old man's face. Most unsettling to me were the deep vertical gouges from chest height to the bottom of the door that looked like

Terror Tales of the Southwest

many years of animal scratches, some of which seemed recent.

The aged door no longer had a knob or latch, but there was no need. The throng of indigent drunks in the yard and on the steps stayed curiously away from the porch and the front door. As some of them stared, I pushed the door open and entered the house.

By the light of a single 40-watt ceiling bulb I could see the doors to two large rooms left and right of the center hallway that bisected the ground floor. The wide hallway had been exposed to the elements and the floors were dirty and naked, bordered by the remains of two sofas whose filthy stuffing was exposed as a result of savage slashes to their dingy upholstery. The doors to the left and right down the hall were padlocked behind rusted hasps, and I presumed that behind them could be stairways to the second floor. There was enough light to see the worn track in the floor leading to another door at the end of the hall. This one had a large knob that opened soundlessly on oiled hinges. The blood was pounding in my head from the fear that now gripped me. I could not help but think of 314 women whose brutal murders in Juárez had never been solved.

The moment I opened that cellar door, I was overwhelmed with fumes and nameless odors coming from somewhere below, along with a jumble of noises. There was no cellar. There was instead a ramp of packed earth, hard as concrete, that declined straight south into a cave-like tunnel. A kerosene lamp provided the only light. It was set into a nicha in the left wall that was roughly stuccoed with cement while crude timbers or vigas shored up the ceiling. It could well be the entrance to one of those border tunnels used to smuggle illegal drugs and aliens under the Rio Grande from Juárez to El Paso. Yet I knew it was something else.

As I walked downward, I was comforted by something else I brought with me and had not mentioned even to Dearing. The .45 automatic in the waistband of my jeans was covered by the bulk of my sweatshirt, and I knew it was an accessory that El Paso city ordinances frowned upon. While New Mexico state law allowed the open carrying of weapons, Texas law was less forgiving if one did not have a concealed carry permit. The pistol was now my only lifeline as I entered an alien world.

I edged down another 25 or 30 feet, my back against the wall as I approached the wan glow of a second lamp set into the wall. The kerosene smell of lamp oil combined with something else— a foetid stench rising from below that caused my stomach to convulse.

The ramp was about five feet wide, but the tamped earthen walkway had narrowed because of what was now piled along the walls as I sidled past. Bones and pieces of bone— vaporous with the smell of decay still clinging to them. I leaned down to look, close to the faint glow of the lamp, and my stomach lurched again. Many of the ribs, skulls, and pelvic bones appeared human, though hideously scored and cracked, but there were other fragments of animal bones, even the remains of rodents suggesting a ravenous appetite belonging to some kind of animal that had been living in the tunnel.

In the dimness of that charnel repository I saw above the niche with the lamp additional black letters precisely painted on the crude concrete plaster, following the tunnel downward:

USOR—DILAPIDATORE—TENTATORE—SOIGNATORE— DEVORATORE—

The words trailed in a single line downward into the descending tunnel leading to a bend 20 feet farther down, from which a glow was emanating. I knew only vaguely what the words on the wall might mean, but I felt their hideous implication. My fear was as much for Amelia as for myself, and I could feel tremors in my limbs as my stomach convulsed, the rancid sweat pooling in my underarms. I stumbled on one of the fang-shaped ribs attached to a decayed form, and it sent up a puff of noisome dust. The smell of decay was now muted by an upward drifting fog of smoke that smelled of cloves, assafoetida, and other sickly sweet incense. A dull, throbbing cacophony welled upward from below. What I sought was just beyond the bend of that intestine-like nightmare tunnel. Fear was joined with claustrophobia as I realized I was 75 feet, maybe deeper, under El Paso.

A nightmare came to life as I edged around the corner, my back still feeling the roughness of the wall. I was inside a cavernous opening whose ceiling was obscured by billowing smoke from four ornate dark bronze shoulder-high thuribles standing at the compass points and each four feet high, glinting dully in the flickering light of candles and torchiers. I could not tell the extent of the underground room, and perhaps my terror distorted the evidence of my senses. It seemed to be oval shaped and at least 95 feet wide and perhaps 125 feet long. I could not see the ceiling, but it was at least 15 feet high, hiding its recesses in the fog of incense.

The entire grotto seemed to glow and throb a ghastly, dirty orange. Vague shapes gesticulated and gyrated in the bluish fog of incense smoke whose tendrils were weaving like serpents. My head was whirling with an inexplicable surge of arousal and rage from some hellish substance burning within those incense bowls. Yet I saw Them.

They were either not fully human or they were hideously changed. Animal noises exploded from distorted mouths as they jostled in their nakedness, cloaked only by the smoky air, their cast-off clothing trampled under the drumming of filthy naked feet. How many? I could not tell but there seemed dozens of them—a congregation of the damned, chanting, jostling, shoving, crouching, and clutching in pandaemoniac abandon.

In the swirling currents of smoke, I saw Him for the first time, standing on a raised ebony dais, holding some kind of engraved sword in his hand. Behind him was a glowing torchier lamp, its peripatetic flame waxing and waning. I thought of the "la plaza" sketch in the damnable *Livro Marbas*.

He was bent over, droning a sonorous ritual conjuration that caused the throng packed into the cavern to move and sway in response when his alien words that reached rhythmic peaks. The words…some of the words were those painted on the tunnel wall and some seemed to be words I remembered reading from the book: "RGAHCULHUACAN… NGLORGAHAHUITZTL…AMIQUI…NGAYTILY."

Two men with bristling beards, still relatively human, made cringing bestial obeisance to the altar as the sword glinted in sweeping arcs, creating currents in the smoke.

The creature on the dais had to be Fernando Valles, but the power of lifelong belief had wreaked a horrific change in him. The voice was a withered, crackled thing of old secrets that cascaded from a sharp-toothed mouth.

The ancient head was elongated, sparse strands of greasy grey hair like a sardonic diadem, and the jaw beneath it was hatefully prognathous. The crooked body was emaciated and covered with irregular patches of coarse grey hair. It required both of his spindly arms to hold the sword he gestured with; those arms were twisted and hairy, the fingernails dark and curling in their unnatural length. He wore a cassock that scarcely concealed his abnormality, and the hairy body was naked below the waist.

It was the legs that most astounded me in my revulsion. In the chaos of that ceremony I could swear that the knees of the gesturing madman were backward as in the canine, the haunches padded with a thick fur under the skirt-like cassock. He spoke phrases in Spanish and then read a jumbled conjuration mixing English, Spanish, and Latin, "En el nombre Beralensis, Baldachiensis, Paumachi, and Apologiae Sedes—of the mighty ones qui regere spiritus…who govern spirits, Liachidae and ministers of the house of transformation…el señor de la transformación."

The smoke from the thuribles—the choking, hallucinogenic smell of that underground tabernacle. A wild thought raced through my brain about how dogs come to look like their owners over the years or maybe the owners came to look like…No, it can't be, but Amelia told me the wizard was over 100 years old. My God! A nighted congregation filing down, down the tunnel into that filthy cavern, even as the waning moon commanded at times known only to them, year after year, for decades, and with every orgiastic ceremony their bodies were twisted and swollen in varied stages of change, evolving into a phantasmagoria of hideous physical shapes that I could see only dimly through coils of smoke. My brain was swimming. Were they changing before my eyes? Or was it the narcotic fumes of the incense deluding me?

And there was something else, another smaller midnight cavity 100 feet from me behind the dais and seeming to continue beyond the cavern I had entered. Perhaps it led through a Stygian labyrinth to some nameless field in Juárez, maybe even to the place where the bodies of hundreds of murdered women were found. Then, for all I knew, it could descend into unimaginable depths below the earth.

The rapt congregation moved rhythmically as though one unnatural body. I understood none of it. Here was howling, there was snarling, and some of the figures turned on each other, clawing and biting. There seemed no purpose, no explanation for this abomination. I hesitate to record what I was seeing, as the fog of incense was dizzying, but the figures stumbling, growling, and clawing at each other seemed to actually be changing before my eyes. Was it a hallucination directed by the sonorous evocations from the wizard standing on the dais or were these humans actually growing hair, their limbs changing and becoming lupine as they responded to the chants, their faces elongating in the swirling clouds? Then again, reality itself was shifting, amorphous, my senses overwhelmed by an undreamed of horror. Such things could not be, but my eyes saw cruel teeth, twitching fur-covered ears.

Nothing in the author Casteneda's drug-fueled separate reality could match what played out before my eyes in this smoke-filled nightmare realm.

Then, through those smoky currents flowing like turbulent grey rivers through the air, I saw Amelia, eyes half-closed, seated on a high-backed oak chair placed at the center of the dais behind the torchier and behind that creature she called father and grandfather.

The waves of her hair flowed onto her soft, naked shoulders, and she wore a low-cut red satin gown that accentuated her figure as though she were dressed for her senior prom. I had no time to stare at her, and she seemed to be in a state of mild hypnosis or, more likely, shock.

The conjurations grew toward crescendo— "Tentatore! Soignatore! … (unintelligible muttering)" Then a gravelly shout: "DEVORATORE!" I knew my perceptions were being warped by the drugs, the noise, and the words of the magical imprecations. There was a humming in my ears like the powerful feedback from stereo speakers.

Yes, I know I saw it—what must have been IT. Hovering near the fogged roof of the cavern, it was a grotesque amorphous face forming and changing in the clouds of smoke from the incense, but I knew that I was looking into the bestial face of Marbas, whose power changes men into animals.

It was the horror of a being who must rule the skinwalker, the man-beast, and he was present this night in the howling chaos of a cave deep below the city, evoked by the sorcery of an evil ancient creature. I saw with my own eyes that infernal demon, the Lord of Lycanthropy. The narrow lambent eyes and snarling jaws of shifting smoke burned into my brain. It had no body, and the parody of a face distorted, devilish and animalistic. The hairy jaws extended and snapped at the smoke while the eyes were one moment reddish and illuminated, then black as the outer Chaos.

My restraint was gone in a frenzy of fear and loathing. Almost without conscious direction, I leapt onto the raised platform from among the throng of milling bodies. Even above the overpowering smell of the incense I could smell the foulness of that animal-man, the fur-covered legs caked with excrement. Amelia looked up and seemed to vaguely recognize me, but my first motion was toward the evil magician.

I was never given to impetuous violent acts, but in one lunge, I yelled and wrested the ancient sword from his hands; its blade was dark from age, blood, and nameless infamies. Without a further thought I plunged it through the chest of the thing that had wielded it, and he collapsed on the dais. For a moment I stared at the twitching body and saw it convulsing… as it yelped, shrieking like an animal.

No time to waste! I grabbed Amelia's hand and yanked her to her feet. Even in semi-consciousness, she rose gracefully, yielding to me.

The ancient Fernando Valles rolled spasmodically from the platform into the milling congregation, wheezing and gurgling in a death rattle, and there was a sudden silence punctuated by muttering growls. In my altered state I could see hideous creatures in the smoke, surmounted by that swirling, smoky image of the demon whose eyes now burned with an infernal glow, but all my will was concentrated on reaching the tunnel mouth whence I had come.

Even as I turned, pulling Amelia with me, I saw some of the creatures, no longer erect, scurrying to the inky hole behind the dais. It seemed that they were running into the blackness on all fours. Howling, three creatures—they were no longer men—picked up the bleeding corpse of Fernando Valles and shambled, hunched over, dragging the dripping burden back toward the dark hole. where they disappeared.

Amelia stumbled, but my grip on her hand was firm as I pulled her past the confused semi-human creatures still stumbling about in the smoke of the cavern; their guttural sounds filled the air. They were repeating the barbarous words of evocation as they howled at the face of Marbas. We reached the bend in the cave where the ramp began, and suddenly one of the congregation was in front of us, blocking our escape and uttering a desperate howl that was picked up and echoed by at least a dozen creatures lurking in the smoke.

The naked, hairy creature ran toward us, and it was young, muscular, the eyes still human despite the hair on his body and the sharpness of the teeth in his slavering mouth. His clawed hands were reaching out…

It was a simple, desperate motion. I yanked up the sweatshirt, drew the .45, firing at the attacker as he lunged. The thunder of the pistol shot was deafening in the cave, and the sight of the bullet striking the middle of his face immobilized the other things in the cavern. The 210-grain hollow point round made a large hole above his upper lip and sprayed the grayish-pink of his brains, and fragments of his skull, onto the grey wall of the cavern in obscene colors. He collapsed backward, no longer howling.

Now shuddering and overcome with panic, I clutched Amelia's bare arm, but she resisted suddenly, trying to escape. She was screaming over the din. "You killed him." Her lovely face was twisted in horror and anger as she came out of what must have been some kind of hypnotic state. "*Qué estas…*What are you doing? I hate you." She tried to free herself.

Confusion battled with adrenaline inside of me as she looked at me, tears starting to streak her perfect makeup. I couldn't believe she wanted to be here, and I stood for an eternity that lasted only two or three seconds. The impulse to leave her to her fate was only momentary, and then I resumed my grip on her arm, overcoming her resistance, pushing her ahead of me with one hand, my other holding fast to the .45. She struggled fitfully, balancing on high-heeled pumps, but she was moving again—up, up the tunnel path that seemed impossibly long and dark, the air stinking and smoky.

From the sound of the howls below I did not have to guess that the creatures from below were following, just behind us. As we passed those frightening words on the cavern wall, Amelia stopped once, turned, crying, as she hit me in the chest with her fist. I shoved, and as she heard the chorus of hideous voices underneath, she kept going, now driven by fright more than anger.

Two hunched over, snarling things were gaining on us, almost shapeless in the cloistered near darkness of the tunnel. I pushed Amelia up the seemingly endless inclined path, my breath exploding with emotion and exertion.

In my fright I imagined I could feel hot stinking breath on the back of my neck, and I loosened my hold on Amelia for a moment, spinning around. Because I was so unsteady, I took the crouching two-hand stance, aiming for the luminous eyes lunging toward us. The .45 bucked in my grip—once…twice…three times, the explosions pounding my eardrums like hammer blows in the enclosed space. Grunts and howls were followed by the sound of something kicking the wall as ill-defined shapes twitched and rolled downward, hairy limbs thrashing. The baleful eyes had disappeared.

Finally, we staggered to the cellar door, panting, and then through the dirty hallway to the front of the house. As we emerged into the chill wind of Halloween night, there was no time for relief. We saw the loiterers and drunks clustered around the front steps, the few *Dia de los Muertos* skull masks ominous in the dark. They must have heard the shots, and all eyes were on us. We stopped, my arm around Amelia as the huddled group advanced menacingly up the steps toward us. The pistol was in my hand, but there would be no time to jam another magazine into it before they were on us.

Suddenly. strobe flashes exploded from the sidewalk. Shouts and epithets filled the air as a motorized Nikon camera recorded the scene to the accompaniment of brief bursts of white light. Almost instantly the crowd dissolved, racing in all directions north into the park across the street. There was Bruce Dearing, grinning with his camera and powerful flash units. He was standing in the street.

"Happy Hallowe'en," Dearing shouted, more at the scattering crowd than us, as Amelia suddenly threw her arms around me. "Ah…Guys, we'd better get out of here. I made a phone call, and those sirens you hear in the distance are headed to this address."

The three of us walked or stumbled to the end of the block as I saw the El Paso Police Department screaming down the street, not just with a patrol car, but with a SWAT team vehicle. A squad of officers wearing Kevlar helmets and camouflage fatigues boiled out of it, racing up the steps of the house. Even from a block away I could hear the rapid staccato of .223-caliber automatic weapons and frightened shouting, guttural howls, and the rasp of orders on intercoms.

Three Hallowe'en revelers walked too casually away from the chaos, one man bedecked with camera equipment, one wearing a grey hooded sweatshirt, and the woman between them draped in an elegant evening gown. I was almost breathless in fear as we moved, and Dearing assured us with his characteristic braying laugh that he had told the police a "good story," but I couldn't help but imagine that he was prescient.

It was a palpable relief to go up the stairs and be back in the safety of Dearing's loft apartment above the butcher shop. Amelia gradually returned to full consciousness, assisted by a hot mug of the green tea Dearing prepared. I asked if she wanted to go home with me, but she shook her head and said she needed to be in her own apartment in northwest El Paso.

For caution we allowed another half hour before we said good night to the photographer who had saved us, and we walked to the church where my car was parked. I drove as slowly as possible northwest on Mesa Street, and Amelia directed me to the apartment complex on the side of the Franklin Mountains where she lived with a roommate. She said she had other family or friends there, so I didn't ask if I could stay with her. She was hugging herself as we walked to her door, my arm around her waist. She smiled at me and touched my cheek before we parted. Despite the streaks of her mascara, I thought she was more lovely than I had ever seen her.

Then too, I was still disoriented and reeking with the stench from the cavern. I knew I would see Amelia the next day on campus, so I reluctantly took my leave. Whatever happened, I knew she would never have to make the awful sacrifice that had terrified her, and I shuddered with the realization that her satanic father/grandfather had almost sacrificed her to a fate that would have condemned her to a darkness beyond description. The 40-mile drive to Las Cruces seemed endless and the night was black.

The next morning, I was watching the El Paso Channel 7 morning news anchor reporting an underground explosion somewhere in south El Paso on Hallowe'en night but that, according to police, it was merely U.S. Army operation at nearby Fort Bliss detonating outdated munitions, the sound mistakenly appearing to come from the border area.

One south El Paso resident was interviewed saying that she thought it was some Hallowe'en prank, while another video clip was from a storeowner who said he felt a minor earthquake. The prelate of Sacred Heart gave his usual *Dia de los Muertos* statement while remonstrating critically about some of the pagan practices of Hallowe'en.

Yet I was certain the men in camouflage who had assaulted the house on Hallowe'en night set charges in that hellish tunnel sometime after midnight, collapsing it along with the mouldering house and the changelings trapped underground—unless some had escaped deep, deep, through the farthest reaches of the corridor that I knew led back to Mexico.

Despite my fondest expectations, Amelia did not come to campus on Friday, nor on the following Monday. When I came to the office Tuesday, I found a letter from her on my desk. I'll not forget the words of her brief note: "You gave me back my life, and my heart will be with you always. I have decided after all to leave the university and to marry Tony. He has a job now. He truly needs me, and the needs of family overrule the wishes of the heart. Please be happy." She signed it with an inked heart.

I wondered—was her boyfriend one of the shape-shifting creatures in the underground cavern? Could he have been one who scuttled through the dark hole, and in Stygian darkness, found temporary refuge in Mexico at the other end of a tunnel? Or was he absent from the diabolical conventicles of Marbas. I was not destined to know.

Life goes on, and it was a long time before I could appreciate the advice of my mother who told me that you don't just marry the girl—you also marry the family. I recall that it was Dearing who told me later, perhaps in a flash of brilliance, "Romance is the refuge of fools and drunks." At least I don't drink.

A week later, the Sunday edition of *The El Paso Times* described the demolition, according to city plans, of an abandoned house in south El Paso that was completed late in the week.

And today El Paso is still a sponge on the border soaking up the poison of the hemisphere, bringing vileness beyond description across in the night and under the ground, with diseases and practices ancient and loathsome beyond description. I for one will never again question the power of belief, for belief is stronger than reason, for good or evil.

As with all media stories, the chronicle of the murdered women slipped into the past with a rise in indiscriminate murder that for years turned Juárez into one of the most dangerous cities in the world. Stories of murdered women disappeared as the journalists who reported crime were themselves shot down in the dirty streets and dumped in fields outside of the city. That drug-fueled bloodbath eventually subsided, but even the drug cartels are known to practice the most disgusting black arts and superstitions, making obeisance to hideous gods and demons. Do they not even today dig tunnels foul, dark, and deep?

As for those barbarous names of evocation I had transcribed, I never made any sense of them, but once I showed them to a professor of linguistics at the University of Colorado, and he identified two or three of the words as "Nahuatl," the language of the ancient Aztecs.

That is unfortunate, because in the wake of the trauma we lived through that Hallowe'en night I took the sorcerer's hellish *Livro Marbas* into the dirt yard of my small adobe house and burned it into a pile of noxious smelling ashes.

Finally, there is the witness of my senses. Indelible in my mind are the images of wolf-like creatures cavorting in the light of a dying fire in the desert long ago; then, that evil night 25 years ago in south El Paso, with my vision distorted by incense fumes deep beneath tainted earth, where I saw a sorcerer with a sword through his chest as the spasms of his dying body seem to revert into lupine form before my eyes.

Even now, despite my affection for animals, I am cautious when I drive at night in the desert, and I will shoot without hesitation any unfamiliar large dog I see skulking around my property.

For I opened *The El Paso Times* on Friday, and I saw a classified advertisement in the personals section:

Esoteric Order; magnes potes-
tas; D. Vargas, Gen. Delivery El
Paso, TX 79905. Muchos son los
llamados.

APPENDIX I

FROM THE *LIVRO MARBAS*:

(Trans.) Howlers in the dark--- drinkers of blood. We take the communion of
the spirits.

We seek the house of corpses (to) feel the power of that spirit of evil. It promises we can never die. In the canyons of Sonora we are baptized. We have trod the
steps of the pyramid and sworn eternal obedience on the skull of Quetzalcoatl in
the secret places of the Aztec. We become the jaguar and the wolf. We (will) rape
tonight, We (will) kill tonight. We walk with the shadow and tear the flesh of the
living.

We bring terror in the night. The sheep of the world (will) crawl before the
power of our magic.

Such are the words:

Drink the potion---

Breathe the spirit of the flame---

With the sword, I pierce the darkness and call forth his terrible majesty.

In the Shadow of Geronimo's Mountain

Summer lightning punctuates the New Mexico night, and sometimes it flickers blood-red behind the three peaks of the Tres Hermanas, that line of three sister peaks on this side of the border just north of Old Mexico. As I drive south from the mining district on U.S. Highway 180 on my way back to Las Cruces, my mind is on my departed friend Ed Alvarado and the horror he found in the shadow of brooding Mount Geronimo on a similar summer night in 1976.

Irony is not wasted on me to know that the little town of Bayard has now established its cemetery just west of the mountain's sheer face.

So much has changed in the district with the end of the smelter and the demolition in 2007 of the iconic smokestacks, one of which had stood for 70 years as a beacon to those who saw copper mining as a godsend in a state where poverty is as much a companion as is the rugged beauty of the state.

Oh, and there are unexplained deaths to be sure. The horrifying end of Martin Simms was neither the first nor the last, and in all the years I lived there, I had both a magnetic attraction and an unsettled feeling when I saw the bluffs of Mount Geronimo turn scarlet with the setting of the sun. On the night Ed Alvarado revealed what he experienced that summer at the base of the mountain, I could never again see the mountain as benevolent. It concealed a horror known but to a few, and it is better left that way.

Yes, I am a native of that cluster of towns, including Hurley, Bayard, Santa Clara (nee Central), Santa Rita, and Silver City. When we were young, we clambered over the hills east of the copper plant at Hurley, and every young man thought it his duty to "climb Geronimo." The climb could be treacherous, and I once slipped during the climb and fell ten feet into a nest of boulders—without injury. But then we always did our hiking in the daytime. It was the summer rule that we were expected back in our yards when the plant whistle sounded at 4:30 announcing the end of the day shift.

Ed Alvarado? He was a mentor who at one time was my Boy Scout troop leader and a guide to many of us who had more energy than common sense in early adolescence. He died a year after the smokestacks fell, in the fullness of his years as they say. That fullness was never placid, not after one singular night. I remember the Bob Dylan song, and the lyrics, "We never much thought we could get very old," and in my retirement I still salute the kindness and guidance given to me by Alvarado in my youth.

I know why Alvarado told few people about what happened that night, and why the death of Martin Simms was whispered about in the community in the aftermath. Some people even said it was Alvarado who was to blame. I just know that a responsible father and husband sometimes went a little crazy on summer nights in his later years.

No, Ed was not a drinker, but there was one exception. Though I had moved 90 miles southeast to Las Cruces, where I taught at the university there, it was my custom to spend summers in the haunts of my youth. In 1989 I rented a frame bungalow with a concrete sidewalk and a yard that was mostly dirt. The original wire fence was still in place, sagging in sections, but it was a good enough place for me to set up my computer and do some fiction writing in the home town of my youth.

The towering smokestacks no longer vomited plumes of SO_2, and I could enjoy the eternal barking of dogs and remember when the jaws of the ore crusher rumbled day and night. I spent some of the days meeting with old friends who remembered my now-relict family, and that included some hours reminiscing with Ed Alvarado and his wife Ermalinda, as their children were now grown and moved away.

It was a Saturday. I was writing a story late into the night, massaging a plot that hopelessly circled the drain. Around 1:30 a.m. I was ready for bed when there came a thudding knock to the front door. Startled, I looked first for my .45 automatic and then found the switch for the yellow bug light on the front porch. Looking out the rectangular glass pane covered with a flimsy lace curtain, I saw a familiar figure leaning against the jamb.

I opened the door and Ed stumbled into the house with the wry lopsided grin so typical of him. Powerfully built, his shoulders had the look of those belonging to an offensive guard, a position he played at Silver High School. His Levi's denim shirt was half open to the waist, a forest of greying chest hair in evidence. Around his neck was a rawhide cord suspending the darkened copper amulet I always remembered him wearing. He raised his eyebrows, brown eyes boring into mine.

Ed Alvarado's black hair and bristling mustache had gone silver. He was retired from the copper company, and his boys were grown and pursuing careers of their own. Alvarado and his wife still lived in town, within sight of Mount Geronimo. The 1 ½" diameter hammered copper disc was a gift from his great grandmother who gave it to him when he was a child, and he never talked about the past, or what happened in 1976; most of us had heard rumors but Alvarado never seemed to be a violent man at any time when I knew him. He did tell his boys stories of Apache lore passed on to him by his *bisabuela*, but they probably did not believe him.

He admitted talking too much on the rare occasion when the beer flowed on the 4th of July or on certain nights when summer storms growled on the horizon. I knew from our candid conversations over the years that his wife more than once had to comfort him when he woke up screaming in the night. But in the years I knew him, he never explained about Martin Simms or the incident. He just said there was an "accident" that night.

I remember clearly his scoutmaster stories to us, as a rapt audience, of how spooky Mount Geronimo could be at times, and I came to agree with him. At certain times the wind can moan and howl as it soughs through the mass of boulders at the southern edge of the mountain or knifes into the vertical blades and crevices of the cliff. At night, the effect could be fearful, and the sounds seemed to be those of disembodied spirits. Perhaps the Apache knew more than modern people can understand.

"Too late for a visit?" Ed belched loud enough to be heard in the street, and I inhaled the fragrance borne of Budweiser.

When I shrugged, I had to smile. Ed walked unsteadily across the hardwood living room floor and jostled the flimsy coffee table that promptly dumped a pile of paper, magazines, and books I had been reading onto the area rug. He stood for a moment, gauging the distance and then dropped onto the couch that was too disreputable to be called a sofa.

"Hey, *Ese*, you weren't here in '76." Though Hispanic, his voice revealed no undertones of his native Spanish.

I was still smiling. "Coffee? Tea? Pepsi?"

"Maybe the first. I'm going to tell you something—need to tell you." He leaned back and looked up at the dark ivory color of the ceiling, turned yellowish in the pool of light cast by a floor lamp, his mouth grimacing as he tasted something unsavory. I went into the kitchen to boil water, figuring he wouldn't notice that the instant coffee would be a poor substitute for what he needed.

When I put the mug of coffee in front of him, I pulled up an old wooden chair with cane back and unsteady legs, leaning forward as he closed his eyes and burned his mouth with a great swallow.

"God, Frank, this stuff is awful." I was still smiling when he sat bolt upright. He was finally going to break his silence about the mountain, and I knew it. "Linda just kicked me out."

My smile turned indulgent, "Don't much blame her. I have to say this isn't like you. Why are you stinking drunk?" Outside the thin walls of the house we could hear the soft rumble of thunder from an approaching or retreating storm.

"I was maybe 6 when my great grandma told me the words. *Ch'in binant'a'*."

"Huh?" It wasn't Spanish, wasn't English, and I grabbed my ever-present yellow legal pad and began scribbling, trying to capture the nasal intonations as best I could.

Ed waved his hand. "Apache. She knew some words. *Nizilhee hát'ii.*" He shook his head as if to clear cobwebs. "It means 'the devil' and 'he wants to kill you'." He grasped the talisman with thumb and forefinger, rubbing it. "Saved my life that night."

I was writing, my eyes watching his fingers. "I wasn't even in the state in '76, but people talked about it. You never said anything to me."

"Never said anything to anybody—except Linda. Even the company got nothing from me. We all know the mountain, but it's a good thing the company hasn't let anybody from the public on the property for the last 15 years. Damn good thing."

Ed took another swallow from the cup and sighed as he stretched, his legs extended under the coffee table, dirty white socks with holes in both big toes. He had left his shoes at home.

"Ed, we kids were all over those hills and bluffs. You even led us out there with Troop 102 in the 1950s. What the hell are you talking about?" I realized I was goading him, getting him to the edge of revealing. Our area folklore told how the nomadic Chiricahua Apache leader Geronimo had at times set a hunting camp atop the cliffs to give the mountain a name.

"That was in the daytime, Frank, in the daytime, before the *ch'lin*—evil spirit—came to me." Suddenly his muscular frame shook as he held back a sob. "Maybe Linda will forgive me…"

Because I knew Ermalinda, I told him she would always forgive him. He was that kind of man, and she was that kind of woman. As he composed himself, I ejected the magazine and cleared the action of the .45 automatic, setting it on the coffee table with a thunk. After his second cup of coffee, there was only the sound of Ed Alvarado's deep voice, the occasional sound of a page on my tablet turning, and the soft grumbling of the dark skies outside. Perhaps he went to the bathroom once or twice, but I scarcely remember the interruptions as I recorded his stark memory.

At the end of the night, sitting in that straight-back chair with a writing tablet on my lap, I must have dozed in total exhaustion, and Ed finally slumped over onto the couch cushions, because it was now dawn, and a bright sun poured through the uncurtained kitchen window. I was dull with fatigue, but I now had a frightening story unlike any I ever could have imagined.

As the morning brightened, I scrambled some eggs and folded in chopped green chile while frying bacon. I could hear Ed waking up with a groan. He ate breakfast with more coffee, avoiding my eyes for the most part. Then there was a knock at the door.

Ermalinda was standing on the porch, smartly dressed, her hair tied in a bun, and she was dangling a pair of soft-soled men's shoes in one hand. She had obviously been to early Mass and was at my door to say "good morning" to her husband, very much as an angel of righteousness. She came into the kitchen and dropped the shoes at Ed's feet; his bare toes were still protruding from the dirty socks.

She put her hand on Ed's back and leaned over, kissing him on the stubble of his cheek before turning to me. "I know he told you. I am asking you not to tell the story, at least not now."

"Family pride?" I was already feeling the enthusiasm that I found when writing an exciting tale.

"Frank, there's also the Simms family. I've talked with them in the last few years, and they are still in mourning. Then, there's something you probably don't know—most people don't. But…" Ermalinda paused and stood behind her husband and began massaging his shoulders.

I put plates into the sink and turned back to her, my hand extended, eyebrows raised.

"There were others." Her voice was calm but filled with portent. Ed stiffened visibly as my attention was riveted on her.

Ermalinda pursed her lips and touched her well-manicured thumb to each of three fingers. "That's one reason the company is so tough on trespassers. There were three other unexplained deaths near the mountain—two of them years before Eddie went up there that night, and one more in 1980."

My last hike to Mount Geronimo was in 1974, but after getting Ed's story, I now felt a cold wash of dread rising in my stomach. "I always thought it was the fear of liability for accidents on company property."

Ermalinda stood erect, arms crossed. "That's what they want you to think. Those dead…dead… men…were on the list as suicides, but I have talked to the families…" Alvarado started to interrupt.

"No, Eddie, I won't be quiet. The last man was a friend of Martin Simms. He went out there because he was curious, and the security patrol found him the next day. Nobody could say why he stayed after dark or what killed him."

I accompanied them to the door and waved as Ermalinda got into her Toyota while Ed climbed into his new Chevrolet Silverado pickup. As for me, I had the secret complacence that I was somehow privy to a horror unknown to the hundreds of people who drove alongside the mountain every day, oblivious to the threat lurking there. Only a writer has that kind of eccentricity. I spent the next two days writing and rewriting the story almost non-stop, obsessed with every detail and knowing that someday I would be released from my promise to Ermalinda and my friend Ed Alvarado.

* * *

A demolition crew sent two giant Hurley smokestacks falling to earth in June 2007, after seven decades, and lifetime company employee Ed Alvarado departed from this life in the fullness of his years exactly one year later. Now, with the permission of his lovely wife Ermalinda, the full story of the invisible thing that skulks behind the stark cliff of Mount Geronimo can be revealed.

The copper mines of southwestern New Mexico have a history beyond the Anglo and the Spaniard. When the Spanish explored the territory in the 16th century, they found Indian-wrought items of native copper, and the Spanish were known to have dug copper and silver from the Santa Rita mines from 1800 until their Apache slave laborers turned terrorists, causing the Spanish to abandon the foothills by 1873 while Anglo interlopers began then to exploit the ore bodies.

After WWI, the open pit mine became one of the largest producers of copper in the United States. So it was, 103 years later, that the Santa Rita open pit was one of the world's largest.

Alvarado was youngest of three generations who had labored for the copper company, and it was his grandmother who had passed scraps of Apache lore down to him. It could have been those traditions that made him one with the land and also brought to him a terror-filled night that never quite left his mind while he still breathed.

During his childhood, Alvarado's great grandmother had told him how the depredations of the Apaches were the result of Spanish brutality, and she told him of Cochise, Geronimo, and Mangus Colorado, who became the scourge of the Southwest.

The Chiricahua Apache roamed the forested mountains, the foothills where the mines were located, and then they ventured south onto the arid plains that stretched into Mexico 50 miles to the south.

Alvarado also knew the tales—no, the reality of the Navajo skinwalker with its fearsome ability to take on the shape of animals in the night to ravage human beings and their livestock. The Diné nation never doubted this spectral enemy, and only the white man was foolish enough to scoff at the reality. These invisible enemies could not be limited to the Navajos.

Though the verbal traditions of the Chiricahua Apaches are not so well known, they accept that humans are at risk from disembodied spirits and even the evil machinations of witches.

The Apache spirits and legends were part of the fabric of Alvarado's world and not dislodged by his college experience. He knew how the Apaches hated witchcraft almost as much as they hated the white eyes and as they distrusted Coyote the trickster. Alvarado's great grandmother had once told him a cryptic story about an invisible creature on the wind, a force even the Apaches did not understand and only kept away by drums and dancing. She told him about these things when she bestowed the sacred copper amulet to him.

The desert night is mostly comforting and benign, but at certain times and at certain places there are manifestations beyond rational description. At those times, the Apaches who camped on the high ground above the cliffs of the hill named Mount Geronimo slept not. They kept the fires blazing throughout the night and they drummed and danced to keep the thing away, sinking into sleep only when the gray of dawn paled the crushed velvet of the night sky.

As far back as he could remember, Alvarado had lived in the shadow of Mount Geronimo, whose cruel bluffs watched over the mining district. When he went to his job at the reduction plant, he was always aware of the changing face of the mountain, gray and impassive in the morning, reddish in the late afternoon.

No wonder it had once been a hunting camp for the restless Apaches, with a commanding view of the other hills and the plains that fanned out to the south. On a clear day, sharp eyes could see a hundred miles to the south.

The environmental engineering department was the newest department in the company, a response to six years of pressure from Washington's new Environmental Protection Agency that had been initiated in July 1970. There were at least a dozen monitoring stations now, with Geronimo station the most difficult to reach. It was the company mandate that the stations record data on SO_2 levels on a constant basis because in those days the acid smoke never stopped spewing from the stacks, and if the numbers went to the pin, operations at the smelter had to be curtailed, according to new EPA regulations.

This station near Mount Geronimo was also the least dependable of the monitoring

Terror Tales of the Southwest

stations, even though the components had been checked again and again. The checking, however, was done in the daylight—the inexplicable malfunctions seemed to happen only at night.

At great expense, the company had sent a D-2 Caterpillar up the rocky hillside close to the mountain, and leveled a 20-foot base dug from the rocky slope. Electrical wire was strung ¾ of a mile to the nearest supply. Data collected at the site was transmitted to the plant office by radio transponder. The station itself was housed in a small white metal enclosure the size of a small camping trailer, with a single door and antennae jutting up from the roof.

Alvarado was happy to be an environmental engineer. He had struggled to be the first in his family to earn a college degree, and the company had promoted him to engineering and the right to wear the brushed aluminum hard hat of engineers and management, even if he sometimes found himself partnered with Martin Simms. It was the nature of shift work that they were sometimes paired together in the plant office.

At 5'9", Simms was a stiff and lanky import from West Texas. His drawn and narrow face could only be described as sallow despite exposure to the sun. He was clean shaven and his hair was always meticulously combed from left to right, struggling to cover the growing baldness creeping from his forehead to the middle of his scalp.

His personality was affable enough, but his Texas drawl was often annoying to Alvarado. When Simms talked, he had an annoying habit of making snuffling noises deep within his nasal cavity. It did not help that he was also a cigarette smoker with the typical hacking cough so common to the type. He was in his 40s and a diehard professional football fan, something that was boring to Alvarado. Yet Simms knew how to restart equipment and "talk" to it via computer when necessary.

Alvarado never admitted being nervous about night-time visits to the Geronimo monitoring station, but he did tell his wife that it was the one duty he dreaded, when the station went off line. It was at those times he preferred to have company, even if it was Martin Simms.

July is the traditional beginning of the monsoon season in the Southwest, when a parched and rugged land had languished under the summer sun, and rain had been nonexistent for two or more months. Cumulo-nimbus clouds began building up in the afternoons, with blowing dust and tumbleweeds blowing across roads and fields. Soon the cloud buildup would grow dark and storm cells would threaten. When the rain came, it lashed the hillsides, filled the arroyos, rushing in angry flash floods that locals knew to avoid. When the water cascaded down the sides of mountains such as Geronimo, it washed out any trails, including the path to the environmental monitoring station.

The environmental engineers could drive the brand new 1976 company Chevrolet Blazer as far as the bottom of the hill, but the engineers would have to go on foot at least 200 yards uphill to reach the malfunctioning station.

That first evening of graveyard shift in that first week of July, it was almost predictable that the signal would be interrupted, and Alvarado was happy to have Simms going out with him to the Geronimo station. The time was 2330 Hours.

The night was turning nasty, and Alvarado felt the prickles at the back of his neck when they stopped near the base of the mountain. The hollow sound of the car doors slamming seemed very loud despite a vigorous wind out of the west bringing the muffled sound of thunder while heavy clouds scudded across the sky.

Under a waxing half-moon, their mutual unconcerned laughter echoed against the mountain when a hot gust blew Alvarado's hard hat off and sent it clanking against a boulder. He grabbed the hat and jammed it back on his head as they started climbing. Small rocks slipped from the path and rattled down the steep hill, with Geronimo's bluff towering above them. Blowing dust made their eyes smart.

Alvarado tried to discount what had happened. They made it to the station, and Simms pulled the metal door open. The interior light was out, so Alvarado held his powerful 6-volt flashlight while Simms tinkered with the transponder. When the green light on the console started glowing, Simms inserted a new 40-watt bulb in the ceiling light and switched it off before stepping out and closing the metal door. Alvarado was now trying to keep a lid on a panic impulse. He wanted to get back to the Blazer as fast as possible. Now the windborne sound reached them. Alvarado heard it as low-pitched howl of pain coming from the giant cluster of boulders wedged against the cliffs above them. To him it was a frightening concatenation of semi-human incantations. Simms just stood and stared into the night, his mouth hanging open. "Let's go—now!" Alvarado barked, trying to maintain control.

As they started down the steep incline, the powerful flashlight flickered and the circle of light turned dim yellow and…died, leaving them with the wind and the vague light of the moon. Alvarado was submerged in primitive fear as they both started yelling, falling, scrambling down the hillside in the dark to claw at the doors of the Blazer. Alvarado slammed the door as Simms ran to the passenger side. The key turned in the ignition. The engine whinnied and failed to start.

Alvarado cursed and Simms slammed his hand on the dash, shouting, "C'mon, you bitch, start!"

Some thing—a THING was with them, just beyond their vision in the dark. It stalked, it slithered, it reached out for them. Alvarado viciously turned the key again, his vision distorted with terror. This time the engine caught, sputtering, then roaring as his foot trod on the accelerator. Tires spun, throwing dirt and rocks against the roar of the wind as the vehicle fishtailed to escape the presence in the dark. A minute later they were on the dirt access road and almost to the blacktop as the headlights pointed to safety.

Suddenly Alvarado felt foolish. Everything was normal, and the off-road tires were humming on the pavement as they headed back to the plant. He was soaked with sweat, and Simms sat in silence, jaw locked, staring out the windshield. They drove down the boulevard in the silent town of Hurley to their office, stopped in a screech of locked brakes, and jumped from the Blazer to get inside the office a little too quickly.

Simms lit a cigarette and drew deeply, exhaling a cloud of smoke. He sat down and leaned back. "Were you scared, Ed?" He squinted at Alvarado's back, folding his arms in a masculine posture, the cigarette in his mouth making him ridiculous.

"Hell no!" Alvarado shot back over his shoulder, his face becoming florid in anger. He busied himself with readying the coffee machine, his fingers shaking slightly as he pulled a white paper filter from the stack. Using a circular motion, he rubbed his eyes with dirty thumb and forefinger as he composed himself and pretended he had indeed not been afraid. The aroma of ground coffee was comforting.

With the welcome dawn and end of shift, Alvarado went home where he could cast aside the mask of bravado that he had worn the remainder of that night. Ermalinda took him to bed and held him until he went to sleep.

On July 14, a small sliver had been sliced from the full moon overhead, and the two engineers agreed that the return to day shift couldn't come soon enough. The overnight hours had become tiresome and yet filled with small data evaluation tasks and nervous anticipation. Alvarado was eager to get past this cycle without another malfunction of the Geronimo station. They had taken turns with solo trips to some of the other monitoring stations, most of which were only simple metal boxes mounted on poles. The trailer on Geronimo was the most elaborate installation of the array, and it was the most unpredictable.

Two hours into the shift, Geronimo stopped transmitting. It had rained in the afternoon, but had temporarily cleared. The two engineers looked at the recorder and mouthed curses. They had to go. The clouds were threatening, so Alvarado threw yellow rain slickers into the back seat of the Blazer, and they headed out of town toward the mountain, quiet and reserved in the vehicle. They cursed technology and the EPA. Simms was taciturn, "If it starts rainin' I'm not getting out of the car." Alvarado just snorted dismissively, resigned to the task at hand.

Raindrops began to spatter the windshield as they came to a stop at the bottom of the mountain. "Let's get up there and get back down the hill before it breaks loose." Alvarado was reticent, but his work ethic prevailed. Simms heaved a sigh and looked through the windshield as the density of the raindrops increased.

As he got out of the Blazer and put on the raincoat, Alvarado was preoccupied with a vague, premonitory sense. In his imagination, he saw centuries of feet that had walked these hills. He slammed the door of the Blazer and took the lead, advancing briskly up the slope, his flash beam illuminating the path. A sudden gust of wind made the raindrops spatter his face. He grunted, putting energy into his legs and hearing footsteps trailing him a few yards behind. The lightning gave a flickering intermittent illumination to two figures picking their way unsteadily up the rock-strewn path at the base of a towering bluff.

Between the stumbling figures and the distant lightning far to the south was the industrial glow from the copper mill and smelter where the never-ending mastication of ore in the great crusher seldom allowed the night to be silent, and every few hours the sky was lighted when a sudden gash of reddish orange magma was poured from rail cars out onto the slag dump north of the plant, its suffused brilliance reflected in the billowing smoke plume from the tall stacks.

Fear was a third figure skulking unseen between the two figures as the moon turned the set of Alvarado's face to wax. After what had happened the week before, he sensed the fear animal slinking along with him. The wind increased in velocity, and he stopped momentarily, picking out the sounds of the wind or…

Simms' footsteps were gaining on him as he pointed the flashlight toward the white trailer. The 1976 company Blazer was out of sight at the bottom of the hill. "Get there—get done—get out," Alvarado was thinking in a cadence, over and over. It could have waited for morning. It should have waited until morning.

Alvarado thought suddenly about Simms, apparently struggling to catch up with him. Let him catch up on his own. He needed companionship—any companionship as the night closed around him like a fist. He didn't mind at that moment if Martin Simms was an ignorant, classic gringo, but being alone on Mount Geronimo this night made the panic swell in Alvarado's throat.

On the short drive to the base of the mountain, Simms' normal self-absorbed talk had been replaced by a dull muttering that even Alvarado's humor did not seem to penetrate.

The night was oblivious to them both. The squatting mesa brutes, grinning from their rocky dragon's mouths, were a faintly outlined pressure in the dark. Puny humans, walking among the boulders, came upon a new obstacle that had been part of the road to the station. Now the path became a knee-deep crevice, razor-cut by a flashflood sometime in the last week.

No, Alvarado thought as his work boots found footholds on the path. No, Simms was not a bad man, just a very noisy, weak one who had come to New Mexico but could not hear the voice of the land. He had not been born here, and one had to live here at least a full generation before becoming part of it.

On the other hand, Alvarado's face belonged to the desert; coarse black hair grew thickly under the hard hat. His deeply tanned face was clean shaven but for the brushy mustache. He normally feared nothing in the New Mexico night, and he fought against admitting the panic that was so real in him right now. Fingering the copper amulet about his neck, Alvarado thought of the secret, invisible world around them, the world Simms was too dense to perceive. He thought of the common legend of La Llorona, that weeping soul who walked the night wherever running water was found. Alvarado had met several Hispanic women who had seen this shrouded figure and heard her wailing. Few Anglos knew the legend, but none of them had ever seen the ghostly figure who sought her dead child. What of the darker legends that nobody but his great grandmother had ever spoken of? Whose reality would they be part of?

Ed Alvarado snorted into that bristly black mustache, his eyes focused on the path. He stopped, his breath coming in puffs. The sound again. It was not a howl or a moan as the wind whipped it into his ears, but the sound of a frightening high-pitched screech—EEEY-AAAWWRAAHHHHHHHHHEEEE—drawn out fearfully longer than a single breath of man or beast. The towering bluff of Mount Geronimo was just over his shoulder, the sheer southern rock face an opaque wall in the howling blackness.

It seemed that time had run out. The skies opened up with a deluge of wind-swept rain. A crash of thunder made Alvarado close his eyes against the panic. "Get there—get done—get out," he shouted out loud, his voice drowned by the fury of the sudden squall. Water was running along the cruel knee-deep gash in the hillside as he leaped across the gap, once again finding the path.

The Indian blood was strong in Alvarado and visible in the width of his nose, the fullness of his mouth. He knew there were things more real out here than the rocks and the desert creatures—things apprehended only the world of rituals.

Alvarado accepted that there were beings wreathed in the smoke of mesquite and juniper campfires, voices that raced with the dust devils, the living creatures of the air that Simms did not believe in, and thus could never sense.

Alvarado cocked his legs to make a dash for the trailer about 50 yards ahead as a solid sheet of water pummeled him. The thud of a collision! He lost his hard hat as something hit him, and he pitched forward onto the rocks, rolling off the path. Simms had obviously run into him from behind, and instinctively, Alvarado reached inside his soaked shirt to grab his copper talisman, while the almost-shapeless figure of Simms seemed to be shambling toward the trailer in the midst of the storm. Alvarado started to yell, but his voice caught in his throat. The idiot had not even put on a raincoat.

Getting back on his feet, drenched and covered in dirt, Alvarado once again put on his metal hat and picked up the flashlight, pointing it. The wash of panic brought the sickening taste of bile into his throat. Alvarado almost whispered, suppressing the urge to spit out a string of filthy names, his fist balled. He wanted scream at Simms, there, ahead of him in the blackness, but he was feeling something else—something soft and downy on his cheek and clogging one of his nostrils.

The flashlight could not penetrate the falling rain, and it painted a dim, wavering circle on a victim painted wetly on the page of night.

The carcass of a jackrabbit was strewn up the rocky path in front of him, ripped, torn and wet, fur drifting in fragments as though it had just been slaughtered; a spurt of terror pierced Alvarado's college education, bringing him face-to-face with the blood knowledge of his ancestors. This dead creature was not the victim of a coyote or a bobcat, and the reeking freshness of the kill in the pounding rain was horrifying to him.

Alvarado's pride was stronger than his fear, and he wouldn't show his fear to someone as contemptible as Simms. His footsteps in the dark were heavy and unsure as he began the last few yards to the monitoring station. He only imagined he could hear Simms raspy, to-bacco-impaired breathing, yards ahead of him near the trailer, but his senses were painfully heightened. The dead rabbit was behind him, and Alvarado could still feel some fragments on his face, still wet and hairy.

The white trailer squatted ahead, a pallid hunchback only dimly discernible in the reflection of the distant lights of the copper plant. The rain drummed on its metal roof

For no good reason, Alvarado remembered a discussion between himself and Simms when the man had first come to work at the plant. He couldn't even remember the words, the subjects. He only recalled how he had danced along the thin line that separates irritated words from impending violence. Did Simms know how thin the veneer of cooperation was between them?

Alvarado pointed his flashlight ahead, looking for Simms. He didn't see anybody, but the door to the trailer seemed to be open. A massive flash of lightning almost blinded him with its brightness. Alvarado found it impossible to control the shakiness of his breathing.

Miles down the canyon, the grumble of the plant concentrator mixed with the digestive sounds of the raging storm. Alvarado felt alone and isolated. The idea of Simms' companionship was no comfort, even though it was just a few more steps to the trailer.

Alvarado cursed under his breath. He sensed something in the air, and blood pressure pounded in his temples. What had the century-gone Apache drums kept at bay in the New Mexico night? What was it, unnamed and indescribable, that had hidden from the pale-skinned invaders and their half-sighted eyes? Yet something still lurked in the hills, in the very air he breathed.

Taut in every nerve and sinew, Alvarado kept his frightened breath veiled behind clenched teeth. He imagined Simms' noisy gasps like those of a wounded animal—perhaps a dying rabbit.

In the moments of deathly silence, broken only by rain sounds, Alvarado's imagination could sense a faint but growing scream, and he knew, had there been more light, he could turn around and see the cliffs of Mount Geronimo glossy with sunset blood, the smell of the slaughterhouse like salt and iron in his nostrils. He teetered on the edge of an infernal pit, the smell of terror radiating from him in waves. Was Simms unaware of what was stalking them on the New Mexico hillside?

Pointing his flashlight at the ground, Alvarado suddenly knew what he had felt in the air, that softness brushing his cheek, the tickling fragments in his nose. He could see at least 200 dead birds, perhaps many more. It was as though they had exploded in flight, dropping in fragments around the white trailer. Feather wisps still swirled in the air, driven to the ground by sheets of rain.

It was impossible to step without treading on the massed, spongy bodies. Alvarado took another glance down the slope they had fled from once before. "Get there—get done—get out." Of course, Simms must be in the trailer and, if Simms did not run, then Alvarado himself could not retreat—but Simms was ignorant, a savage in the true sense of being unaware. He suddenly thought of Simms—let him die!

Alvarado's legs yearned to send him plummeting back down the hill to safety. The rabbit, those birds…death wrapping around him like a choking garment. His yellow rain slicker was speckled with feather fragments and fur. He wanted to think of the warmth and light of daytime, the breath of life, but he could find nothing in his mind but here and now. He called out, "Simms. Hit that light switch," but he knew that words could stop nothing. His mind was screaming to know what had drawn the birds to their destruction in the middle of the storm.

It was only for an instant that he tried to seek a "logical, scientific solution" as the last meaningless classroom discussions dwindled into mumbles. He knew better. It was just here, large as the mountain, as inexorable as time and shaped with the minds of all those it had possessed since the creation.

"Madre de Dios, Holy Mother of God." The words were his own, pumped from his throat as a tremendous burst of wind shrieked through the rocks, driving the rain before it, insane with roaring, tearing at hair and clothes. Alvarado heard his hard hat skittering down the hillside making faint, hollow metallic sounds until it was gone. He crouched, spittle slobbering his lips. Needles of grit and water scoured him, digging at his face. He gagged as feathers clotted in his mouth. The sound of the mountain was a natural cataclysm, blinding him, deafening him. The flashlight had gone out again.

Desperately, Alvarado fumbled with the 6-volt flashlight trying to work the switch. His fingers were almost useless sausages as he stabbed at the switch. The light came on again. His eyes stung with the pain of the grit in them. Simms had to be inside the trailer, but the howling river of wind and rain had coated the flashlight lens with muck and turned the light beam gray and mottled.

The figure was standing in the open door of the blacked-out monitor trailer, face grinning without a smile, eyes empty. This was not…Alvarado coiled in self defense, his primal scream torn from him by the night wind.

That sallow face and limp strands of soaking hair—the misshapen, jagged brown teeth and sagging skin—reaching hands like talons and a soaked shirt unbuttoned and hanging open to hide a mockery of human form. The blank eyes were looking at Alvarado as his flash beam was fading, dimming, irretrievably lost like the lives of the birds and the rabbit. With the whip of his right arm, Alvarado threw the useless flashlight in Simms' direction. The hard rain was still slashing in on him, stinging his face and peppering the raincoat. Footsteps came pounding toward him while the mouth gaped in a frightening screech— EEEYAAAWWRAAHHHHHHHHEEEE.

Like an animal, Alvarado fought as the thing threw itself upon him. His hands clutched flesh and tore. The wetness, dirt, and terror formed a glutinous suffocating mass that was trying to kill him. He rolled upon the ground, kicking, biting, vomiting at the foetor of an unholy smell.

Alvarado did not know which were his screams and which was…the other. And the open door of that white trailer banged hollowly in the wind while hard-driven rain created a din on the aluminum shell of the station. He called for help in the ancestral network of his racial memory and redoubled his desperate fight for life. The rain was a hammering bombardment, turning the soil into wriggling watercourses down the hillside, its intensity welling, the grappling forms turning the ground a hideous pink mercifully hidden by the black night.

Alvarado's hands clutched at a leathery throat. There was a gurgling, a crack of bone, and then Alvarado rolled away from the twitching, dying loathsome form. His only thought was that Mount Geronimo was glistening with blood but, when he regained some sense of composure, the blackness still surrounded him. He had won. His fingernails were broken, and he throbbed with the pain of bruises, abrasions, and cuts. His clothes were sodden and sloppy with dirt, the rain, and—other wetness.

The rain softened, the wind abating to a cool breeze. Alvarado's eyes were clogged with debris, and this was probably the only reason that he sobbed. The whole world was black, and he sought only to escape.

Alvarado stumbled down the hillside, falling. Every time he fell, he did not care because his limpness did not allow him to be hurt. There was no steel left in him. Through the arroyo. "Get there—get done—get out." Find the path. Get to the safety of the company vehicle. He dared not think what he had done, whom he had killed during the frenzy of madness, or what he had left behind him.

Water was running ankle deep in the arroyo, and he leaned against the rocky, crumbling bank, exhausted and panting. He had left Simms dead up there, or was it Simms? Alvarado's stomach retched with the memory of flesh yielding to his raking fingers.

It seemed almost beyond his ability, but he clambered out of the shallow arroyo. Twice he stumbled against large rocks in the dark. He could still hear the banging of the trailer door in the night, like the distorted tolling of a miscast bell high on the hill, still flailing in rhythm with the thing that walked on the wind. The clouds parted briefly, and the moon lent a dim pallor to the hillside and the towering bluff behind him.

The next thing he felt was shiny and cold. The spasm of fright subsided. The fender of the Blazer! Alvarado was too spent to care about what had happened as he leaned against the cold, wet metal.

They could do what they wanted to him. He was still alive. He leaned there for at least a minute, gathering strength to extract the car key from his sodden trousers and wincing at the pain in his damaged and bleeding hand.

Alvarado stumbled to the door on the driver's side, and he crawled inside, eyes closed, feeling the comfortable projection of the key into the ignition and the thunk as he pulled the car door closed to shut out the madness in the night. As the engine roared to life, he leaned against the steering wheel, its cool, hard pressure a caress on his left temple.

Alvarado's next scream was just a croak.

Sitting in the passenger seat was Martin Simms, unsullied, and noiseless. Simms' lips were pulled back into an empty grin, his clothes unwrinkled and completely dry, eyes staring at nothing through the windshield. Alvarado screamed again from the bottom of his soul as a hollow rattling sound bubbled from the throat of creature in the seat beside him.

* * *

The smelter furnaces are long since frozen, the smokestacks reduced to rubble, and the excavation in the great open pit has slowed after at least two centuries of continuous work. Nobody is allowed to go to those rocky hillsides behind the plant. Some say it is because the security goons of the copper company arrest interlopers and sometimes assault them, but others say there are secret reasons why people have been barred from the hills near Mount Geronimo for the past four decades.

Of course, no charges were laid against Alvarado in 1976, even though he delivered Martin Simms to the ambulance in a catatonic state. There was no physical damage or cause for Simms' malady, but within a week, the man's condition changed without him ever regaining consciousness—the deterioration of Simms' body was said to be "startling" to the doctors at the regional medical center who looked after the empty shell, though they mumbled something to his family about a "myocardial infarction" and a "possible brain aneurysm." Simms was unresponsive to any stimulation, and it was only a matter of another week before the febrile life processes stopped abruptly, and the body collapsed in on itself as though there was nothing inside. Alvarado only knew that he drove back to town accompanied by an empty husk of a man. He fingered his copper amulet and prayed to his bisabuela for salvation.

Alvarado said only that he had fallen on the hillside that night, and when the company abandoned the monitoring station at Mount Geronimo, they found some fur, bird corpses, but nothing else on the disturbed ground outside the trailer when they hauled it away. And I have done my part to tell the story as it actually happened all those years ago.

As a postscript, a lifelong friend of mine is a private pilot in Silver City who offered the service to families of scattering ashes of their loved ones over familiar landmarks in the district or in the forested mountains.

One of his most recent clients was a counter-culture woman whose long-time companion was a full-blooded Apache. When the man died, his last wishes were fulfilled when my friend flew the woman in his Cessna 172 low over Mount Geronimo, and the white cloud of sacred ashes settled on the bluffs to make him the last Apache to hold watch on the mountain.

As for Alvarado, the sanguine color on the late afternoon rock bluff of Mount Geronimo told him where Simms had gone, and no words would ever explain it. He was content in his retirement to look toward that stone mountain from a distance, and he stayed indoors on stormy summer nights when the lightning flickered blood-red behind the three peaks of the Tres Hermanas on this side of the border just across from Old Mexico.

Terror Tales of the Southwest

In the Treasure Room of Verdez

"There are many properties that remain after death; and these are things in which the idea of the matter is less swallowed up, according to Plato, in them even after death, that which is immortal in them will work some wonderful things—" **The Grimoire of Albertus Magnus**

Camino Real, the royal road that led from Mexico City to Santa Fe, was traveled by Conquistadors who were steeped in the lore and barbarism of the Inquisition. They slaughtered the Aztecs and punished shamanism and witchcraft they encountered in their path; however, there was a gap between the settlements of Old Mexico, the Paso del Norte (now El Paso), and the northern New Mexico Indian pueblos with their own witches and legends. Santa Fe was the Spanish imperial outpost, but to get there, one had to traverse the Jornada del Muerte, one hundred miles of death south of Socorro, the town named for relief. It was more the miasmic bosques of the Rio Grande and the swamp sicknesses than it was thirst and heat that killed the travelers. South of Socorro, the cruelties of the Spaniard were destined to turn the Apache into an unprecedented force for terror in the 19th century West.

The Indians learned their tactics from the disciples of Toledo, and some of the Conquistadors were rumored to follow even darker beliefs. It was in their relentless search for the treasures of Cibola that the Spaniards wandered from the Rio Grande valley and westward into the southern New Mexico foothills, where they were given land grants by the King of Spain to mine gold, silver, and copper in the shadow of the iconic mountain named The Kneeling Nun—*monja arrodillada*—can be seen throughout much of the county, with an almost-human shaped rock pillar facing a cliff as though in prayer.

In the late 19th Century, the Territorial Government of New Mexico voided the grants and opened the way for American exploitation that became a major industry in the 20th Century. Tantalizing stories of Spanish treasure became part of the oral tradition, persisting in the decades after WWII.

The Remarkable Narrative of Peter Whitcombe

"I suppose you came to hear about the treasure." A pair of faded, blue, rheumy eyes peered at the younger man standing at the door of the room. The eyes were set in sockets creased like bellows; the face was bleached leather, and the stubbled beard was white.

"Yessir, I'm doing some research for an article I'm writing, and I've heard you knew something about a treasure in somewhere around the Santa Rita open pit mine. I saw that article in the Silver City Daily Press..." For Peter Whitcombe in 1977, the article was provocative enough for him to drive almost six hours from Silver City, through Albuquerque and to the New Mexico city of Las Vegas, the location of the State Hospital. The article itself was written by a Rick Peterson whose news beat was usually positive news about the copper corporation working both the Santa Rita operation east of Silver City and the Tyrone mine west of town. There is no doubt that the copper industry was the life blood of the community for most of the 20th Century.

HURLEY MAN STILL MISSING
Trespassing charge leads to mental evaluation for alleged artifacts looter

SILVER CITY—A Hurley man is still missing while his companion was remanded Monday to mental health evaluation after being charged with trespassing on Phipps-Dodd property late last week.

J.W. Shelley, of Silver City, remained in custody after appearing in Magistrate's Court on the charge, while Grant County Sheriff's Department officials question him concerning the whereabouts of H. McGrath, 34, of Hurley, who was reported missing by his family Saturday.

From the police report, Shelley was reported as having told PD security agents that he was treasure hunting on copper corporation land, but he was found wandering in a canyon south of Santa Rita late Friday.

Sheriff T.J. Ryan told reporters Saturday that Shelley was "disheveled" and that he had no hiking equipment. Ryan also said that Shelley's clothes were blood-stained and that he was disoriented and incoherent when taken into custody.

Phipps-Dodd Security officer Luis Apodaca confiscated metal and wood scraps from Shelley when he was apprehended.

The company prohibits entry onto posted property for "safety and environmental reasons." He said that looters and pot hunters are a problem for them.

Unfounded treasure legends are common in the county, but historians discount them as fantasies.

(see "missing" p.6)

The younger man, perhaps 28, held the lined legal-sized notepad a little too tightly while he allowed Shelley to read the clipping from the previous year. It was Peterson who told Whitcombe how the case had been resolved, with Shelley committed to the State Hospital, diagnosed as schizophrenic with hebephrenic tendencies.

Whitcombe was not certain what that diagnosis meant, but he was interested in the tale of hidden treasure that local residents connected with the case, and it intrigued him enough to decide upon writing an article for *Treasure* magazine. It also required that he find J.W. Shelley and get an interview with him, much as Whitcombe disliked the idea of visiting an asylum, even if such installations were euphemistically called "mental health facilitieis" in the modern parlance.

Las Vegas, N.M., lies northeast of Santa Fe on Interstate 25 on the way to the Colorado border. After driving from Silver City the better part of a day, Whitcombe left the interstate and located the dour rectangular three-story hospital with its center entrance topped by a roof peak that had stood since the turn of the century and previously called more honestly the state insane asylum. Every state had at least one, until compassionate and enlightened post-1960s legislators turned inmates out onto the streets to found the generation of the homeless.

The reception staff members at the State Hospital were cordial and accommodating. They told him that Shelley certainly claimed to know about a "hidden trove" in the time he had been in their charge, but they told him nothing else as he was escorted him down the waxed hallway of the second floor under banks of fluorescent lights. A burly nurse with short, steel gray hair escorted him, assuring him that Shelley was not dangerous while under medication. Now, standing in an 8-bed ward at the foot of the man's bed, Whitcombe felt a sense of anticlimax. Shelley was just an aging desert rat in a hospital gown, his mouth moving regularly, probably in response to some antipsychotic drugs. A white-painted straight-backed wooden chair was against the wall by the bed.

When Whitcombe sat down in the chair it wobbled either from a missing tip on one leg, or a floor out of level. It made him all the more uncomfortable as he rubbed his cheek and felt the perspiration gathering at his armpits.

Shelley read the article Whitcombe offered to him, mumbling as he read, "That article? I remember that. Those newspaper hacks are in the back pocket of goons at the Phipps-Dodd Copper Company. I'm telling you, they sure roughed me up when they caught me, I'll tell that much. That's why the newspaper article talks about trespassing. It was all lies. C'mon, c'mon and pull the chair closer. I told about it before and I don't mind talkin'. I don't think anybody believed me though. Guess that's what happens when a fella puts on the years. Oh, before I start, get up and pull those blinds. For some reason I can't stand too much sun any more." The mid-afternoon sun was fiercely shining through grime-hazed west-facing windows. The protective iron mesh grill on the outside made chessboard patterns on varnished wooden floor of the ward.

As he drew the blinds, Whitcombe glanced at the man's face. He was old, true, but his teeth were even and strong, and the face, though traced with the well-earned lines of middle age, was still full. The overhead fluorescents were off, and in the dim light, Shelley grunted approval and began his well-practiced tale in a strong, even voice. The only other sound in the room was the whisper of Whitcombe's cheap BIC ballpoint stick pen. There were four other patients in the ward, all sleeping.

"Back when I was younger I lived down near Silver City, and exploring old mines was a hobby of mine. By the time I was in my 20s, I had visited just about every hole in the ground that wasn't still being dug—ah, of course the biggest hole in the state is that giant hole owned by Phipps-Dodd. You shoulda met that friend of mine, Herb McGrath; he and I used to go out on weekends, sometimes following treasure descriptions in hopes of finding even a trace of the Spanish loot left there between 1800 and 1873. Before Phipps-Dodd bought out the old Kennecott Copper Corporation, the company was tolerant of employees who wanted to hike in all that country they owned between Santa Rita and Hurley. Then, those P-D bastards bought them out and hired patrols like they was a secret government installation…

"Guess it was McGrath one year who came up with the information on Emilio Soliz Verdez." Shelley mentioned a book, and Whitcombe scribbled down the title.[1]

"The book only had one paragraph on Verdez, but who the hell would care about one of Carrasco's irresponsible lieutenants. Anyhow, as I remember—and it seems like a good time back—the book hints that Verdez didn't think no more of Indians than he thought about grasshoppers, unless they were women. Verdez wasn't too orthodox in his religion neither, according to the stuff McGrath found in that book.[2]

"Anyway, Verdez really piled up some loot, getting ready to move the whole pile back to Chihuahua and over to Spain when the time was right, but Carrasco did him in and left the treasure where it was. Naw, I didn't believe it at first either, but McGrath, he persuaded me that we should set out looking for it. From the only surviving documents from Carrasco, we know that he disliked Verdez and nicknamed him 'the Moor' because he was darker than many of the Spaniards, and he had some Moorish blood to go along with what Carrasco described as a 'mutinous disposition'.

"Now, you have to understand that there's a lot of public land under the Bureau of Land Management in New Mexico, but those Phipps-Dodd people who bought the mines in the 1980s never cared about the people of New Mexico, and they kept people from crossing their land, even by force when their so-called 'security patrols' found anyone on their property. Still, McGrath and me had lived in the area most of our lives, and we knew ways to avoid the armed patrols. We started by looking for the traces of where the Spanish used to haul their copper south from Santa Rita and then we spent months studying books and those big ol' USGS survey maps. We spent weeks walking up and down every cussed canyon for 20 square miles.

---

[1] Vaskov, Samuel P. The Conquistadors and the Settling of New Spain. Southwestern State University Press, Las Cruces 1923.

[2] Vaskov, op. cit. p. 139-140: (by permission of the publisher) "General Manuel de Carrasco discovered the mountain of copper at Santa Rita after an Indian revealed the secret to him, but the development of the mines was left to Miguel Elguea, a businessman from Chihuahua. Carrasco had problems with some of his officers, including Emilo Soliz Verdez, a particularly troublesome lieutenant who seemed to have heretical ideas.

"…Verdez and several of his men split off from Carrasco in May 1803. He and 22 followers went south from Loma del Cobre that was to become the Santa Rita mine. They pillaged more than one Indian village and established their own feudal autocracy that stood for two years before Carrasco's troops suddenly descended upon them and all were ruthlessly extirpated by Carrasco's men. This battle seemed to have been bloody and wearing on the Spaniards and, while their records mention the contact, they sedulously avoid any descriptions of what they found.

"Some historians claim that the story of Verdez and the battle that resulted in the deaths of every Verdez man must be an imposture because Carrasco was not one to spill Spanish blood unless it was a threat to his existence. The Verdez colony and mine was not such a danger and could have easily been ignored by Carrasco. Most accounts gloss over the general's stay in Santa Rita, mentioning that he went back to Chihuahua; however, this punitive expedition of three days was certainly possible, and facts support the account as given here.

"A cryptic account of Carrasco's letters to Spain also mentions the 'richest treasure of all, the location of which died with Verdez'.

"All the foregoing contributes to the opinion of many historians that Carrasco's aversion to Verdez' peculiar form of worship explains the thoroughness of the massacre as well as the neglect of Carrasco to take back the treasure that Verdez had amassed. One surviving letter, however, addressed to his business partner Elguea contained a description of the location of such a treasure. It was never explained why Elguea did not send his mine managers to look for the treasure supposedly so close to Santa Rita."

Terror Tales of the Southwest

"What started us was a reproduced document in one of those books on lost mines and buried fortunes. Why not? Ol' Doc Noss found the treasure of Victorio Peak down in Doña Ana County in '37 didn't he—for all the good it did him." Shelley's laugh was a cackle. "Noss got himself shot—then came the war, and the government finally took out that treasure in '69 in a top secret operation. Why not? Noss never figured on the government turning New Mexico into a missile range. Anyhow, I remember the translation of that Verdez letter word for word, even after all this time:

> **…From the place called Loma del Cobre, go south to the place where the ten Indians were killed, then look for a wooden cross atop of a rinconada. Go to this and at the bottom you will find another cross chiseled in the rock face. Sit with your back to it and you will be looking between two mesas to a third almost half an hour's walk distance. The entrance to the cavern is covered and well guarded, but the believer will not pay the price. Find inside 25 burro loads of gold and silver. Offer part of it as sacrifice to Astarte lest she be angered, then take the treasure to Paso del Norte where I will meet you for the journey home. Do not hesitate to kill anyone you encounter on the way.   — Verdez**

"The book labeled the description as a phony, but McGrath and me, we figured it was a little too strange to be false, and very few people had ever heard the name Verdez. We figured the map position of the original hill of copper, even though it's now that giant open pit mine, and we positioned ourselves in the hills south of the mine. We figured, what if Carrasco wiped out Verdez and his band before Verdez could meet the retrieval crew he summoned by that letter. They were supposed to bring burros and take the goods down to the Camino Real…at least we figured it that way."

"I remember that Sunday in July. It was damned hot, and we'd just sat down in the shade of a cliff face. It was almost like being at the gum line of a giant line of teeth, and I was running my hand along the smooth rock, when I felt an unnatural indentation. We moved some small rocks and some of the fill, down about 18 inches, and there was an indubitable faint cross cut into the rock. I sat down with my back to the rock face; I can still feel how warm that rock felt on my back. As I sat there, with McGrath squatting beside me, we were looking across at a non-descript mesa about a mile away, where the treasure cave was supposed to be.

"Yeah, you can bet we were excited as we drank from our canteens and shouldered our packs, but when we made our way to that mesa 25 minutes later—just like the letter described—all we got was a letdown. We couldn't find anything like a cave or a cave opening. So, what'd we do? Of course, we came back off and on for three months running—folks thought our brains were baked, and we always ran the risk of getting caught crossing company property to get back into the hills. We were bone-tired that day in October, and we were losing confidence, But then—but then we found an opening. We were giddy as school girls." Shelley's laugh was almost a cackle, and Whitcombe was startled at Shelley's intensity.

"It's been said that when the Apache hides something, the white man will not be able to find it. Now they learned treachery from the Spanish, among even worse traits, but there is no doubt that the Spaniards were a lot more clever than we consider today."

Whitcombe scribbled furiously, certain that this man was just as insane as the doctors suggested, but the Silver City newspaper had missed a feature angle that was a sure reader magnet. He thought if he could find Shelley's partner McGrath, he could tie up some loose ends and end up with a fascinating magazine article. Whitcombe interrupted the thread of the interview, asking Shelley about McGrath, but the man in the bed just waved impatiently in the semi-darkness.

"Like I was saying, 180 years of wind, dust, rain, brush, hid all traces of the opening, but we finally saw a crevice between two closely wedged rocks buried in the ground. Those rocks were too regular, about five feet in length, with facing edges almost parallel. With a little imagination, you could almost see them as a pair of cellar doors at the back of a house. They looked like boulders, but we found they were actually rock slabs and so thick they couldn't be moved. We could get close to the crack between 'em and see an opening that seemed to go down at a steep angle. We could also smell the dank air inside the opening. Higher up on the slope, above those rough slabs, we could see that a pile of small boulders arranged like they was covering what must have been a larger opening at one time.

In the Cavern of Verdez

"Anyhow, on the next trip we brought electric lanterns, rope, pick and shovel, all the gear we could carry, and all we'd need to make us both rich. God, it seems so long ago now, but we dug in the hot sunlight for hours, sweating and aching, palms blistering, until we cleared enough dirt to put a lever between those two wedged rock blades and to gradually pry them apart. It was on the next trip that we were able to move them apart about 40 inches. Now we had a hole big enough to let a man down and leave some breathing space. I mean, if you saw McGrath's waistline, you'd know we needed that extra space. He was all muscle, but never skinny like me.

"I'd say it was a little before noon that day when McGrath took the lantern, and I held the rope as he eased down into the blackness; it wasn't a minute before he called up to me, and I went skinning down after him, my heart pounding.

"There we were inside the hill. We'd gone from noon brightness to total blackness except for that bright oblong of the entry slit above us. It looked to us like we was in a small chamber. We had to push past a dirt pile—probably the original entrance that had been blocked up, maybe even by Carrasco himself. We didn't care, and I guess we had a raging case of the gold fever. We didn't care about anything so long as we got out of there with a fortune. Now, as I remember, we went down a slope to the right—no, it was my left—I remember because we wanted to make sure we didn't get lost."

Shelley's voice had become almost hypnotic for Whitcombe, and the young writer knew that Shelley's story was about something that really happened to him. Perhaps there could be a treasure after all.

"What with it being 90 degrees outside, it felt cold inside this cave. Ya know, if you're in a cave where the air is colder than the outside, you know there's bound to be some underground water running through it. Anyhow, we started pussyfootin' in the dark passage when we saw the first signs.

"We musta been the first ones down there since Carrasco dealt with those heretics and

Terror Tales of the Southwest

sealed the main entrance. The passageway was about 50 inches wide, and the ceiling receded into the blackness, formed by rock that seemed to form praying hands under the earth. In the middle of this hard floor were the scattered bones of a skeleton, and a rusted breastplate punctured by the remains of a lance.

"Now I was getting kinda jittery, what with seeing the bodies of a man dead since the time of Napoleon. The solid rock walls of the cavern were black in places where they had been scorched by torches once set into chiseled crevices in the living rock, but moss and lichens crusted heavily over most everything else. The air smelled of mold and a faint noxious odor.

"We walked downward into the hill another 25 feet or more when we came to an open place and, even in the orange light of the electric lanterns, we could see enough to make any man sick. I'm telling you, Son, it was like a tornado in a graveyard, with bones and pieces of axes, helmets and the like, mixed up and standing in heaps.

"There was about an inch of slimy green water on the rock floor, and I can still see the way a sickly white fungus covered most of any bones protruding upward, mixing with the foul water to form yellow-green mounds where bodies had fallen. I could almost hear the cursing as Spaniard fought Spaniard in religious frenzy; I can almost hear the screams of the dying even now."

Whitcombe kept writing, but he fidgeted in his chair, seemingly torn between the desire to finish the story, and the urge to leave this room that he began to imagine as having an unwholesome smell.

Shelley never stopped talking, sometimes his voice hollow and other times sere and sandy, like rice cascading onto aluminum foil. "We walked careful-like, and still we could feel things beneath our boots crumbling like sodden chalk. Beyond that open place—we couldn't even see the ceiling now—were two doors, or what was left of doors anyway. Those doors probably led to the mining tunnels. I picked the left-hand opening, and McGrath chose the right. I pushed aside the collapsing rotten wood and stepped inside the left-hand passageway. All I found was more skeletons...or scattered bones that used to be skeletons; they was piled against walls along with rusted chains and manacles. It looked like a damned torture chamber. No wonder this Verdez wasn't liked so good!

"When I walked back out into the main chamber, the only noise I could hear was the soft crunching of what was under my wet boots. I didn't know whether McGrath had found anything because I couldn't see his lantern in the other shaft. I stood there listening for what seemed a very long time. I started thinking ugly things, and...*que no*...the other room...I won't go in there! Not me!" Shelley's voice was suddenly booming, filling the hospital room, dominating, demanding.

There came some confused muttering from two other patients who were awakened by the rising tide of Shelley's monologue.

Whitcombe had stopped scribbling on his notepad. From the beginning, he had been almost lulled by the earlier rhythms of Shelley's voice. But now, now he snapped to attention.

The voice had changed pitch and intensity; Shelley was obviously no longer aware of the dim hospital ward but was living again in the darkness of the subterranean cavern of Emilio Soliz Verdez. Shelley's slip into Spanish seemed alien, almost as though adopting the voice of some other man, someone sinister and threatening. Whitcombe remembered the psychological label the hospital had given for Shelley.

After a few moments of wheezing and shuddering, Shelley seemed to struggle and then gain control again, his voice dropping back to normal tone and volume as he shifted in the bed. "I listened for a coupla seconds—didn't hear nothing—so I took a deep breath and went through the second door where McGrath had gone. The door was probably crude pine planks strapped together with copper bands, but the whole thing was rotten and crumbling. The wood was just about gone, and the strapping was twisted and wilting, drooping where I touched it. There was a greenish-black copper plate nailed to one of the fallen door planks with some Spanish words inscribed on it, but my Spanish was never too good and, besides, the corrosion would make it impossible to figure out."

Shelley's voice was changing again, getting more cracked and urgent. Occasionally it would break into a deep, almost bass, then wind up to a febrile tenor. "That room...that shaft...so big that a man couldn't see the end of it, nor either side. I was alone in that circle of my lantern light and, Son, I didn't like it too good. I yelled once for McGrath, but I couldn't stand hearin' the echoes go bouncing from wherever that cave ended. I stood there, wondering whether I should go down into the blackness looking for McGrath or just stay there close to the door. I made up my mind to stay, but then I heard the echo of something bumping against a rock far, far, down from the circle of my light. It musta been McGrath, so I took off walking in a straight line toward the noise. The dark dissolved the light from my lantern like water dissolves sugar, but I kept goin'."

The Legacy of Astarte

The man in the bed breathed with terrified excitement. "But wait, I did find the treasure of Verdez! I was there, and I saw plunder piled up, waiting to be taken out...and I...I..." Even the bed was shaking now.

Whitcombe bolted out of his chair, wondering whether to call for a nurse or an attendant. The fear feeling in the room was contagious. The other patients were mumbling in the ward—a disturbing undercurrent as though conspiring against him.

Shelley was in another world, though. "I saw a form ahead—it was McGrath. His lantern was dead in his hand, and he turned around to look at me. 'Emilio?' He said it in my direction and, in the light of my lantern, I could see his eyes was empty, his face slack and vacant.

"McGrath! I shout, but he slings the lantern at me and begins to run deeper into that massive cave, moaning like a crazy man. I followed quick as I could. I wanted to grab him and get us both outa there, until I heard somethin' else. I stopped and listened. It was like a whisper, getting louder, and I could hear some of the words now."

Whitcombe had backed away from the bed now, unable to believe the distended tale of the older man in the bed, but it did not stop the younger man's breath from being ragged, nor his heart from thudding. The cheap ballpoint pen had fallen to the floor, and he clutched the yellow legal pad against his chest.

Shelley was speaking to the darkness now, and Whitcombe no longer existed for him, if indeed he ever had. "I don't care what the hell you're sayin'...*Madre de Dios*...I can see the gold. No, don't say that...I couldn't kill my friend, not for all the *Escudos* in...

"*Si! Muerte por…*only those who believe with us can live forever. Wait. Your voice is fading! The gold! What about the gold? It drips with ancient blood. Yes, I hear you now. General Carrasco was a fool. In the end he ran and left us here with our goddess. *Astarte nostro.*" Was Shelley listening to voices in his head or the ominous mutterings of those other patients who were now sitting up and looking in their direction.

"Astarte? What the hell is this? I'm not listenin' to you no more. You deserve to be dead." Shelley's voice changed pitch again. "Ah, but I have known the joy of seeing blood running from the sword! *Muy Excellente!*" It was a dialogue between two men coming out of one mouth.

But then, Whitcombe thought in spasms of fright, what of those other voices in the ward. They were now exchanging phrases in Spanish, conspiratorial, threatening.

Whitcombe was sweating, his breathing labored, and he felt the mantle of exhaustion falling over him like a suffocating wool blanket. Still, he tried to keep up as Shelley coughed up phlegm onto the white hospital gown, and the sheet now pulled up to his chest. But Shelley was ready to talk again, his voice changing again

"I've held a bar a that gold in my hand, blackened with old impurities, twisted at the end like a piece of taffy…musta weighed 60 pounds or more. Time I was leavin', but Verdez is just out of sight, talking, and his compadres are mumbling in the background. They are lookin' in my direction. He's right about this sword—it has a good heft to it, but I wouldn't…still, Maldonado is not a true believer. Those who don't believe must die. I must find him—I will find him even in the darkness. I know this shaft so very well, and Astarte will surely be pleased."

Again, Shelley's voice shifted gears, now urgent. "Verdez, you Moor *bastardo*! You're not getting my mind or my soul…" Shelley was twisting in the bed as though wrestling a doppelgänger. His legs beat a muffled tattoo under the rustling sheet.

Whitcombe furrowed his brow, now confused as to who was speaking in the semi-darkness now that the late afternoon sun had dipped behind the hills surrounding the New Mexico town of Las Vegas. The voice he heard was now sonorous and measured, its phrasing literate and menacing.

"But time is a river in my veins, and the old joys of rape and murder are like a blazing fire before my eyes. There is nothing to compare with the glories of the past. *Dios*, but the power is in me! The things I have seen would wither and blast an ordinary man. The blood sacrifice shall expiate his heresy. We shall take Maldonado to the altar. *Magna Astarte*, may his screams be pleasing to you as his blood…runs…out."

Shelley was sitting erect in the bed now, and Whitcombe listened in terror and fascination, his back against the wall, looking toward the door. Shelley's voice abruptly changed again. Now it was weak and cracked, dry as sun-baked mud.

"Did I go ta sleep on you?" Shelley's head was slumped down, chin on chest, but Whitcombe just wanted to get out of the room, and he was paying little attention to the figure on the bed.

"Sorry, but an old man does things like that, I s'pose. Anyhow, nobody ever saw McGrath again. They questioned me, but I swear I never saw him again. I don't even know how I climbed the rope to get out of that cave. I'll tell you one thing: I know the treasure is still down there, even to this day.

"I was told at the time that they found me wanderin' around one of the canyons below Santa Rita. It was that damned company patrol that grabbed me and called the Grant County Sheriff's office. They took me into Silver City, first to jail, and then to the hospital. I guess they didn't believe my story 'bout the hill, and the cave size. They say there isn't any such place out there. Those company goons sure did question me, I'll tell you that. I had bruises to prove it. My bet is that they went after the treasure just like the military went after the treasure ol' Doc Noss found in Victorio Peak down by Las Cruces. They'll get more than they bargained for if they go down there. I can promise you that." Shelley's sentence ended with an obscene tittering sound—a secret laugh.

"Think I'd best sleep a bit now. The older you gets, the more rest you need. I'll sketch you a map of the place if you want it—even split with you 50-50 if you dare to go down there."

Whitcombe declined the offer nervously and began his farewells to the man hunched in the grey dimness of the room. The other patients had settled silently back into their beds.

Shelley stopped him one more time. "Oh, before ya leave, open those blinds again. I'd sorta like to get that last little bit of daylight in here while I'm restin'."

Whitcombe approached and nervously pulled the cord on the vertical blinds. Then he suddenly swallowed his breath, almost gasping. The man he was looking at now in the salmon light of late afternoon fading sun was a caricature of the J.W. Shelley he had introduced himself to an hour before. Dry skin was pulled tight in a scabrous brown mask across the man's skull, and the bones were clearly outlined in the shrinking flesh of thin, skeletal hands. The mouth was a nest of discolored, misshapen teeth, and one incisor, black with decay, clung obscenely to the front of the man's hospital gown where it had just fallen.

Shelley's voice reached Whitcombe as he opened the door. "We will share a great treasure when you come back to get me…" There was menace and darkness in the wheezing voice, suddenly turned deep— "…*compañero*…" A desiccated hand stretched out in Whitcombe's direction as the frightened writer fled from the ward.

Later, when Peter Whitcombe sought to make sense of what he had seen, he only found in books that the Pagan worship of Astarte also used the infernal name of Ashtaroth, and her worship was widespread in the ancient Pagan world. What Whitcombe experienced convinced him that the Christian crusade against Paganism after 300 A.D. had some justification. Tumescent Christianity led to the utter destruction of the Pagan temples and the torching of the Libraries of Alexandria.

The true history of Astarte's devotees was razed in the frenzy of conversion. He never even contemplated further research. The day of the interview put an end to a story he would never write for a treasure magazine. For it was the eyes that hastened Whitcombe edging from that hospital room, almost fleeing, without a further word. In the late afternoon sunlight, piercing eyes of angry brown-black showed no temper of pity or humanity as they followed him hungrily to the door of the ward.

As Whitcombe was leaving the State Hospital, he remembered asking at the main nursing station about the patient's illness. Though she said it was against policy, the nurse who had escorted him to Shelley's room pulled open the Steelcase grey metal cabinet and removed a thick file folder with a white 4"x6" white label pasted to the outside. She looked at

Terror Tales of the Southwest

him and shook her head slightly as he locked eyes on her briefly, pushed the file back across the counter, and turned toward the entrance. Whitcombe swallowed hard and rushed from the hospital.

The newspaper clipping that he had brought with him was crumpled in his hand, and he now knew that Shelley had been committed to the hospital only the year before. The label read:

J.W. SHELLEY
SILVER CITY, NEW MEXICO
Admitted: 6/28   Diagnosis: Schizophrenia
Age: 26

Postscript: It was 31 years later when Whitcombe pulled the legal pad from his manuscript file with a plan to type it into his new Macintosh computer. His features were still youthful, but his hairline was starting to recede.

Though he knew that Shelley was long dead, Whitcombe could feel again the queasiness from that long-ago afternoon in a room of the State Hospital. The copper mines of Grant County had been sold again, this time to a firm with headquarters in Indonesia, but a friend told him that trespassers on the thousands of acres still controlled by the company were forcefully detained and prosecuted, just as interlopers on the White Sands Missile Range Victorio Peak property faced federal charges. Whitcombe wondered again about the reasons.

As he looked through the notes for the unfinished treasure story, he was reminded that Shelley's friend McGrath was never found, and Whitcombe knew where he had gone, sacrificed to Astarte in the blackness of that nitrous cave under the hills south of Santa Rita where a foul charnel wind blows upward from a place of demons.

Terror Tales of the Southwest

The Cure

*"Those unwittingly...consuming what a witch proffers...find to their sorrow
that some animals alive and gnawing forms in their stomachs."*
Marc Simmons' 1974 Witchcraft in the Southwest

The Healer of San Vicente

San Vicente is an incestuous town so much like hundreds of others with deep
roots, but it is my town. Underneath the veneer of normalcy on its streets, I saw
with my own eyes a thing churning in Lalo Hernandez's belly, and I cannot forget the loathsome shape of it as it destroyed him. That night I became a believer in the *curandera* and, as
well, in a harsh justice as old as the hills of New Mexico.

For me it began at the high school and a visit from sophomore student Amelia Valles.
In the early 1980s I was employed by the school system to do career counseling and aptitude
testing among other duties.

I met Mirabel Valles, Amelia's mother, at the fall open house, and she told me of her
concern that her daughter should have an ambition in life beyond a boyfriend. Mirabel con-
fided in me that, even though she was college educated and an administrative employee in
the city offices downtown, her calling was as a *curandera*. I confessed to her that I could not
even pronounce the word, much less understand what she did.

Mirabel formally introduced me to her daughter, who smiled pleasantly but seemed to
have more interest in a gaggle of her fellow students whom she joined as her mother talked
with me.

She chuckled as I revealed my interest in the occult. I asked if her therapies had any
overtones of magic. Mirabel raised a well-manicured finger and looked at me with dark and
piercing eyes as though she were going to impart a secret. "No, Dear, most of my work is
as a volunteer midwife, and I am a *yerbera* —you know, a worker with herbs."

"How does a cur...and...er...sorry, I messed that up...does that have anything to do
with the bruja? I know how to pronounce that one."

Mirabel smiled, "I go to Mass, and that is the difference. Father Simone blesses my
work, and I can just look at a person to know how they need to be healed." She was looking
at me, and I was suddenly a little uncomfortable and feeling the strength of her personality,
even though the room was filled with parents and some students.

She took my hand a second time, "Anyhow, my Amelia will come see you for some career counseling, and I think we will talk again."

"I hope so," I blurted out, quite out of my normally reserved character. She walked away with fluid grace in high heels without looking back, and I realized that my eyes followed her. I remembered later how Mirabel struck me. She could only be described as a large woman, voluptuous, almost as tall as I was and in her early 40s. Though she was full-figured, her hips were well defined and her stylish dress was molded to her figure. Even hours later I could remember the fullness of her lips and the size of her dark brown eyes under flawless makeup. The upper ridge of her nose carried that attractive, subtle peak I always associated with Native American or Aztec heritage. Her dark hair was drawn up into a bun. Later that night I tried to analyze my fixation and felt a sudden flash of fear that, in our brief conversation, she could read my insecurities and the failures of my relationships that made me favor the relative solitude of a writer's life.

On a sunny October morning two weeks later, Amelia brought her hall pass to my small office in the counseling complex of the high school.

When Mirabel Valles introduced her daughter to me, I could not deny that I thought Amelia was destined to be a burden to her family. I did not know then that Amelia's father had died in a car wreck three years previously, and the mother was saddled with the responsibility of guiding her only child through the frightening maze of adolescence.

Well she should have been worried, because Amelia bore the curse of beauty, a fearful symmetry that can open doors with a smile as well as destroy families. Amelia had the tall, slender build of a model at 5'9", with narrow Castilian nose and a regal face. While obviously Hispanic, her eyes were green and piercing, her full lips painted in modest pink. Her open smile was welcoming, but I sensed an amusement in her posture that was not quite flirting but possessed of an easy self-confidence beyond her age.

We spent an hour as I administered the standard Princeton Review Career Aptitude Test battery and promised to get the results back within a week. Amelia seemed unconcerned, and what little she said was typically about Homecoming and her boyfriend on the football team. Later in the day, I dropped her name in a conversation with Principal Vance Koger. He gave me a wry smile and suggested that Amelia was going to give her mother heartaches.

"Hey, she's a sophomore, and I've heard she already has our quarterback Tommy Sanchez in love with her!" I wanted to impress on him my awareness of school gossip.

Koger crooked his finger. "Come with me." We walked down the long hall to the front doors at the west side of the building. "See that?" He pointed directly across the street at a primer grey 1979 Chevrolet Monte Carlo lowrider with chrome-plated rims. A dull thump-thump carried the bass track from whatever was playing in the car. Smoke of some kind rolled out from the driver's window. "That's Lalo Hernandez—I know him by his other name, 'Under Indictment.' He's there every day, and when her boyfriend's at football practice, she's in that ride, and off they go."

"Amelia?"

"Amelia."

"A drug encounter?"

"God, I hope not. Mrs. Valles would be crushed."

I avoided an expletive. "Does her mother know?" The endless human tragi-comedy was displayed before our eyes.

"Not yet, but you know how the San Vicente story goes. This place is smaller than anybody thinks it is." Koger stood at the doors, arms crossed, legs spread. "Hernandez dropped out in 8th Grade, and today he's one of, let's say, the wealthy unemployed."

I just shook my head and went back to finish the day with other student files.

The following week I sent a note to Amelia's home room and asked that she come by to pick up the profile and discuss the aptitude results. The reply from home room reported that Amelia Valles had not attended school any day that week, so I made a call to City Hall and was transferred to Mirabel's desk, since she had initiated the request.

I offered sympathy for her daughter's absence and was rewarded with a reply that was tinged with fury. "What do you mean she is absent? Are you sure about that?" As I back-tracked, we talked about the aptitude tests, and I told her I would bring the results to her house when she got home from work.

The Remarkable Demonstration

As I drove west on 6th Street, the sun was disappearing behind the hills surrounding San Vicente. The Valles home was set down below street level, and four steps led down from the city sidewalk to the front walk. Behind the house was a ravine shaded by juniper and scrub oak. The pleasant white stucco adobe with upscale red tile roof presented a turquoise blue painted wooden door frame. The front room window sported the same blue trim around the typical 1950s metal framed panes. Visible through the glass was a hanging *Ojo de Dios*, Eye of God, woven from multi-colored yarn.

Mirabel Valles answered the door at my first knock. She was still in her business dress, and she shook my hand when I entered. She showed me to the plush sofa and insisted that I join her in a glass of ginger ale. "Amelia left me a note that she would be late at school working on a project for the football team." She pursed her lips in a frown. We both knew it was a lie. As we talked, I realized what I recognized in Mirabel, and though I did not say so, I mentally compared her with the 1950s film star Katy Jurado as she appeared in the movie "High Noon."

After spending a few minutes discussing Amelia's profile and her aptitude to work as a bank teller and a florist, among other possibilities, Mirabel asked me, "What is that on your left hand? I instinctively dropped it beside my left leg as if to hide it, feeling my face flush in embarrassment.

"No, let me see it." She crossed her legs and leaned forward as I stuck out my hand to show her that I had three stubby warts, each fully 3/8" in size—one in the web between thumb and forefinger, one between second and third knuckles, and another at the side of my left wrist. Mirabel's fingers were warm as she touched the excrescences.

"How long have you had these?"

I admitted that I had tried all manner of remedies, but the warts had remained for about two months.

Mirabel took the hand between both of hers. "I will buy these from you." Under her blue eye shadow, her large eyes were intense, and I could not look away from her.

"I don't understand." I could feel my brow wrinkle in confusion.

Her black vinyl purse was leaning against the coffee table leg. She, opened it and took out a change purse. She handed me a quarter and two dimes. "That OK with you?" I was flustered, wondering if she noticed how I stared at her breasts under the trim blouse she wore.

I nodded, feeling a little foolish, but I stuffed the coins into the watch pocket of my jeans; then the conversation went back to her daughter, and I could tell that Mirabel's self-assurance was more tentative when she talked about Amelia, as though the stakes were very high. Twice while we were talking, she got up and went to the front door to look up toward the street. I told her we could talk about her daughter's future any time, as I found myself being comfortable with this woman who had the knack for setting her guest at ease without catering.

When I got up to leave, Mirabel rose gracefully and accompanied me with lithe strides. She did not smile, but she said, "I would like to call you if that is acceptable. I want to know if there is any change." Somehow, I did not think she was talking about the warts on my hand.

At the open door, I could hear the faint thump-thump of a car stereo down the block, and as I mounted the steps to the street, I saw Amelia walking briskly toward the direction of the sound. As I got into my car, I heard Mirabel's parent voice, "*MIJA!*" I was happy to escape an impending skirmish. I certainly would not risk the ire of a formidable woman such as Amelia's mother.

The following Friday was a home game against the team from Socorro, and San Vicente handily defeated the visitors 38-27, with Tommy Sanchez throwing three touchdown passes and running for a fourth from 28 yards out. The unique ambience of the Friday night lights has a look and a fragrance all its own. The slight chill in the night air is invigorating. I wondered if Amelia was in the stands cheering for her boyfriend, but I couldn't make out her face in the packed stadium. Tommy got headlines in the *San Vicente Daily Enterprise* on Saturday.

Tommy also got headlines on Sunday. A SVPD report listed Tommy Sanchez in stable condition after a drive-by shooting on Saturday. He was sitting in his parents' car outside his house when an unknown vehicle drove past and an occupant fired at least five shots at him. None of the bullets struck him, but glass splinters from a shattered front windshield went into his right eye and required surgery. The Sanchez family was concerned, because Tommy, a junior at SVHS, was seeking a service academy appointment. No suspects were identified, and the shots were fired from a small-caliber weapon, possibly a .25 automatic. As I read the story, I jumped to a conclusion I could not prove.

The school was awash with rumors the following Monday, while the week started busier than usual; Tommy Sanchez did not return to school until Wednesday, and then with a heavy patch over his eye. The SVPD made visits to campus to speak to Principal Koger, and students seemed restive in the halls.

Tuesday afternoon I was leaving the building early to go to the head office of the school system, and Amelia was leaving alone among the throng of chattering students. Her long auburn hair fluttered with an October breeze, and her smile was glistening. She greeted me, and I stopped to ask if she had spoken with her mother about the tests. Her face darkened "No, we haven't had the chance…" Her glance went over my shoulder.

I was in the presence of Lalo Hernandez. I first sensed the faint odor of marijuana mixed with that of tobacco, and I turned to see a young man almost a head shorter than Amelia, his sallow right cheek marked with a gang tattoo I had seen but could not decipher. He was wearing chinos low on his hips, a soiled tank top t-shirt loose on his narrow but muscular shoulders, his arms rich with arcane jailhouse tattoos such as skulls with serpents emerging from the eye sockets, lettered names with daggers penetrating them, and the recognizable cross tattoo w/three rays extending from the top. His feral eyes had a puffiness that reminded me of fetal alcohol syndrome, and he wore a wool watch cap over what I presumed to be a shaved head.

His hostility was palpable as his head jerked as if to say, "You're in my way, Esé." His hands were in his pockets and his eyes were on Amelia. I was thinking about Tommy Sanchez as the beautiful Valles girl followed Hernandez off campus from a slight distance in order to provide deniability if she were challenged. I could only imagine how her mother had interrogated her and how Amelia was probably seething to rebel even further.

That night I read some old love letters and went to bed feeling the frustration of confused and unrequited love. My fantasies reminded me of the tortures of Tantalus.

Friday morning, I woke up just before dawn and went to the bathroom where the sink was littered with toothpaste tubes, hairbrush, mouthwash, and used lengths of dental floss. I splashed water on my face and grabbed a washcloth, looking into the bright, lighted mirror.

Why hadn't I noticed it before? When had it happened? I felt a flash of incredulity as I lifted my left hand in front of the mirror. The uncomfortable, ugly warts had vanished. I looked into the mirror, but I was seeing the penetrating eyes of Mirabel Valles, her full red lips slightly smiling, and when I remembered the three coins still in my pants pocket, I had to tell her of my amazement.

The week before Homecoming, San Vicente had drawn a bye, and with no game on Friday, the building was as calm as a high school can ever be. When I talked with Mirabel Valles by phone that morning, I jabbered like a schoolboy in my excitement, as I kept inspecting the back of my left hand. She asked me to meet her after she got home from work.

Just before fourth period, Vance Koger called me to his office. His face was grim and ruddy, and I knew he must have been visited by a disgruntled parent. I didn't bother to sit down, and he advanced a delicate case. "One of Amelia's friends, Michelle Goins—her mother came in 20 minutes ago and said that Amelia's mother had performed an abortion on her daughter. She's 17."

"And why doesn't she go to the SVPD?"

Koger pushed backward in the swivel chair, rolling on the carpet protector. "That's the rub." He massaged the sides of his face. "She says she's scared—scared to death."

"That's weird. Hey, I've met Mrs. Valles on more than one occasion, and she seems pretty strong willed, but I don't think..." I stopped suddenly as I reconsidered.

"You know that more often than not, I am the court of last resort concerning these kids. I talked with Trammel in counseling, and apparently, nobody knew Michelle was pregnant. She's absent today, and Adele Goins says that her daughter is very sick and almost hysterical."

My stomach was rolling with a sudden queasiness. "So why are you dumping this on me?"

"Goins says that our Mirabel is a witch." His eyes rolled.

Mine didn't, but I covered by saying, "A *which*?"

"You heard me. What do you think?"

I lie badly, and so I did the next best thing; I dissembled, "I've been told that no such thing exists in 1980s America. She says she does herbal medicine and calls herself a cunander... or, uh, you know what I mean." I was rubbing the back of my left hand, not comfortable mentioning my private interest in magic and other occult practices.

"There's more than one *curandera* in San Vicente, but they don't usually inspire the kind of fear I just saw in Adele's face. No doubt in my mind that something rattled her. I'd like to get some information on Mirabel Valles, and I think you might help."

I nodded and promised I would say something to Amelia's mother, although I had no idea how I would broach the subject. Even if Mirabel Valles had helped the Goins girl terminate her pregnancy, why would that cause her mother to be afraid? If anything, it would be Mrs. Valles who would fear prosecution or a lawsuit.

The Inner Sanctum

It was just past sunset when I parked on Sixth Street and walked down the steps to the Valles house. The fall evenings in San Vicente cooled quickly as the breeze flowed down from the forested hills to the north of town

An older woman was coming out the front door, holding a plastic bag and a small tied bunch of what appeared to be sage. Mirabel gave her a parting hug and stood in the doorway as I approached. I know I was smiling, but her lips barely turned upward in self-satisfaction.

She ushered me to the sofa and asked to see my hand. I could hear music coming from another part of the house. "It's Amelia. She is grounded." Mirabel's voice was clipped and terse as she raised her long, dark eyebrows, still not smiling.

I feigned ignorance as I changed the subject. "Can you believe they're gone?" I offered my left hand, and she took it, inspecting the healed skin.

She shrugged and sat back, her full figure swelling the sleeveless white silk blouse that she must have worn under a suit jacket and which glistened in the soft light of the floor lamps. On her upper left arm was a three-inch tattoo of a scorpion looking toward her breasts. "I told you—I know what is wrong with people."

Again, I did not think she was talking about the disappeared warts on my hand. I studied the strength of her face and its almost dramatic makeup. Her cheeks were full and round as is sometimes the case with Scorpio natives, and though her lips were thin, bright red lipstick was thickly applied.

She crossed her legs in my direction. "Did you know about Hernandez?" She demanded.

"Uh oh. I had hoped that was not going to be a big deal. I mean, Amelia already has a boyfriend." I was smiling ineffectually. After all, it is common knowledge that every girl in San Vicente had a boyfriend from the time she reached puberty.

"I caught her in his car when I came home early yesterday. Lalo Hernandez will not be part of my world." Her gaze was almost glowering, surrounded by styled midnight hair that glistened in the same manner as the stretch of her silk blouse. A few almost-invisible grey strands wandered through the dark waves lapping on her shoulders.

A door opened in the back of the house, the music suddenly getting louder, and Amelia stalked into the living room, dressed to go out. She was pouting. "Mama, I have to go see Michelle. She is still not better." I sensed an accusatory tone.

Mirabel was cold, her face dark. "*Mija*, you stay in this house unless I go out with you. You can go to school on Monday."

"Whatever!" Amelia snapped, her perfect mouth twisting, her fists clenched. She did not even acknowledge my presence.

"We will talk about this later when I can trust you again. You are lucky I still allow you to use the phone."

Amelia exhaled loudly and stomped out, the door to her room slamming.

Now we faced each other on the sofa, and I jumped in without preamble, "My boss says that Mrs. Goins is afraid of you for some reason."

Mirabel did not answer. She only shrugged.

"OK, now I look at what you did for my warts—no question you did something—and I have been thinking about this. You say you use herbs to heal, and that you help women in childbirth."

Her expression was impassive. "Yes, I told you I was also a *partera*…" She lifted her hand and rotated it to encourage me.

"Well, what I want to know is if you use magic…" I was suddenly uncomfortable at the blunt sound of the word.

Her expression did not change, and I could hear cars going by slowly out on the street and the muffled rock music from Amelia's room. Mirabel's hand came up in front of her face, bright red nails forming a knife blade, one edge touching her nose, and the other pointing at me. "Anglos see medicine as acceptable therapy on one side, with magic on the other side having no power to affect anything." She made her fingers close and then fly open in a small explosion. "In fact, there is no dividing line. Anglos do not believe in magic, even though it surrounds them. Look at your hand."

I nodded and leaned forward as she sat up. "So, are you practicing magic?" I blurted out the question.

"I heal people. I told you that. Scientists are still scratching their heads over the placebo effect that works with some people—you know, sugar pills that cure everything from anxiety to indigestion. Then, sometimes terrible cancers just disappear. They call it remission, but it is still a cure. The curandera was here long before modern medicine, even in San Vicente. Remember that aspirin was first discovered in a mountain herb."

It seemed I was approaching tentative friendship with this enigmatic woman. "Why is Mrs. Goins afraid of you?"

Mirabel rose and straightened her tight skirt. She took a few measured steps toward a closed door at the east end of the living room, whose frame was painted in the same turquoise blue as the front door frame. I was telling myself I could never be attracted to her, but I watched her hips sway as she walked.

She opened the door to the room and looked back at me. "Come over here."

I followed her into a darkened room. At the north wall was a desk upon which sat a small gooseneck tensor lamp that gave a small circle of brilliance on the green desk pad but to little else. On the east wall was a sideboard with a marble top and carved cabinet doors below. At elevated platforms above the marble were votive candles whose glowing glass containers depicted the blessed virgin. Two more candles sat on the right and left sides of the marble surface. A few items could be discerned on the waist-high milky stone surface including a mortar and pestle, and several clear spice jars with labels not clearly legible. Centered on the backsplash of the sideboard was a 15" tall metal crucifix that appeared to be light, stamped metal. It gleamed in the candlelight. A cabinet door beneath the marble top was open, and I saw a shelf crowded with glass jars and paper packets, all carrying inked labels. As I looked around the room, the faint but pleasing fragrance of sage wafted into my nostrils, producing a feeling of calm despite the tension I felt from being around Mirabel.

"Your altar?" I broke the temporary silence.

She did not look at me. "Sometimes it is. Everybody needs to pray, even atheists."

"What about Michelle Goins?"

"I won't talk about that except to say that my Amelia cried to me asking me to help her friend. It is a bad situation. I think the girl blabbed everything to her mother, and the mother called me at work during the day, threatening to send the cops after me."

Her profile was illuminated by the candlelight, and I offered a final comment. "You weren't worried?"

"I just politely told her to go to hell, and I hung up on her." She snorted in amusement but did not smile. The candle flames wavered. It was a story half-told. A rumbling of a car exhaust could be heard in the street as we went back to the living room.

As we walked back into the living room, Amelia came running from her room toward the front door, her long hair flying. Mirabel reached out and barred the way.

Amelia pleaded, "Mama, I just have to go outside for five minutes. That's all. Let me go." There was an engine revving on the street.

"Back to your room." Mirabel's voice was quiet but menacing. It was a standoff, and tears were welling in Amelia's eyes as she weighed the cost of advancing toward the door. I just stood by in uncomfortable silence.

Amelia hesitated and then spun around and stalked back toward her room. In a stage whisper, she softly mouthed the word "bitch," that made Mirabel start to follow her, but thinking the better of it, she stopped, clenching her fists. She was looking at me with her dark eyes.

"Maybe I had better go. We can talk about healing and magic when things calm down." My instincts told me that Amelia's need to go outside was more than emotional, but Mirabel was blind to the signals.

"No, it would help if you stayed for a few minutes. Let me get us a soda." Now she smiled faintly as if hiding something behind her flawless makeup. Music was booming from behind a closed door at the back of the house.

Terror Tales of the Southwest

The fizzy sweetness quenched my thirst, and I did not realize how dry my throat had become. Mirabel sat back on the couch, stretching the blouse as she took a deep breath and stretched her left arm across the sofa top. She looked at me, unblinking. "You know a few things, don't you?"

I felt a challenge as I tried to explain. "What you do…uh, what you did for me…is brand new for me. I have just read books on magic and witchcraft—even a book on witchcraft in the Southwest."

She shook her head imperceptibly, "I'm not a witch, but our traditions recognize *brujas*, including cops and councilmen. Anglos, not so much, but they have much to learn."

"Mirabel, look at my hand! You didn't give me any herbs, no poultices, no drugs, but the warts are just gone."

Her face softened. "You did what you could for Amelia."

"Is it magic?" I leaned toward her, rubbing my left hand.

"What is magic? Do you even know? I tell you that some things work, but not everybody can make them work." She looked away as if thinking about what to tell me next.

"I know I grew up being told there was no such thing as magic; maybe that's why I have read so much about it." I'm sure my face reflected my consternation. The Valles living room was eerily quiet. Even Amelia's music had faded.

"You grew up here, didn't you?" It was a rhetorical question. "When I was just out of high school, I found my talent. Do you remember Aaron Padilla? It was 20 years ago." She paused as I tried to place the name and suddenly knew she was talking about San Vicente's best known disappearance.

The Unsettling Case of Aaron Padilla

I felt an icy finger going down my spine and a tightness in my abdomen as Mirabel stretched her arm along the back of the sofa and crossed her legs.

I was now remembering one of San Vicente's signature mysteries, "I was out of college by then, but I remember the cops were clueless. Padilla was the son of the police chief, right?"

Mirabel nodded forcefully. "What most people don't know is how Aaron stalked me. From the time I was 17 he tried to date me. He was a big guy—about 6-feet, 200 pounds, and mean because he could get away with it. He beat up a guy I wanted to date, and he sometimes parked across the street from my parents' house all night."

"You could charge him!"

"Ha! You know better. The cops here back each other to the wall. My parents were told to keep quiet and that Aaron was just a romantic young man."

"So, he just disappeared. Doesn't make sense."

"My dear, I prayed to the Blessed Virgin day and night, but she didn't help me."

I sensed something terrible emerging from her memory, but I didn't want to hear it. "That is awful. I don't want you to remember if you don't want…"

Mirabel's face softened, and she lifted her dark eyes toward the pale ceiling, moisture in the corners as she cut me off. "He raped me one night, OK? I was walking home from the movies downtown. He had a knife, and he hurt me. His father warned my parents to keep quiet and told them it was my fault."

A leaden weight dropped into my stomach, and I closed my eyes in disgust. As I recovered, I wanted to ease the pain of her memory. "They never found him. I remember now—his black 1961 Chevy Impala was found abandoned in the Cherry Creek campground. It was locked, and his wallet and watch were found locked in the car. No keys."

"That was the way the story appeared in *The Enterprise*." Mirabel closed her eyes, still leaning back.

I reached out and put my hand over the scorpion on her arm. The flesh was cool, and she did not react. "Maybe you can tell me more about your…your, uh, abilities when your daughter calms down."

Mirabel nodded, and we both stood. We walked slowly to the front door, and she opened it to the burst of cool outside air. I turned to say good night, and she was leaning against the turquoise door frame arms crossed under her breasts, her figure silhouetted by the living room lights. She did not turn on the porch light. I just lifted my hand and said nothing, turning to walk toward the street.

Her voice was clear and low, chasing after me as I left. "Aaron Padilla committed suicide."

The shock washed over me, but I quickened my pace, feeling relieved that I was only unsettled by, not attracted to, Mirabel. Preoccupied, I got into my Volkswagen Rabbit and pulled out into the street, my mind full of what I had learned at the Valles house. It was only a mile to my small house, and I was still fully concentrating on the Valles situation as I pulled into my dirt driveway, suddenly finding the steering becoming sluggish.

I quickly locked the car and went into my silent home, now aware of an uncomfortable feeling in my solar plexus. I checked for messages on my answering machine, not really expecting a call, and then I fixed chocolate milk and turned on the TV to watch something, anything, before I went to bed. I should have known that sleep would be hard won this night. I lay in bed, turning and hearing Mirabel's words from hours before, while I imagined investigators peering into a black Chevy Impala hardtop coated with frost on a November dawn 20 years ago. Now mostly forgotten, the Padilla case was never solved, and he was never found. Much as I resisted it, I could not banish the image of a voluptuous silhouette and its connection to a genuine San Vicente mystery that excited my writer's instinct.

Rolling out of bed with the dawn, it was time to take care of a multitude of housekeeping tasks, such as grocery shopping. My kitchen counter was cluttered with tortilla chip bags and a saucepan half full of red enchilada sauce. It would be the base for Saturday's supper. I looked at the old linoleum flooring slightly yellowed by somebody else's wax job before I rented the house.

After exercising and reading the newspaper, I went out to my car, only to see it down in the front end as though exhausted. Both front tires had gone flat. Kneeling in the dirt of the driveway, I saw a very small slit in the sidewall of each tire, and no epithet would repair the damage. As an Automobile Association member, I next called for a tow truck to take me and my car to the only tire dealer in town. I knew that it would be a half day down the drain.

There was no doubt in my mind who had stuck a knife into my tires, and I was glad that I could rely upon a pistol for self-defense, if this particular push turned into a shove. After using my credit card to purchase two brand new Continental tires, I sat in the office in front of a rack of new tires, smelling the hard rubber and listening to the rattle of air wrenches in the repair bay. I felt that Lalo Hernandez was more of a danger to the Valles family than to me, but I still had a fantasy of firing a hollowpoint .45 slug into his exposed breastbone.

As I sat waiting for the tires to be replaced, I looked out the plate glass window and to weekend traffic on Main Street. I wondered how many of those people went to healers such as Mirabel instead of local clinics. How many of these people believed implicitly in the powers of magic and witchcraft in this 20th Century? In my studies, I had found very few works on witches and necromancers in the Southwest, though I had read Simmons who surmised that traditional black magic was practiced in New Mexico by the *brujas*, who supposedly began their rituals by rejecting Christianity with such invocations as *"Sin Dios, Sin Santa Maria…"* or, without God and without the Virgin Mary.

Certainly, Mirabel wasn't one of those. Simmons said that people in the land of the Rio Grande had a great fear of witches, and I was now faced with a reality I had always enjoyed only as theoretical. Reality is not usually very entertaining. I looked at my left hand and thought about every word Mirabel had said as I left her house the night before.

It was afternoon before I finished grocery shopping and tackled the laundry, something that men rarely do, and after supper I promptly fell asleep on the couch until the phone jostled me awake around 10 p.m. For a moment, I thought it was a call I had long hoped for, but instead it was the intense voice of Mirabel Valles.

"I don't want to bother you, but I couldn't reach my mother in El Paso. Amelia isn't here. Can you believe that she went out the window of her room?" Mirabel was seething.

As I attempted to placate her, without success, I wondered if beautiful Amelia was Mirabel's blind spot. "You know she will come back before morning."

"Oh sure! But how will she come back? I am sad and so angry. I know she is with—him. How can she do this when a nice, handsome boy like Tommy is in love with her?" As she talked, I wonder if she was only enraged or if she was crying as she blurted out her frustration.

Mirabel began to talk about Amelia's father. "I worried about this three years ago when Diego died in the motorcycle accident. That Harley was only three months old when a drunk crossed the line out on the highway. I didn't think Amelia would ever stop crying. She was always her daddy's girl from the time she was five years old. She couldn't blame me, but our life has been rocky ever since then. And if I ever talk with another man, she is furious. Oh, but you don't have to worry—you're an Anglo." Even in subtle humor, her tone did not change.

We talked for 30 minutes, and I avoided asking her what she intended to do. I was sitting in my own small house with a table lamp for company and a genuine wish that Amelia would not throw away her future for a lowlife loser. After she hung up, I sat in my solitude, thinking about how often this story was repeated. Perhaps Mirabel could do something…but I had read once that magical intervention was usually temporary and human forces in situations always returned to *status quo ante*, unless the person comes to an interior resolve and makes changes to long-established patterns of behavior.

I imagined Mirabel as a teenager, fighting against Aaron Padilla and losing. I wondered what I could find out about Padilla and his disappearance 20 years ago. It would make a fascinating article if I could find time to write it.

Sunday was bright and mild, with cool mountain air tempering the warm sun, and a faint odor of wood smoke tinging the atmosphere of San Vicente. Remembering the hours, I waited until noon and then walked to College Avenue and up to the city library, an unassuming brick building with west-facing windows and red painted front door with eight wood-trimmed windows.

I asked about the 1962 files of the *San Vicente Daily Enterprise*, and long-time librarian Adrian Moody took me to a table at the back. I could not help but notice that she wore sensible shoes, and she was always pleasant to researchers and browsers.

Adrian brought me the bound volume of the newspaper, as the library did not have the budget to have the newspaper microfilmed. I realized I had no idea exactly when the Padilla incident happened, so I asked her about it. Adrian smiled and took off her dark-framed glasses, rubbing the lenses with a handkerchief she took from the pocket of the beige button-up sweater she was wearing. "Ummm, let me see. I remember it. People talked about it for weeks, and they never did find the poor boy."

Of course, I could not think of him as a "poor boy," after what Mirabel had revealed.

Opening the heavy board covers of the buckram edged binder, Adrian licked her finger and rifled through pages to September, October. And she stopped. "Oh yes, I know exactly. It was the first days of November. She turned to Thursday, Nov. 1, 1962, Friday, Nov. 2, Saturday, Nov. 3. There was nothing. There was no Sunday edition at that time, and she opened to the next edition, Monday, Nov. 5, and there it was on page 1 in the left column, underneath a headline about an impending visit by some dignitary to President John F. Kennedy's White House.

Padilla mystery deepens: abandoned car found in forest belongs to Aaron

by James Walz

Authorities confirmed Saturday that a car found in the Gila Naitonal Forest was registered to a missing San Vicente man who disappeared three days ago.

Forest Service Rangers identified a black 1961 Chevrolet Impala at the Cherry Creek campground as being registered to Aaron Padilla, 19, of San Vicente. They alerted N.M. State Police and the sheriff's office.

San Vicente Chief of Police Reynosa "Ryan" Padilla, Aaron's father, said that his son had failed to return home Thursday evening. "We just want him to come home and will do everything in our department's power to find him."

Preliminary investigations revealed that Aaron Padilla's car was locked, but police opened the car up and found a wallet, empty beer cans, foil wrappings with the remains of food, a small quantity of marijuana, as well as dried blood on the steering wheel and on the driver's side seat

Padilla, 19, is a part-ttime university student and a graduate of San Vicente High School, where he played tackle on the football team.

Chief Padilla said in an interview Saturday that Aaron had no enemies and was well-liked in the community. He indicated that because the abandoned vehicle was found on federal property, the FBI could be brought into the investigation.

"Oh yes, Jimmy Walz. He was so ambitious. You know he went on to *The Albuquerque Journal*." Adrian always seemed to be enthusiastic about information, and hundreds of people enjoyed her company during their library visits. With her help, I put the binder face down on the copy machine and made a copy to show Mirabel Valles.

Now I was intrigued, and I asked Adrian what else was written about the case. I put the binder on the table and turned from one edition to the next but saw nothing.

Adrian's voice had a lilting tone, and she tilted her head slightly. "You know, that's the funny thing. There weren't any other stories other than a repetition of what is in this one. There were one or two small items with Chief Padilla's request for the public to call in with information, but the case just died." Her choice of words was appropriate.

"You know, I looked for books here on magic and witchcraft, but I have never seen any on the shelves." I made conversation as I paid her for the copy and thanked her for her help.

Adrian's smile was prim. "We don't even try to keep those subjects any more. No matter how we tried to monitor them, every book on the subject is stolen, one way or another." Neither of us was surprised. She stuck her hands in the pockets of her sweater as she walked me to the front door. As I looked at the red trim on the door, I wondered why blue wasn't more common as a treatment for door and window frames.

Later that afternoon I called Principal Koger and asked what he knew about Aaron Padilla, even though it would have been long before he was a school administrator, probably before he was out of school himself. Koger said that his long-time predecessor Lindauer Haggerson had told him stories to the effect that the younger Padilla was "an untouchable son-of-a-bitch" who wore his father's police shield as perfect immunity. Neither students nor faculty were able to say anything against him. Poor boy, indeed.

Sunday evening I was chopping onions, grating cheese and shredding lettuce while the oil in the skillet warmed and the enchilada sauce began to simmer. I hadn't decided whether to include ground beef with the evening meal, but there would be a lightly fried egg as the crown on the dish, covered with red chile sauce. Enchiladas are a traditional Southwestern dish, and local legend has it that the addition of a fried egg on top was invented in San Vicente around the turn of the century.

Sharper Than a Serpent's Tooth

While I was deciding, I dialed the number for Mirabel Valles. I recognized Amelia's voice, and I asked for Mrs. Valles, hearing Amelia shout, "Mama…" and I could tell she was annoyed.

Mirabel's hello was crisp and veiled until I told her who it was. "Did your daughter get home OK?"

Her voice was low and controlled. "She was out all night. I could have killed her." It was sarcasm, but I had that old unsettled feeling from the way she said it.

I read the article to Mirabel and related what Koger had told me about her abuser. She was silent as though not comfortable in having a horrific memory recalled.

"If you don't mind telling me, did the cops talk to you after Aaron vanished?"

"Sure, because Padilla told his father that I was his 'girlfriend'— the bastard." The venom was undiluted after all this time.

"Sorry to bring it up, but I'll bring the clipping to you anyhow. I hope Amelia has begged your forgiveness." I felt the urge to make her feel better.

Mirabel paused and cleared her throat, "No, she is defiant, and she uses lies to get past me. She tells me that Hernandez is misunderstood and that he has had bad luck since he was young. Amelia says that she knows she can help him."

"What about Tommy Sanchez? That kid is aces."

I recognized Mirabel's characteristic snort. "You know what she told me? She said that Tommy was such a nice guy…" She paused, and I was thinking that when girls say you are a nice guy, that means they would never have sex with you.

Apparently, Amelia had come into the room, causing Mirabel to delay her sentence. There was a pause, and then she continued, "…so, she told me that he was such a nice guy, but he didn't need her the way *Lalo* did. I wanted to strangle her." Mirabel's pronunciation of the name was venomous.

"OK, maybe I can drop by next Friday after you get home from work. Good luck with your daughter." She gave me a time and then interjected, "By the way, I think there is a woman at a distance you have been thinking about. I don't think she is ever going to call you."

"What? Are you trying to go psychic on me?" I was instantly covering for myself, wanting to deny her realistic prediction.

"Uh-uh. I'm not a *vidente*, but I told you I very often know what is wrong with people—except maybe with my own child." With that exchange, we agreed to meet when the new week was finished.

Passing in the halls Wednesday, Principal Koger mentioned to me that Amelia Valles had used false hall passes to ditch school. The forged passes were to visit me in the counseling office, and I was not amused. I wondered what Mirabel would say now that she had been notified of her daughter's non-attendance. As for Tommy Sanchez, he had recovered and was back at football practice with at least one cheerleader comforting him between classes.

I didn't have time to think much about Aaron Padilla or Michelle Goins, but now and then I visualized the dark eyes of Mirabel Valles in the room with the crucifix on the wall, votive candles and jars of herbs.

Though San Vicente had no more than 10,000 residents, the downtown was always bustling with traffic that gave way on weekend nights to a stream of cruising adolescents whose cars crept up and down the main drag at a snail's pace. Errands and conversations with friends at the grocery store brought me home in time for evening news from the El Paso TV channels. Cable TV afforded me a luxurious 24 channels—only three of which I ever watched.

The mundane world was jostled just after 6 p.m. when Mirabel called to say she had come home late. I said I had not eaten dinner, and she asked if I would join her. It was a welcome invitation, and I grabbed the Aaron Padilla newspaper clipping, heading out the door with a mixture of anticipation and apprehension.

The sun had just disappeared beyond the western hills as I parked at the Valles address. As I approached the front door, with its blue trim, a friendly grey cat walked over from the corner of the house, tail straight up in eagerness. A neatly coiled green garden hose sat beneath the outside yard faucet to the right of the front porch, bordered by a 3-foot tall rosemary bush.

Mirabel opened the door and the cat scooted inside, taking the shortest route to the kitchen. As she invited me in, I brushed against her and entered the living room with its subtle fragrance. She turned off the TV set, and I handed her the photocopied article.

"I know you don't want to talk about it, but you made me very curious, not just about Padilla, but about your work. I've done a lot of reading…"

She looked toward the ceiling and shrugged, "We can talk during dinner. She gestured to the right and led the way around to the dining room where two places were set.

I didn't hear the sound of music coming from the hallway to the left, "What about Amelia?"

"Thank God for *abuelas*," She said. "Her grandmother came up from El Paso and took her down there for the weekend. Did you know she skipped school three days this week?" Mirabel gestured to a chair next to her place at the head of the table. "Now, sit."

I winced, and my mouth twisted, but I didn't have to say anything. She already knew.

Mirabel's heels clicked as she went from the carpeted dining room to the tiled kitchen floor. She brought plates with meat burritos smothered in a sauce rich with pieces of chopped green chile, the plate then sprinkled with cheese. She brought in frosted pilsner glasses and cans of Mexican Tecate beer. We poured the beer, squeezed lime juice into the beer and added a dash of salt.

"To good health," Mirabel toasted, lips pursed, unsmiling.

"And to your daughter's future," I added awkwardly, as Mirabel looked at me, her mascara still perfect after a day at work.

The food was superior, and I realized how hungry I was. Mirabel sat in a long-sleeved blouse with her elbows on the table, the beer glass held delicately between the fingers of both hands, the red of her fingernails contrasted with the effervescent amber inside the glass. Suddenly I realized that I was staring and felt my face flush when she turned her head to look at me.

As we finished eating, Mirabel looked at the clipping, her eyes narrowing. "That bastard. Hell is too good for him."

"So, are you willing to tell me about Padilla's disappearance? I think you know."

She held the half-full glass up to the light, looking into it. "He was left with no choice. I can't even describe it. My mother taught me. Let's talk about something else." She put the glass down, lifted her fingertips to her chin, and tilted her head slightly as she looked at me, unblinking.

I leaned forward, "You know some people say the cure-eran…" I stumbled and she began to smile.

"Let me try that again. What you do has been labeled witchcraft by some sources."

"Those are Anglo sources, of course. I know you have done research, and I read books too. The *curandera* is not a *bruja*, but the *bruja* can heal while perhaps the *curandera* can curse. What's the difference? Perhaps the Hippocratic oath? Tell me that Anglos don't do abortions." Mirabel was challenging me and enjoying it.

"OK, so you are not talking about basil, rosemary, and thyme, but you know things about herbs."

"Sometimes herbs and prayers make a powerful combination. Thoughts are things, you know." She raised her accented eyebrows. "You still have the coins?"

My silence was agreement and confusion at the same time, and I nodded.

We were interrupted by a knock at the door, and Mirabel stood, straightening her skirt. "I forgot. I need to speak with Rafaela Espinoza. I have a poultice for her skin. She has a rash on her stomach that Dr. Henderson has not been able to control. Finish eating. I'll be right back."

As I listened to the mixed English and Spanish from the front room, I heard Mirabel bid the Espinoza woman good-bye, saying, "Don't forget—*nuestre Padre cada noche*!" I was sure it meant saying "our father" prayers each night.

Mirabel returned to the table as I asked, "Will it work?"

"Of course." She picked up her glass and drank the last of the beer.

"How about herbs? I told you about the book I have on witchcraft in the Southwest. Can you use herbs to hurt people? Maybe kill people?"

Mirabel took a deep breath, her chest expanding, and then she exhaled. "You know as well as I do that killing people is easier than helping them. Anyhow, there are herbs not known to botanists. My mother gave me the secret of cachana. It is rare and found in the foothills of the *Sierra Madre Oriental*. I don't think botanists have described it, but some call it a witch plant. It's not the same as the common plant of that name in the U.S."

"I thought locoweed—jimson—was a witch plant."

"Oh, a little knowledge can be dangerous, my dear. Datura is one of the most dangerous plants in the world, and it is growing right under our feet."

When I was young, I learned that every part of the jimson weed was poisonous, from the roots to the leaves, the flowers. I told her about the two girls who came to the high school one day wandering the halls aimlessly with delirious hallucinations, and when they were taken to the hospital they admitted they had made a tea from datura leaves. If they had not found their way to the high school in their delusory state, they might have died from the decoction.

I helped her take the dishes to the kitchen where she told me, "I use datura for several things. It does wonders for asthma if used correctly."

As she talked, I was hearing a Gene Autry ballad from my youth, "…where the longhorn cattle feed on the lowly jimson weed…" Back then I had no idea what the lyrics meant. Mirabel rinsed her hands and beckoned with her finger. We went to the back door where she flipped on the back-porch light.

Fate and Darkness

When we walked onto the concrete back porch, I felt a gentle but very cool breeze. Mirabel clasped her arms under her breasts and shuddered. Then I looked down and saw the datura bush. It was at least five feet wide and in the last stages of its cycle. The flowers were dry and brittle. I bent over and picked up a devil's claw, the best-known artifact of the plant. It was half the size of my palm but the two hook-like prongs extended beyond my hand. It looked like the head of a goat.

"You use this?"

Mirabel just looked at me and ushered me back inside. "You have studied witchcraft, so you know about the witch's ointment that they used to 'fly.' The Southwest shamans use an ointment of datura to have visions and to fly through the night sky. Datura is from the nightshade family."

"That's what the book says too."

Mirabel settled on the sofa, leaning back as her blouse again tightened. I tried to make a point not to notice, but I took the opportunity to come back to the mysterious disappearance of Aaron Padilla. I was looking toward her front window, "You said Aaron Padilla committed suicide. They found only his car…"

She was looking at her fingernails, "I know because the alternative was even worse."

I turned toward her as her eyes, under lowered lashes, met mine, "I don't understand at all."

Mirabel's voice was clipped and precise, "I didn't see it, but my mother, Amelia's *abuela*, avenged me back then, and it is a terrible thing."

"You are saying you mother is a witch?"

Mirabel glared at me. "She is my mother, and I was grateful to her for ridding me of that monster. What happened to him was only justice."

I nodded and smiled. "I like to think it was, but I wish I knew…"

Mirabel shook her head imperceptibly and said, "No you don't. Now, you have made me curious about this book of yours." She crossed her legs in my direction.

I was quick to explain that it was not my book, and it was published by the Northland Press in Flagstaff, Arizona. "It covers all manner of witch tradition: New Mexico, Arizona, the tribal lands and south into northern Mexico. Many of the unique references are about enchanted food…"

Suddenly Mirabel uncrossed her legs, sitting bolt upright. "Would you let me read it?"

"Well, sure. I can drive back to my house and get it for you. It's still early."

Mirabel turned toward me, "That would be really nice. It's no trouble?"

"You made a delicious dinner. I'll be back in about 20 minutes." I was feeling some eagerness at having her read a source book familiar to me, and she escorted me to the front door as her cat emerged from a back bedroom to lead me outside. The rapidly cooling air was bracing, and I drove the back streets to avoid being mired in the Friday night Main Street cruise.

It was something I should have expected in that it was taking me longer than I planned. At first, I couldn't find the book within the double pile of reading material I kept by my bed. Then I was back in my car and headed toward 6th Street. On the way, I saw the unique Monte Carlo lowrider belonging to Lalo Hernandez, expensive chrome rims on 14" wheels glinting under the streetlights, as he headed for the main drag along with three other passengers. After what had happened to my tires, I saw a cunning malevolence in that vehicle. I wondered how many times he cruised slowly past the Valles house in a night, and as I watched the vehicle, I could see his silhouette slumped down in the driver's seat, chin raised as he peered over the small diameter chain-link steering wheel. I allowed myself to indulge a murderous fantasy.

It was now fully dark as I parked and walked down the concrete steps toward Mirabel's front door. A 30-watt bulb lit the porch and the door, and the interior light from the closed living room drapes was faint. I knocked and looked down to see her cat waiting alongside me.

Mirabel opened the front door and ushered us both inside the room, lit only by a single floor lamp in the corner. I could still smell the green chile sauce I had tasted not long before; it was blended with another elusive fragrance that made my breath quicken. I had the book in my hand.

She said nothing as I stared at her in the semi-darkness. In her heels, she was nearly at my eye level, her black hair glossy as it framed her full lips and eyes rich with mascara. She was wearing a long black negligee. Then she opened it, and she was naked as she came into my arms enfolding me in the dark lacewings of the robe. Her breasts were against my chest as the book fell to the floor, the taste of her lipstick sweet, the lure of her perfume overpowering.

Wordlessly she led me to the hallway and the bedroom where scented candles burned. I was dizzy with confusion, my heart pounding, my hands sliding over her generous body as she helped me undress. Dazed, I found myself overcome by frenzied desire when she took me, wrapping herself around me until I lost track of the time, wanting only to stay inside her without limits. Her moans and cries filled the silent bedroom as I thought of nothing but pleasing her.

Afterward we lay in each other's arms until I could recover enough to talk. "I thought—I mean, the book…"

"To hell with the book." She pulled me against her again and our tongues met with the subtle taste of the dinner we had shared. Something about her created a wild surge of desire I could not resist, even had I wanted to. Her full body intoxicated me, although I had told myself that I was not attracted to her. Then she was on top of me, and I welcomed her voluptuousness as well as the emptiness she made me fill.

We must have fallen asleep, because it was very late when we awakened, still entwined in each other's arms. I cleared my dry throat, "I can't remember why I came here." My chuckle was insincere.

Mirabel's breasts pushed against me. "I said I knew about people. I tell you that there is nothing wrong with you now." Her hands roamed on my body, making me gasp involuntarily. She was smiling in the candlelight.

Later she fixed glasses of cold ginger ale as I reluctantly prepared to leave. The book was still on the living room floor, and the cat was sleeping peacefully on the sofa. Once again, Mirabel enveloped me in the folds of the diaphanous negligee, kissing me deeply. "If anything happens, can I count on you?" She whispered.

She knew the answer, even as I nodded without comprehension, my arms under her robe, pulling her warm body close to me.

When I walked outside, the air was sharp and chilled. I took a deep breath and walked up to the street. I went to my car and looked back toward where Mirabel parked her car. From the glow of a streetlight 50 yards away I saw the reflection from glass fragments. I took another deep breath and went over to her car. The rear window of the car was caved in like a crystalline crater, and I thought, "The little bastard…" as I went down the steps again, but there was no need to knock.

Mirabel was still in the doorway, and I pointed toward the street, telling her what had happened while we were lost to reality. Her lips formed a smile as though it did not matter. She shrugged, "It is nothing, and I can get it fixed tomorrow."

"Can I help?"

She kissed me firmly on the lips. "Yes, you can—but not right now. I will be all right tonight." Her calm was suffused with a deadliness.

I drove back to my house in the post-midnight darkness, parking in the yard and going into the silence of my living room, dazed by the evening's events. I paced through the house and came back to the stereo. Song lyrics were coursing through my mind, and from my stack of 45 rpm records, I found the classic from seven years ago and set the needle on the spinning disc. The words played on my churning, almost unwelcome emotions: "Nights in white satin, never reaching the end…" then, "Just what the truth is I don't care anymore, 'cause I love you…" I wondered how long that song would remind me of this night.

As I lay sleepless and energized, the avalanche of thought shards surrounded me: the long-ago disappearance of Aaron Padilla, the vicious enigma of Lalo Hernandez and his hold on Amelia Valles, the fear of Adele Goins after her daughter's unfortunate miscarriage. Then there were the veiled abilities of Mirabel Valles, who was part of it all. It came to me before dawn that the words "cure" and "curse" are separated by a single letter. Too soon it was dawn.

A Weeekend in San Vicente

The morning streets of San Vicente were already bustling with traffic, and people, mostly unaware of the early 20th Century roots of an Old West community. High concrete sidewalks had been poured to make it easier for people to dismount from horse-drawn wagons, and some iron rings remained embedded in the concrete for tying up horses. I knew that inside the Palace Barbershop I had seen the ornate bathtub in the rear where cowboys came for a weekly bath and a shave many decades ago.

When I looked at the four *faux* Corinthian pillars flanking the doors of City Hall, I felt an emotional flash, remembering Mirabel's body against mine as I thought of her office therein. It always amused me that the city's oldest bar was next door to City Hall, and the smell of stale beer flowed out onto the sidewalk even at 10 a.m.

I crossed the street and into the bakery that had been in business since I was a child. I bought a dozen of their unique dollar-size shortbread cookies, some of them white and some chocolate, each with a nickel-size fudge button on top. These too I remembered from my youth. One of the freedoms of a sunny morning was the fact that the night crawlers like Lalo Hernandez slept most of the day. My last stop was the San Vicente Office Supplies conveniently across the street from the bakery and three doors down from City Hall. I needed typing paper, and it was my plan to record the Aaron Padilla story, and my own, as they unfolded. With my purchases, I walked around the corner and headed west up Broadway as it inclined toward the courthouse at its summit. My car was parked outside the hotel.

On the sidewalk at the hotel entrance was a sheet of 8.5x11 foolscap obviously ripped from a tablet. Without breaking stride, I bent down and scooped it up as a breeze lifted one end of it. I recognized it immediately as a page of writing from a woman I knew as "The Scribbler." She was an ordinary woman who wore her hair neck length and was probably in her 50s. She usually wore green slacks and a tan jacket as she walked the streets of San Vicente.

Sometimes she could engage in pleasant exchanges about the weather, but other times she walked thoughtfully, writing furiously with a pencil on the tablet she carried with her. I looked at the sheet and saw one or two recognizable words, but the rest of the page was crowded with fierce angular strokes spaced as though they were secret words urgently scrawled until the page was crowded like a bowl of black spaghetti. Then she ripped the page off the tablet and discarded it.

I had seen the intense look on her face, her eyes concentrating on the pages, and I wondered what secrets she was disclosing that nobody would ever decipher. Often, she smoked cigarettes as she walked, the smoke wreathing dark brown hair that was streaked with light grey. Friends had told me Margaret was once a registered nurse in a Veterans Administration hospital, but now she wrote prescriptions no pharmacist could fill, and she lived in an alternate world that some called mental illness. A century ago, she might have been labeled as one possessed. What if those pre-Freudian alienists were right? I thought about how fragile the mind can be and how susceptible it is to the influences I labeled as magic.

As I reached my car, placing the ream of typing paper on the floor, and the cookies in the passenger seat, I realized that I was smiling broadly. For some reason, I was free of the long-term longing that had obsessed me for more than a year. I was also feeling uncomfortable arousal as I entertained the image of Mirabel Valles wrapping her negligee around me. No, I was not immune to subtle influences either.

When I pulled into my dirt driveway, it was impossible to miss the black 1980 Chevrolet Malibu parked at the front gate, and I walked to the sidewalk as Mirabel emerged from the driver's seat carrying a brown paper bag. The rear window was still smashed. She was wearing jeans with silver studs and braid on the front and back pockets that looked stylish on her generous hips—eye-catching with her black pumps. She approached me and offered me the bag. "*Biscochitos*—for you. Try one."

The lard in those special New Mexico cookies was already staining the paper bag. "For me? Hey, I love those. How'd you know how to find me?"

"Mine are better than others. I put Kahlua in my recipe." She held a cookie up to my mouth, and I took a bite, savoring the faint coffee and anise flavor mixed with sugar. I ate the whole thing and accepted the bag, not mentioning that I had bought other cookies earlier. "You are in the Bell Telephone Directory, but you know that anybody with a utilities connection is an open book down at City Hall." It made sense to me.

Mirabel patted my cheek, and the absence of a smile did not lessen her appeal. "Could you go with me to the auto glass place. I have an errand, but I have to get this window fixed before tonight."

"OK, I'm your guy. Let me put this stuff in the house first." I trotted to my front door, wishing she would come inside, but she was already back in her driver's seat. I dumped everything on my kitchen counter, and then banged my elbow on the kitchen door frame in my haste to get back outside.

I backed out of my driveway and followed Mirabel's Malibu downtown. With losers like Lalo Hernandez abroad, auto glass companies will always thrive. I remained puzzled why Mirabel did not show more outrage to the vandalism of the night before.

Custom Glass on College Avenue was bustling when Mirabel pulled into the bay. I parked on the street and walked into the small waiting area, surprised to see quarterback Tommy Sanchez behind the counter. Of course—his father owned the business, and his son worked at the useful skill of replacing broken glass, from plate glass to auto windshields. When Mirabel entered the waiting room, Tommy grinned and they hugged each other, with Mirabel patting him on the back as though he were her son.

Sanchez shook my hand and called me "sir," to befit his upbringing. I remembered the first time a young person called me "sir," because I realized at that moment my youth was gone. I was only 24 at that time. With Tommy Sanchez at work on Mirabel's car window, I figured the work would be accomplished quickly.

Mirabel and I walked out to my car, where I opened the door so that she could slide into the passenger seat. Once I got behind the wheel, I asked her where we were going.

"Go around to Broadway, up Arizona Street onto the hill. I want to spend a few minutes with Hermina Sandoval." She held up a small packet. "Hermina is an aunt of my husband.

She has cancer, and I am going to help her."

"What is in the packet?" I was curious.

"Verbena. She will drink it as tea. It will fortify the liver and fight the cancer."

"Is the herb that strong?" My natural skepticism toward herbal remedies was emerging.

"The herb is the carrier. The doctors at the clinic did not offer anything, but I know I can help her." She did not offer to say what rituals might have gone into the herbs inside what appeared to be a plastic sandwich bag. I wondered idly if the herbs would have an effect on mental illness such as that afflicting The Scribbler.

We headed south up the hill on Arizona Street where the paving was poorly maintained and marred by small potholes and crumbling borders. I stopped in front of a modest adobe house with a sagging wire fence and relatively new black-painted ornamental iron gate. A dog was barking in the bare front yard with its 30-foot spruce tree standing sentry inside the gate. I would wait in the car.

Before she got out, Mirabel looked through the windshield, her face inscrutable, "Do you have a gun?"

I snorted as I voiced the old cliché, "In San Vicente, guns are like freckles. Everybody's got at least one. Why do you ask?"

Mirabel gave me a dismissive wave with her left hand, then she placed it firmly on my thigh, her red nails gripping me. I felt the heat through my jeans. The gate squeaked, and I watched the glitter from the moving back pockets of her jeans as she walked to the front door of the Sandoval home, and then I shut off the engine while I opened the driver's side window. The day was brilliant, with light cirrus clouds high in a turquoise sky, the quiet broken only by the occasional barking of San Vicente's dogs and an occasional vehicle going to and from Saturday errands. Smoke coiled from a black metal chimney across the street carried the fragrance of juniper and mesquite. I could overlook the town's business district down the hill from here.

In the 15 minutes or so that I waited, I wondered if Lalo Hernandez had friends in this neighborhood, and I thought again about the mystery surrounding the disappearance of Aaron Padilla 20 years ago. An incestuous town holds its secrets very close, and I sometimes felt I was on the outside peering into an intricate genetic network that did not welcome me, even though I spent most of my life here.

When Mirabel came back to the car, she was silent as I made a U-turn and went back down the hill to the Broadway intersection. Turning west onto Broadway, we passed the Rainbow Café with its single window and painted tricolor logo arcing over the entrance that was reputed to be a place to find a drug connection.

Two young men were leaning against the wall of the café, and one of the them was Lalo Hernandez. I looked in his direction as we passed, and he pointed at me with his finger, thumb raised as he sighted along it. I could feel his hostility and decided it was a good thing that I did have a .45 automatic. I resolved at that moment to start keeping it as close to me as my own San Vicente secret.

Over a hill and down to College Street we found Mirabel's vehicle parked on the street with a new back window. I wanted to talk, but Mirabel seemed eager to get on with her Saturday. She put her hand on my thigh again before swinging out and walking around to the driver's side of her Malibu as I watched. She didn't look back or wave.

I went back to my house, ate several rich *biscochitos*, and typed four career narratives based on tests given the previous week. One of them was for Michelle Goins who took the battery at the insistence of her friend Amelia Valles. The test showed her aptitude for working with children. The fear described by her mother was another issue that still perplexed me.

As the afternoon lengthened, I took time to field strip and clean my pistol as I sat on the sofa. When it was re-assembled, I listened to the satisfying "snap" as a loaded magazine was inserted into the butt. Then I turned on the TV to catch any old movie that the cable company could provide. My thoughts turned to the relationship of herbs to healing. I wondered if prayers and conjurations affected the nature of reality.

I must have drifted off to the alpha waves from the 24" luminous screen because I was jolted awake by a tapping on the front door, and late afternoon light was light grey through the windows. I shook my face awake and went to the door.

Mirabel was the last person I expected to see, but I motioned her into my front room. "My daughter will be home tomorrow evening, and I want you to have dinner with me again tonight. Without preamble, she put her arms around me and I felt dizzy as her lips sought mine. Was it the taste of the cookies or her lipstick that was arousing me?

"Come with me. Besides, I wanted to see your gun." Her eyes were dancing, but she did not smile.

"You have already seen my gun, but you haven't seen my pistol…" I embraced her and kissed her again, holding her close so that I could feel her breasts against my chest. She responded without hesitation, and I could feel a genuine eagerness. This time, a faint smile lifted her full lips when she stepped back.

I retrieved the .45 and shoved it into my jeans pocket before following her out the door.

She drove to 6th Street, and this time my hand was on her thigh as she leaned against the driver's side door half looking at the streets and half looking at me through long, dark lashes. At her house, we walked to the front door, her arm around my waist and mine a little lower on her as her heels clicked on the front walk. Her cat was waiting patiently at the front door and probably expected immediate food service. He missed his guess.

The Night Visitor

Inside, we went directly to the bedroom and took each other hungrily, our clothes strewn on the floor. It was almost dark when we paused. She was lying on her stomach in the darkness of the bedroom, one arm across my chest. The bedside clock radio was the only light, and its numbers advertised a luminous green "6:47." Waves of well-being seemed to wash over me, and I wanted to stay here. My voice seemed very loud in the silent afterglow of our passion. "Mirabel," I paused. "Did you learn everything from your mother?"

"That is the way it always has been. Magic is not learned from books. The herbs must talk to you." She turned on her side, her hair down in her face.

"How does it work? Why does it work?" I was staring at the ceiling, my heartbeat still elevated.

"Life must be given to the herbs, each to its own nature, just as all food should be blessed to a purpose. The herbs are alive and the prayers turn them into medicine. They reach into the patient and find the good within them. I believe most people are good. Of course, there are some who have no good inside them." Her dark eyes were on me, and my first thought was of Aaron Padilla and Lalo Hernandez. I was going to ask more, but her lips were too close, and I wanted her too much.

Finally, we lay quietly, our bodies damp, our breathing the only sound, until…

Suddenly came a metallic rattle from the front room, and we both jumped. Mirabel gasped and whispered, "The front door."

There was a rock in the pit of my stomach, but I reacted, rolling off the bed onto the floor. I found my discarded jeans and pulled the .45 from the pocket. All I heard from Mirabel was "Go," as I scrambled to my bare feet and padded silently in darkness to the front of the house. Wavering light from the candles in Mirabel's shrine room to my right outlined the metal crucifix on its east wall and dimly played on my naked torso.

The front door was opening, and a figure was edging into the room. The first thought flashing into my mind was that Lalo Hernandez was invading the Valles home. Blood was pounding in my temples, and my throat was as dry as the Namib desert while terror washed over me.

With my thumb, I pulled back the hammer of the .45, and it was the loudest sound in the room. The figure coming through the door went flat against the jamb, uttering a pitiful wailing sound. Beneath a bulky sweatshirt with hood was an obviously terrified female who was entering Mirabel's home.

Suddenly I felt ridiculous, standing in my underwear in a woman's living room with a pistol in my hand, while the female I was confronting was obviously unarmed and was now starting to weep.

"I…I…have to get it back." The woman wrapped her arms around herself for security. As the hood fell back, I recognized Adele Goins, with her short hair and a face contorted with tension, even though it was veiled by the night.

I backed up as Michelle's mother sidled into the room, her back against the wall. "Mrs. Goins, I don't understand. What are you looking for?" I could feel the heat of embarrassment replacing the fear I had just experienced. I could already hear the stories that would race through town when this lady got back to a telephone.

Adele Goins choked off a sob and extended her hand, "Tell her I will do anything, but I can't go on this way."

I was, of course, speechless, because I had no idea what she meant. I just stood there in the dark, staring at a distraught woman, remembering what Principal Koger had said about her. Then I heard the click of Mirabel's heels and could feel her enter the room. She did not turn on a lamp, and the faint glow from the shrine candles lent an eerie definition to the characters in this set piece.

"Michelle gave you something, didn't she? I know it." Adele Goins voice was supplicating, not accusatory.

"Did you see something?" Mirabel's voice was flat and cold. I glanced toward her and could see that she was wearing that midnight negligee and seemed a vengeful female spirit as she crossed her arms.

Adele nodded her head fiercely. "It's so awful. It will not let me sleep. My husband doesn't see anything, and I can't wake him when it comes into the room."

"You were going to call the police and have me arrested. You told me that when you called me at my office in City Hall."

Adele went from nodding to shaking her head. "No, no, I never did. I was just so angry. She is my daughter."

"She is better off now." The voice behind me was implacable.

Adele's voice cracked with emotion. "Michelle gave you something, didn't she?"

Mirabel said nothing, and I felt myself in the presence of a praeternatural event.

"Nothing like this ever happened to me. I think I am losing my mind. That's why I came here. Go ahead, call the police. I don't care any more." Her voice was strained with emotion.

Mirabel's voice was slow and measured. "You have learned something, and if you apologize, you can be blessed for it."

The cringing woman against the door jamb reached out, "Mrs. Valles, I am so sorry. I don't want to die."

Mirabel walked past me into the room with the candles, her negligee floating eerily in the dimness. Another candle was lit, and I could see Mirabel with her back to me, arms spread, intoning softly with words I could scarcely discern, "*Santa Maria, nuestra madre, escucha mi oración…perdonar*" I caught the word "pardon," and I could see the haunted eyes of Adele Goins staring into the darkness. The front door stood open and cold air was uncomfortable on my exposed skin.

Then, so slowly, Mirabel came walking back to the living room. She was carrying a 5"x7" inch color photograph that I could tell, even in the candlelight, was of a younger Adele Goins, and I could see a dedication and signature.

A narrow black ribbon had been wrapped three times around the width of the picture, and suspended from the ribbon was what appeared to be a locket. It was obvious, even to me, that Adele's daughter had purloined these personal items at Mirabel's request. It seemed ominous.

Eager almost to desperation, Adele Goins took the photograph and its attachments and clutched the package to her chest, her eyes fixed on Mirabel Valles. Mirabel's look was imperious. "You were not here tonight. You may go in peace." She lifted her right hand and made the sign of the cross with two fingers, reciting: "*In nomine patre, filius, et spiritus sanctus—amen.*" I felt an almost-electrical charge pass through the room and heard Adele Goins exhale in a sigh. No other words were spoken, and Adele Goins scuttled from the house, departing from Mirabel's life.

We stood alone in the darkened living room. Mirabel looked at the front door, "She is not a bad woman, but she understands very little." As for myself, I was suddenly aware that I was cold and almost naked.

As suddenly as turning off a switch, Mirabel changed the subject. "It is too late to cook, and I know somebody working at Pizza Hut who will deliver—the son of my husband's brother-in-law. She went to the phone as I thought that San Vicente is indeed an incestuous town. We then dressed and waited for the pizza to be delivered.

It was close to midnight when we sat on the sofa. With the taste of pepperoni in my mouth I asked, "What did she see, Mirabel? Was it some kind of demon?"

She looked at me with a slice of pizza delicately held and poised for a bite, and she shrugged, "I don't know. My mother said we cannot know these things. We only know they exist, just outside of our normal vision." I glanced down at the coffee table and saw the *Witchcraft in the Southwest* with a bookmark protruding from its pages.

I took a swallow of Pepsi and picked up another slice of pizza. "I wonder if Aaron Padilla saw something years ago."

"That was very different. What happened to that woman is nothing in comparison to what visited Padilla." She was looking toward the front window as she spoke, speaking as from a great distance. "It still waits."

It was 2 a.m. in San Vicente, and Mirabel drove me back to my house. I watched her taillights disappear down the street and stood in my disreputable front yard. I could smell wood smoke drifting over the town and see the glow from the downtown district where the stream of Saturday night cruisers was winnowing to its inevitable end. In less than two hours, Main Street would be empty. I wondered if Lalo Hernandez was out there, nursing his sullen attitude.

Then I entered the silence of my messy house and threw myself onto my unmade bed, careful to unload and place the pistol on the nightstand. I did not wake up until high noon on Sunday.

There were still four *biscochitos* in the bag on the kitchen counter, the brown paper sack now thoroughly saturated with lard residue, and I wolfed them down with a glass of milk, all the while thinking of my strong and unusual attraction for Mirabel and feeling disappointed that Amelia would be back with her mother before the day was done.

With the sun overhead, the home invasion I had witnessed the night before seemed more and more surreal—the weeping and distraught mother of a girl who had conveniently miscarried—the prayers or incantations of an exotic woman in a negligee who released the mother from a spell or curse—the effectiveness of a folk healer in the middle of a modern Southwestern town. Could medicine and magic have the same roots? I began to doubt the normal world I had believed in. What if the apparent normalcy of San Vicente was an illusion. It was possible that under every street, under the basements of brick and stucco houses ran a swollen underground river running down, down, into daemonic oily black sea beneath the earth.

As the day progressed, I wondered if Mirabel would seek her own mother's counsel after Amelia's return to the Valles home. It was obvious that not even magic could intervene when a rebellious child defied her mother. I wondered if it was the tragic loss of the father exacerbating the hostility Amelia had developed toward her mother so quickly after the year of her *quinceañera*.

The weekend gave way to a busy work week. Several times I saw Amelia and her friend Michelle Goins in the SVHS hallways. I gave Michelle the narrative I had worked out from her aptitude tests, and was relieved that she did not seem to look at me with any kind of suspicion, but my mind kept going back to the Saturday night confrontation in the dark, and I wondered if Adele Goins could keep the secret. My other memories of Saturday night brought me far more excitement.

By Thursday, I could not help but notice Michelle was alone in the halls, and I had not heard from Mirabel. I was intensely curious, but it was not my situation. The other side of me suggested that I was just avoiding the insoluble conflict between mother and daughter. I had learned long ago that the outsider was always a stranger when involved with the family of another. Blood is the only destiny. Perhaps Mirabel would call.

I had been running late Thursday morning and did not read *The Daily Enterprise* when it landed in my yard, but I picked it up when I returned from the day at the high school. I removed the rubber band and opened the newspaper while still standing inside the front gate. Below the fold on the front page was a story that suddenly made me feel weak with apprehension.

Rock cleft in forest yields grisly find for hikers at Cherry Creek

by Marcia Kinnear

SAN VICENTE—Unidentified human remains were recovered in the Gila National Forest Sunday morning by hikers in the general vicinity of the Cherry Creek camping area,.

Grant County Sheriff Leslie Goforth announced the discovery Tuesday and said the bones and personal items were turned over to the FBI to be processed by their laboratory at Quantico, Va.

While few details were released, Goforth said in an interview that the skeletal remains were of a male and had been exposed to the elements for at least two decades. He said that personal items recovered at the scene indicate an identity that is being withheld until next of kin can be notified.

Along with fragments of clothing and jewelry, authorities recovered a rusting .38-caliber Police Positive revolver. The weapon was loaded and one chamber had been discharged.

One of the GCSO deputies was interviewed Wednesday who said he was at the scene and observed that the skull found appeared to have an entrance bullet hole in the right side of the cranium as well as an enlarged exit hole on the left side.

If the story was accurate, there were only three people who knew what it could mean. I could still hear the words Mirabel used to describe the hidden finish to Padilla's life, and I hastened into the house to dig out the Xeroxed Nov. 5, 1962, article. I sat at my desk, looking at my typewriter and comparing two newspaper articles separated by decades, making a connection that would probably dawn on the rest of San Vicente very much later. My desk chair was an old straight-back piece with a slightly padded red leatherette seat, and it wobbled with age despite the glue I had used to extend its life. It did not do to be too comfortable when writing, but I could still tip it backward when I was contemplating. I wondered if Mirabel had seen the paper. I had to ask her.

After a makeshift dinner of local tamales and beans, I began to type a narrative that described Aaron Padilla, a young Mirabel, and I could sense a floating horror that moved in the juniper smoke over San Vicente. It was more than my imagination, but it defied proof. In the background, the TV was broadcasting a re-run of "Hawaii-5-0," and I did not have to watch because most of the episodes were familiar to me.

On the cluttered desk was the recent book *The Roswell Incident*, about an unquestionably factual flying saucer crash and recovery in 1947. An open bottle of Pepsi was beside the desk lamp, and for some reason I craved another biscochito that I could still almost taste. The metallic clatter in the rhythm of my typing was comforting, and I was making good progress as the evening progressed. By the TV, I could tell that it was 9 p.m.

There was no knock at the door. Mirabel stormed in, surrounded by fury. I'm sure I just sat and stared open-mouthed as she stood there, still dressed for work, except that her sleeveless carmine silk blouse was untucked at the waist on one side, falling over the waistband of her tight black skirt. She had a black purse over her shoulder. Then I stood up as she lifted her manicured hands to her face, the little scorpion on her left arm flexing its tail.

"She is defying me, the little..." Mirabel stopped before adding a name to describe her daughter's rebellion. I stood, hands at my side, waiting for her to explain as her face contorted with emotion known to thousands of parents in thousands of towns in America. I wondered, idly, why she could not use her secret power to bring Amelia to her senses.

I invited her to the couch and offered her the inadequate soft drink refreshment I had in the refrigerator. When I brought her a glass, she put it close to her face as the carbonation sparkled over the ice. When she did drink, she left a generous trace of lipstick on the rim of the glass.

"If my husband were still alive, this would not happen." Her voice was sepulchral, and she was looking at the front door as she spoke. "I found a note when I got home from City Hall this evening. Amelia has gone to live with..."Her hands were in front of her, vibrating in frustration. "—him."

I did not ask "who." Mirabel's anger was almost frightening to me. At that moment she did not seem to be a wielder of inner powers. She was just a mother whose love for her child clouded her every thought right now. I asked her, "Do you know where she is?"

"Remember, anybody with a utilities connection..." She clenched her fists and her body compressed as waves of anger and concern assailed her. "She wrote that she had taken most of her things and that HE would take her to school every day." Mirabel threw her arms into the air and turned to face me. "He is evil. He deserves something terrible." The words were icy and spoken like an incantation. She picked up the glass of soda and took a long drink.

"If I can help, you know I will." When I said it, I thought the words were banal, but Mirabel just looked toward the front door and nodded solemnly, lips pursed. I could only imagine the deep convictions seething in her heart. I knew she was not a woman who forgave.

"Some things are meant to be. Amelia left a crumpled note Hernandez sent to her. He scribbled it in his own hand." She reached into her purse and pulled out a wadded piece of note paper as though it was a trophy.

My mouth was dry, and I swallowed noisily, still unnerved by her unanticipated visit. Earlier, I had wanted to ask her about the newspaper article, but now I had forgotten it.

She put the glass on the coffee table, pushing aside a pile of magazines. She turned to me and began unbuttoning the silk blouse. As she looked at me, I found myself inflamed with irresistible desire as she reached over to me and took my head in her hands, her tongue pushing into my mouth as she kissed me. I don't remember how she helped me undress, but I pushed the skirt over her generous hips and we took each other fiercely. I felt her red nails digging into my back, her legs hooked around my own. Her moans drowned out the irrelevant noise of the TV set, and it was a long time before I was too exhausted to continue. Mirabel had a depth of passion I had not experienced before, and I did not know if it was the Scorpio in her or the reservoir of suppressed rage.

It was growing late, and my breathing was still labored. "Aaron Padilla...I have to ask you..."

"What about him? I already told you." Her tone was curt, and she obviously had not seen the newspaper. I struggled to my feet, almost tripping over my pants lying in a heap on the floor and went over to the desk, bringing the Thursday edition over to her.

She read the article as though I were not in the room. Her face betrayed a look that took her to another time, but her lips were almost smiling. When she was done, she threw the newspaper on the coffee table and leaned back against the couch cushions, breathing deeply. She seemed to consider the subject closed.

This time I sat close to her and put my arm around her shoulders. "I thought about this, and I want to know how you could have known..."

Suddenly, Mirabel put her arms around me, her face against my chest. I could feel hot, silent tears on my skin. Her body was shaking with emotion, and we sat like that for at least five minutes.

"The women of our family pass the magic from one generation to the next. When that *cabron*—Aaron—raped me, I had nobody but my mother. She avenged me. Oh, he was so arrogant, and he had his chief of police father making sure he would never be arrested."

"But that doesn't explain..."

Mirabel put two fingers on my lips. "Yes, it does. My mother was known to everyone in San Vicente. Some even feared her. Even though I was badly hurt, my mother made nice with the Padillas. She taught me to pretend that I liked him and one evening invited him to our house for dinner. Afterward, she gave him a package of burritos to take with him. He was so arrogant, bursting with pride. I was not the only girl he hurt. He saw himself as a *macho enamorado*..." She used the local slang for a womanizer.

It was obvious what she was leading up to, but I wanted her to tell me everything.

"My mother prepared the sacred herbs and said the words of the ritual, and she made me repeat the words as we prayed together in the candlelight before the food was prepared. I knew only that he would never bother me again. He vanished a week later."

"...And they found his car in the forest. There was blood...but you were never there."

"Something was there, and it was too horrible for him to bear. He had only one escape." Mirabel leaned back and pulled my head to her breasts. The smell of her perfume was intoxicating me again.

"And you knew, even though you weren't..."

"Yes, and that story in today's paper is not news to me."

Mirabel kissed me, stood up with her purse and went to the bathroom to adjust her clothes and her makeup. I heard the sound of the toilet flushing and then she came out, ready to leave for home. She kissed me on the mouth and said, "You could do a better job cleaning that bathroom, *mi amor*." I was suddenly reminded of the burden that came with finding myself in what women called a "relationship."

I put on my pants, and I accompanied her to the door in my bare feet. "How about Amelia?"

She paused, "I don't know. She is my daughter, and I love her beyond reason. Hernandez has an apartment on Cooper Street—a duplex out past the courthouse and near the cemetery. My husband may be dead, but I can count on you."

Although I saw her as ultimately formidable, I knew she was right, and I walked with her down the sidewalk to her Malibu, with its new rear window, parked on the street. The concrete of the sidewalk was cold on my unprotected soles. I went around and opened the driver's side door for her. She slid in and reached out to clasp my hand before going back to Sixth Street. I watched the taillights disappear. I was hopelessly entangled in a drama that could not end well. It was only when I went back to the house that I realized I had stepped on a painful goat-head sticker—that pernicious plant pest of the Southwest. It probably had some herbal purpose of which I was ignorant.

A Gathering Storm of Magic

The next day, Friday, I was relieved to see Amelia in the hall with Michelle Goins. Her beauty was only slightly dimmed. Her hair was slightly tousled and her face seemed pale. Perhaps there was a new normalcy setting in until Mirabel could talk sense to her. The authorities would not be called to the Valles home, and Lalo Hernandez would be picking up Amelia after school. San Vicente's interconnected families would be drunk with gossip

I did not hear from Mirabel on the weekend, and I spent some time writing my semi-fictional narrative about the Padilla case. I learned that former San Vicente Chief of Police Reynosa "Ryan" Padilla was retired at his elaborate home south of town in a development called Ridge Estates. Many had speculated about how a retired policeman could afford a four bedroom, three bath home with an in-ground heated swimming pool, and an 8-foot stucco wall with iron gates surrounding the property. But then San Vicente is an incestuous town, and it does not pay to ask too many questions.

For a day or two I toyed with the idea of calling former Chief Padilla, but a newspaper reporter took care of that task in my stead. Monday's newspaper story began, "Authorities confirmed on the weekend that the skeletal remains found in the Gila National Forest last week were identified through dental records as belonging to 19-year-old Aaron Padilla who disappeared in 1962. No other details were released, but an interview with his father…"

The rest was predictable boilerplate of parental grief and sympathy for a "fine young man" whose life was cut short. The world as presented in mass media was too often at odds with the gritty pockmarked reality of human life.

In my reading and my reflection, I began to think of about the mechanisms of magic as discussed by Simmons in his enigmatic book about witchcraft in the Southwest, as well as those classic tomes and grimoires of more remote times. I had also heard many stories about Mexican witches living in Vera Cruz, and of the evil women of Ixtmal.

And what of demons? The pale yellow light in my very ordinary living room told me what my parents had said: Demons do not exist. Yet I had learned better. The question was not whether they existed, but how they entered the world of humans. I had come to see them, not as manifestations of a tortured imagination, but rather invisible beings shambling in the darkness of a dimension close to ours and waiting to be called forth by substances and rituals. Did they come to The Scribbler in the midnight hour? They were often present in mental disease, but I did not like to think of them as being able to take on physical substance. Our religions have spent millennia building barriers to keep the demons away from us, and yet…and yet…did some of Mirabel's prayers evoke something other than the saints and the Holy Mother? As I prepared for bed, I realized I could not be objective, because I felt a subtle magic she exerted on me.

I lay awake realizing that the tortured images of Hieronymus Bosch were perhaps not imaginings. What if he had intentionally invoked the images he painted? Even now, the misshapen hordes of demonic entities clawed at the barriers, seeking entrance into the world of naïve humans. Perhaps this was the hidden meaning of *The Key of Solomon*, and the goal of ceremonial magic. While Solomon controlled the demons who built his temple, what hope had the rest of us in the presence of a horde of hideousness beyond our capacity to visualize?

As another hour passed, I stared at the ceiling, thinking about the mystery surrounding the death of Aaron Padilla. What had stalked Padilla in 1962 and had driven him on a wild ride into the forest? He must have been convulsed with terror to flee his vehicle in the dark—running, stumbling, and then jamming himself into a crevice in one of the cliffs. Then he blew his brains out. I still could not explain the presence of blood found on the driver's seat and the steering wheel. Was the newspaper story of that time in error?

Then I fell asleep to wake for another long week. Mirabel phoned me on Tuesday to say that her mother was coming to stay with her for a few days while the crisis with Amelia was all she could think about. I felt immediate disappointment, realizing that I wanted to see her, but she needed to talk with me about her daughter. She used clipped phrases, "I am so angry. The girl cannot even cook. She is as helpless as a kitten. I prepared her a tray of rolled enchiladas. She does not even know how to cook beans properly. *Cabron* waited for her in his ugly car. To think I am feeding both of them." She launched into curse words while I dutifully listened, wanting almost desperately to get her to come to my house. I said nothing.

And I dreamed that night in a manner alien to my experience. I saw the infantile scrawl of Lalo Hernandez on a crumpled sheet of paper, the string of words lifted off the paper in a long black thread, woven within Mirabel's fingers like a cat's cradle as her invocations were offered before the candlelit crucifix in her sanctuary, her floor-length sheer negligee hanging open. I asked her what the words meant, but she only stared at me meaningfully and turned back to her altar. Then, suddenly, I was in the forest, kneeling under a rock crag and holding a grinning, dirt-encrusted skull with two ragged holes in it. I was overcome with terror because its jaw opened to speak—and then I woke up with a start, my heart pounding. In the silence of my bedroom I clearly heard Mirabel's heels clicking on the parquet wood flooring in my living room, and I did not sleep for the remainder of the night.

The rest of the week found me occupied at work. On Thursday, Principal Koger mentioned to me that Adele Goins had called him to apologize for being so distraught in her previous meeting with him. He shook his head, grinning. "San Vicente—gotta love this town." I also saw Tommy Sanchez in his letterman's sweater, talking to two of the cheer squad, and I thought him better off where he was now.

All else was ordinary in a town where I couldn't buy a green light in traffic and where nobody used their turn signals. I remembered asking a long-time resident why he didn't signal, and he shrugged. "Hey, Ese, everybody knows where I live." End of conversation.

Mirabel called me late Friday afternoon and said she was phoning me from her office. "*Querido*, I'm sorry I haven't seen you, but you know my mother is here right now. We are making some preparations. My mother doesn't like Anglos very much, and you know that Hispanics do not want their daughters to have anything to do with Anglo men."

"Yeah, it was one of my major frustrations in high school." I chuckled at the truism, but my mind was stuck on the word "preparations."

"It won't be long. I find I still have to cook for my useless daughter. She says that her boyfriend is not feeling well. She wanted me to make menudo for him—she won't eat it herself, but she knows I only make it on Fridays."

As usual, my emotions oscillated between desire and apprehension. "I hope Amelia comes to her senses."

There was a pause on the other end as I heard her talking to a co-worker, then back to me: "I will be with you soon. I can count on you?"

"I meant what I said, but I don't know what you are thinking…"

Mirabel ended the conversation abruptly. "I will call you." It made little sense to me that she would continue to help her daughter after the girl ran away and should have been arrested and brought back home. That she would actually provide food for the abductor who had certainly smashed her car window and seduced Amelia made no sense to me.

Coincidence is the rarest of circumstance, and I long ago ceased to believe that events and encounters can be written off as "coincidence." Because life is intentional, human activity necessarily affects events in a large or small manner. Magic was once defined as the art of causing change in accord with will, and history is replete with events writ large that show how powerful will can even affect the world. I had read much and accepted that magical operations must necessarily be accompanied by unusual events that alter the normal flow of day-to-day events.

For the next few days, I became aware of "coincidences," and I scrawled some notes that even now sit on my desk at home. I saw Adele Goins three times in as many days—once coming out of The Model Shop, the fashionable clothing store for married women on Broadway; then again at the grocery store where our carts passed in the canned vegetables aisle, as she avoided my eyes; and for the third time at the Shell station where I was refueling as she pulled into the bay.

That was not the end of it. Every day I saw the Lalo Hernandez lowrider somewhere in town, always with young Amelia in tow as they pursued their private lovers' errands. On Thursday I found myself at a stoplight with Hernandez next to me. I glanced across and was surprised to see Amelia driving, looking ridiculous as she hunched over the 12" diameter chrome-plated chain link custom steering wheel. Hernandez was slumped in the passenger seat, head lowered, an unlit cigarette drooping in his mouth. Amelia stared straight ahead, waiting for the always-overdue green light.

And I saw Tommy Sanchez in town at least twice, not counting his presence in the SVHS hallways. He was friendly and respectful as usual. Of course, there was a logical reason for these encounters, because all are coincidence—it is a favorite word of Anglos.

The only person I didn't see during the week was Mirabel, but I was not about to walk into City Hall to remedy that. I admitted to myself that I wanted to see her more than anyone else I could think of. She telephoned me briefly Thursday evening to say that Amelia still had not returned home but had called to say that Hernandez had taken sick and wasn't getting better. Mirabel then told me that Amelia had come to pick up a special dish that might help Lalo, because her daughter knew that she cured so many of San Vicente's own. Mirabel's tone of voice was difficult to assess, but I sensed a discordant undertone. She rang off hurriedly after I heard another female voice in the background. No doubt it was Amelia's *abuela*.

Friday at the high school included a pep rally 6th period in the gymnasium as the final game of the season loomed. I stood with Principal Koger at the north end as hundreds of students created a cacophony of cheers. I wondered how many hundreds of high schools across the nation were going through the same eternal rituals. The prospects for the evening were not promising as most of my friends were married and Friday evenings in San Vicente were for family nights at the local restaurants, and husbands dressed formally with shirts that buttoned or snapped.

That evening, sitting on the sofa and changing channels every five seconds, I decided that TV dinners were aptly named, but I did not want to reduce myself to watching the new television channel MTV, even though I could not resist watching the video version of ZZ Top singing "Gimme All Your Lovin'." I promised myself that I would finish my story of the Aaron Padilla mystery, but it always brought me back to Mirabel.

Then the phone rang, startling me.

For some reason, I let it ring four times before picking up. I had learned that when the phone rings, it usually is bad news or somebody wanting money. It was Mirabel, and she wanted far more than money. She was compelling, "You said I could count on you. I need you to go get my daughter. You know where she is? You have a gun."

"I know where she is, but why not the cops?"

"This is San Vicente. I would never tell them."

I did not question her reasoning, and I felt a peculiar emotion akin to loyalty, but perhaps it was just normal lust. "I'm going now." As with most human misery, I knew this crisis was precipitated by drugs, something Mirabel did not seem to recognize in her maternal concern.

"Please hurry, Querido. I know what I'm saying."

Next, I jacked the slide on the .45 and shoved it into my Levi's pocket. I was wearing a long-sleeved blue denim work shirt, and it would have to do. I grabbed my 6-volt flashlight, tested it and left the house lights on as I rushed out the door to find a blast of cold air and stinging drizzle. I trotted to the light blue Volkswagen Rabbit and put the flashlight on the seat. My senses ramped up as I smelled the rich ozone smell of electrical discharge in the air. It was good weather for high school football but not much else. The pistol dug into my mid-section as I turned the ignition key.

The Nameless Horror

The engine turned over with the first burst of the starter. I hit the headlight switch and almost cursed because the windshield was a mix of dotted rainwater and the film of dust. When I turned the windshield wipers on, the dried blades protested and smeared the glass. No time to fix that.

I slammed the transmission into reverse and rocketed out of the drive, spinning the wheel, then shoving it into first as I headed for the main drag. The rain was dampening the traffic, but it was still early, not even 9 p.m. I turned west onto Broadway and sped up the wide street toward the courthouse, ignoring the stop sign when I turned left onto Cooper Street. I was just barely able to see out of the windshield because of the streaking, but as the drizzle increased, the spitting sprinkle washed the dirt away.

When I swung into the dirt area in front of the duplex, I shut off the engine and vaulted out of the car. I didn't see the lowrider Monte Carlo. Lights were on in one of the apartments, the front door standing open. I approached slowly, almost casually. I did not regret carrying a weapon, knowing what I did of Hernandez and his drive-by history. I knocked

Terror Tales of the Southwest

on the open door but got no answer. The TV inside was blaring, and it was tuned to MTV. I heard Pat Benatar singing, "Why don't you hit me with your best shot…"

I burst into the room, the .45 in my hand. The ceiling light illuminated every corner and my nostrils were assailed with the stench of tobacco smoke and the unpleasant sweet smell of marijuana. The beige wall had no pictures, but Hernandez had apparently used a black marker to draw a large cross w/three rays—the same symbol I had seen on his arm. A low table was littered with empty beer cans and a half-full fifth of vodka. A large ashtray was piled high with butts, and cast-off clothing was draped on the black leather sofa whose cushions displayed rips in two places. The only item that did not fit was a half-full glass of milk. I picked it up and saw the trace of pink lipstick on the rim.

A pair of high heel shoes and a carry-on size beige leather handbag lay beside the sofa, and a pan with half-eaten burritos sat where people had been watching TV. To my left was the kitchen, lit by fluorescent ceiling fixtures. Nothing there, but the sink was piled with dishes and a half dozen glasses lined the counter. I looked into the refrigerator but there was nothing but a blue cardboard carton that had contained 18 cans of beer. The linoleum floor was grimy.

I went back to the living room where two doors—one to the bathroom, and one to the bedroom stood open. I looked into the bedroom to see a mess of tangled sheets and…a splotch of blood as big as my hand.

In the bathroom, the sink was littered with cosmetics and lotions. The smell of feces told me the toilet had backed up, and I did not have to look. On the tank top I saw three used pencil-diameter syringes, and in the sink, was a Johnson&Johnson empty package for a gauze bandage.

Back in the living room, I paused. They had been there, perhaps within the past half hour, and I tried to think where they would be. I looked down at the front door sill and my breath caught in my throat. It was a blood trail on the threshold. Had that evil bastard hurt or killed Amelia? Time was now my enemy.

I took a chance. If they had left within the past 10 minutes or so I would have seen them driving down Broadway from Cooper. In the other direction, the street led past the cemeteries and to U.S. Highway 90 heading south. That was the direction they had taken.

For some reason, I scooped up the handbag and stuffed the shoes into it before running to my car. Outside, I felt the denim shirt tight on my shoulders as the cold rain spatter darkened the denim. I had to be right, and I stabbed the accelerator, making the front wheels spew gravel as I aimed for the paved road. Behind me the apartment door stood open, a yellow rectangle of light getting smaller as I went from first to second, to third gear, my headlights lancing ahead, searching.

It was only a mile farther that I hit the brakes. I glimpsed the shine of chrome rims on a parked car at the entrance to the Catholic Cemetery. As I pulled to a stop off the pavement, I could see that the distinctive lowrider was not parked—it was wrecked, listing slightly to starboard where it collided with one of the 8-foot tall white-painted brick gate posts, flanking the 10-feet wide paired iron gates. The car had struck with some force without damaging the gate, but the nose of the vehicle was bashed in and slightly raised, the passenger door hanging open. The dirt entrance approach showed a cruel grooved scar in the gravel where the driver had slammed on the brakes and swung into collision with the closed entrance. Could I be too late?

I killed the ignition and climbed out of my car 60 feet from the Monte Carlo, with a flashlight in one hand, the cocked .45 in the other. The moment I opened my car door I heard piercing screams as I tried to control my panic, my heart thudding against my ribs.

That 60 feet seemed as far as a mile as I advanced in a crouch, pistol extended. The first thing the flashlight showed was the girl in the passenger seat. Her arms were flailing, and her voice was a shrieking wail, a combination of terror and despondency in an endless night. It was the scream of a lost soul, and I was now her lifeline.

I approached the open car door, my car headlights shining through the cold drizzle, projecting my shadow onto the car. I could see my breath. The cold rain was soaking my denim shirt. I shouted, "Out of the car, Amelia. Get out now!" She just sat, her hands shaking furiously in front of her face, while her screams came in waves.

I got close to the car door when I heard another sound. It was a low grisly howling. It must be Hernandez, and perhaps he was injured when his car hit the cemetery gatepost.

In the beam of the flashlight I could see blood on Amelia's jeans, and then I pointed the beam deeper into the passenger compartment. Dear God! The steering wheel was wet with blood and a red smear was emblazoned on the inside of the windshield. My light went to Hernandez's face; his head was thrown back, his gaping mouth in a twisted "O" shape. From deep in his chest came the ghastly howling sound. Then I saw IT as the flashlight descended to the man's midsection.

Amelia now covered her face with both hands, but her screams never stopped. What I saw then can never be erased from my memory. The horror of it will stay with me for the rest of my life. Amelia! Get out of that car! I don't know if I actually said it or thought it, but I was transfixed on the thing that was Lalo Hernandez, his black eyes sightless, his mouth yawning as the unearthly howling sound waxed in volume.

That was when I saw the chrome-plated .25-caliber pocket pistol in his hand. Hernandez was raising the gun!

Simultaneously, I raised the .45, following the flashlight's beam. My pistol was cocked, and I was filled with revulsion and terror, wanting to extinguish whatever life I saw in that caricature of man. I never pulled the trigger.

Before I could squeeze off my first round, Lalo Hernandez abruptly turned the gun and jammed the chrome plated muzzle into the roof of his mouth, blowing a hole in his brain. Even then the howling would not stop.

The odor from inside the car was indescribable—that of the slaughterhouse and worse. There was a smell of putrefaction, and I dropped the flashlight to the ground, reaching into the car with my left hand and grabbing the forearm of the unresponsive teenager. I shouted her name and yanked with all my strength. I felt my gorge rise, vomit sour in my throat.

I pulled her from the car while she stumbled as though having no strength in her legs. I threw her to the blackened gravel of the parking area, and she rolled onto her face in the grime. Now I backed away from the wrecked car, retrieving my flashlight from the ground.

When I pointed the flash beam into the Monte Carlo for the last time, I saw the form in the driver's seat wracked with spasms, the unearthly noise hollow and hellish. It could not be, but the pistol was still inside Hernandez's mouth. The howling was issuing from…

Suddenly I was vomiting, retching until only sour bile dripped from my mouth. The sounds from that car, the indescribable foulness of the odor, and what I was witnessing, became too much for me to withstand.

Terror Tales of the Southwest

I heard a soft moan from Amelia and was once more aware of the near-freezing rain on my face and shirt. I shoved the 45 in my right jeans pocket and wiped my mouth. I put the flashlight on the ground and went to the teenager who was still sprawled, motionless, on the wet ground. I lifted her gently and half-carried her to my car where I dumped her into the passenger seat before going back for the flashlight.

When I returned to my vehicle, I could still hear the daemonic noise issuing from the wrecked Monte Carlo, and I got into my driver's seat, slammed the door, and punched the accelerator, making the wet gravel growl, trying to be anywhere but sitting at this gate to the netherworld. I pointed my car back into town. I would take Amelia to my house before doing anything else. I avoided Main Street because the post-game cruising parade would be in full swing.

I pulled into my driveway and helped Amelia out of the car before grabbing the beige handbag. She was whimpering and unsteady. I noticed for the first time that her feet were bare. I half-carried her through my front door and placed her on the sofa. The lights were still on, and the cluttered living room seemed too normal for what we had been through.

Her clothes were rain-soaked and spattered with blood, but I did not think it proper to undress her. She was shaking from the cold, and I went to my bedroom to retrieve a heavy wool blanket that I almost smothered her with. I got a towel from the bathroom and knelt down to wrap her bare and dirty feet. Despite the trauma, her toenails were still showing careful pink nail polish. For the first time, in the light of my living room, I could see that Amelia's right cheek sustained an ugly abrasion from my rough handling getting her out of the Monte Carlo. She still seemed oblivious to her surroundings as she hugged herself and cried softly.

My next move was to the telephone. I dialed Mirabel's number, and she answered on the first ring. "Mirabel, come get your daughter." She just said, "Ten minutes."

Not knowing what else to do, I went to the kitchen and poured milk into a sauce pan, adding powdered chocolate milk mix and turning on the front burner of the stove. In a few minutes, I was pouring the steaming cocoa into a large mug and taking it to the living room, where I wrapped Amelia's hands around the warm cup and guided it to her dry, pale lips. She had that objectionable odor of a woman who uses perfume that does not quite mask the acrid smell of cigarettes. She opened her eyes, and I saw for the first time that the pupils were pinpoints, the pale green of her irises no longer luminous. That slimy son-of-a-bitch had lured her into drugs, probably cocaine, during that short time he had power over her. It was a triumph of vengeance to know that Lalo Hernandez was dead or even worse than dead.

Ten minutes later, Mirabel walked in without knocking. Wearing a tracksuit and running shoes, she looked at me briefly and went to the sofa, sitting down and taking her daughter into her arms, "Mija, Mija," Mirabel murmured as she rocked her little girl whose tangled hair and pale face had transformed the teenager into a child.

"Do you know what to do now?" I caught Mirabel's attention and she replied with a slight nod, closing her eyes. I handed her Amelia's handbag with the shoes sticking out, and she removed the towel and slid the shoes onto her daughter's feet.

They stood up and Mirabel asked if she could borrow the blanket, keeping it wrapped around the girl's wet clothes. I nodded as the three of us moved toward the front door. I wanted to tell her about the horror at the cemetery, but she asked nothing. I followed them out of my house to the front gate. The drizzle had stopped, and the air was tinged with frost.

The cold penetrated my wet shirt.

After putting Amelia into the passenger seat of the Malibu, Maribel went to the driver's side and her lips formed a silent "thank you," and lifted her hand with thumb and little finger extended—the universal symbol for "I'll call." I wondered what was planned when she got back to 6th Street.

Back inside my house, I had to wash the sour taste from my mouth as I tried to calm myself. Sleep evaded me again, and every time I dozed, I found myself looking inside that wrecked car looking at something too horrible to describe.

The next week I heard nothing from Mirabel, and the story about the wreck at the cemetery did not make sense. Yes, they found the car, but there was a phrase about a "charred body" that could not be right, unless somebody set the car on fire. I never learned what happened after I took Amelia away from the horror. My conflicting emotions about Mirabel found me longing for her and feeling an undercurrent of dread as well.

When I finally got a call from Mirabel, she told me that a much-chastened Amelia was back in school full time, stripped of the evil habits Hernandez introduced to her. Amelia still woke up screaming, but she remembered less about that November night than I did. She no longer defied her mother, and I noticed her in the halls having regained much of her previous fair skin and lustrous hair. It may have been my imagination but she did not seem to behave as frivolously as she did before. Mirabel told me she had invited Tommy Sanchez to have dinner with them in the near future. Everything seemed to revolve around the mysteries of food, and I had a craving for *biscochitos*.

Then, in a late November night, I sat bolt upright in bed gripped by a nightmare, finding myself once again at the cemetery. My flashlight painted the slack form of Lalo Hernandez leaning back, his mouth open as he jammed the little .25-caliber auto pistol into the roof of his mouth and shot himself to escape the indescribable. I saw the demon for myself, though that word may be inadequate.

The author of the book had spoken of a creature gnawing inside the stomach of the accursed, but he was loathe to describe the fulfilment of it. Aaron Padilla had died alone in the forest, driven to madness and suicide by the thing inside him that was gnawing its way out, leaving his blood inside his car before he ran screaming into the forest night and killed himself to stop the agony and the terror.

Twenty years later, Lalo Hernandez fought the demon that grew inside his stomach, with Amelia Valles as the witness. As she screamed, I saw the thing burst from his belly, spraying blood onto the windshield and onto his passenger.

It was a horror beyond my descriptive abilities. Hernandez's peritoneum was rent asunder, the skin ripped and organs extruded. The thing—the thing I saw was an oily black blob wrapped in Hernandez's intestines. It throbbed and pulsed like a growing black liver, shiny with a viscous excrescence and a second protrusion growing from the first blackness. That second abomination opened its mouth to reveal glistening razor-sharp teeth that gnashed and chewed, even though Hernandez was already dead. The blasphemous mouth in the lump with no eyes spewed blood and organ fragments as it destroyed its host's torso. It was undulating, expanding as it answered the curse that called it from its nighted dimension beyond our reality.

As I pulled Amelia Valles from that car and retreated in horror, I could still see the glossy black unnameable thing, swollen and growing as it consumed its human host. My nostrils were choked with a smell so noisome and sickening that I vomited in my revulsion. As I picked up the supine Amelia to get her away from the charnel evil, I heard the low-pitched howling and knew it didn't come from Hernandez. That blasphemy was coming from the faceless mouth as it called to the cosmic chaos from whence it came in a voice that no human could replicate. As I relived that dark moment, a phrase entered my mind: "and corruption shall return unto corruption." I could not remember where it was written.

* * *

With the coming of Thanksgiving week, I had begun to regain my sleep habits, though the nightmare returned occasionally, just when I was sure it had been exorcised. Now it was the night before Thanksgiving, a school holiday. Putting some clothes into the laundry basket, I felt something in the watch pocket of a pair of Levi's I had worn at least two weeks before. Inside the pocket, I found a quarter and two dimes, leaving me to sit on the bed remembering.

Still clutching the coins in my left hand, I lay down heavy with growing fatigue and only a bedside lamp burning while I seemed to doze. I did not know how much time passed, but suddenly I was awake as I heard the front door open. I had forgotten to lock it! As I lay there, my breath came quicker, but I did not reach for the .45 on the nightstand.

There was the clear sound of heels clicking on the parquet living room floor. She walked into the bedroom and she threw the folded wool blanket onto the bed as she shrugged out of her coat and let it drop to the floor, revealing something silken and clinging underneath. My blood was racing when I felt the press of her soft warm flesh against me under the covers. All else evaporated inside my mind as I celebrated her power to cure.

Missions To Venus

There was a golden age of science fiction, in which writers filled the solar system with rocket ships blasting off to Mars, the moons of Jupiter, the asteroids, the Moon, and especially Venus. That golden age of science fiction lasted from the late 1920s into the 1950s, creating Buck Rogers, Flash Gordon, and many other space adventurers. Before man actually went into space, the romance of science fiction found endless adventures, with intrepid rocket pilots leaving the White Sands Spaceport and seeking the exotic beings waiting for them on alien worlds.

Such pulp magazines as *Fantastic, Amazing Stories, Planet Stories, Wonder Stories*, and others, supplied a monthly diet of space operas, and some of the magazines were certain to feature at least one Venus story on a regular basis. There is little doubt that these stories and the movies they spawned created a generation of space devotees whose offspring never stopped believing in the possibilities of space travel and continue to seek the exploration of the universe today, leading to the space stations predicted by Wernher von Braun and the eventual bases on the Moon and Mars. Despite the growing body of data claiming that the mist-shrouded planet could not support life as we know it, classic sci-fi writers were obdurate in their support of the possibilities waiting behind the cloud curtain of Venus.

The reading public had a voracious appetite for these adventures, and movies began to reflect this interest of life on Venus and Mars without expecting scientific precision. "Rocketship XM", "Angry Red Planet", "Forbidden Planet", "Queen of Outer Space", "Quatermas and the Pit", were some of the many- movies that made travel to other planets seem normal and ordinary. It was only the beginning. As for Venus, its mist-shrouded surface was known early on to be inhospitable to life, but as late as the 1950s it was speculated that Venus might even be the home base of the flying saucers and their occupants. Some even speculated that the poles of Venus would have almost livable temperatures and hidden civilizations.

So, revisit the technology of the 1940s and its speculation of how easy it would be to pilot a rocket ship by dead reckoning across 36 million miles with the navigation, communication, and military equipment would be carried in the missions to Venus in the succeeding decades. Ingenious developments would make it possible for intrepid explorers to survive and enable human triumph in the far-flung reaches of the universe. So, we invite you to blast off for Venus and the high adventures lurking on the second planet!

Terror Tales of the Southwest

Blast off to Venus

The thunder wrapped around him like a blanket, and the capsule began to vibrate as the rocket lifted from the desert launch pad at White Sands. As it lifted, gaining velocity, he felt himself gaining weight as though a giant hand were pushing him down into the cushions of the pilot seat that kept him at a prone position. His stomach churned, and a flash of panic overcame his rigorous training for a moment. Col. Mark Chennault was on his way to Venus.

Desperation lay in the capsule with Chennault, and the three-month journey could not pass quickly enough. This was the third rocket to Venus, but what had happened to the first two? The advanced science of 1954 had made the Top Secret Venus program possible, and the Hyperborea, as Wernher von Braun had whimsically named this giant ship, was both a supply ship and a rescue vessel for the first two missions that were supposed to send signals back from the cloud planet but had not reported in.

The thrust of the liquid-fueled booster was sending a 250-foot giant into the night sky and pushing it inexorably eastward to the outer edges of the atmosphere where Chennault would jettison the first stage and ignite the experimental fission engine that would continue acceleration to approximately 20,000 miles per hour. He would have his rendezvous with Venus at its conjunction with Earth orbit, about 30 million miles from Earth.

Chennault felt consciousness slipping away as the acceleration pressed him down, down, into the stiff cushions of his chair. He forced himself to think about the Venus Project. It began with mysterious signals picked up by radio and emanating from Venus in 1946 and 1947; the regular, repeated and complex pulses were never deciphered, but the office of Vannevar Bush tasked the German scientists at White Sands to begin a plan to send men into space. As secret as the Manhattan Project and as closely guarded as the study of flying saucers, the Venus Project grew from the Von Braun design of a Nazi rocket in 1944 that would have been powerful enough to reach New York City. It was rumored at war's end that Von Braun had also begun designs on a Mars rocket before Germany's defeat.

It took seven years, but with the help of Los Alamos and Kirtland laboratories, no expense was spared to build three rockets capable of traveling to Venus. The first two ships would each take a crew of four scientists to land and explore the polar area of Venus. Accommodations on board would allow the crew to live in the ships, but there would not be insufficient fuel to take off again from the second planet. The third rocket was twice the size of the first two, and it would be capable of the return trip, bringing the riches of scientific research, as well as retrieving the exploration crews.

Von Braun's original V-2 had sent a 1-ton warhead into the stratosphere, and his Venus ships had doubled that capacity. When Chennault looked at the pre-flight inventory for Hyperborea, he found not only spare suits and personal items, but weapons, ammunition, and a locker with 24 cases of C-rations in the military wood boxes, each box with sufficient canned and packaged food to feed eight men with three meals each for threee earth weeks. The other two ships were similarly provisioned.

Chennault had been awe-struck when he approached the launch pad at midnight. A lift inside the towering gantry crane elevated him to the cockpit of the rocket. The searchlights focused on the rocket tonight in the desert had made his elevator ascent surreal, and there was no escaping the importance of his mission and its tremendous expense. He had lain alone in the dark cockpit for at least an hour, strapped into the cabin as the crane crept slowly away from the ship on massive metal treads. His only company was the glowing dials of the instruments in the panel in front of him. Only when the waiting was over did his stomach convulse as the rocket motors exploded into life, creating instant daylight at the launch pad.

Now, the shining projectile had left Earth behind and was knifing past the stratosphere. Warning light on the console—30 seconds to Brennschluss.

As he watched the second hand sweep, Chennault wondered what had happened to the first two expeditions. Did they die crashing into Venus? Were they surviving and waiting for the Hyperborea to rescue them? The Celestia and the Thule lacked the ability to return from Venus; they were designed to glide to the surface and to depend upon life support systems that would maintain the crew until the arrival of Hyperborea. It would not be until the successful return of this third mission that the government would decide whether to reveal the facts to the public.

Five, four, three, two, one, and Chennault hit the release switch. The ship shuddered as the massive exhausted rocket booster fell away, arcing in flames back to Earth. The second toggle switch ignited the nuclear fission engine, and the vehicle continued its acceleration into the blackness of space.

As he slowly raised the pilot seat to vertical position, Chennault reminisced about the endless discussions he and the research staff had pursued about the hazards of space travel. Tonight, regardless of the risk, his ship was a silver needle, threading infinity. It was a far cry from WWII when he flew the night skies in his Northrop P-61 Black Widow twin-engine fighter, strafing German trains and sometimes glimpsing the unsettling Foo Fighters flashing through the night sky. Other pilots said they were German secret weapons, but Chennault was smart enough not even to report them. In the cauldron of war, he and his Air Corps friends had jokingly decided that all war was directly related to the scarcity of women, and he had retained this view as an item of personal conceit that he seldom voiced.

Strange, but he had never mentioned this philosophy to his fiancé Teresa, and tonight he imagined her perfectly permed hair that curled just below her ears, while her common sense enthusiasm was even now focused on planning a wedding upon Chennault's triumphant return.

Teresa had been frosty when he told her of being selected for a long, secret mission, but Chennault didn't tell her that, of all the pilots tested, Col. Turner had told him that he was probably the best suited for a solitary mission. That was not exactly what a prospective bride would find inspiring.

Terror Tales of the Southwest

The fate of two four-man crews on a strange planet now hung in the balance waiting on this one flight of the best product of human ingenuity. The nuclear fission engine supplemented by eight reserve solid fuel rockets were welded to the fuselage between the rocket fins, capable of slowing descent to the tail-down landing on Venus, then blasting off from the planet, and finally landing back at White Sands.

The radio crackled, "Hyperborea 1, Hyperborea 1, do you copy?"

"Roger, Mission Control. I read you five-by-five."

"Perfect trajectory, Hyperborea. Check all gauges and prepare for sleep."

"Roger, Mission Control. I have strapped on the intravenous armband and set the timer."

"Hyperborea, as a reminder, from what we learned with the other two ships, you could find within 24 hours your radio signals may not get back to us, but the homing beacons on Celestia and Thule will guide you once you are within 1,000 miles of Venus. Then it's your baby. We still don't know whether Earth radio signals are reaching Venus."

"Roger that, Mission Control. I can't wait to do some real flying." Chennault knew that his pilot skills had put him in this seat. He always said he could master any flying machine ever built.

"Over and out, Hyperborea."

It sounded so final, and Chennault found himself alone in the blackness, illuminated by the greenish glow of the instrument panels, surrounded by the digestive hum of the panels and the thrumming sound of the fission engine as maximum speed was attained.

Suddenly the fission tubes went silent as Chennault hit the kill switch in synch with the tremendous velocity of 20,000 miles per hour showing on the dial. Yet, as he sat in near-zero gravity, it seemed that the ship was suspended, motionless. Barring collision with space debris, his next awareness would be the approach to Venus, using reverse rocket thrust to slow the ship, skidding into its atmosphere, and homing in to the location of the other two rockets.

Chennault set the controls of the intravenous device that would drip sedative and saline solution into his arm to maintain his body fluids and keep him asleep for the bulk of the interplanetary journey. Alone with thoughts of home and the adventure ahead, he eased into unconsciousness as black as space itself.

Descent to Another World

The world turned red and pulsing, and Chennault felt weighted down and aching. A buzzer sounded intermittently as he clawed his way to consciousness. Training took over, and he pulled off the armband, switched off the alarm, and surveyed the gauges as though he had just looked at them moments before. Through a porthole, he could see the pale luminous disc of Venus, as large as the rising moon on Earth. He was racing to meet her. Or was she racing to meet him?

The next days were occupied checking the rations and armaments stowed beneath the cabin floor, practicing the loading of film in the cameras, making entries in the logbooks, and doing tension exercises to regain condition of the muscles that had atrophied in zero gravity.

Day and night could only be measured by the hands of the cabin clocks, but soon the unmistakable faint pull of gravity told Chennault that his flight skills would soon be tested as never before, when the hydraulic ailerons on the ship's four vanes would push the rocket into position for landing. The final day was spent firing retro bursts to reduce the rocket's speed in preparation for entering the cloud atmosphere.

The radar unit showed a distance of 4.737 miles when the faint beacon tone sounded through the speaker, and its waveform appeared on the oscilloscope. It was time for the pilot to fly his ship. Venus swung in its orbit toward him, and the ship was being slowed to be ready for entry.

Soon enough, friction with the atmosphere of Venus aided Chennault as the speed on the velocimeter dipped below 900 miles per hour, but his ears were tuned to the beacon signal, his eyes on the peak of the signal on the scope. It was encouraging as the beacon was positioned near the pole of the planet. Scientists had very much agreed that the planet was too hot for human existence on most of the surface of Venus, but mysterious radio signals from Venus had been monitored, so it seemed likely that the polar regions were the source.

Circling the planet once, Chennault watched as the beacon signal grew toward its peak, and he pulled back on the stick, feeling the hydraulics working in the rocket vanes. The ship was pushed perpendicular to the surface, hurtling downward through growing mist.

Now! The instability of the Hyperborea's attitude was sending it downward. Too fast! Too fast! Chennault hit the toggle switch of the fission engine, its powerful thrust fighting the increasingly powerful pull of Venus.

Speed was 600, 400, and the ground was 15,000 feet away, 13,000, 10,000. Descent was too fast. Chennault was looking upward at the dials. Speed was 250—altitude 3,000. Too fast. He felt a sudden panic. The thrust was not enough. Though the g-forces pulled him down into the seat, Chennault reached out and hit the switch for the solid fuel thrusters. The roar startled him and the ship lurched, He could taste a trickle of blood flowing from his nostrils. This was the moment. Live or die!

The dials started to blur, and suddenly it all seemed so impossible. Could velocity reach zero at the same time as altitude disappeared? The rocket shook with the combined explosions of the combustion chambers. Nothing was visible outside the ports, even if Chennault had time to look out the portholes. Involuntarily he was trying to yell against the roar of the rocket motors.

The shock of contact with the surface of Venus banged Chennault's head against the headrest. The motors! Instinctively, he slapped at the toggle switches to shut down the engines. The roar was replaced by a sudden silence, not unlike the quiet of space. The rocket pilot lay in the command chair, panting in exhaustion, perhaps for five or ten minutes, throbbing with pain and fatigue. Outside the portholes was a pearly grey light, a luminous mist. Yet, there was no time to waste; the beacon sound reminded him that he must find Celestia and Thule as quickly as possible.

With some difficulty, Chennault pulled on the thin rubber sheath over his flight suit, designed to protect from the theorized acidic atmosphere of Venus clouds. He stopped only to open a can of beans and wieners from the stored C-rations stored under the cabin floor, and then he strapped on the canteen belt and pistol holster before drawing out the Thompson M1A1 submachine gun and spare magazines.

The exterior gauges were promising. The exterior temperature was 120 degrees Fahrenheit, and droplets of moisture were forming on the 6" thick glass of the portholes. All

Terror Tales of the Southwest

Chennault had to do was don the headpiece and oxygen apparatus. With the submachine gun slung over his shoulder, he was ready.

The long lever inside the first of the two airlock doors was drawn down, and he felt rather than heard the ladder rungs extending outward below the outer door. With a swoosh, the exterior door swung inward. Chennault looked out at an alien planet. Though the clouds seemed impenetrable, the light penetrating the mists was considerable. He took a photograph with the Leica camera and its fast 50mm f2.0 lens. Visibility was at least 150-200 yards, even with the swirling currents of a strong breeze. The smell of Venus penetrated the oxygen mask, sulfurous and cloying, overlaid with the choking smells of decaying vegetation.

Slowly, Chennault descended the round, staple-shaped ladder rungs. The final 12 feet was an extension ladder that went to the ground. The ground was soft, and he swiftly backed away from the cooling blast tubes, remembering the warning about radioactivity associated with the fission engines.

Chennault was sweating already as he looked around at the black soil covered with a lacework of yellowish lichens among clumps of blackish-green moss that glistened. A sudden burst of rain swept across the tableau, and he could tell that the water was acidic, yet probably diluted and not of great danger. He began walking across the spongy surface and had progressed about 150 yards when he saw the dull projection of a rocket fin. His breath came quickly, and he trotted eagerly until he could see the entire form. Identification was instant, as both Celestia and Thule used three fins in an elevator/rudder configuration whose tips ended in retro rockets; the ships' undersides were flattened and reinforced in anticipation of a belly landing.

It was the Celestia, but Chennault's heart fell, a lump forming in his throat. Metallic debris was scattered in a trailing pattern showing how the craft had come in for its landing on the belly skids, but there had been an explosion. The guts of the craft were strewn in a broad ribbon.

The nose of the V-2 shaped rocket was intact, but as Chennault approached, he grimaced. Through the windows he could see two bodies still strapped into their seats in a state of advanced decomposition. The seats behind those were gone as if the center of the ship had been punched out from within. Looking more closely, he could see that the entire hull of the ship seemed to be partially eaten away, as though the aluminum skin was corroding in patches. The Celestia could not have been here longer than 16 weeks, but it looked as though it had been there for decades.

Where was Thule? It was obvious that the beacon signal did not come from destroyed Celestia, so Thule must be somewhere just beyond the limits of the mist-bound extremes. Chennault felt the perspiration dripping down into his boots, the hothouse temperatures were now causing his temples to pulse and ache.

Suddenly Chennault froze as a vortex of wind spun the mist cloud and lifted it momentarily. He had a glimpse of a cliff of black granite, its immensity took his breath away. It seemed to slant backward from the vertical about 10 degrees but, as he advanced toward it, he could see that it jutted upward from the soft soil almost as if it had pushed up from the depths of the planet. He could not begin to see the summit, as clouds collided with the rugged black walls, then swirled as an updraft created a vacuum that left a widening field of vision. The rock colossus could only be described as a mountain range of undetermined extent, more abrupt than the Himalayas, so cyclopean that very little detritus or build-up could be seen in its approaches.

As far as Chennault could see, to the left and to the right, the gray and black rock formations were unbroken, their summit still invisible to him, perhaps miles high. He was awestruck as there was nothing like this on Earth.

The shifting mists played with his vision as he walked along, now about 300 yards from his ship. There was something else on that endless mountain cliff, something amazing. He glimpsed it before the mists closed in again, and he stood there gaping before recovering his wits and starting off again on his primary mission—to find Thule.

Hyperborea disappeared into the mists behind him as he slogged forward, now finding the soil wet and slippery, but he found what appeared to be a broad skid mark, fully 70 feet wide that plowed a furrow into the earth. He followed it, and there it was—the oversized V-2-shaped Thule just at the limit of his vision.

Chennault tried unsuccessfully to run across the soft turf toward the ship that had obviously landed successfully, then slid sideways for more than 200 yards, pushing a wedge of wet soil ahead of it before coming to rest at the base of the towering cliff face. By the time he reached the Thule, he was winded, and he leaned against the metal hull, his face pressing against one of the rocket's cabin portholes.

The crew was gone, the storage bins wide open and half empty. Restraint belts dangled from the seats, and it was plain that the four men had survived and had left the ship. Chennault was elated; all he had to do was find them. They must be out conducting the scientific experiments that their expedition had been charged with. Chennault was suddenly eager to hear another human voice, and he raised his mask to yell "THOO—LAH" into the mist, hoping to hear a response.

The call echoed eerily off the face of that towering cliff, and the response came almost immediately from deep in the mist. The sound was a wave of ululation, flowing from east to west, rising and falling in volume. Chennault felt alone and suddenly frightened at the inhuman tide of sound coming out of the luminous cloud.

Then came a rain of projectiles. Small stones, chunks of what seemed to be wood or pieces of bone peppered the metallic hull of the Thule, and also striking Chennault's suit. Some could be ignored, but then he felt the sting of some pebbles hitting him with dangerous force. He saw shapes coming out of the mist, and he rushed to the starboard side of the ship, knowing where airlock door was located. A torrent of stones and other projectiles set up a din as they struck the sturdy hull of Thule. The catch was depressed and Chennault dove through it, pushing the airlock until it hissed shut, sealing the compartment.

Now through the inner door, he secured it and shoved the security bar into place. The hull vibrated as it was swarmed by an army of living creatures. Chennault crouched, and looked through a porthole, seeing small misshapen animals rushing the craft, throwing themselves against the sturdy hull. The faces were distorted hybrid of human and animal features. There were eyes and mouths, hands and possibly legs, but the chaotic onslaught never allowed one form to be visible through the port long enough for him to fully define the shapes. The noise swelled to a crescendo mixture from the projectiles striking the ship and the high-pitched throat noises of the attackers that accompanied their frenzy.

Chennault stripped off his mask, peeled back the rubber covering of his suit, and he lay

Terror Tales of the Southwest

down on the cabin floor of Thule, exhausted, and overcome by the heat and by his inter-planetary journey. Lying there, he struggled out of the suit, turned on the air conditioning switches, and lay naked on the metal floor, letting the horrid vibrations set up by the twisted horde of Venus batter the hull furiously. Sometime during the next hour, as shown on the hands of the cabin clock, he slipped into unconsciousness.

Chennault was next aware of the soft hum of the air system. Somehow, the horrifying attack had ended, and when he got to his feet, he saw nothing on the sward outside the rocketship. Perhaps the ghastly creatures were waiting for him deep in the mist outside, but he was more concerned about the fate of Thule's four-man crew. No matter how he felt about the threat, he had to go out there one more time. Grateful that the electrical systems of Thule were functional, he switched off the power.

Once he had climbed into the suit again, he pulled the lever on the airlock bur, after he pulled down the facemask, he picked up the Thompson and inserted a 30-round magazine, pulling the bolt back. He also jacked a cartridge into the chamber of the .45 automatic pistol. After pulling the inner door shut behind him, he opened the door to the hot blast of Venus air.

The light should have changed. It had been hours since he had left the Hyperborea, but there was no change in the luminous, misty world. Was it noon? Twilight? There was no way of telling. A sprinkle was falling on him, warm and sulfurous. Though the earth was soft, there were tracks still visible by the hundreds, one of them very clear next to the hull with a roughly triangular heel pad and a squat oval extending to three long toes with claws. He shuddered and began walking.

Wait. Chennault remembered seeing something before the onslaught of the misshapen horde. It was something on the cliff, and he backtracked, looking upward. There it was! He had seen it. Perhaps the towering mountain cliffs were astounding enough, but it was im-possible to explain what he was looking at now. It was a perfect rectangle, probably 20 feet wide and at least 70 feet tall. The color of obsidian, it glistened in the featureless light, black as outer space and polished like a mirror, set into the cliff face. How could it be a natural feature?

Chennault approached the cliff, realizing that the lower edge of the silent rectangle was probably just above his reach. There was no seam, just an even cut in the granite with the massive sheet of unknown material inserted into it. Once he found the crew of Thule, he would make certain they had done photography of what Chennault wanted to call "the monument." It could be natural, just as quartz on Earth was formed in geometric shapes.

He walked on, submachine gun at the ready, estimating how long it would take him to retreat to the Thule again if he had to. The cliff face on his right was trickling with rivulets pouring down from the hidden summits deep in the clouds. Another hundred yards along the cliff, Chennault saw the glint of metal. Half buried in moss growing around it was the compact aluminum and leather of a Leica 35mm camera. The expedition had come this way!

The camera was showing some patina to the aluminum, but seemed intact when Chen-nault plucked it from the damp ground and stuffed it into the sample bag attached to the rear of the pistol belt. His footsteps were muffled by softness of the lichen-laced moss. Suddenly, he was startled by what he saw on the cliff face. He swung around and gaped at a second giant obsidian rectangle set into the granite. His turn was so sudden that the barrel of the submachine gun struck the rock face with a "chunk" sound.

The great rectangle was identical to the first one, and now Chennault was certain that this was an intelligent construction, its polished face gleaming in the light. But, there was no time to stare or contemplate the architect of these mysterious monuments. Something struck the cliff close to him. The small sound of his weapon on the rock had alerted the frightening enemy.

Horrors in the Mist

A trill issued from the mists, and at least a dozen stooped, naked creatures came rushing into view. Their lumpy bodies were grayish-white with yellowish patches on wet and glistening skin. The horrific faces were twisted in fury as they threw stones and elongated rods that looked like miniature spears. Chennault grinned and said out loud, "Here's a present from Earth," as he shouldered the Thompson and squeezed the trigger.

The weapon recoiled against his shoulder as it spewed .45-caliber slugs, the stuttering explosions echoing against the cliff face. Chennault fired timed bursts of four rounds, the bullets tearing into naked alien flesh. All of the charging creatures took hits, bowled over by the impact of multiple rounds.

At least a hundred yards away, a massive trilling and tittering rose as a wave of sound that was almost as loud as the sound of the machine gun. Chennault changed magazines and looked back. His retreat was cut off by a swarm of the horrible things advancing toward him. He fired two short bursts, cutting a swath through his attackers.

His only path was further along the cliff face, and he took it, trying to run while objects hit the cliff face next to him, sometimes stinging his back and shoulders. They were advancing on him, cutting him off from refuge at the rocketship Thule. The hellish high-pitched sounds now were coming from somewhere ahead of him as well.

At that moment, Chennault spied a cleft in the granite, a gap that seemed wide enough for a human body and tall enough for his 6-foot frame. There was no time to think—only moments to act. He pushed into the darkness of the cleft and faced the opening, backing up until he felt the end of the recess, scarcely five feet from where the Venus creatures were stampeding toward him.

Chennault drew the .45 Automatic and waited. The first horror jammed itself into the mouth of the chamber. Calmly, he aimed the pistol at the misshapen head. The resulting "Boom" was deafening, and a hole appeared in the middle of the creature's face, blowing out the rear of the head. The body was wedged into the opening, and another of its kind climbed on top of the soft, wet corpse. Chennault aimed and fired again, killing it instantly, while the legion of its fellows clawed and screamed to clear the opening and get at him. He aimed at the next invader, his back firmly against the wall. He squeezed the trigger, the pistol kicked in his hand, and then he was falling backward to the grinding sound of moving rock.

He fell with a thud, his breath explosively driven from his chest. One hand still gripped the .45, but the submachine gun held in the other hand was sliding out of reach, and a sharp pain in his backside told him that he had fallen directly on the camera. As he looked upward, he saw figures bending over him, and his fingers tightened on the .45.

"Welcome to Venus, Colonel." The deep voice filled Chennault with exultation.

"Brenner, it's really you! Carlson! Agar!" The faces came into focus as Chennault scrambled to get to his feet. They slapped him on the shoulder and shook hands all around.

"Sorry we couldn't make room for your friends out there, but this is a limited occupancy establishment," Maj. Charles Brenner, command pilot of Thule, was grinning. "Take a look around."

Chennault's nervous laugh was contagious. Now he took Brenner's suggestion. They stood in a megalithic passageway of astounding dimension. Worn stone formed the floor, close to 15 feet wide, and the walls were closely fitted blocks of granite. As far as he could tell, the walls were canted inward perhaps 15 degrees and were designed to meet at an apex perhaps 75 feet above in the darkness. The spectacular skill of the masons who built this reminded him of photos he had seen in The National Geographic magazine showing the pathway to the King's Chamber of the Great Pyramid at Giza.

Inhabitants of the Caverns

Yet it was not dark in this interior passage. Chennault saw the reason. A giant luminous rectangle west of where they were standing flooded the passageway with natural light. As he approached this powerful skylight, he realized that it was the interior of those obsidian mirrors he had witnessed as set into the cliff. Here, the rectangles served as a view of the outside, clearly showing the exterior features he had just walked through. He looked at Brenner, obviously waiting for an explanation.

"We don't know, Colonel. We have learned almost nothing, but we have met the inhabitants of Venus. They are not at all like the welcoming committee outside. At least we learned how to operate that sliding rock doorway."

Chennault was still gawking at the amazing cathedral ceiling of the passageway. "How far does this go?" It was all he could ask.

Capt. John Agar answered, "We don't have any idea. You'll understand when you see what's down the corridor."

His companions still wore their pistol belts, and Chennault picked up the Thompson, slinging it over his shoulder. Slowly they began walking, in step, along the corridor. The next thing Chennault noticed was the cool air wafting through the corridor. Then he heard the rush of water and an entire segment of the north wall revealed a narrow flume ten feet above the floor and fully 15 feet wide; cold water cascaded through the slit down into a shallow aqueduct, flowing along the corridor to some unseen destination. The cool air circulating was a distinct pleasure and, on the other side of the corridor, shoulder high began an elaborate frieze of sculpted symbols. Chennault looked at the others.

"Nope. These things look sort of like hieroglyphics, but I don't have a clue as to what the symbols are. I don't think they know, either." Brenner seemed intentionally obtuse about who "they" were.

At intervals, the great rectangles looked out on the hothouse planet, suffusing the corridor with bright light. In between, the walls were incised with the peculiar symbols, telling a story Chennault wished he could read.

As they walked, the three crewmen explained to Chennault how they had landed successfully, set the homing beacon and then began to venture out of the Thule to take readings. They too had been assaulted by a swarm of the outside creatures, retreating into the ship. It was then that the Venusians had emerged from within the cliffs and held the horde at bay with some type of whistle or horn whose high frequency squeal dispersed the attackers.

It was only when the Venus people had ushered them through the rock slab door that they realized Lt. Crabbe had been wounded. A white metal shaft, the size of a bolt from a crossbow, had penetrated his thigh. By the time they were safe inside the cavern, his leg was already pained and swelling from infection.

Their hosts had taken them to the interior and given them quarters, where they dressed Crabbe's wound and where he was still recuperating. From what they had learned since, they were being chaperoned by leaders of this society.

As for the crew of the Celestia, Brenner shook his head. Apparently the crew had not survived the explosion when their ship crashed into Venus.

Now the stone floor descended measurably as they strode briskly, the chilled water in the narrow aqueduct rushing noisily downward. The last massive rectangle window was behind them, and darkness grew. Brenner looked at Chennault, "Prepare yourself for a surprise." Carlson and Agar were following close behind them.

Chennault could see a different kind of light as they descended on the path. He remembered walking inside Carlsbad Caverns back in New Mexico and how the path descended into the bowels of the earth. Yet he was not prepared for what was opening up before him.

The splendor of the underground vista made Chennault gape once more. It was a polar cavern so vast that he could not see the extent of it. As with the corridor, the roof of this vault was invisible to him, perhaps because of a mist the hovered a hundred feet above the floor or perhaps because of the wondrous light source that seemed to replicate the sunlight he knew from Earth.

Clear crystal cylinders approximately 10 inches in diameter and made of some artificial material extended like precise stalactites from the hidden fastness of the ceiling. What that artificial daylight revealed was too much for Chennault to take in. For here were the people of Venus. Brenner seemed to know exactly where he was going, and they walked straight ahead, looking side to side at what could only be described by Chennault as cliff dwellings. In the distance, figures were moving along walkways and standing in groups.

"Colonel, we have not yet begun to understand this culture." Carlson spoke from behind him. "We don't see a scientific culture and yet they have built all these massive structures. They have remarkable textiles and an agriculture that puzzles us." He directed Chennault to look off to the right, at a distance that could have been as much as a mile away.

"My God, that looks like corn." Chennault was aghast.

"Just what we thought," Brenner interjected. As they looked around, they saw figures inside the dwellings, peering out at them. Some others were dimly descried in the distance where the tall stalks of the crop were growing. They were obviously human or human-like, but they were also obviously cautious of these aliens from another world.

"Hey, Guys, look at those light tubes, or whatever they are. They must be hundreds of feet long and weigh a ton. Stuff like that required manufacturing facilities. They must be an advanced culture." Chennault was also thinking about the architecture that made the caverns and which had formed the elaborate dwelling places, and then there was the radio equipment powerful enough to send signals intercepted by Earth.

"You'll see, Colonel. They are coming to greet us, but you won't hear very much. Their speech is…well…you'll see." A group of individuals emerged from a multi-story dwelling built into a relatively close cavern wall, perhaps 200 yards to their left.

Chennault strained his eyes, watching as these people approached. The officers and scientists at White Sands could have no inkling of the wonders now unfolding before the explorers. He glanced upward and saw a dozen birds gliding just below the mist above them. Were they ducks or perhaps even flying reptiles? Some kind of insect flew around his head, and Agar swatted at it, "You should see the swarms of bugs down by the lake. Oh, the lake is a couple of miles from here."

Carlson chimed in, "Lake, swamp—it's all the same thing, but we haven't seen half of what's under here."

"But the air here is breathable, while outside there's hardly any oxygen." Chennault was still awe-struck.

Brenner pointed upward. "See the mist swirling up there? There's a downdraft coming from way high up in the ceiling. These mountains must be as tall as Everest, and Agar here says that it is possible that oxygen is concentrated at higher altitudes, downdrafting with the high altitude winds."

The reception group slowly approached, walking in a leisurely manner. Chennault got his first look at the true Venusians. He glanced at Brenner, "You know them?"

Brenner nodded, "Four out of the five."

Five figures drew close to the space explorers, two of them male and three female. They were all of medium stature, standing almost 5'8", mesomorphic in form and straight of posture. They were not broad shouldered, but seemed sturdy.

The two males wore one-piece close-fitting coveralls that appeared to be fine leather, buttoned at the front with seven plain, gilded metal buttons from throat to waist, and they wore boots with long shanks. They were beardless, with slightly enlarged skulls and hair that grew naturally down over their ears. Their eyes were subtly elongated and slanted. To Chennault, it seemed they were staring at him intently. Suddenly he was feeling agitated, his mind a jumble of images.

"Hello, I am Col. Mark Chennault, pilot of the Hyperborea."

"Welcome. We knew you were coming here to join your companions." Chennault heard the words, but the speaker's pursed lips never moved." He looked at Brenner.

Brenner smiled at Chennault's surprise. "Yeah, we didn't know what was going on, but they talk directly to our minds. Oh, they can do vocal sounds, but they tend to use their vocal chords for musical sounds, and communicating emotions. We're not sure if they read our minds, but we learned real fast to pay attention when they projected words and pictures."

After adjusting to the oral/mental exchange medium, Chennault was still left wondering if they had names. He formed the strong mental sentence, "Who are you?"

"I am Artheme." He could hear the words in his mind as the two males parted, and Chennault got his first look at the women of Venus. The woman who spoke her name to his mind stepped forward and was looking at him from eyes that were a brilliant green beneath long, flowing straight black hair that fell in bangs over her forehead. Those oval and slanted eyes were framed by lids coated with luminous metallic shadow, the lashes and brows emphasized in a style that could only be described as Egyptian. She wore a shimmering silver ground-length gown that seemed almost liquid, her generous breasts jutting forward, her full hips stretching the metallic satin fabric. Her full lips were a glossy deep ruby color.

Chennault was instantly transfixed; his concentration was upon the unspoken words forming in his mind. Impressions were followed by sudden images of deep space and remarkable disc-shaped silver ships hurtling toward the cloud planet, descending to the surface in a dimly remembered past.

Artheme lifted her lustrous lids and the trace of a smile caught the corners of her closed red lips.

From behind, Carlson clapped his hand on Chennault's shoulder, startling him back to the moment. "Venus women are…different, but you'll get used to it."

"I don't think so…" Chennault ran a hand through his sandy hair and then felt the growing stubble on his face. His pulse was racing unaccountably, his eyes fixed on the woman Artheme. His mind was grappling with the images she had sent him of other visitors to their planet.

Brenner interjected, "We'll get you up to speed on that later." Now Carlson and Agar approached the other two women, both wearing similar garb to Artheme, but of differing colors. One gown was emerald green, and the woman's hair was a waterfall of gleaming platinum. The third woman's long hair was a different shade of blond, with a metallic fuchsia gown rippling with her movements. She and Carlson were looking at each other, and she was humming to him in a haunting musical tone that Chennault found almost mesmerizing.

As a group, they all now began walking toward the dwelling complexes at the south side of the immense cavern. Brenner walked ahead with the Venusian men, while the others followed, side by side. At one point Artheme's hand touched his, and he felt an electric surge course through him.

They entered what could only be described as an apartment, softly lit through two crystal cylinder tubes projecting through the ceiling. Brenner was obviously in wordless communication with the senior male, and Chennault looked around at the interior, appointed by a low grayish-green stone table and corresponding stools fixed within the smooth floor of the same stone. Stone pallets or bunks lined the walls of the apartment whose ceiling was gracefully domed over the entire enclosure, perhaps 55x25 feet. The pallets were covered with fabric cushions of varying colors, mostly beige and brown.

Various stoneware receptacles and shallow bowls were set on the table surface, as well as some unusual utensils that resembled spoons.

Agar spoke, "Before you ask, that door at the end leads to the facilities…" They walked around the apartment, and Chennault noticed gear belonging to the crew stacked by the inviting bunks. "…and food is distributed every day, brought right to the door. It's prepared at a central kitchen for hundreds of people living in here."

"But, how did they build all this? I don't see any machines or…" He was talking to Brenner.

The Eyes of Aratheme

Artheme was looking intensely at Chennault, commanding his attention, and pictures formed in his mind of the great circular silver ships penetrating the Venus clouds and landing in the polar region, just as Celestia, Thule, and Hyperborea had done. The image Artheme was showing him was from long ago, but he did not know how he knew this.

"Then, who…"

This time she spoke a word, her lips softly moving, "Anisaz." All three of the other crewmen turned to look at Chennault.

Carlson was the first to react to the word, "That's the mystery we haven't made any progress with. Then, we still are not sure who built some of the ancient stone buildings on Earth, are we?"

The reception committee showed that it was ready to withdraw, and Artheme reached out and touched him on the chest of his tunic. As she turned to leave, Chennault desperately wanted her to stay.

Left to their devices, a normal buzz of conversation ensued as Chennault picked a bunk to call his own. "When is it night around here?"

Brenner laughed, "Well, we have learned something to take back to Earth with us. Nobody could tell because of the clouds, but we now know that Venus is the only planet that rotates clockwise, and we figure that the days—not the years—are about 250 earth days. It's a little shorter in the polar region, but we are now beginning twilight and the time when the Venusians go outside to hunt and gather materials. They say that, even during the long night, the light tubes continue to function in here, even if the sun doesn't provide the source. We think that the cylinders extend through the granite, up to the mountain peaks and through the cloud cover. Astounding."

"But how?"

"You heard the babe—Anisaz. Now you know everything we do."

Chennault shook his head in wonderment and made ready to flop on the inviting cushions. He removed the magazine from the Thompson and laid the gun on the bed beside him. The rustling of men rummaging in their gear, the clink of metal, all subsided, and sleep came quickly to Chennault, although his thoughts remained on the woman in the silver gown and her magical gaze.

The pilot of Hyperborea awoke to the sounds of splashing water, spirited conversation, and the tramp of boots on the apartment floor. He felt more refreshed and energized than he had at any time since leaving Earth.

Mission Into Venus Hell

"Welcome back, Colonel," Brenner said as he emerged from the place where the water was flowing, some kind of towel wrapped about his midsection. "You might want to borrow my razor until we get a chance to visit your ship. Then we can get moving."

"We're going somewhere?" Chennault thought he wasn't going anywhere until he had eaten something. There were no C-rations in sight.

Brenner jerked his thumb toward the table that was piled with exotic fruits, some round; puffy loaves of bread or cake, and Chennault threw himself at the food, not thinking about its alien origin. Everything he tried was delicious, but he attributed that to his hunger. The notebooks of the rocket crew were also sitting there, filled with the observations the explorers had recorded since their arrival.

After breakfast, he washed and shaved, feeling as though he had spent the night in a five-star hotel. A few minutes later Brenner picked up Chennault's Thompson and tossed it to him. "To answer your earlier question, we're going outside, so strap on your oxygen gear."

"Why are we going out there? It's not very friendly."

Agar explained. "That's something else we've learned. Nice as it is in this cavern, the Venusians have to go out frequently to harvest certain plants, minerals, and also to capture certain kinds of creatures they use for meat. Pretty gutsy bunch."

"How about those things I was dancing with?" Chennault shuddered involuntarily.

"Nah," Carson chimed in, "those slimy things are toxic, even to the Venus diet. These guys have lost some of their number when those things find a way to surprise them. Our armament may help pay for these accommodations." He jacked a round into the chamber of his own .45 service pistol.

Chennault wasn't eager, but he was willing. "Maybe we can get to the ships and get more ammunition and oxygen bottles." He also had the errant thought that they could get into the Hyperborea and blast off from Venus before they took any further casualties.

"We're ahead of you, Colonel, That's on our agenda." Brenner spoke as they helped each other strap on their gear. "Jontheme, the leader who showed up yesterday, has shown us how to find each of the several gates to the inside. There are a couple of them very close to where our ships landed."

The Venusians entered the apartment wearing belts that suspended empty satchels and there was a leather pouch strapped to their backs from which a tube looped over the shoulder, the nozzle opening suspended at chin level. It was obviously a breathing supplement. At least eight Venusians were equipped and ready for the foray, but Chennault only had eyes for Artheme who had changed into metallic tights and boots; her top was that same liquid silver material, and her breasts jutted into points. She was looking at him through lowered lids, and perhaps she was smiling, but Chennault couldn't be certain. The other women, their strange high frequency whistles hanging like aiguillettes from their shoulders, were similarly attired.

Brennan told him that Lt. Crabbe was still unable to walk and was in a separate apartment, but that they would have a reunion after the twilight expedition outside.

Chennault and his companions squared their shoulders, checked their weapons, and followed the Venusian patrol up the path into the long corridor away from the cavern, listening to the rush of the cold-water aqueduct that cooled the interior of the hidden civilization. Too soon they were divided into two groups at two separate stone gates leading to the hostile outer world. In between the gates, the giant one-way window in the wall showed the forbidding landscape they were about to enter.

The window was like a huge visi-screen, but it revealed only the coiling mists and the gusts of wind that occasionally revealed the secure hull of the Thule rocket, whose shiny exterior was starting to discolor from the acidic atmosphere. Nothing else was visible. Thoughts from the Venusians seemed optimistic

"Colonel, I suggest that your team go to the left, toward Hyperborea, and our team will go directly outward to that field to the right where they need to pick herbs and mushrooms."

"I have to assume that the only danger is those little horrors that attacked me." Chennault grinned.

Brennan grinned back. "If only that were true, Colonel. Be ready for anything." Each team moved to the stone doors, ready for simultaneous exit. Carlson went with Brennan, while Agar accompanied Chennault. One more look through the window and they pushed aside the silent stone gate, slipping through the angled crevice in the granite.

The air of Venus hit Chennault like a steamy, squishy fist, burning his lungs before he could pull the mask down over his mouth. After the placid atmosphere of the cavern, with the sound of its rushing waters, the whine of the steamy Venus wind was malevolent, while its dangers lurked beyond their field of view.

Quickly the other team strode into the mists, and Chennault's team walked testily on the soft ground, moving toward the Hyperborea whose vertical spear shape slowly emerged from the swirling hot fog. He was apprehensive, but the Venusians showed no nervousness at all. He realized that it was the silence of their progress that was their greatest ally.

Attack of the Venus Horde

Breathing occasionally from the tubes extending from the packages on their back, the four members of the team worked swiftly as they moved to a field thick with domed mushrooms, or what appeared to be mushrooms. Despite the oppressive heat and acrid mist, each of the four filled the sacks hanging from their belts. Chennault and Agar stood alert and scanned the billowing fog curtain for movement.

The calm concentration of the Venusians was contagious, and the two Americans started to relax while still peering into the thickening mists that limited visibility to about 50 yards. It was obviously the natives' silence that protected them from being discovered by whatever lurked beyond the field of vision.

The Venusians seemed to handle the fearsome heat without noticing, but Chennault felt the sweat soaking the inside of his flight suit, while his head throbbed from the smell of acid and decay. There! A noise.

There was no time to seek the source of the noise. A shrill ululation swelled out of the fog eddies, and Artheme grabbed Chennault's hand as the party of six backed toward the granite wall that suddenly seemed very far away. As they backpedaled, a fusillade of metal shafts descended in their direction. He heard a few hitting metal—something had struck the hull of the Hyperborea.

Several dozen whitish dwarves surged into view, throwing objects and producing a deafening trill. Artheme blew into her high frequency whistle just as Chennault slipped on the wet moss and fell to his knees.

The horde paused. Agar and his female companion followed the two male Venusians, rushing toward the safety of the granite fissure while Artheme helped Chennault to his feet. The slimy horde advanced.

Now standing again, Chennault sneered and pulled back the bolt on the Thompson. Turning the submachine gun on its side, he pulled the trigger. The explosive stutter spewed .45-caliber slugs into the creatures from left to right. The sound of the gun overwhelmed the sounds from the attackers. He emptied the magazine as at least a dozen of the misshapen horde fell backward, heads split, inner organs spilling out.

As he changed magazines, Artheme's urgent message filled his mind. Their companions had almost made it to safety. He looked back and saw another swarm of the creatures spilling out from his right flank. Agar was backing toward the fissure, firing his pistol into the mass. Everyone was through except for him, and then the mass struck him like a rogue wave.

Chennault realized that they were now cut off from escape, and he yanked Artheme toward the rocketship. The Hyperborea was their only chance. It was only 50 yards away, and Chennault only stopped long enough to spray the charging creatures with another burst of tommy gun fire.

The ladder rungs were still extended, but suddenly a monstrous figure lumbered around from the rear of the towering rocket.

Artheme screamed aloud, and as Chennault spun around, he was confronted by something taller than he was with a terrifying, gaping mouth lined with recurved fangs and fearsome eyes. The thing loomed over him and scooped up Artheme in greenish muscular arms, its finger-like claws digging into her. The creature, with its prize, bowled the rocket pilot over and strode past him, the girl struggling in its grasp.

Chennault sprang to his feet in fury, his back to one of the support vanes of the Hyperborea. Did he dare shoot for fear of hitting Artheme? Rage washed over him, and he let out a battle shout that rose above the sound of the fray. The hulking creature stopped momentarily.

The Thompson was at his shoulder, and Chennault aimed deliberately at the thick neck of whatever had seized Artheme; he knew the muzzle would rise, and the range was closer than 10 feet. A spray of bullets thudded from behind into the neck and head of the thing, and Artheme tumbled to ground, finding her feet rapidly and running to the ladder.

She was remarkably agile, and she climbed rapidly. Halfway up, Chennault looked down. The whitish throng was following! No time to waste.

The Thompson was pointing straight down, as a whitish thing grabbed at his boot. The short burst tore pieces from the thing's head, and those clambering behind it were drilled. They fell with a messy thump onto the mossy ground, clearing the ladder.

At the top of the ladder, Chennault gave Artheme the mental picture of how to release the catch on the airlock. More of the creatures hopped on each other's shoulders and onto the ladder, climbing over each other to reach their intended prey. Artheme reached down and pulled him up into the airlock. Just as the creatures reached the door, he pulled the lever to retract the ladder rungs. As the rungs disappeared back into the body of the ship, the white horde fell headlong among the corpses of their kind, their hideous cries dying with them.

Chennault was gasping with exhaustion and relief, his chest heaving from the exertion. Artheme sat, her head on her knees, her silken hair falling down in disarray as a mask to her shock. The heat was almost unbearable and suffocating.

He went to the panel and pressed the toggle switches. The generator whined into action as he started the cooling system. Then he opened a storage cabinet and took out several items. As cool air rapidly made the cabin habitable, Chennault opened the airlock door one more time.

What he saw horrified him, his gorge rising. The white things were swarming over Capt. Agar's body like maggots. A few turned to look up at Chennault, throwing whatever they could find but unable to reach that high. It was the others that sent a bolt of fear down his spine.

Now he got a good look at the true monsters—at least seven feet tall, four of them huddled around the heap of white things tearing at Agar, their fifth companion sprawled near the ship, its exploded head spilling black fluid. Greenish-gray, they were scaly reptilians with extended snouts and teeth that seemed crocodilian. They stood erect with powerful legs and arms that ended in four long, cruel digits. Around their necks were bands of metal, with cords that were fixed to the sides of their heads where their exposed tympanic membranes glistened in the dull light. They carried long metal tubes that looked like small bazookas with grid-like sights on top.

SWACK. One of the tubes discharged with a distinctive sound, and a ball of electrical fire struck the pile of small monstrosities, burning and scattering the creatures these frightening beings seemed to command. SWACK. Another tube fired into the mass, and the shrill cries reached a crescendo. SWACK. They seemed to be eager to get their hands on the fallen Earthman. SWACK. Suddenly a glowing ball slammed into the hull of Hyperborea not three feet from Chennault, and the reptilians turned their toothy snouts upward, pointing at him.

Chennault's eyes narrowed as he yanked the metal ring from the object in his hand. "Nice to meet you," he muttered as the lever on the pineapple-shaped hand grenade sprang loose when he tossed it down into the center of hideous action.

The explosion shook the ship and the ping of shrapnel against the hull was a welcome sound as Chennault huddled on the floor of the airlock. When he crawled to the opening again, he was welcomed by a scene of carnage.

Two reptilians were dead, ripped open by the grenade explosion, and the other two writhed on the ground, missing limbs or rent in their abdomens. The soft-skinned white things fared worse, and there were many corpses piled together. Chennault retrieved the Thompson and fired single shots into the wounded reptilians until they stopped moving.

Artheme squeezed in beside him and blew her whistle. Those of the small creatures who had survived the grenade now shambled, tittering, back into the mists. Chennault then pushed her back into the cabin and secured the airlock. They sat down, looking at each other until their breathing normalized.

Chennault raised a finger and went to the panel, switching on the radios, waiting for the tubes to heat. Artheme's brow furrowed as he formed the thought, "It was a radio signal we heard on Earth that brought us to Venus. Was it you?"

Artheme seemed perplexed but did not send an answering thought.

"As quickly as possible, we need to get our crew on this ship and leave your planet for our return to Earth." He spoke the words as well as thinking them, and then he thought, "Perhaps you can return with us."

Her smile was sad, but she did not reply. Instead, she leaned over and removed Chennault's mask and pressed her lips against his throat, her voice musical and harmonious, His arms were around her voluptuous body, feeling her silver-clad breasts against his chest.

"What are those…those… things?" He said aloud, shuddering as he luxuriated in the comfort Artheme lavished upon him.

The thoughts she sent were fear tinged, and the words came into his mind, "They are of the City in the Mist. They are very many and they have always tried to destroy us."

"They have weapons—but what else?"

"We have not even named them, but we have seen their dwellings and their machines." Artheme's thoughts were so clear that Chennault could see buildings and networks of something that could be cables, or perhaps they were vines. The images included pictures of great turning wheels and pipes that belched clouds of steam. Maybe they were even now organizing an assault against his ship.

Artheme's fingers were pressed against his lips, and she was asking him to talk about Earth. He relaxed in her arms. Twined together in the cockpit of Hyperborea, Artheme and Chennault spent perhaps an hour, maybe more, exchanging knowledge of each other's worlds, but they spoke not.

Finally, Chennault went to the airlock and looked at the ground around the ship. The threat had passed, leaving the ground littered with the dead, including five reptilians and Capt. Agar. Though it was futile, he picked up the microphone and sent a series of terse voice messages to White Sands. As soon as possible they would all be on the way home to Earth. He flicked all the switches to the "Off" position as they prepared to make a run for the interior.

The ladder rungs extended, the two climbed down to the ground, knowing that they would be seen from the great window that gleamed in the face of the granite. They ran to the scene of battle, and Chennault picked up the mutilated body of Capt. Agar, taking him into the crevice in the rock.

When the stone door slid away, the two found themselves surrounded by friends. The blond woman ministered to Agar, her luminous eyes running with tears as he was lifted up and solemnly borne deep into the cavern. It was explained to Chennault that there was a place for the dead in a farther reach of the cavern beyond where he had even seen. The atmosphere was somber and subdued; even Artheme's thoughts to him were shrouded.

Now Chennault was certain that the entrances in the granite, though natural in appearance, were carefully contrived to deny entrance to the reptilian monsters from the forbidding City in the Mist.

Much later, after a long walk deep in the cavern world and a requiem for Capt. John Agar, they returned to the apartment. Artheme walked with Chennault, having donned again the clinging silver gown. Brennan surprised him, now accompanied by a tall, statuesque woman with honey-colored hair who walked arm in arm with him.

Carlson finally spoke, "Colonel, so much has been happening that we haven't had time, but we should check in with Lt. Crabbe."

"I'd like that."

They went up natural stone steps to the second level in the wall complex and entered an apartment. Chennault saw the familiar face of a fellow member of the Venus Project. "Lindy, it's good to see you."

Crabbe threw him a salute from the prone position. "Pardon me if I don't get up, Colonel, but my Venus sawbones tells me I have to keep the leg elevated. I'll be up and around in no time now. It turns out that the little devil's metal shaft cracked my leg bone." The two shook hands and, from the room at the rear of the apartment, another woman entered.

"Your doctor?" The astonishment was apparent in Chennault's voice, and the question was rhetorical. The woman wore a metallic gown similar to those worn by the others, differing only in color; hers was glittering gold, fitting tightly on her perfect figure.

Lt. Crabbe smiled broadly. "Yessir! Don't you wish you were sick?" They all laughed. It was then that Chennault notice that the gold gown worn by Crabbe's female attendant showed a slight bump in the abdomen.

"Not polite to stare, Colonel, but you've got it right." Carlson was looking at him with a "What now?" expression.

The men traded glances, and then Chennault smiled. "Some guys know how to make the most of an excursion." Crabbe lay there and put his hands behind his head. "These infections are worse than anything on Earth. These people do have something like Penicillin, and it is a good thing. My leg festered within minutes of getting hit by those little darlings out there. Did they tell you how quickly things decompose out there?"

"I sure can understand it, but we'll talk about it later after you're ready for another trip in a rocketship."

After a few more pleasantries, three men went back down to the apartment to organize Agar's remaining possessions, and later, Chennault explained the need to organize their departure from Venus at the earliest possible time—as soon as Crabbe could get to the ship. Brennan and Carlson shared some of their stories about their own Venus experiences, but they clearly avoided talking about the women who had befriended them. Chennault reminded the men of their duty and those loved ones waiting for them back on Earth. Not only that, but the millions of dollars expended by the U.S. Government to build the three ships dwarfed any previous commitment save the Manhattan project. The men in this room were the custodians of those millions.

After cleaning off the smell of conflict and the acrid substances of the outside, they dressed again. Brennan and Carlson left Chennault with his thoughts as they left the apartment singly for their own reasons.

He sat at the stone table, sipping an effervescent wine-like liquid and shaking off the violent combat of hours before. He paged through the crewmens' notebooks that included temperature readings, air composition, as well as cryptic comments such as "No written language or industrial development. Jontheme says they can't read the inscriptions on their walls."

The Cool Green Fire

It was then that Artheme entered the apartment, her silver gown shimmering, and her black lustrous hair pouring down over her shoulders. Her full lips were wetly scarlet, and her heavy-lidded eyes were heavily shadowed with metallic purple.

Chennault rose to greet her, and her faint smile brought with it the thoughts of welcome. He gestured to the stools as she approached. A wave of intoxicating fragrance engulfed him. Artheme lifted her arm and extended her hand, and he saw that her nails were the same color as her lips.

He stood and took her hand as she led him from the room, down the walkway and up another set of stairs. Chennault could hear activity on the cavern floor, but he felt as though there was no one in the world save himself and Artheme. Walking close to her, he could sense the sway of her hips as they stretched the tight gloss of the gown.

Artheme led him into her apartment whose cool light tubes illuminated a distinctly female environment, with flowering plants and water trickling in a fountain at one corner of the room. The domed ceiling was adorned with hanging ornaments. Two of the walls were painted with rows of multi-colored hieroglyphs such as those etched into the cavern walls.

Chennault's mind was filled with cool green fire, the color of Artheme's eyes, and he slid his arms around her supple body, feeling her instantly pressing her full length against him. She nuzzled his neck, and he then raised her full lips to kiss her—awkwardly at first, but then she sought him with fierce hunger.

They went to Artheme's bed, soft with embroidered cushions. They lay together, and the images in Chennault's mind were those of intertwined coils of shining fire, twisting around the naked bodies of him and the beautiful Venusian woman. Then, the gown was sliding upward, the images in his mind becoming physical reality beyond all of his experience. Her musical humming turned to cries of joy, and they stayed there for a very long time.

He must have slept, but he awakened to Artheme's gaze and caresses. Still holding her, he pointed to a band of three-inch-tall pictographs that marched across the wall above her bed. What did they mean?

Artheme again said the word "Anisaz," and her mind told him that they did not know what the hieroglyphs meant, only that they were brought on silver ships at the beginning of their time. They had no need of writing, as their life and culture was alive, transmitted from mind to mind, generation to generation.

"Will you come back with me—to Earth?" Chennault asked her aloud, and Artheme nestled against him, humming the intoxicating musical sound that seemed the embodiment of happiness. In his mind, he understood that these people had not created the giant caverns, nor had they built the walls of dwelling places.

Their "Anisaz" had built the megalithic caverns, brought them fruitful plants, the light transmitting cylinders, and the secrets of agriculture that their stable population had maintained for unknown ages.

Chennault realized he had seen no children while in the cavern. Artheme responded to his thought, "Ours will be the first in many cycles." She put his hand on her stomach as he also thought of Lt. Crabbe and his very affectionate doctor.

Much later, when the fire in his mind was banked, he told Artheme that his crew must prepare for leaving Venus. She held him, saying nothing, but leaving the image seared in his mind of the two of them together in her soft bed.

After leaving her, Chennault returned to the apartment and found Carlson and Brennan quietly writing in their notebooks. "Are they all pregnant?" His question was sudden and demanding.

The two other spacemen did not even look up from their work.

Chennault grunted. "Better get Crabbe on his feet, because we're heading home as soon as we can get our gear aboard. There's room for eight people on the Hyperborea. We can take the women with us."

Brennan got up and smiled faintly. "I told you, Colonel, these women are different. You'll see."

"OK, Colonel, I know that orders are orders." Carlson sounded suspiciously resigned.

Chennault continued, "Final thing—we need the source of those radio transmissions, and I can't find any evidence that our friends have electronics or internal combustion engines…no vehicles"

Brennan grimaced, "You're catching up with us now. The Venusians don't even comprehend radio, so those signals are coming from…" He pointed to the south cavern wall.

"Are you saying that those scaly horrors…?"

Carlson spoke up, "What did you think of their fireball tubes? Obviously they've got electricity, no matter how ugly they are."

"Did you ever think, Colonel, that even though they haven't got astronomy, that those ancients who built these caverns might have left some gifts to the outside race? We think they are sending blind signals trying to lure the ancients back to them."

Planning the Return to Earth

Chennault squinted, his sharp blue eyes narrowed. "I don't care what in the hell they are, but I do know we are getting on the first stagecoach out of Dodge City, before the Hyperborea can be compromised." At the same time, he found himself curiously unable to form mental images of home or his fiancé.

The other two seemed reticent, but they went up to see if Crabbe could get up on his feet and into his suit.

Within the hour, Brennan and Carlson brought Crabbe down to the apartment. He just said, "I'll make it, Colonel." Then, they all strapped on their equipment, loaded their weapons, and prepared to say good-bye to the Venusians.

While there was no sign of the Venusian men, when four intrepid spacemen emerged from the apartment, they found their Venus companions waiting, as though this turn of events was expected.

"Please, come to Earth with me," Chennault said to Artheme in a mental surge. She averted her head, looking at the floor. The others seemed just as adamant. Chennault was filled with a cold longing that was almost unbearable. It couldn't be helped.

The rocket crew moved up the passageway, accompanied by the females. Dozens of other Venusians were following up the walkway. The men looked at each other, clearly unhappy with this sudden departure order. Crabbe limped, but the others dragged their feet, and Chennault found himself loathing his own commands.

They took a last, long look through the marvelous one-way window to see that Hyperborea seemed intact, its ladder rungs extended. Moss and fungus was already covering the heap of corpses left from the previous battle. The coast was clear all the way to the limits of their vision.

"All right, Guys, lock and load." Their firearms ready for action, they paused and looked at their Venusian companions who stood back, unwilling to join them or to help them. Chennault looked one more time at Artheme, a lump growing in his throat, and then he and Brennan pushed the silent stone gate aside.

Four men edged through the angled granite fissure and out into the hostile and miasmic atmosphere. They walked cautiously toward the giant spear of Hyperborea that pointed toward home.

The mists were silent as they stepped briskly across the fetid soft ground, single file, weapons at the ready. With every step, vaporous fumes bubbled up from under the moss, and only their oxygen masks kept the odor from overwhelming them.

The ship was almost close enough to touch when the ambush was launched. The monstrous creatures had been patiently waiting, and they charged from the fog of the Venus twilight, lumbering, their strange weapon tubes extended. Guttural shouts came from their scaly throats, sibilant and threatening.

Chennault could not tell how many there were, but the spacemen were outnumbered at least five to one. "Let 'em have it!" He shouted through his mask, and he raised the submachine gun to mow down the hideous throng.

The air exploded with bursts of fire as one Thompson and three service pistols opened up. Heavy slugs tore through armored breast scales and punched holes in soft ventrals. Deep grunts turned to hisses as several of the reptilian brutes fell face first onto the field.

Now the attackers fired their charged tubes, and electrified fireballs spewed out toward the crew. Several balls struck the ground, dissipating, while others flew over their heads. Like heavy roman candles, these tubes sent their balls of death as the monsters came closer.

One of the rounds struck Carlson in the side. He yelled and fired a .45 round into his assailant's face before doubling over in pain, almost immobilized.

Chennault pressed the magazine release button, dropping the expended magazine, and he shoved another 30 rounds into the gun. He fired a staccato burst, and the seven-foot giant stumbled, falling to the ground, motionless.

Sizzling electric balls flew through the air as the spacemen dodged and fired. Could they make it? Chennault was ready to make a final spring when the white things emerged from the fog, surrounding the landing vanes of the Hyperborea. No, it was impossible.

"Back!" Chennault yelled, and they all reacted, seeking the safety of the granite cliffs, firing as they went. At least 12 of the giant reptiles had fallen, but more were emerging from the mist, and a hail of metal shafts and stones were being pitched by the countless misshapen dwarves scrambling past the rocketship now out of reach to its retreating crew.

Fireballs were striking the granite walls, discharging. Crabbe was the first to reach the fissure, and he emptied his .45 Auto pistol before scrambling through. Carlson, though injured, was next. His pistol was already empty, and he was bleeding through his suit.

At the mouth of the fissure, Chennault opened up on the front rank of the greenish gray monstrosities, every one of his bullets tearing flesh. The magazine was empty.

Brennan reached out and shoved the commander. "Go! Now!" Off balance, Chennault plunged into the fissure just as a sizzling fireball struck Brennan full in the chest, knocking him backward. Chennault was in the fissure as he saw Brennan falling backward. He threw the Thompson behind him and reached out.

Chennault's hands clutched Brennan's suit; he dragged him into the fissure, pulling him backward and feeling the rock scrape his hands and elbows. Thank God the stone door was open, and he felt multiple hands pulling him into the cavern with a rush of cool, fresh air.

Brennan was unconscious, maybe dead, and Chennault was exhausted as he lay on his back, staring upward into the darkness of the steepled ceiling whose apex was so high as to be invisible. He was aware of many shapes standing around him, and he had the sense of concern from all those gathered around.

It was the face of Artheme he recognized first, crouched down, her slim hand on his cheek. Chennault smiled through cracked lips, seeing as in a silver haze. He was helped to his feet, and he saw that Brennan was still breathing, though his chest was burned from a five-inch black hole in the center of his suit. The electric charge had probably carried the force of a miniature lightning ball, shocking him into unconsciousness while causing a serious burn. The suit had saved his life, the rubber lining preventing the discharge from stopping his heart.

The Venusians crowded around them until they were able to begin walking toward the open cavern, each lost to his own thoughts. The Venus males were carrying Brennan, and the honey-blond woman in glistening bronze was applying a creamy poultice to his chest.

Artheme was leading Chennault toward her home, and he stopped at the bottom of the steps as Brennan regained consciousness. Brennan reached out and tugged on Chennault's sleeve, "Colonel, you know we discovered the length of the Venus day—250 Earth days?" Chennault nodded.

Brennan cleared his throat and motioned for his litter bearers to let him stand. "Well, we found something else: a Venus day is the human birth cycle here."

As they ascended the steps, Artheme's cool fire entered his mind, and it said, "Our child will be born tomorrow." Then they were in her home, his suit discarded, his only thought to join Artheme in her bed as the Venus night so slowly approached.

* * *

After Brennan had recovered, the men gathered in the apartment to speak of their plans to recover the remainder of the supplies from Hyperborea and Thule, and they made further entries in their notebooks.

Deep in the darkening mist, a fearful race was sending signals through the solar system, luring others to Venus for purposes the Earthmen could only imagine. They wrote in the notebooks with a shudder, and they described, with furtive phrases, the terrible plans being made far away at the City in the Mist.

Never again did the men speak of duty or the expense of the marvelous rocketships designed by Von Braun. Perhaps they would think of these things tomorrow, just as they might, tomorrow, recover the memories of their interrupted lives on Earth. Chennault looked deeply into the green fastness of Artheme's eyes, consumed by the cool green fire she stirred in his mind.

In the deepening twilight, the Hyperborea leaned like the Tower of Pisa. By Venus morning it would topple like a dead tree to meet its end on the field of the second planet. from the Sun.

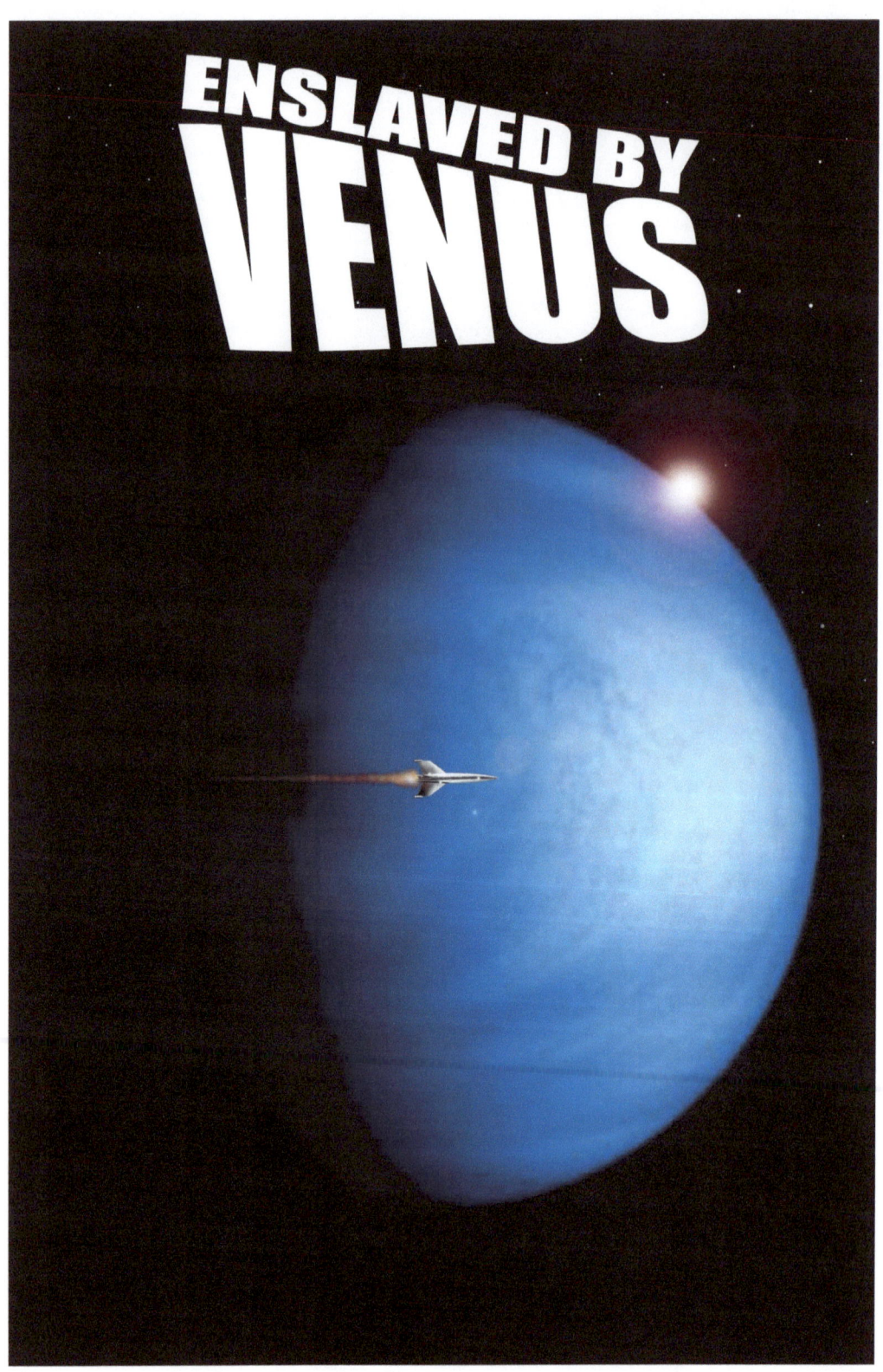

Terror Tales of the Southwest

Crash Landing on Venus

What now? Corbett unclenched his teeth as the ship shuddered to a halt. The last half mile had been a careering bobsled ride, caroming off unseen terrain features and sliding on what seemed to be slick, swampy mud, while he yelled involuntarily. Now he was stranded with the unknown horrors lurking in the mists of Venus.

What now? There was just silence except for the crackle of the useless radio panels and the soft hum of oxygen generators keeping the air breathable, but there was only silence from the rear of the ship where the great rocket engine and steering thrusters had once roared. The thermal insulated windows were fogged, dripping with condensation as were the gleaming concave walls of the hull, and Corbett felt sweat trickling under his tunic armpits as the temperature rose. He looked down and saw his strong hands still gripping the dead controls, knuckles white. On the floor of the cabin, his eyes caught the glint of silver from the gleaming Rocket Forces qualification badge that had somehow come unpinned from his breast. It had never happened before, and Corbett wondered if it was an omen.

The ship groaned softly and he felt it rotate slightly, settling into whatever was outside. This was Venus, and Corbett knew better than to land here, but again, he couldn't go back to Earth either. His head was throbbing, and as he removed his magnetic soled boots and struggled out of the form-fitting contour station, he knew he'd better come up with a plan—fast. He had heard the stories about Venus and why the United States military stopped all travel to the second planet.

The radios brought in nothing but static on the ultra-short wave 25m band, so Corbett switched them off to cut the heat from the bank of tubes behind the panel. The visigraph showed an outside temperature of 115 degrees Fahrenheit, with humidity at 98%. The external camera view revealed nothing but moving clouds of mist. Somehow he had managed to land near the planet's pole; anywhere else would have meant a painful and hopeless death. How many of the earlier explorers and colonists had learned this to their sorrow?

Corbett was in his final year as a cadet at the Space Academy when the United States first landed on Venus. After the Third World War in the 1950s, the move to space was a true American crusade. The first men landed on the moon in 1965, and the Schmitt-Yeager team touched down at the Venus pole in 1987, followed by three private expeditions funded by United States Steel and Boeing. Corbett had studied many of the scientific reports sent back from the research teams by tele-viewer. As part of his training, he learned how to survive on Venus in preparation for U.S. expeditions in force scheduled to begin in 1989.

Then the reports stopped, and all signals from the luminous planet ceased less than six months later in 1988. The newspaper headlines screamed their questions about lost scientific teams, but the brass at the academy put an embargo on any further talk about Venus expeditions.

Corbett whispered curses as he began to follow the gangway ladder to the storage compartments, his lonely footsteps making hollow sounds inside the hull. He didn't want to think of the stupid decisions that put him out here, trapped millions of miles from home. It was not comforting to remember that Schmitt and Yeager were the only Americans to make it home from Venus, and they had both died gurgling from hideous alien fungus growths inside their lungs.

The metallic sound as he yanked open the equipment locker was earsplitting against the silence that permeated the ship. While the U.S. Rocket Forces used moon shuttle runs to train their rocket pilots, the limited knowledge transmitted back from Venus had led researchers to produce new weapons and gear to be carried in all space-bound ships. There was a compartment in the medical kit with ampoules labeled "Venus Serum", and Corbett stripped down to his underwear, wincing as he plunged one of the syringes into his thigh, and then he crawled into the one-piece protective suit that was guaranteed resistant to spores and fungus. A close-fitting fabric helmet sealed at the collar of the suit and a filtering mask completed the protection. There was nowhere to go but outside.

Corbett pulled the lever to break the hatch seal, shouldered the strange-looking flame cartridge weapon and belted on the sidearm with spare magazines. He wasn't the kind of guy who hesitated—there was a dead man at the White Sands Proving Ground and Rocket Base who could attest to that—but now he stopped, remembering his training and Colonel Armstrong who had lectured them: "No man gets dressed in the morning thinking that he is going to die today."

The hatch door opened with a hiss, and a wall of drenching heat like a steambath enveloped him. The wide profile rubberized boots touched the soil of Venus. A portable oxygen generator on the weapons belt was ready, but the scientists had done their work well. He could breathe, but his stomach revolted at the overpowering odor of decay and death. At first it seemed the mists were without feature, just an envelope of bright obscurity, with a mother of pearl lustre. He could hear a strong, hot breeze that stirred the mist into fantastic serpentine shapes that shifted and beckoned kaleidoscopically.

It was impossible to see much more than ten feet ahead, but Corbett was staring at the sleek, projectile-shaped rocket ship lying helpless in the muck. Its gleaming hull appeared as though it had been here for 50 years. Greenish tendrils of mould were crawling up the side of the hull and he knew what to expect from the scientific reports. So that's what the pressurized chemical device was for. He walked testily back to the hatch, opened it, and went back into the ship. He sprayed the interior, creating a fog, then outside again where walking on the spongey soil felt to Corbett as though he were walking on human bodies. He sprayed the length of the hull and the racing mould became ashen, flaking off to become part of the seething carpet of soft moss that bubbled wherever he placed his boot.

Now it was time to put the magnetic audio beacon on the hatch and begin a grid search of the area. He kept the battery powered mini-receiver attached to his belt. Within five steps he lost visual contact with his crashed ship and he was drenched with moisture. The mist currents disoriented him, and they raced ahead, swirling, then folded back on themselves as though to come back and beckon him forward. He had no compass, but it would be useless on Venus anyway.

Corbett walked a hundred paces perpendicular to the hull of the ship, then turned right for a hundred steps before making another 90-degree angle. On his third turn, he was headed back toward the ship and feeling relieved because the luminous mist clouds were causing him to see strange images of things that could not exist. His step count grew uncertain. Was it 39 or 49? His eyes grew heavy as his body throbbed with wet heat.

He didn't see it coming, but something slammed into him like a Notre Dame tackle, with a hellish buzzing that he felt as much as heard. Corbett reacted as though he were spring loaded, rolling on the swampy earth, reaching for his weapon; he could taste blood in his mouth, and he dreaded the possibility of a wound exposed to this foetid air.

Corbett yanked back the slide on the hand weapon. A dark form was floating right toward him, less than 8 feet away. He pulled the trigger, and heard the firing. THUMP. The low velocity 37mm round sailed into the attacking thing.

The explosion of the rocket projectile was deafening, and Corbett was thrown backward. He didn't realize how powerful the new Tektonite really was. Just for a moment he imagined that he saw this flying horror, a lumpy bulbous thing with frail wings at least 8 feet in span.

Dizzily, Corbett clambered to his feet. The head of the thing was on the ground in front of him, its mouth still working frantically side to side like that of a crab, but monstrously large, the eyes mere slits. Then the head died, and the buzzing trailed off into silence.

He shook his head, squinting into the mists. The ship should be straight ahead of him, but a vague outline he thought he could see to his left, shimmering in obscure luminosity, appeared to be metallic. He lurched, started to change direction, but his training intervened, and he began counting steps again, trusting the friendly signal from the beacon that sent a faint beeping sound in his earpiece.

The Lost Expedition

Here it was! He was somehow disoriented or had counted incorrectly, but there couldn't have been two ships. The beacon signal had led him finally to his ship, but it was in a direction opposite to the grid he was certain he was following. His mind had fallen prey to confusion, and without the beacon, he would have been lost. But then, was there something else in the mist?

Almost panicked, Corbett found the hatch and clawed it open, throwing himself inside his ship, jamming the lever closed with the airtight seal squeezing out the unknown horrors of Venus. What now?

There were enough food capsules and water bottles to last probably another 15 earth days. The supplies were supposed to take care of a normal crew of three on a moon shuttle flight of no more than seven days. The length of Corbett's life was measured in days, and his only hope was the story of a marooned expedition whose few reports from Venus had stopped after three months.

Col. Armstrong had labeled the scientific team's expedition as "optimistic arrogance," and they had followed Schmitt and Yeager too soon, backed by the Smithsonian Institutions, National Geographic Society, and the Carnegie Insitute. No expense was spared, and Corbett remembered the team's photograph in LIFE magazine the week they blasted off.

Armed with the serums and devices developed from data accumulated by the first U.S. penetration of the Venus clouds, they were confident they could set up a survivable station on the planet.

It was the theatre of hope after a devastating war, as radio and television broadcast the launch of eight silver rocket ships—the most ambitious project civilized man had ever attempted. Corbett remembered the excitement of fellow cadets when newspapers carried the radio messages from the scientists who reported no measurable planetary rotation and no detectible magnetic field. The speculation was that the leeward side of Venus was one endless day.

Corbett switched on the Mayday signal, though nobody was within 26 million miles of him, none but those who had come here to explore and found only death. The fog of the herbicide in the ship still lingered, and the fatigue of the harrowing flight was dragging him down. Sinking into the pilot's contour seat, his thoughts drifted to that last night at White Sands Rocket Base, the girl Deanna, and the fight, as the tide of sleep lapped at his consciousness. Then oblivion.

Corbett didn't know how long he slept, but his first sensation on awakening was being roughly lifted out of the seat. Two figures had grabbed him and were dragging him out of the chair. He tried to struggle, but they were strong, and they were accompanied by two others...frightening, hulking figures that loomed in the foggy air. Perhaps they were human, but he couldn't tell. Also, Corbett realized that his strength was failing, and he couldn't have resisted them anyway. Were they Venusians or some other frightening alien race?

The creatures were enclosed in some kind of dark bulky suits with ominous rectangular face plates as black as onyx, and they roughly clapped Corbett's helmet on him as they dragged him through the hatch of his own rocketship and out into the steamy hell of Venus. He vaguely heard two of the creatures rummaging in the ship and emerging with weapons and gear. When he finally gained his feet, he was deep in the mists, lost and dependent upon these silent, plodding creatures dragging him along. There was no choice but to cooperate.

Then there was a door opening in a mould-covered wall, and Corbett went sprawling onto a smooth floor, sliding for about five feet. One of the creatures fell on top of him and another pulled off his helmet. The next thing he saw was the flash of a needle as it stabbed for his neck, injecting fire into his jugular.

A Vision on the Second Planet

Then the creatures backed off, and Corbett staggered to his feet, ready to fight. The wave of resignation hit him as he saw in front of him something that looked like a bench. He sat down in a heap and looked at his tormentors. One of them was human! A man in a gray tunic was smiling faintly at him, his thinning hair somehow comforting to the kidnapped rocket pilot. The embroidery on the breast of the tunic read "Grolier Society."

Slowly the others put down their booty from Corbett's ship and removed their hoods revealing three men with beards. When the fourth hood came off, Corbett gasped involuntarily. A mass of titian-colored auburn hair fell down around a pale, oval face, her green eyes electric, red lips full.

The other men stripped off their environment suits, and they just stood, until the woman spoke to them, "Sit down and eat." The men finished removing their outer garments and sat down at a makeshift table obviously constructed from shipping crates.

Corbett was shocked at the rasp of his own voice. He had not spoken to anyone since escaping from the rocket base millions of miles away. "Who are you? What is this place? Why did you inject me?"

The woman surveyed him coolly, and the older man spoke. "One thing at a time, young man. We heard your mayday signal on our radio set, and you have no idea how excited we were to be rescued. It seems we were premature."

The woman looked up and blew a stray curl of her luxuriant hair away from her eyes. "It looks as though you'd better tell us who you are. We're a research facility, but there's something not quite right about you and your ship. We need to know when our re-supply is going to arrive, and when are we going back to Earth. I gather that our transmitter has failed, but we have received strange bulletins from earth about suspending all voyages to Venus. Is it true?"

Corbett watched her intently, only vaguely aware that the enclosure was like a prefabricated quonset hut made of some lightweight material, with skylights in lieu of electric lights. The luminous mist outside shed an even illumination to the interior.

Before Corbett could speak, there was a sudden crash that shook the building. He ducked, but nobody else moved. "What th…"

The woman smiled enigmatically, "It's just a flacker, or at least that's what we call them. They're carnivorous, but they're not very dangerous. Monstrous insect is as close as I can come to a description."

"Yeah, I think I met one. We danced." Corbett felt the sting on his neck where the needle went in. "Why did you have to…"

"Well, Mr. Space Cadet, we know next to nothing about Venus. Before we came here, we knew about the lung fungus, but there are other nasties out here that Schmitt and Yeager didn't encounter. If we hadn't inoculated you, you would probably have died within a week. Certainly you must have noticed that your energy was being sapped."

Corbett nodded.

"I'm Bernard Kretschmer, in charge of the colonizing mission to Venus, and this is my daughter Eva. What you see here is what is left of 73 crew and eight ships that originally came here. Now it's your turn."

Corbett realized he'd been staring at Eva. Underneath the shapeless environmental suit, she wore a one piece form-fitting coverall that could have been green silk but was probably a nylon or dacron synthetic.

"Sir, I'm 1st Lt. James Corbett of the U.S. Rocket Force, or at least I was when I left earth."

Eva raised her eyebrows. "There's more to it than that. Yours wasn't an organized mission."

The Fugitive From White Sands Rocket Base

Corbett rubbed the stubble on his square jaw, grateful that this enclosure was kept livable by a unit that blew cool, oxygenated air, powered by the soft thrum of a generator. In one corner of the enclosure was a large pair of tanks connected by tubes that probably was distilling water from the moisture being retrieved from the outside. He squirmed slightly and looked down at artificial floor, "You want the rest of it? Okay. You remember White Sands? You guys left in a blaze of glory when I was finishing my training. I remember that night when all your rockets lit up the desert night, and the press took some of the most important photos ever published. White Sands is a military base, so a guy can go crazy in the Bachelor Officer Quarters there. For recreation, we went into the little town of Alamogordo. You know, close to where the first atom bomb was tested. The base was so busy that there were rockets going up almost every week, and Alamogordo is a boom town.

"I had a girl friend there, or I thought I did. I had made two moon shuttle flights with veteran pilots as part of my training, and that night was scheduled to be my third. I was going to lift off at 0300, but I had to see Deanna, so I commandeered a car and drove the desert highway to surprise her. Well, she was surprised all right, and so was her other boyfriend. Yeah, I got hot under the collar, and I should have got out of there—but I could see from the look on his face that he didn't know about me either, and he started hitting her. I reacted, of course—it's just something I do. It wasn't much of a fight, but I hit him pretty hard. He went down, striking his head on the sharp corner of the chest of drawers in the bedroom.

"That's right. He was dead, and I recognized him as an admin officer at the base. He was a captain, and I was a lieutenant. If I have a talent, it's for improvisation. I ripped the telephone cord out of the wall, scrammed without saying a word to Deanna, and raced back across the desert to the base, driving 100 mph.

"I drove right to the launch pad. With the logo on the car door, the sentries weren't concerned. The supplies hadn't been completely loaded, but I knew the routine. The fueling cycle was finished. It was 0100, but nobody questioned me showing up two hours early. The gantry crane had been moved aside temporarily before the final loading of supplies was to be effected. If only I could get aboard before a police dragnet was sent out from Alamogordo or somebody called the base."

Father and daughter watched Corbett intently, but the others sat the table, eating, as though nothing else existed for them.

"Go on, Lieutenant." Eva lowered her eyelids as though they were a force field to protect her. Corbett was fascinated by the way her breasts jutted against the green silk of the coveralls.

"The remaining supplies were lined up on the tarmac, with men doing inventory, awaiting the final gantry approach for loading. I knew from previoius flights that ignition could be started from the cockpit or from the blockhouse. With this rocket it is possible to climb the external hull ladder, even when the gantry was removed. While the ground crew retired to the blockhouse for a meal break, I climbed, hand over hand, up that ladder, disappearing through the cargo hatch into the crew compartment. I did a quick preflight check. I was sure I could manage the ship without my two flight crew members. At 0120 I shut off the radio, remotely closed the cargo hatch, and started the pre-ignition sequence.

"A gantry crew fired up their diesel engines and had just started creeping toward the ship again. The exterior ship TV camera showed the supply crews racing from the block-house yelling and scattering as the first flame came from the rocket tubes. Even through the hull I could hear the shriek of sirens, and I knew that desperate voices were trying to raise me on the radio. I was looking only at the black sky above me when I hit the red button.

"The thunder of ignition shook the ship, and it lifted slowly, gradually gaining momentum. At about 1,000 feet the acceleration began to pull at me, that grinding force of gravity that made me weigh about 600 pounds. Then I blacked out as is the normal process. When I regained consciousness, I could see the curve of the earth and the main engine had shut down automatically. I was in space.

"The controls were preset for the moon, but I knew that I didn't dare go there. We were still waiting to hear the reports from the first mission on its way to Mars. Mars was out, and so I went to the navigation table and turned all six of the computation wheels to the Venus setting. Almost immediately I felt the directional thrusters pulsing as the ship came around. Then I was travelling about 5,000 mph and, with each pulse of the thrusters, the speed increased. The rest you know. What now?"

Except for the sound of the men eating, the crackle of the radio, and the occasional burst of wind against the insulaed quonset, all was silent. Eva paced, her hips swaying, her brow wrinkled in disapproval, and her mind obviously working.

Dr. Kretschmer pursed his lips and sighed. "There were a couple of hours after your landing when we were certain we were being rescued. Have they forgotten us completely?"

Corbett remembered the orientation lectures he had sat through endlessly during ground school at Lackland Army Air Base in Texas. "Wait a minute. This was the most ambitious space project in the history of mankind. Our hopes were so high, and the newspapers headlined every scrap of information you sent back. The world held its breath when your ships were buffeted by the stratospheric winds of the planet and nobody exhaled until you reached the surface. It was bad luck that four of the eight ships were damaged on landing, but some damage was expected.

"You have no idea how fascinated we all were about Venus, and I visualized your brave team unloading the building panels in the face of unknown dangers. Your team was productive from day one, and the reports sent back became a precious part of our scientific literature. What I never understood is why your narrative about the life of the crew stopped after the first week or so."

Eva was still pacing, but Kretschmer shook his head, "My boy, you have no idea what it was like here in those first days. The main job of Eva and myself was setting up the radar mapping operation for the National Geographic Society. With no visual capability, we had devised a way of using radar beams and then sketching the terrain from the scope images. At the same time, the pilots, security staff, and project engineers finished the shelter and began to range out into the mist. Looking back, that was our mistake—our eagerness to explore." He nodded toward the men sitting at the table.

The soft light emanating from the skylights never seemed to change, and Corbett could see that the shelter was probably 75-100 feet long, 35 feet wide, and there were pieces of canvas hanging from the skylights, obviously to block them during sleep periods. He couldn't hold back any longer, "My God, what about the rest of those 73 people—the scientists, the armed security people? They didn't starve to death…" He could see that there were still stacked cases at the far end of the quonset labeled "C Ration/Space Package."

They were interrupted by a sound at the door. There was a pushing accompanied by the scrabbling sound of dozens of claws. Eva picked up the flame gun and tossed it to Corbett. She went to the door, threw the metal bar and retreated to the middle of the room. The thing that fell into the doorway horrified Corbett, its soft, shiny body pulsating along a six foot length. Its entire bulk was lined with claw-like legs that scraped frantically on the floor. Corbett had seen that mouth before, however, and he squeezed the trigger.

A pipeline of intense blue-white flame shot forward and engulfed the creature, incinerating it instantly in the doorway. Dr. Kretschmer picked up a shovel and pushed the carbonized thing outside before securing the opening and replacing the metal bar.

"That's the larval stage of the flacker, Lieutenant, and it's just a sample of the horrors we have faced in the past year."

Corbett's stomach was jumping, but he said he wanted to know what had happened to the scientific expedition.

Eva broke her silence. "Lt. Corbett, I'll tell you the whole story, but first we need to make another trip to your ship. The timing is critical, and you'll understand before we're done. Right now I still think you're a dangerous man, but danger is relative. You're fortunate that you cannot see everything hiding in the mists. My only advice is that you not look directly into the mists while you're walking." She turned away and began talking to the silent, bearded men at the table. They got up and donned the bulky environmental suits. One was issued to Corbett as well. Eva was talking to the men as they put their suits on; they didn't even nod toward her. Corbett was burning with curiosity about the men's apparent mental affliction.

Into the Mist

There was no time for reflection. Eva pulled on the shapeless hood, motioned to Corbett to do the same, and they prepared for the outside. When they stepped through the door, the group was enveloped by the mists, but Corbett was amazed at what he could see through the faceplate. It was a bluish filter that allowed him to see almost 20 feet ahead, twice what he could see without it. His body was adjusting to the heat and almost visible humidity. He was sweating profusely, but it seemed almost normal.

Now he could see that the ground was alive with motion, with forms wriggling, crawling, and hopping. No wonder that initial walk on the Venusian soil had seemed so soft and unstable. Eva had the directional finder, and she was walking in a straight line. To Corbett's left was a tree with limbs curved like the ribcage of an animal that seemed to be embracing the remains of a flacker. A disembodied voice inside the hood startled him. It was Eva.

"That's the most common tree form. *Narcolepsia gigantis* as we named it. Anything stumbling against its trunk is secured by an adhesive sap that is also narcotic in effect. Of course the tree then penetrates the captured creature with sharp tendrils and drains its body fluids. Stay alert, Lieutenant."

Corbett just wanted to make sure he didn't lose sight of the woman who was in the lead of their little column. At first he watched either her back or the ground, but then he glanced at something in the mists. It couldn't be. Eva had said he shouldn't look at the mists. But something was there.

The wind was blowing at about 5 mph with gusts up to 10 mph, yet Corbett saw the mists curl into corkscrew patterns and flow with an artistic rhythm. He could see the mists congeal, and as he squinted through the faceplate, a human form was becoming clear—a reposing, naked female form, ever more concrete, detailed… and beckoning to him as he stared, slack-jawed and mesmerized.

"Lieutenant!" A crackling radio voice stabbed at his ear, and a hand yanked the sleeve of his suit. Suddenly, Corbett realized that he had somehow turned away from the others. It couldn't have happened, but somehow he must have become disoriented. Impossible, yet…

Corbett stumbled dizzily as Eva dragged him along. The others plodded ahead, apparently unconcerned. Eva gave each of them, by name, terse commands that they followed without comment.

The path ahead was blocked. At first Corbett thought it a terrain feature, until it moved at the far limit of his filtered vision. What seemed to be a ghastly mound of mould-covered earth was moving!

Now, Corbett reacted to his training, suddenly very protective of his beautiful guide. He pushed Eva aside and extended the flame rifle, its selector set to full power.

"Stop!" Eva's voice in the ear speaker was a command. "It's virtually harmless to us, and we don't want to attract anything else's attention."

The thing resembled a dark brown manta ray with a giant hump on its back, almost shapeless, and it seemed to flow along the slimy surface. A toothless slash of a mouth, at least three feet wide, moved forward, engulfing all the wriggling things on the wet ground in its path. As they walked close to the creature, Corbett could hear the churning of its massive digestive processes, and he could see that the outer surface, be it skin or chitin, was caked with mould, soil, and swarms of tiny glistening insect-like creatures that clung to it like a shawl made of beads.

"Hurry—we haven't much time." Eva urged them onward, and Corbett was irritated that he was being told so little.

The ship loomed out of the mists, and Corbett gasped. The hull was dented and scarred as high as a man could reach, with long gouges making brilliant cuts along the strengthened aluminum alloy hull. Particularly unsettling appeared to be a concentration of rage against the hatch area. He imagined yet-unseen horrors still lurking in the mists who had taken out their fury on the spaceship. Only the integrity of the ship design had prevented the mindless vandalizing creatures from finding a way inside. Eva had a weapon in her hand, and Corbett kept his at the ready. She had the standard issue tool for unsealing the hatch, and they crawled through the opening. When the hatch was closed again, Eva made a motion with her hand that they could remove the hoods, and Corbett looked around at his ship.

"Your ship is doomed, you know." Eva looked at him in brutal honesty. "We're here for a reason. I just hope it's not too late."

Before Corbett could protest, the other men went silently to the cockpit and began to dismantle the control panels, the navigation calculation unit, the bank of radios, and other instrumentation. One of them loaded up rations, medicines, and water containers. The men wrapped the components in cargo netting and hoisted the heavy loads onto their shoulders. Somehow they seemed stronger than they looked.

"No time for anything else. The sound carries." Eva motioned them back to the hatch and out into the hostile atmosphere.

Back under the hood, Corbett missed the comfort of his own ship, and his stomach lurched as his feet slid on the teeming, living surface of the planet. "They'll be here soon. Hurry!" It was Eva's voice crackling in his ear.

Corbett was almost running to keep up with his determined companions, his breath hot and steamy, his head throbbing with the heat. There was a noise behind! It was more than a noise—it was a vibration he felt through the soles of the suit. Something tremendous was following.

Not given to panic, Corbett found himself mentally clawing to get out of the suit before he was overtaken, but instead he followed doggedly the backs of the suits pacing ahead of him, fatigue advancing as quickly as whatever was gaining on him. Then the mist was like a hand passing across his face, a funneling, swirling tendril that encircled his waist as might a serpent, and then it dissipated into the steaming grayness.

A rectangular opening appeared ahead, and the team ran for it, but it was going to be too late. The ground was shaking, and Corbett turned to see the mist turn dark and overwhelming. The behemoth towered above him, its outline becoming hideously clear as it approached.

Fully 40 feet high, the great creature lumbered toward them, its bulbous head at least six feet in diameter, with slitted vestigial eyes and a cruel beak for a mouth, a beak that seemed to extend at least three feet in front of the head. The top of the head was covered by a forest of cilia-like antennae that quested and writhed, pointing and searching, constantly moving like long grass blown by the wind.

The monstrous body, large as a whale, lurched forward and actually lifted off the ground, its clawed forelegs clotted with the wet, black humus. Suddenly, most of the squirming antennae were curved downward, pointing in Corbett's direction. No time for hesitation!

The flame rifle spewed its hissing high pressure jet of fire, striking the thing in the middle of what must have been its chest. The flame penetrated instantly, and a flood of gas and liquid vomited outward as the creature actually caught fire. Corbett fired twice more, and this towering animal was engulfed, almost as though its body was full of petrochemicals. A rain of hot liquid doused Corbett's suit as he stumbled backward, and a voice in his ear almost screamed, "Inside! Now!"

Even the protection of the suit didn't prepare Corbett for the heat and the choking odor that enveloped him. He staggered drunkenly toward the doorway 20 feet away, surprised when he could no longer control his legs. The hulk of the giant creature was still burning and spewing noisome fluids into the mist as Eva pushed the door closed and then ran to him and began to pull the suit off of his body. His head was swimming, but the fresh air inside the shelter was an elixir that brought him around. A hand was on his cheek, and two brilliant eyes looked down at him; the red lips formed a faint smile.

Eva pointed, and Corbett watched as the discarded suit began dissolving before his eyes. She climbed out of her own suit and stripped off the contaminated gloves. The close fitting green body suit was dark and glossy with perspiration, clinging to the curves of her body as she knelt beside him. She shuddered visibly.

"The most monstrous creature we have found on Venus. We named it 'devorazoid' because it seemed to be the dominant carnivore in the area we have explored. It's not a mammal, not a reptile, not an amphibian. Earth has nothing like it." When Corbett put his hand over hers, she didn't take it away.

"So that's the greatest danger on Venus, and we beat it." Corbett tried his reckless grin on her.

"If only that were true." The smile faded. You still don't know the worst."

"That's because nobody tells me anything." He was able to stand now, still grinning, and he pulled Eva up with him. "But, if that creature is the smartest and most dangerous thing on this planet, we've got a chance."

There was a tinge of anger again at the corners of her eyes. "Nobody said anything about 'smart,' and we thought the same thing a week after we set up camp. The whole truth is almost unbelievable." Eva's hand on his upper arm was gentle, but firm. She led Corbett to the water processing machine.

Corbett was surprisingly thirsty, and drank deeply as he watched as Eva's father poured chemicals on what was left of his environmental suit.

Eva was watching him. "Sulfuric acid—it seems to be one of the most common substances here. It's even in the moisture that's part of the mist of Venus."

"Venusian perfume," Corbett quipped.

On Eva's instructions, the other men were working with the items cannibalized from Corbett's rocketship. The pair then went to the camp table and sat down so that Eva could tell her survival story.

"I guess you know the beginning. And, after the beginning, we were never sure when our transmitter first failed. Now I know that we were not prepared to colonize an alien planet. We were so foolish, but the first victories made us reckless with pride. All of the ships made it to Venus, and all landed within a mile of each other. Yes, several of the ships crash-landed, but nobody was killed, and we had the experience of Schmitt and Yeager that made us believe we were inoculated against unseen microbes.

"Oh, we were so filled with excitement. Seventy-three proud explorers who were covering themselves with fame and glory—that's what we were thinking. Look over there. Those three men are some of the finest scientists of our age, and their lives are over. They might as well be zombies. They don't eat, sleep, or function without our verbal direction. Whatever humanity they might have had inside them is completely gone. At least we were able to save their physical lives. The rest were not so lucky. You'll know what I mean very soon. We're overdue for an attack."

Corbett shook his head and rubbed the dark stubble on his face. "I can see a few casualties before you learned how to deal with the creatures I've seen, but I don't see any intelligence there. Those creatures aren't crafty enough to fool those highly trained people."

"I didn't say they were. You have to remember that my father and I helped build the shelter, and then our job kept us inside with the radar scope and the map table after the first week. Nothing happened to us. There were a few cases of infection that required penicillin injections, but they were rare. The inoculation like that I gave to you protected every one of us against the diseases of Venus. Our microbiologist found that most of the organisms on this world are more primitive than our own. Our radar detected a body of water four miles away, and our exploration team found what seemed to be rudimentary water life, probably pre-Devonian in Earth terms. The excitement never seemed to end, and the first two weeks made us almost giddy with our own success, and we drank a toast to the idea that we were the dominant life form on Venus. We were such fools." Eva stopped suddenly as though listening for something. Her father looked at her from a dozen feet away. He shook his head, and Eva seemed to visibly relax.

Corbett felt the frustration of not understanding everything around him. "Those guys are doing technical work at the work bench. This is nuts."

"They haven't lost their skill or their intellectual capacity. It is their will and their humanity that's been stolen." Eva's tone was condescending. The damp silken cloth was still clinging to her breasts as they rose and fell with her breathing.

Corbett's frustration overcame him and his fist pounded the table, startling himself and Eva's father. She didn't flinch. "What kind of microbe does that?"

Eva reached out one perfect finger and pushed against Corbett's forehead. "You're as dumb as we were when we came here. You have to stop thinking in Earth terms. Yes, the flackers got two, killing them horribly. We had another three who were invaded by a protozoa that destroyed them from the inside out. One day we lost five from our military contingent—that was the day we first met the devorazoid, and all of them were killed when they blew up the monster with a bazooka rocket. They were too close. One man died when he ran into the sleeper tree, and three idiots died when they ate fruit from a plant that looked too good to be true. Have you been counting?"

Corbett knitted his brow and added the 14 casualties to Eva and Dr. Kretschmer, plus the three sad cases working silently at the work bench. It left 54 scientists, doctors, and military personnel unaccounted for. He was just about to ask the obvious question when all hell broke loose.

A Bastion Under Siege

A hurricane of blows struck the shelter from all sides, thumping against the reinforced metal panels, shaking the sturdy building, testing its reinforcing studs. Corbett jumped up, his hand groping for a weapon, anything with which to defend himself.

Eva's father ran to the table, while his daughter could not help but show her terror.

Corbett glanced toward the three scientists at the work bench, and it was chilling to him that, for the first time, they stopped, and were staring blankly at the walls, nodding as if they were listening to something Corbett could not hear. Outside, it seemed as though bodies were throwing themselves in abandon against the sides of quonset structure, and Corbett remembered the violent scratches and gouges visited earlier upon his hapless rocketship.

Now began a low-pitched howling noise from every quarter. What creatures could be doing this? Had they finally discovered the highest form of primitive life on Venus?

The pounding was deafening and the three mere humans huddled together beside the camp table. Despite the fear that was dampening his armpits, Corbett was suddenly aware that Eva had taken his hand, squeezing it desperately.

"We don't understand," Eva began in an unsteady voice. "This happens every six earth days, almost to the hour. We don't know what makes them attack like demons, but it coincides with the temperature cycle. Here at the poles, we find that temperature varies regularly between 105 degrees and 125 degrees.

The attacks come every time the temperature hits the low point. The first two or three times caught us unprepared, and they took away some of our best men who were outside when the attack came. This has been going on for months, and someday they may break down the shelter. No matter how strong it is. Their first attacks were on the rocketships. If you wonder why we never tried to escape from Venus in the ships that brought us here, now you know the reason."

The blows against the shelter, and the unearthly howling reached a frenzy. Dr. Kretschmer breathed shakily, "At least the door is secure."

Eva's eyes went wide. "My God, the door. I forgot to bar it." Eva ran toward the entrance while Corbett dove for the pile of equipment on the floor hoping that his hand could find the butt of the 37mm rocket pistol. At that moment the metal door slammed open, and the entrance was filled with things crowding to get in.

Like the other creatures Corbett had seen, these things were covered with verminous soil and mould, grayish green with sick yellow patches and swarming with parasitic insects; yet, they had humanlike appendages, their open mouths toothless and suppurating. The stench turned Corbett's stomach as his right hand instinctively found the smooth butt of the pistol.

Chaos erupted in the shelter. One of the things leapt forward eight feet, grabbed Eva, and as she screamed, Corbett fired into the doorway. He was ready for the explosion this time, but nobody else was. The tektonite blew two of the things backward through the doorway and into oblivion. The next shot caught three more, dismembering them before they could approach the door, The howling and pummeling stopped, and the one creature left alive inside dragged Eva out toward the roiling mists. She fought furiously, and Corbett knew the pistol could not help now. Corbett lunged forward blindly, yelling until he landed with all his body weight against the back of the retreating horror. Its howl was cut short as the 180-pound man struck it with full force.

Eva was knocked clear, and the creature rolled into the mists, apparently stunned. Corbett scooped her up into his arms and carried her back into the safety of the shelter, his skin stinging from the droplets of mist.

Despite what she had been through, Eva seemed remarkably composed as Corbett allowed her feet to descend to the floor. Together they barred the door and stood close, looking at each other. Despite the odor of the Venus things, Corbett sensed a delightful fragrance emanating from the waves of Eva's hair. For a moment, he forgot everything they had just gone through, and the whole world of Venus seemed focused on a pair of glossy red lips.

Eva's lips seemed to move toward his, but then she backed off. "Well, Lieutenant, I knew there had to be a reason for saving you." She smiled impishly.

"Even if I'm a fugitive from the law?" Corbett felt that impulsive grin pulling at the corners of his mouth.

"We're too busy surviving to worry about the law on a planet millions of miles away." Dr. Kretschmer broke the spell, while the three autistic scientists went back to the workbench as though nothing had happened. The attack was over.

Corbett was still looking at Eva, who was looking back. "What now?" He asked. She answered by throwing a tube of ointment to him so he could salve his irritated face and hands.

"I can tell you what's going on, or I can show you our landing area and tell you what we've been planning in case somebody ever dropped in for a visit."

"Can't we do both? Now that I've met the Venusians and decided that they're not very friendly, I am starting to wonder how we'll ever get out of here alive." Corbett didn't relish ending his life in a misty steambath.

Eva opened a carton and brought out another environmental suit and hood for him. "Let's go." She then went to the men at the work bench who put the instrumentation into boxes and began to don their suits again. "I want to show you something that could save us."

In minutes they were leaving the shelter again for the hostile mists, each carrying a box of items stripped from Corbett's rocketship. The pearlescent mists converged and parted; Corbett kept imagining familiar forms and faces emerging in the air currents.

"To your right, Lieutenant. Ship number one." At the edge of his faceplate-enhanced vision was a rocketship, blast tube pointed toward the sky, buried halfway, nose down, in the Venusian soil. The cone of the rocket tube looked forlorn and wasted, covered with greenish mould. A few hundred feet further was a ship that had pancaked the way Corbett's ship had come down—except there was a difference. This ship had almost been torn apart, its hull panels torn away the rocket engines exposed and smashed.

Eva's voice crackled in his ear, "That was ship number two, and there are three more like that. The other three landed by the book." Ahead was a ship sitting on the tripod of stabilizer vanes, its blast tube pointing to the ground almost as though it were ready to launch, or so it seemed until they came closer.

Corbett saw that the control surfaces had been wrenched from the trailing edges of the stabilizers, the nacelles of the thrusters punctured and ripped open. Someone or something had climbed the tower of the hull by the retractable metal ladder rungs, and the access hatches were open. Eva's voice intruded on his hopes: "That's right. They got in and destroyed the cockpit. What's left of the interior is three feet deep in soft, pulpy fungus. They never just attacked the shelter; they always attacked the ships as well. Following the Schmitt-Yeager regimen, we sprayed the hulls with herbicides to stop mould and algae, but we began to lose hope when the attacks began."

A Ship Named Hope

They kept walking, and though the sweat poured from Corbett, he felt as though he was adjusting to the punishing climate of the Venusian pole. Another ship loomed in the mist, and he concentrated on the three-storey space vehicle, avoiding the temptation to stare too closely at the shapes he imagined in the shifting mist blanket.

Eva inserted a tool into the skirt of the blast tube and turned, causing the ladder rungs to extrude themselves from the smoothness of the gleaming hull that shone wetly, but had resisted the plague of mould and fungus that attacked everything else. There were signs of scarring and a few dents, but the ship was not yet damaged beyond spaceworthiness. They opened the boxes and hoisted the hardware, wrapped in cargo netting, hanging from straps on their shoulders. The strength of the unfortunate scientists was prodigious as they hauled the loads upward.

They climbed the outside of the ship, and Corbett felt the weakness coming back while the eddies of mist taunted him. Above him, Eva deployed the hatch tool and it opened. One by one, they entered one of the famous ships whose rockets had been silent for a year.

Inside, they removed the bulky hoods. Corbett grunted in despair. Everything here had been smashed. He looked at Eva who was wiping perspiration from her face, her hair still remarkably in place. "Get to work." She was talking to the scientists who followed her instructions without a word.

Corbett's frustration exploded. "How could you have let those Venus monsters have access to your only means of escape?"

"We didn't do anything of the kind. Here, help them get those wrecked panels out of the console."

Now Corbett began to hope again. The instruments from his crash-landed rocket might just give them a chance.

"It didn't happen overnight, you know, and those Venus monsters you blew up in the door to the shelter—well they weren't Venusians. They were once our crew, our protectors, and our friends.

"The hideous lung growths that killed Schmitt and Yeager were an easy death compared to what happened to our colleagues. My father and I worked in the shelter, drawing the increasingly clear maps of the Venus landscape, but everybody else set out to take soil samples, photograph animals or look for mineral deposits. We thought the environmental suits and inoculations fully protected everyone, but there was at least one thing that the first expedition wasn't here long enough to discover."

Machine screws in the console came loose and a rack of shattered vacuum tubes fell to the floor with a crash, a floor that became a bulkhead when the ship was in horizontal flight. Corbett lifted the matching good set and the silent scientists slid the rack into the appropriate metal tracks.

Eva had lifted another panel and was replacing bent and twisted thruster levers that had been savagely attacked. "It happened gradually. First our people were dizzy and tired, but we knew it could be the heat or the dehydrating nature of being inside these suits, and when the shelter was finished, there was a celebration, and people acted a little crazy, but they were entitled, but then…"

Corbett responded to Eva's gesture, and lifted the heavy and complex geared wheels of the navigation controls that mated to the hydraulic control guides and the directional thrusters. "You mean those bloodthirsty things covered with stinking fungus was your crew? Why would they attack their own kind?"

"You haven't figured it out yet?

Corbett held the panel while the bearded scientists tightened the machine screws holding it in place. "I read a story once about Kansas in the frontier days. Those early wheat farms were so isolated, and the wind blew through the stalks, never stopping. It was said that many farm wives went insane from being alone in an isolated farmhouse all day while their husbands were out plowing, reaping, whatever it took."

Eva's hands were busy reattaching wires while she answered. "We kept our clocks at Greenwich Mean Time, and we kept our calendars because Venus has a period that keeps it in the same relationship to Earth, so I know how long it took. A day on Venus is longer than its year. After the shelter was built, the teams went out for short periods, accompanied by armed patrols. They killed hundreds of Venus creatures, but there was something they couldn't kill.

"They all began acting strangely, almost sullen, and within two weeks, they started staying out longer and longer, sometimes not coming back for 24-26 hours. Then came the silence as though their personalities had been stolen. We were so busy that we didn't have time to pay attention. My father and I weren't in charge of the work parties or the military. Our job was to stay inside on that radar scope and draw the charts of Venus."

Corbett was looking at her intense concentration as she reassembled the main thrust control. "What about these guys? We're acting as though they aren't even here."

"They aren't, Lieutenant. They would have been like the rest if we hadn't seen it coming. They worked inside more than the rest, so the change came to them slowly."

"What change are you talking about?" Corbett's voice was demanding now.

"There is a dominant species on Venus, Lieutenant, and it has been ruthlessly working to wipe out the invading aliens that penetrated its home. It's done a pretty good job, and our only hope is to escape. There was not even a shred of hope before you arrived, and now we have a fighting chance."

Corbett finished installing the navigation table, sweat pouring down his face, and he rubbed his close-cropped hair, thinking that the hair was not so short as it was when he blasted off from White Sands. "I guess we have a few earth days before the next attack."

Eva looked up as she replaced the rocket control panel cover. "The mind of Venus is fickle—like a woman's. You can't anticipate what she's going to do. We were wrong every step of the way, and now we have time for about one more decision."

It was suddenly silent in the rocketship. The replaced controls were marginal, and the cabin was still a mess, but given a fuel supply, they just might be able to get off the planet.

"My father is getting everything ready. We can't wait any longer now that we know what all our fates are likely to be. Let's go. We'll leave the men here to tighten all the bolts and get rid of the trash."

Corbett suddenly put his hands on both her shoulders and gripped. "We're not going anywhere until you finish the story. You've hinted at it ever since you pulled me out of my ship and introduced me to your nightmare."

Eva looked down and then raised her eyes to meet Corbett's. "We were so slow and unbelieving. We first expected random encounters with alien creatures, but when our own kind were turned against us, we didn't expect what happened. They attacked the ships, one by one, while they kept us cowering in our shelter. The outside things seemed to forget how to use weapons, and they were reduced to using sticks, rocks, and pieces from the ships as they destroyed them.

The Mind of Venus

"Venus is a young planet—younger than we thought. The consciousness of Venus, its dominant species, isn't in the creatures. It's in the mists."

Corbett let her go and turned to face the bulkhead, throwing his hands out. "Oh, come on, Eva. That's as looney as your boys here."

"Is it? The mists started to work on you the moment you first stepped out of your ship. In three or four earth weeks, you would have been almost a zombie. Give it two months and you'd have gone native, rubbing narcotic moulds on your body, rotting out your teeth, and eating larvae while your mind hears only the whispers from the mist."

Corbett turned around again, his eyes wide. "You mean these things are ghosts? Spirits?"

Eva smiled her maddeningly faint smile. "Call it what you will. We think the mists are pure mind stuff, and this is its first experiment with possessing physical bodies. We would call them parasites, but there's no way of knowing what the true explanation may be. The mists are an alien intelligence—or maybe a single intelligence. That's all this terrible expedition has taught us. Now you see why we have to move fast. What if they can also read our thoughts?"

As he digested the information, the rocket pilot suddenly understood. "You're saying that Venus is primitive the way the Earth was before the Devonian era. This means…"

Eva's father nodded, "Certainly, Earth may have gone through the same evolution. In the beginning there must have been pure, unstructured consciousness, without form or differentiation. Then the energy developed concrete thought and sought to indwell organic forms as those organisms changed and developed. Perhaps in a hundred million years, Venus will cool and become a host for intelligent life, the way Earth is today."

Corbett felt a chill despite the throbbing heat, thinking about the implications. Eva gave the silent, bearded scientists their orders, and they kept working silently while Eva and Corbett swung through the hatch, closed it and began climbing down the rungs of the ladder and back into the living mists.

As they walked swiftly back toward the shelter, Corbett could now see menace in each sworl of luminous vapor, and he would not allow his eyes to accept the fantastic forms that seemed to waft more insistently in front of his faceplate. It was a relief to find the dented steel door of the shelter opening for them.

Inside, Dr. Kretschmer had assembled the papers of the expedition into four rucksacks, along with water and minimum rations. "When your ship crashed, Lt. Corbett, we finished our long and arduous transfer of fuel from the vandalized rockets into the one ship they had yet to incapacitate. I feel that we have only hours…maybe less."

Corbett was still breathing heavily from the walk. "But the temperature is on its way up. There will be no attack until the next cycle. You said so." He realized that he sounded like a kid asking for reassurance from his father.

"You may believe what you wish, but keep your hands on your weapons nonetheless." Kretschmer pointed to the rucksacks and they each shouldered their load. There was no time to waste. Within minutes they were leaving the shelter for the last time and plodding relentlessly toward that ship whose pointed nose was waiting to return to the heavens.

Corbett felt waves of fear as copious as his sweat. The mists surrounded them in furious currents, bright, luminous, and deadly with suggestion. Thick tendrils of mist reached out, and he felt ghostly fingers closing over his arm like a lover trying to pull him into an embrace. Eva's radio voice in his ear was comforting. 'We're halfway there."

The creatures attacked suddenly, without warning, their horrible forms masked in mist. Surprisingly agile, they raced forward, but they found their intended prey on guard. Corbett pressed the trigger, and the flame rifle spewed its thick strand of lethality. The cylinder of flame reached out 20 feet and drilled through the midsection of the charging howler who fell like a stone into the muck. His second shot sent fiery death into the midsection of another attacker that blossomed into an instant torch. Dr. Kretschmer and Eva were firing also, he with a standard service automatic loaded with .45 cal. explosive bullets, and she with a rocket pistol.

Two, three, five, seven once-human things exploded into flames or fell in pieces. They'd had enough, and Corbett's jaw went slack. It was not an illusion. He saw rivulets of mist beckoning to the remaining creatures, backing them into the invisibility of the luminescent curtain.

With the weight of the rucksacks slowing them down, Corbett's lungs were on fire from exertion, yet he kept up with Eva and her father, knowing that a hellish horde was reorganizing and reforming behind them, preparing for another assault.

The rocket ship was an obelisk in front of them, and they each grabbed the retractable ground access ladder to reach the metal rungs extruding from the body of the monster rocket and which led three storeys upward to safety and possible escape. Corbett was the last on the ladder, and he heard each one springing back, retracting into the hull as he grabbed the solid rungs above him. He heard something else too—the howling of mad beings as they approached the ship. Could it be too late?

The Only Rocket Pilot on Venus

His oxygen-starved brain was reeling as he struggled upward, feeling the rucksack as it tried to pull him off the ladder and back onto the hell of Venus. It seemed forever before he found the maw of the open hatchway and hands pulling him aboard.

Eva was first on board, and it was she who was turning the handle to retract the ladder rungs just behind him. Corbett heard a howling form losing its purchase and falling 30 feet to the ground. "Get us out of here, Lieutenant." She pushed her hair out of her face as Corbett pointed to himself.

"Me?"

"You don't really think we saved you for your looks, do you? We were missing a lot of things, including space expertise. Right now, you're the only rocket pilot on Venus." They swiftly abandoned the bulky environmental suits, throwing them out of the hatchway before sealing it.

Corbett felt the reckless grin coming back, and he settled into the left hand countour seat while Eva and her father buckled the three silent team members into crew seats. Eva climbed into the right hand seat, but Corbett had no time to appreciate the way her curves flowed underneath the silky green coveralls. He was busy flipping switches in the pre-ignition check.

They heard the pounding as determined attackers struck the hull and the stabilizing vanes. One of the creatures had found a piece of metal from a wrecked ship and the frightening sound of determined blows vibrated through the ship.

Eva was looking at him with steady, brilliant eyes. "Now would be a very good time, Lieutenant." She was grinning.

Corbett nodded confidently, pushed the thruster levers all the way forward for pre-igntion, and reached out to hit the red button that seemed as large as a grapefruit. He pressed it and waited for the explosive response from the engines. The only noise came from the battering against the hull that was louder and more insistent now. Corbett knew they could be doomed for want of a wire connector.

His fingers flew above the button to a screw knob that opened a metal flange. Whoever had piloted the ship had taken care to close the safety switch that prevented accidental ignition. The toggle switch clicked loudly when he pushed it, and his finger hovered once more above the red button that seemed to throb in his fatigued vision. The hull was vibrating and a sound like chalk on a blackboard made him wonder if they might totter and fall over into the mud in a fireball of exploding fuel.

His finger pressed the button with all the strength he could muster.

The blast. THE BLAST! The rocket exploded into life in a cleansing typhoon of roaring fire, a pillar of irresistible, brilliant force. Because there was no flame tunnel underneath this makeshift pad, the avalanche of thrust made an instant crater and boiled the Venus mud into vapor. The flame blossomed out fifty yards in every direction, carbonizing everything in its path. The creatures from the mist died almost instantly while the ship vibrated and shook. Eva screamed, and Corbett couldn't help from yelling, although the roar of the main engine drowned out everything.

Corbett felt vomit in his throat as the ship overcame its own inertia, then teetered as though it might still fall over and roast them in the juices of Venus. The ship started to rise, imperceptibly at first, then picking up speed. He felt the pull of gravity welding him to the chair, and now the projectile was unstoppable, accelerating inexorably with those familiar forces immobilizing him. A trickle of blood was coming from his nose, and then he passed out. It couldn't have been more than a few minutes before Corbett regained consciousness, and the ship was knifing into the blackness of space. The camera lenses showed a luminous arc behind them while ahead were the diamond pinpoints of infinity. The ship was in horizontal attitude, and Corbett looked over at Eva who moaned softly as though she were awakening from a pleasant night's sleep. He craned his neck and saw the others stirring.

As the earthlike gravity of Venus released its hold, Corbett propelled himself out of the seat and grabbed handholds to move himself to the navigation table where he adjusted the six wheels to a setting that would take them back to Earth, much as he wished there was somewhere else he could take them.

Eva was looking back over the seat, watching him. Corbett grinned and shrugged, "Out of the frying pan, they say…I'm sure the MP's will have a welcoming committee for me when we touch down."

Dr. Kretschmer laughed. "My boy, you're going to be an international hero for rescuing the first interplanetary exploration team. I think things will work out fine."

Corbett eased his way back to the pilot seat, and Eva was leaning toward him, her hair lifting in the zero gravity. Her smile was warm and genuine, an expression he had not seen before.

She touched her red lips with her finger and brought it to his mouth, still smiling. "I don't know, Lieutenant, maybe you haven't escaped from Venus after all." As the two looked at each other, the navigation thrusters pointed the ship toward the tiny disc of the brilliant green planet they called home.

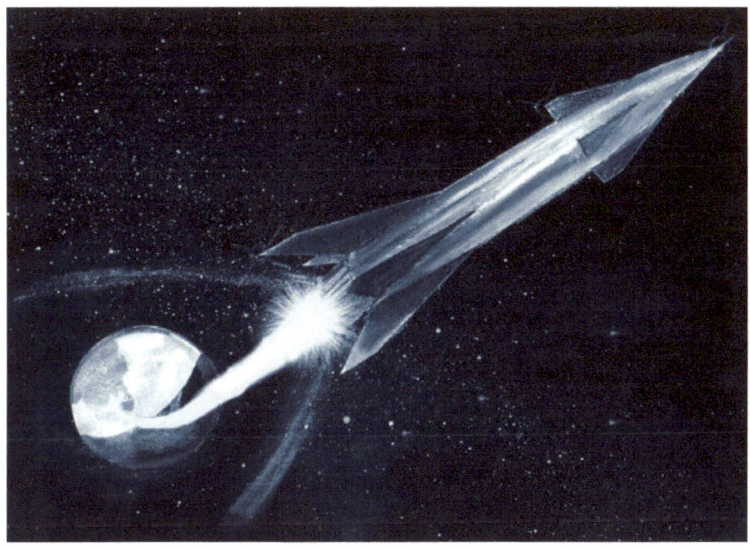

THE AUTHOR'S STORY

For most of his life, the author has ventured into the twilight realm of supernatural horror, both as a reader and as a writer. Now he brings his stories home to the desert Southwest. Born in the mining district of southern New Mexico in 1939, Frank Thayer grew up exploring the country that now becomes the setting for a set of supernatural horror tales.

Thayer was in the cadet corps at Texas A&M University for three years before transferring back to New Mexico State University where he graduated with a degree in journalism. He worked as a reporter, photographer, weekly newspaper editor in Las Cruces, New Mexico before serving with the National Guard.

On his return from active duty, he was writing stories for men's magazines in the early 1960s, Thayer was mentored by August Derleth of Arkham House Publishers. Derleth was a member of the original Lovecraft circle of writers and became the publisher of all Lovecraft's work in the decades after his death. Derleth subsequently selected and one of Thayer's stories to be anthologized in a Derleth collection *Travellers By Night*, and Thayer since considered himself part of the secondary level of that august circle. Later in this period, he traveled to Canada, searching for work in journalism, and he served as a college journalism instructor and department head at the first community college in Ontario, Centennial College of Applied Arts and Technology in Scarborough (Toronto), Ontario, remaining from 1966 to 1977.

After his return to New Mexico in 1977, Thayer wrote stories and did photography in locations that now are part of the fiction in this volume. He went back to NMSU to earn his advanced degrees and to spend 30 years as a journalism professor and department head at that university. Today he is professor emeritus and still teaches in the department while devoting much of his energy to his fiction writing.

Contiguous to the writing of horror fiction, Thayer has also published three journalism textbooks and is a co-author with Scott and Suzanne Ramsey, of North Carolina, in two ground-breaking books confirming the crash and recovery of a flying saucer near Aztec, N.M., in 1948. Their books *The Aztec Incicent: Recovery at Hart Canyon* in 2012, and *The Aztec UFO Incident*, released in 2015 have sold thousands of copies and are complimented as being the best researched flying saucer books ever published.

Born and reared in southwestern New Mexico, the author takes his part as a guerrilla warrior against the ordinary world, keeping one foot in everyday reality, and the other in the realm of cosmic horror. A lifetime of devotion to the supernatural horror field culminates in this book *Terror Tales of the Southwest*. Frank Thayer has walked in the places where these stories unfold.

A cosmic abomination from the Old World festers under an unsuspecting Canadian town, rising to afflict four generations of its residents. From the author of *Terror Tales of the Southwest* comes a trilogy of horror tales in an illustrated volume that includes the facsimile of a 1679 dissertation from the British Library in London that documents the dead who chew in their graves.

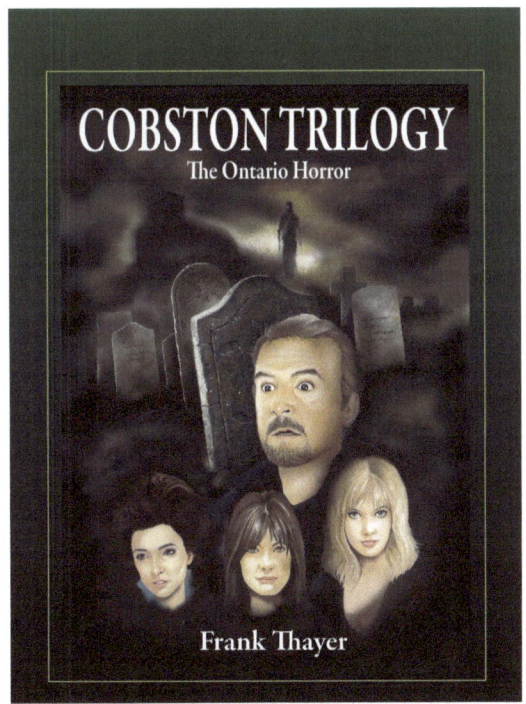

Order Cobston Trilogy: The Ontario Horror Today!

$19.95 plus $3.00 domestic media mail postage
$12 shipment to Canada and the UK
PayPal payment to: gticruiser@aim.com
Check or Money Order by regular mail

Order from: Frank Thayer
Sun Cross Publications
P.O. Box 3136
Las Cruces, NM 88003
USA

www.ingramcontent.com/pod-product-compliance
Lightning Source LLC
Chambersburg PA
CBHW040820050726
47507CB00019B/83